THE LOST KING

ALSO BY ELIZABETH CREITH

THE SWAN HARP
SHEPHERD IN RESIDENCE
ERIK THE VIKING SHEEP

PRAISE FOR THE SWAN HARP:

"A spellbinding fantasy romance… The human and swanfolk cultures united in harmony through the marriage of King Tir and Queen Tianis created an intriguing foundation for worldbuilding within the story's introduction. I loved diving into the swanfolk's culture and seeing how the transformative magic intertwined with Kiar's story, creating tension and suspense… Princess Kiar bears the weight of the kingdom on her young shoulders. With many lessons to learn, Kiar has to prove that she has the strength to rule and make difficult decisions, especially when the most ominous threat comes from the least expected place.

I recommend *The Swan Harp* to readers who enjoy slow burn fantasy romance, shapeshifting magic, medieval fantasy settings, and subtle political intrigue." —*Reedsy Discovery*

"When her sisters Adana and Orla both gain the ability to transform into swans like their mother, Kiar feels left out. As Princess of Valenia, she will inherit the kingdom from her father King Tir—but becoming queen is nothing compared to the ability to fly. This feeling intensifies when her family fosters three cygnets and it turns out that Orla is a black swan, a once-in-a-century phenomenon with powerful magic… An uneasy peace with the neighboring kingdom of Noermark hangs in the balance as its King begins to make attempts to take over, by marriage if not by force. Every decision the young queen in waiting makes must balance the needs of all her subjects, human and swanfolk alike.

Fantasy skirting fairytale, Elizabeth Creith's young adult novel *The Swan Harp (Wings of Valenia Book One)* uses an unusual premise and some original and tender world-building to draw readers in." —*IndieReader*

"Elizabeth Creith is an exciting new voice in fantasy fiction, creating an entire new world full of beautiful, fragile and powerful creatures, as yet unseen anywhere. You'll stay for the magic, but you'll live for the story." —Susie Moloney, author *The Dwelling, A Dry Spell, and The Thirteen.*

"Family, betrayal, tragedy—there is so much to love about this exciting coming of age fantasy! The…resonance of the old tales, with a heart we expect from the best stories of today." —Anita Daher, actor and author of *You Don't Have to Die in the End.*

"In the medieval world of Valenia, humans and swanfolk live in harmony. Author Creith tells the story from Kiar's point of view-a young girl growing up quickly because of her circumstances. The book is full of beautiful, powerful, yet fragile creatures—human and otherwise. Creith's storytelling is relatable and descriptive, yet simplistic enough that younger readers won't lose interest. Creith was inspired by a 500-year-old ballad about two sisters in love with the same man, and also by Lorena McKennitt's song, 'The Bonny Swans.' If you love old fairytales and myths, this might be the book for you. It's a new version of an ancient tale full of shapeshifters, medieval life, hidden magic, family drama, and it's 5 stars from me. —Linda, Amazon reviewer

"This is Book One of the *Wings of Valenia* series. Amazing world building that is detailed and imaginable. Fascinating characters that are well developed and diverse. Twists and unexpected turns keep you reading. The storyline is fast-paced and very well written, filled with magic, betrayal, danger, death, politics, intrigue, and subterfuge. The plot thickens, the suspense builds, and the passion erupts! I can't wait to read the rest of this series. —Jennifer, Amazon reviewer

ELIZABETH CREITH

WINGS OF VALENIA
BOOK TWO

ISBN 979-8-9908030-2-2 (paperback)
ISBN 979-8-9908030-3-9 (ebook)

Published by Type Eighteen Books
www.typeeighteenbooks.com

To the memory of Ravi Nair

CHAPTER

ONE

The morning my sister Adana came to say goodbye for the winter, I was up early. Willow, my foster sister and friend, muttered something in her sleep from the other side of the bed when I got up, and then she fell silent again.

I dressed quickly and washed my face in the cold water from the basin. I combed my hair out and braided it, then slid behind the curtain that covered my window to breathe in the autumn air. It hadn't snowed yet, but the smell of frost and dying leaves announced that winter was on its way.

My mother stood in the courtyard, almost directly below my window. She was easy to recognize; no other woman in the castle wore her long hair loose instead of braided or coiled into a knot. Bands of white streaked her black hair. They'd widened in the half-year since the death of my sister Orla.

She faced out toward the wall. Nobody else stood as quietly. Even the guards on the wall and the one at the gate shifted or

paced to keep warm and limber. She might have been a young tree, or a woman carved of stone except for the way the slight breeze stirred her hair and clothing. She might have been watching for Adana. I hoped she was. I hoped she hadn't started believing once again that Orla was still alive and on her way home. Those times were hard on her and everyone around her, and hardest of all on my father.

I stepped back into the room and pulled the curtain closed. Willow sat up and swung her feet out from under the blankets.

"I'll see you downstairs," I said, and she nodded.

In the great hall, my father and Tuan sat at the king's table, nearest the outer door of the hall. Six months ago, the king's table had been full every morning. We all sat there—my father and mother, my two sisters Adana and Orla, along with Willow, Gil, and Tuan, the three swanfolk my parents had fostered.

Now Gil and Adana were married and gone to live with the swanfolk, my mother's people. Orla was gone, too, never to return. She'd always been Mother's favourite. Mother ate little now and didn't linger at the table with Father as she once had.

There was less on the table than a year ago, and not only because of our family's diminished size. The spring planting had gone as usual, and the crops had grown well. But in the last weeks of summer and into the fall, the fields had been plagued by deer, rabbits, even boar. Nothing seemed to keep the creatures out—not clippings of hair hung around the fields, not the dogs, nothing. The intruders ran, but always returned.

The boar were the worst; they trampled what they didn't eat and were dangerous to confront and drive off. Father and some of his men had gone out six times to hunt boar, bringing home five. Only one had run; the others had stayed to fight, although I'd never heard of boars defending food. Wild pigs ate everything; there was always something for them, whether it was acorns or beech mast, or the root vegetables in the fields.

Nias, the cook, had begun to serve less at each meal, and while nobody went hungry, little was left over. The chickens were still laying; they would stop for winter, but without a good supply of table scraps, they would stop sooner. I didn't know if there were fewer eggs already; Nias had said nothing about it. The boar, thinner than usual and tough, would not make up for the crops they'd eaten and ruined, and the same was true of the deer and rabbits, grouse and other wild birds we snared in the gardens.

Every day I expected Nias to say something about the food stores. I worried we had a lean winter ahead, and a leaner spring.

"Good morning, Father," I said, and leaned to kiss his cheek.

He put his arm around my shoulders and hugged me. "Good morning, Kiar."

He tugged on my braid, and as I slipped into my place next to Tuan, he smiled at us. Tuan squeezed my hand under the table.

That was something else that had changed. A year ago, Tuan had been my friend; now he was much more. We hadn't spoken of betrothal, nor had he said any of the formal things a suitor was supposed to say to my father. All the same, he now sat next to me at court occasions. Father had ordered a chair for him, not as elaborate as my own throne, but carved and cushioned and clearly a seat of honour.

"You're dressed up this morning," Father said.

I raised my eyebrows. He'd put on the embroidered surcoat he wore for feasts, and his beard and hair were freshly trimmed.

"I thought I'd wear something pretty for the occasion," I said. "We won't see Adana now until spring. Do you think Gil will come, too?"

"He'll come," Tuan said.

"They'll be cold without feathers," I said. "We should have cloaks for them."

Father lifted a fold of blue wool from the empty chair beside him—Mother's chair. "I asked Elena to bring their cloaks down. Your mother is out there watching for Adana."

"Has she eaten?" I asked.

"Yes," Father said. "She had some bread and fruit before she went out. I think she'd like to go down to the lake and say goodbye to her parents. I thought I'd take her after she's seen Adana."

"That's a good idea," I said, although privately, I wondered if it was. My grandfather, king of the swanfolk, had banished Mother, his own daughter, from the flock. He was the first to say she was mad, that her presence frightened and angered the rest of the flock, and he had decreed that she could no longer come back to the people she'd grown up among. Even now, my father wouldn't admit Mother was not simply deep in grief for Orla.

Sianna, the wisewoman who lived half a day's ride from the castle, had said that Mother would probably get better. My father, I thought, clung to the hope that she would return to being the woman he had courted and married, the swan princess who had kept her human form to be with him. She was better, but that didn't mean she'd ever be cured. I no longer hoped for the mother who had loved me to come back.

Willow came in and sat on the empty bench opposite Tuan and me. She eyed my clothes. "You're dressed up."

"I think Adana will come today," I said.

The swanfolk had been restless over the past week; small groups circled and came back to land on the lake. On the autumn breeze, their calls carried from the lake to the castle, an unceasing gabble of sound that signalled the fall flight.

"Eatha told me she wants to bring in the cloth from the bog today," Father said. "She'd like a guard with her. Do you have an idea about who should go?"

Every spring, Eatha placed lengths of woven cloth into the shallow, peaty pool at the edge of the bog, and every fall at the early frost, she pulled them out. The bog-water dyed the wool a soft, dark brown, lighter on white, darker on grey and black. Moths didn't seem to eat holes in the peat-dyed wool as much as they did in undyed cloth.

"I'd like to," Willow said before I could answer.

"We three could go," I said. Of course, Eatha would want a guard. This summer and fall, the wild animals had been behaving strangely, coming closer to the fields and the castle than usual. It wasn't only the deer and the wolves who preyed on them, but bear as well, even the shy wildcats.

Wolves mostly left us alone, but bears sometimes attacked one or two people. Wildcats were unpredictable. Until this year, we hadn't seen them around the castle or fields. Even the outlying

farmsteads usually heard wolves at a distance, and seldom saw bear or wildcats close by

"Did she see anything in particular?" I asked. "What should we watch for?"

"She said she didn't," Father said. "but she still felt uneasy going to the bog alone."

He didn't say "after last spring." Nobody talked about it, but the things Orla had done, or nearly done—before she died and after—had shocked and frightened people. Her dark magic had created an aura of fear, and it had faded slowly.

"Weapons are no good against magic," Willow said, spooning honey onto her bread.

"True enough," Father said, "and I'll thank you not to say that to Eatha, Willow."

She ducked her head. "Yes, Sire."

"Orla's gone," Tuan said. "nobody needs to be afraid. Not with—" He stopped.

"I know who keeps this country safe," Father said, "whether or not you say it."

So did we all, and for a few moments, we were all silent. I felt my cheeks burning. It should have been Father who cast Orla out of Valenia. The fact that I'd been the one to do it still made me feel uncomfortable, as though I'd somehow betrayed him.

"Then you'll go with her, all of you?" Father said at last.

"Yes, of course," I said.

He nodded. "It's good to let her know we take her fears seriously. You don't leave a candle burning in a child's room because there are monsters in the dark. You leave it so the child knows that if there are monsters, she has protection."

I was drinking the last of my hot mint tea when one of the guards on the wall called out.

"The princess! The princess!"

"Adana!" Father picked up the cloaks from Mother's chair and almost ran to the courtyard. Tuan, Willow, and I followed.

The two swans were still in the air, gliding down to land in the grass in front of the castle. Almost as soon as the first one touched the ground, the blue-white glow of magic flared up around her. When it faded, my sister Adana stood there, her long black hair settling around her bare white body.

"Welcome home, Adana," Father said. He shook out the blue cloak he'd brought for her and swirled it neatly over her shoulders, and she slipped her arms through the two slits in the sides and fastened the silver pin, shaped like a rose, which held the cloak at her throat.

"Thank you," she said, smiling. "I'm happy to see you, Father. Are you well?"

He kissed her forehead and hugged her for a moment. "I am," he said. "Gil, it's good to see you looking well."

As the glow of magic around the second swan faded, Adana's husband stood slightly behind her.

"Thank you, Sire." He took the green cloak Father offered him and draped it over his own shoulders. "It's good to be well." Gil had been very sick all last winter, first from the lung fever that happened sometimes in cold weather, and then from Orla's enchantments. He and Adana had married at midsummer and taken their place in the flock as heirs to Mother's swanfolk parents.

"How is Mother?" Adana asked.

"She's well. She eats, and she sleeps indoors. It's hard for her to be under a roof for long." Father glanced back through the gate, but Mother wasn't quite in sight.

Adana held out her arms. "Kiar, you look beautiful! Did you put on that dress for us?"

"Yes, I did." We hugged, and slender as she was, she still squeezed the breath from me.

She kissed my cheek. "It's a pleasant change to see you dressed prettily. Tuan, don't you think so?" She held out a hand to Tuan and Willow and drew them into our hug.

"Can we offer you something to eat?" I said. "Nias has made your favourite cakes every morning for the last three days, in case you arrived."

"I'd love that," Adana said. "but we can't stay. Grandfather wants to leave today. He's waiting for us to come back."

"It was good of him to let you say goodbye," Father said.

Grandfather was the Swan King; he could take the flock south to the winter grounds at his pleasure. Even Adana, his granddaughter and heir, had to obey him.

"It wasn't only to say goodbye," Adana said. "I have a message from Grandmother."

"Then we'll talk in private," Father said.

When we were all settled in his council chamber, with a plate of cakes still hot from the oven, Father said, "What is this message?"

"Grandmother says the past has come back," Adana said. She crumbled the little cake in her hands. I hadn't seen her so troubled for months. "She says it's angry and dangerous."

"How can the past come back?" I said.

"I know," she said. "It doesn't make sense in human speech. She told me in swan form, and the meaning isn't the same."

None of us asked why Adana hadn't simply asked Grandmother to repeat her warning in human form. A human could make such a request, but among the swanfolk nobody asked the king or queen to change form, or to explain themselves again.

"What might it mean?" Father asked. "Someone from the past is coming back to make trouble? An old enemy?"

"Maybe," Adana said. "But the way she said it didn't sound as though she meant someone from Noermark, or a person at all, or even another swan."

"You mean, nothing alive?" I asked.

"I suppose." She frowned. "Gil, didn't it almost sound as though she might mean something dead? Or at least, not really alive?"

"A ghost?" Father said. His frown matched Adana's. "Was she speaking of—"

"No!" Adana said. "It wasn't Orla. Besides, Kiar banished her. It couldn't be Orla." She reached to take Gil's hand.

"Are you sure?" I asked. Orla had been more powerful than any of us had known. She'd used her magic to make places around the castle where she could stand among us, unseen and unheard, and she'd used them for years. I wasn't altogether confident her spirit was banned from Valenia, even though she'd left when I'd thrown her out.

"I'm sure," said Gil. "It's not Orla, Kiar. Nobody will see her back here for a long, long time. And if she came back, I'm sure I'd know. What she did to me, that kind of magic, it leaves a shadow. I think I'll always know if she's around. And I say she isn't."

"You're certain of that?" Father asked.

"Yes, Sire," Gil said. "I'd stake my life on it."

"I think we have to believe you, then," Father said. "But if not her, then what? Or who?"

"I wish I could tell you," Adana said. "I don't know whether Grandmother will say any more, and I won't have time to come again before we leave."

"When will that be?" I asked. Once the flock left for their wintering grounds in the south, there would be no way for Adana to send us a message.

"Perhaps today, or tomorrow. Grandfather flew around the lake this morning, and I thought he'd give the call to leave, but he came back to feed. He knew I wanted to say goodbye. And one more thing," Adana said. "I think the bog is growing larger. The edges have moved out in some places—a little, but they have moved."

"Bogs move and change," Father said. "There was no alder or willow growing along the creek until perhaps twenty years ago. The dyeing pond was bigger, too, if I remember rightly."

Adana smiled and shook her head. "I suppose Grandmother's warning made me nervous," she said. "and I was looking for something to be wrong. It hasn't changed that much, after all."

"No long, boggy arm crawling up the hill to the castle?" I asked.

She laughed. "No, nothing like that. Grandmother didn't say anything about the bog, but I noticed it from the air."

"Never mind," Father said. "I'd rather you let me know. It's good to have a swan's-eye view of the world."

We talked for a while of smaller things, and then Adana rose. "We have to go."

"Of course," Father said. "We'll see you off."

We walked back out into the sharp autumn air.

In the courtyard, Adana stopped. "I want to speak to Mother, or at least try."

"She was around that corner when we came in," I said, pointing. "She was watching us. Maybe she's waiting for you to speak to her."

Adana's look said she didn't altogether believe me. "I'll meet you outside the gate." She walked along the wall and around the corner. She was gone long enough for my fingertips to get chilly. When she came to the gate, her eyes were pink-rimmed, as though she was holding back tears.

"She wants to come with us," Adana said to Gil. "She asked if she could fly back with us, and I had to tell her no."

"Will she listen?" I asked. "Maybe she'll try to follow you."

Adana shook her head.

"Adana is the heir," Gil said. "The voice of the king when he isn't there. I don't think your mother can disobey her."

The word *can* was a blow. Mother as we had known her would probably have chosen to obey Adana's word. More likely, she wouldn't have wanted to fly south and leave us. But now Mother was so much more her swan self that she couldn't choose to defy Adana. She might look human, but in her heart, she wanted to be back in her swan form, among her true people.

I wanted to comfort Adana, but I couldn't think of anything that would help. Gil put his arm around her, and she leaned her head against his shoulder, only for a moment. Then she straightened up.

"I'll come and see you in the spring," she said to Father. She hugged him, and he held her tightly and kissed her hair. Then she hugged me and kissed my cheek, and did the same to Willow and Tuan.

"Take care of yourself," she said to Father.

"Look after her, Gil," Father said.

"I will, Sire."

Then he and Adana unpinned their cloaks. Willow took Gil's cloak. I reached for Adana's, but Father got it first. He folded the cloak over his arm. Then Gil and Adana called up the magic, and two swans stood where two human people had been a few seconds before. They flew away without a backward glance. We watched until their wings were a scribble in the air. I didn't dare look at my father's face; I could feel tears in my own eyes.

I had thought that no winter could be more terrible than the last, with the lung fever and Gil slowly dying under Orla's enchantment. Now what I remembered was all of us—Orla still alive, Mother still herself, and Adana and Gil with us, even through all the bad things.

I walked back inside the gates, but Father stayed where he was. Tuan and Willow fell into step beside me.

"I'm glad you didn't go south, too," I said to Willow.

"I like the snow," she said. She was biting her lips, trying not to laugh.

"What's so funny?" I asked. "I wouldn't mind something to laugh about right now."

"Oh, Kiar," she said, "It's funny that you'd think I'd leave. You and Tuan are as much my flock as the swanfolk are. More, maybe. How could I fly away and never see you all winter?"

"This is going to be a strange winter," I said, "with only the four of us."

"Five," Tuan said, glancing towards the corner of the castle. Mother stood there again, but this time she wasn't watching the sky. She was looking towards the gate, and Father as he gazed at the place in the sky where their eldest daughter had flown away.

CHAPTER

TWO

We found Eatha in the storeroom where lengths of cloth were folded and arranged on shelves once they were finished and dyed. The little room smelled of the plants used to dye the different colours. Skeins of wool for embroidery hung in bundles from the ceiling.

Eatha was winding a rope around a heavy peg in the wall, pulling it taut across the room just above head height. She was short, with dark, greying hair that stood out in wisps from her braid, and strong from working with heavy, wet lengths of cloth. I waited until she'd tied off the rope before I spoke.

"Father told me you wanted to pull cloth from the dyeing pond today," I said. "He asked us to go with you."

"I feel foolish asking for a guard," she said, dusting her hands on her apron, "but the last time I put cloth in the pond, I felt as though something was watching me."

"A wildcat?" Willow asked.

Eatha shook her head. "No, and I didn't smell or hear an animal. Not so much as a peep from the little birds, Lady, and maybe that's why I was uneasy."

"We'll come with you," I said. "But in case we need to move quickly, we should all be mounted."

"Thank you, Lady. I'll speak to the hands at the stables."

"What do you make of that?" I asked when she'd left.

"I don't know," Willow said, "but it can't be anything good. First Adana says the bog is getting bigger, now this."

"And your grandmother said the past is returning," said Tuan.

I shrugged. "Father said the bog has been bigger in the past. Maybe that's what Grandmother meant, the bog getting bigger, taking over pasture."

"Do you really think that?" Willow asked.

"No," I said. "But I don't know how to explain it. And the only angry thing from the past I can think of is Orla, but Gil says it isn't her. Whatever is going on, all we can do is watch what happens and be ready to act. Maybe we'll find something out this morning."

"Swords and spears?" Tuan asked.

"Bows, I think," I said. "If something is there, I don't want to get close enough to spear it. I'd rather shoot it before it gets near."

"Me, too," Willow said.

"I thought you said people tell stories about the bog to scare children," I said.

"It might not be something from the bog," she said. When neither Tuan nor I spoke, she threw up her hands.

"Oh, all right!" she said. "Maybe they're to scare children. But no harm being prepared in case they're real."

"They might be the kind of real that can't be hurt with weapons," I said. We all thought of Orla's spirit, floating above the hearth and the ruins of Aren's harp.

"Magical things can't stand iron," Tuan said. "Orla avoided your knife."

"That's true," Willow said. "Maybe ghosts have to avoid iron, too. Or marsh-feys, or bog-walkers, or whatever is scaring the birds."

"Well," I said, "if it has a body, we can hit it with arrows or swords. If it doesn't have a body, we should be ready to get away as quickly as possible. And who knows, it may not show up at all."

"I hope it does," Tuan said.

"Why?" I asked.

"Then we'll know what it is. Isn't that better than not knowing?"

"I'd be happy not knowing," Willow said. "At least, as long as it never came back."

Privately I agreed with Willow, but I thought it likelier that whatever had spooked Eatha wouldn't simply go away quietly. Eatha was sensible and practical, and she carried a knife as long as her forearm and as sharp as a sword. I'd never seen her nervous, or heard her admit to being afraid of anything, even wolves or bears. If she was nervous enough to ask for a guard, she was honestly scared.

We saddled our horses and found Eatha waiting near the gate. She had a sturdy, little brown mare and a grey pack pony carrying two basketwork panniers, one on either side, and Aislin, her apprentice, held the reins of another grey. Both she and Eatha were dressed, like us, in woollen trousers for riding. Theirs were patched and faded, dark brown to the knees and lighter above, from wading into the peaty water to fetch out dyed lengths of cloth.

"Three of you for the two of us and a pack horse," Eatha said, "I'm going to feel silly if there's no trouble."

"And I'd feel terrible if trouble came, and you didn't have help when you needed it," I said. "Maybe nothing will happen because we're there. You never know."

I checked Kestrel's girth again and patted her neck. Willow was whispering to her horse Whiffle, and Tuan stood with his bay, Lightfoot.

We mounted and rode out the gate, then turned north and walked the horses down the dun. Ahead of us the grain fields were broad stretches of brown stubble. The grain was in bags in the storehouse, and the straw stacked in the barns and stable. The last handful cut from each field had been braided into Grain Women, dolls with the full ears of barley and oats standing up in a shock of hair. They were stored in a special room in the ox-barn. In the spring we'd bury them in the new-ploughed fields, as we'd buried last year's Grain Women this spring past.

"I wish there was a charm against deer," I said. The Grain Women might ensure a good harvest, but they wouldn't keep the deer from eating it. It worried me to think of the end of winter, when bread would be scarce.

"Less grain, more venison," Willow said. But she knew as well as I the deer we'd taken had been thinner than they should be in the fall, their flesh tainted with the taste of fear, even the ones killed cleanly with a single shot. The rabbits and hares snared in the gardens had been the same. For every five bags of grain we'd stored last year, we had four this year. The thin deer wouldn't make up for that.

With the grain harvested, at least there was no need to keep the horses in single file down the path between the fields. We fanned out and rode that way down to the bottom of the dun and then up the long, gentle slope that led to the top of the next rise. Once we started down the other side, the castle gradually fell out of sight, and the land sloped down to a low, flat, broad expanse crossed by the creek that fed into the bog.

"Whoa," Willow murmured to Whiffle. The white mare shuffled her feet. Kestrel lifted her hooves and set them down, one after another. The pack pony tossed his head and jigged in place, and all the horses blew and snorted softly. Their nerves made me edgy, although there was nothing to see or hear to disturb us.

The grass was mostly pale brown and yellow here, and it rustled around the knees of the horses. The blades should have been much shorter, grazed down by deer and nibbled by rabbits and hares. We didn't hunt this meadow for exactly that reason; the good grazing here kept the deer well-fed and out of our fields. I couldn't understand why they'd abandoned it.

Along the creek that flowed east from open meadowland and forest into the bog, the sharp fringes of sedge and reeds stood up tall and still green, although faded from their summer brightness. Clumps of willow, mouse-willow, and alder grew along the bank, along with waterleaf, a shrubby bush with wide, oval leaves Nias used in cooking. Here the creek was halfway to knee-deep and ran quietly. We stopped at the water's edge, and Kestrel stepped closer and put her head down to drink, but lifted it again before she touched the water.

I scanned the dying brown grasses rolling away to the dark mass of forest to the north and west, then glanced up into the sky. Everything looked as it always did, but there was a ticklish spot on the nape of my neck, and I wanted to check over my shoulder. I edged Kestrel around and glanced as far back to my right as I could without turning my head. Nothing. Two crows flew from somewhere beyond the forest to the north, straight and fast over the dark green, then veering off to the east, no more than moving black shapes in the pale blue sky.

"Grawk, grawk." The sound came small but clear from the birds. Not crows then, but ravens.

"Warblers," said Tuan.

"Yes." I hadn't noticed them before; the "weet, weet, wee-eet" of the little brown birds was a constant sound during a quiet day. Only when they stopped singing did you notice they'd been singing at all. Now that Tuan had called my attention to the birds, I heard the warblers, and the kingbird pipping, and the trill of the redthroat.

I clucked to Kestrel and walked her past the others until I was leading our group along the creek.

The water grew both wider and shallower as we approached the dyeing pond at the edge of the bog. The water there had a brownish look, tingeing the pebbles under the surface, then turning dark with the peat swirling through it from bank to bank. A few feet before the edge of the dyeing pond, the creek spread wide and was no more than a sluggish, muddy stretch, without a ripple.

Peeled sticks stood up from the water; some were as thick as a finger. Others around the edge of the pond, where the peat was thicker, were notched. Those marked kegs of butter. Peat-soaked butter made a soothing ointment for dry skin. Other sticks stood out farther in the pond, each one wrapped with a cord that disappeared below the surface.

Eatha and Aislin dismounted and walked past me, leading the pack pony. Eatha found a stake in the ground and picketed the pony, and Aislin took a coil of rope from one of the panniers.

I still heard birdsong from the creek behind us, but nothing closer. I looked around, and as I turned my back on the bog, the skin on the back of my neck shivered. Again I felt as though something was watching me, staring at the spot between my shoulder blades, but when I turned back to the bog, there was nothing to see—only the mists, a bowshot past the dyeing pond that showed where the bog properly began.

I put an arrow to my bow and felt a little better. The feeling of being watched didn't go away, but at least I was prepared for anything that came at us, provided an arrow would stop it.

Eatha stood counting, her finger moving as she muttered numbers. While she counted, Aislin began shaking the rope onto the ground. One end was grubby from long use, but the other end—and about half the length—was stained dark brown.

I could feel Kestrel shifting her feet. She swung her head and a line of white showed in her eye.

"Steady, girl," I said, patting her neck. Willow rode forward and pulled Whiffle to a stop short of the pack pony.

"Does anyone else have the feeling someone is watching?" she asked.

"No," Tuan said.

"It's nerves," Eatha said. From the sound of her voice, she didn't believe it.

"There's nothing here," Aislin said. "We're out in the sun, and nothing from the bog can come out in the daylight. It burns them." She went back to laying out the rope, completely unconcerned.

Willow glared at Aislin's back. I knew she was probably annoyed at being nervous, and Aislin's calm would make her irritation worse. On the other hand, Willow's nerves made me feel a little braver about my own tight shoulders and the ticklish spot on the back of my neck. It wasn't only me, then, who felt alone but also watched. The horses would catch nervousness from us, too.

By the time Eatha finished her count, Aislin had flipped the rope onto the ground in wide, loose loops and slipped a neat harness onto the other end. It went over her shoulders and crossed front and back before tying around her waist. She saw me looking as she tied it snugly.

"If I have to be pulled out, this won't cut me in two," she said.

"Have you ever had to be pulled out?"

"Well, once or twice. There isn't a proper bottom to the bog, you know—only places where the peat is more solid and holds my weight. It took us a while to find those spots, and they move a bit, but if I'm careful, I land on them. If I miss my footing, the rest is too thin to stand on and too thick to swim in."

She kicked around in the grass and found a heavy stake, and another a few feet away, each with a hole cut through. Both were pale and weathered, with shallow splits up the sides. Aislin tested the hold of each one, kicking them. "Still solid," she said.

"All twelve of the markers are here," Eatha said, "So we don't have to poke around looking for anything because the stick has fallen over."

"Do you have another rope?" Willow watched Aislin thread the free end of her rope through the two stakes and then knot it. "We could keep hold of the ends, and there'd be two of you to pull the cloth in."

"If one of you could hold the rope," Eatha said, "I'll get the cloth loaded while Aislin brings it in. That would help," Eatha said. Tuan had dismounted before she finished. He took the knotted end of the rope from Aislin.

"Stand there," Aislin said, pointing. Tuan moved into place and took up some of the slack in the rope. When Aislin walked towards the pond, I saw the stakes were arranged so that both she and Tuan were at an angle to the length of rope running between the stakes. If Aislin had to be pulled out, there were two corners to brace against.

Eatha pulled a long, hooked stick from a pair of loops on the pack pony's harness. "Let's get on with it," she said.

Aislin nodded and waded into the water. In two steps, she was over her knees and reaching for the cord attached to the first stick. She hauled it up in a loop and turned as far as she could with her legs mired in the peat.

Eatha reached with the hooked stick and caught the cord, pulling it towards her until she could grasp it with her hands and pull. Hand-over-hand she pulled, and a fold of cloth emerged from the bog, trailing over the surface in a muddy, rippled sheet.

Before Eatha could get the whole length of fabric to shore, Aislin pulled up a second cord. Eatha stopped pulling on hers and reached out for the loop with her stick.

"Here." Willow dismounted from Whiffle, dropping the reins to the ground. She took the stick from Eatha and hooked the loop Aislin held out.

"I'll help with that," I said.

Willow shook her head. "You stay back there, where you can watch. Someone needs to be on guard."

"Against what?" I muttered to myself, but I had to agree that someone should keep watch. Tuan, despite what he'd said about not feeling watched, kept looking around. The rope was looped once around his waist, and he held the knotted end in his left hand, keeping his right free. He watched our surroundings, the fields and the forest, the bog to the east. I couldn't keep my eyes from the bog, either. It seemed a safe distance away, but whatever was unnerving Eatha and Willow was unlikely to come from anywhere else.

Dark and peaty as the dyepond was, plants still grew around it. Short, upright leaves in patches marked where bog-orchids bloomed in the spring, and low mounds of dark green bogberry bushes, dotted with blood-red berries, made cushions around the edges of the dyeing pond. I'd seen kingbirds and redthroats eat the bogberries, but no person would risk it. Anything that grew this close to the bog was tainted with the uncanniness of the place.

However clear the day, the air around the bog always held a dimness. The border of the bog itself was a curtain of dark air—not exactly mist or smoke—but as hard to see through. Like a curtain, too, it seemed to hide a watching presence, and one that bore no good will to human folk or swanfolk.

I bore the bog a grudge on my own behalf. Over two years ago it, or something in it, had reached out to pull Willow down when she flew too close. She'd bolted, and I'd followed her across the sky and over the borders of Valenia straight into our neighbour and enemy's territory, Noermark. When my father found out how close I'd come to being captured, he'd made me wear an iron necklace to stop me changing to swan form. I hadn't flown for a year.

My own rebelliousness toward my father and my loyalty to Willow had led me into trouble, but a small part of me blamed the bog. Every child, and every adult, knew the stories of things that lived in the bog—not birds and frogs, but marsh-feys and bog-walkers, restless spirits, and vengeful ghosts. Willow doubted these tales, although the swanfolk had their own legends about the bog and its victims.

Now she was acting more nervous than I'd ever seen her, masking it with impatience and activity. She hauled on the cords quickly, hand over muddy hand, as fast as Aislin could drag them up from the peaty water. Eatha folded the dark brown lengths of cloth roughly and laid each one in a pannier on the patient pack horse as she did. Brown water trickled out the sides of the wickerwork and dripped off the bottom. She laid the cords neatly on the ground with the ends together.

"One more," Aislin said. It was the farthest one, and she pulled the final loop of rope out with her as she waded, waist-deep now, the last step to reach the cord. She leaned forward against the thick ooze and stretched her fingers, flicking the ends at the cord.

"Just a—little—farther." She leaned more and hooked two fingers of her left hand around the cord. She was perilously close to overbalancing, and I opened my mouth to say so.

Then everything seemed to move in slow motion. It happened as I opened my mouth to speak, and before I had drawn in my breath.

Every bird stopped singing, cutting off as sharply as if a door had closed between them and us. A breath blew from the bog. There was no other way to describe it; it wasn't a breeze or a gust, but a long, cold sighing, as though someone, or something, were letting out a breath it had held for a long time. It smelled of nothing—not rotting vegetation, or peaty water, or autumn air. The closest thing I could think of was the air of a cold winter day, carrying no scent at all. As the last of it died away, I smelled something like smoke and leather, a familiar odor from the day Willow pulled away from the reach of the bog with the edges of her wings scorched and blackened. It turned my stomach, and acid rose in the back of my throat.

It seemed the birds had stopped singing hours ago. The very ripples in the pond stood as though they'd been cut in stone. Aislin leaned forward, a strand of her hair hanging motionless over her ear while that breath blew out, and then stopped. The birds flew up all around us in a whirr and rustle of wings, and time started again.

And Aislin, with a short, startled shriek, disappeared into the dyeing pond as though a hole had opened beneath her feet. She didn't fall forward, as I'd feared she was going to do, but straight down. The cord she'd grabbed pulled taut; the stick tied to it leaned and bent towards the surface of the pond, and the other end of it, attached to the cloth, sprang to the top of the peaty water. The rope that anchored her to shore snapped straight.

When Aislin shrieked, Kestrel started but stayed in place. The other horses, without riders to steady them, shied and danced away, and the packhorse, picketed in place, jerked on his rope and snorted. I glanced at Tuan. He leaned hard against the rope and backed up. The curve and loop the rope had made on the grass was gone; it had pulled into a taut line that slanted towards the dyeing pond. At the edge of the pond, Eatha and Willow hauled on the rope, Willow backing out of the dark water as she pulled. At each pull, Tuan backed and took up slack. Drops sprang from the rope, wrung tight.

In battle, you seem to see faster. This was the same; even as I saw these small details, I was off my horse. Drowning is fast; if Aislin had sucked in a lungful of that dark water, she could already be dying. I slipped my bow back over my shoulder as I ran the few steps to Willow and Eatha.

They'd pulled in a few yards of sodden rope, and Aislin's hand reappeared above the surface as I grabbed hold behind Eatha and hauled. Aislin's fingers were still clenched around the cord attached to the last length of cloth, then her other hand came up, flailing, and caught the rope we held. We heaved again, and her head broke the surface, hair plastered down, skin splotched with peat, and she coughed up a gout of water, gasped, and coughed again.

We hauled again, and I felt the thrum of the rope behind me pulling tight as Tuan took up the slack. The three of us pulled Aislin, still submerged to the waist and clinging to the rope for dear life, back to shore. Willow caught Aislin's arm and pulled her to her feet. She bent over, coughing, but she was alive.

"You're hurt," I said. Blood seeped between the fingers of her left hand, still clenched around the cord that held the last length of cloth. The cloth itself had come up with her; part of it was still underwater, but a few feet lay in wet folds on the peat surface.

"No wonder you were heavy," Eatha said. "You could have let that go; we wouldn't want to lose you for a length of wool!"

"I forgot," Aislin said, and spat. Her lips were flecked with peat, and she spat again, trying to clear it out of her mouth. Then she retched twice, but only a little water came up.

Eatha took a water-skin from her horse's saddle. While Aislin rinsed out her mouth, Willow hauled in the last piece of cloth and splashed to shore.

"Do we need to stand in the water?" Willow asked.

That was when I noticed at last. I stood in the dyeing pond, in water halfway to my knees. Underneath the surface, the pale, dry meadow grass gleamed dimly. Eatha had tethered the pack horse six paces away from the edge of the pond. Now he stood fetlock-deep in brown water.

As I looked around the bog, a shudder went up my back. Had the murky air, the chill and watching presence, been this close when we arrived? I didn't think it had.

"The bog," I said. "Whatever happened right now, it's bigger than when we arrived."

CHAPTER

THREE

Tuan had pulled the rope free of the stakes and was winding it in loops. Willow held the last length of cloth spread out between her hands to fold. Eatha held the waterskin while Aislin fumbled at the knot in her harness. For a few seconds, everyone stopped what they were doing, and we all looked at the bog and the newly expanded edge of the dyeing pond. I took my bow off my shoulder and put an arrow on the string. Step by step, I backed away from the bog, Something moved at the edges of my vision, but when I looked at it directly, it slid away. Or had it been there at all? The back of my neck still tingled, and I felt goosebumps on my arms.

"We should leave." Willow stuffed the last piece of cloth into the pannier, not bothering to fold it. One corner trailed down the side of the basket, a thin stream of water running off the lowest point.

"Yes," said Eatha. She picked up one of the trailing cords, no longer neatly on the ground but washed apart in the spreading water. "If I don't knot these together first, we won't find them next time."

"Forget about next time," I said. "Let's move."

Willow untied the packhorse from his picket and led him out of the shallow water towards the other horses. They all, even Kestrel, stood beyond the new shoreline, ears pricked and nostrils wide, looking towards the bog. Tuan coiled the rope all the way to Aislin and pushed her hands away from the knot on her harness.

"Here," he said, and dropped the coil of rope across her shoulder. "Take it off later." He took the water-skin from Eatha, who still gazed at the dyeing pond as though stunned; he pulled her by the arm towards the horses. It seemed to take forever to get everyone out of the water and mounted. Finally I heard the sounds of horses trotting then cantering away.

Tuan came up beside me on Lightfoot, Kestrel's reins in his hand. I handed him my bow and took the reins, and he watched the bog while I mounted.

"Thanks. Let's go," I said. That moment of turning away from the bog made my whole back shudder, as though ranks of archers were waiting for me to turn my back before they shot. I felt as if someone, or something, wanted me to look back, but I kept my eyes forward, I flicked the reins and clucked to Kestrel. She needed no urging, and we galloped after Eatha, Aislin and Willow. We didn't pull up until we reached the crest of the rise.

"There, now," I said and patted Kestrel's neck. She blew though her nose and shook her head, jingling the rings at her bit. "We should be safe here. Aislin, do you need something for your hand?"

"I'm all right," she said, letting go of the rein. She'd held it curled in her fingers and away from the palm. Now she opened her hand, still oozing blood. Then she slumped sideways, and Willow barely managed to get hold of her arm before she could fall out of the saddle.

We eased Aislin to the ground, but her legs wouldn't hold her. She sat blinking and speechless on the cold earth. Tuan brought his water-skin over, and Eatha coaxed Aislin's hand open and trickled water over the palm. Blood-stained water and flecks of peat ran off the side of her hand.

Tuan went back to Lightfoot and flipped open the saddlebag. When he returned to Aislin, he carried a strip of linen smeared with green salve. He dried Aislin's hand with one end of the strip, then wrapped it around her palm.

"Ow," Aislin said. She shook her head. "I'm sorry. Did I fall?" Her mouth twitched, and her eyes filled. "I thought I was going to drown," she said, and the tears spilled over. She slumped a little sideways, and her horse jigged away.

Tuan felt her hands. "She's cold."

I could see she was shivering. Her clothes were still dripping water, which was enough to make anyone cold on a brisk autumn day. More than that, her narrow escape had shocked her spirit. I remembered my own feelings of chill after my fight with

Hafor, one of the sons of King Gythorn of Noermark, when he'd trespassed in the spring.

"I have dry clothes," Eatha said, "and a blanket. Changing out of those wet things would help. Food, too."

"Do it, then, but quickly," I said.

Tuan pulled Aislin to her feet and supported her. Willow dismounted and undid the knots of the harness, lifted it off her, and hung it from her horse's saddle. Then Willow and I helped Aislin out of her clothes. She shook in long shudders, staring at nothing. With her back to her horse and the two of us in front of her, she was at least shielded from any breeze. When all her wet things were off, Eatha draped a blanket around her and rubbed her back and shoulders dry before pulling a long linen shirt over her head. She followed it up with a grey woollen gown, wide-skirted enough to allow riding, and put a piece of dried apple into her mouth.

Aislin chewed and seemed to wake from her stupor. Her eyes moved from me to Willow.

"I wish we had some spirits of wine," I said.

Tuan pulled a small flask from his saddlebag.

"What else do you have in there?" I asked.

He shrugged and gave me a small smile. "A needle, thread, bandages. Dar always carries these things," he said. "I learned it from him." He put the flask to Aislin's lips. She took a drink and sputtered. "Better?" he asked, and she nodded.

"You should ride with someone," I said. "We don't want you falling off on the way home. Can you hold on until then?" Aislin's face was blank, and she didn't answer.

"Get up behind me," I said. Kestrel was the heaviest of the horses with us, and Aislin was small and light. I mounted, and Tuan boosted her up, still clutching the blanket around her shoulders. She wrapped her arms around my waist, and we started down the other side of the hill and back towards the castle.

Willow stood up in her stirrups and gazed back at the bog.

"It doesn't look different from here," she said. "You'd hardly know it happened."

"Did anyone else hear—a breath?" I asked. "Or smell anything—smoke or, I don't know, burning feathers?"

Tuan shook his head.

"No," Eatha said.

"Me either," said Willow.

"Aislin?"

"Not me."

"It was right after you fell in. The birds stopped singing, and then started again, and I felt a breeze only, somehow, I thought it was something breathing in the bog."

"I noticed the birds," Willow said. "All at once. I heard a kingbird stop in the middle of a chirp, as though it suddenly disappeared. I didn't feel anything of what you're saying."

"What happened to you?" I asked Aislin. "Did you miss your step?"

"No," she said. "The ground moved under my feet. I was standing on a firm spot, but it slipped away."

"It's a good thing you wear that harness," Willow said.

All the way down the hill, and back up the dun to the castle, I wondered what exactly had happened at the bog. Nobody else had heard the breath or felt the air move. Nobody else had smelled burnt feathers. Maybe they simply hadn't noticed. But Tuan, at least, had been paying as much attention to our surroundings as I had, and Willow had been nervous, too, and would have noticed anything out of the ordinary. Why hadn't they noticed?

I could think of only two explanations. One, I'd imagined the air moving and the smell, the feeling of someone watching and waiting, and then noticing me. My own nerves had played tricks on me. I didn't want to think I could be so easily spooked. We'd half-expected some kind of trouble, but we'd all been looking for something more tangible. A wolf, or an ogre, or a bog-walker attacking us from the mist would have been less unnerving.

The other explanation I liked much less. Ever since I'd spent a year wearing iron, any magic directed at me, or even done near me, made me feel sick. If I hadn't imagined the bog breathing, and if nobody else had noticed it, then it meant that something magical had noticed me, and sent that air especially to me. For what, I couldn't imagine. I also couldn't imagine it would be for something good.

CHAPTER

FOUR

I went looking for Father. The sudden expansion of the dyeing pond, and maybe the bog itself, was something he needed to know. I found him in the armoury, looking at a boar spear.

"Has somebody seen another boar?" I asked.

He turned the spear in his hands.

"Kiar! No, just remembering. I hope we're done with boar for this year."

"So do I," I said. "At least the harvest's in. They can't do any more damage there. And there was lots for them to eat this year. It doesn't make any sense."

"No, it doesn't," he said. "In other years there's been less, and we haven't had this trouble. And they're so thin. Hardly worth going after, if they weren't into the crops."

"You'll be careful, though, if you go after one," I said.

"I'm always careful, as much as you can be hunting something big and dangerous. What's this about, daughter of mine?"

I looked at him. His face, too, was thinner than it had been last year. The grey in his hair had increased. I didn't know what to say.

As though he'd read my thoughts, he said, "We all get older, Kiar, but I can still handle a spear and keep the boar's tusks out of me and my horse. Something Gythorn won't be doing for a while."

King Gythorn of Noermark, our enemy to the north, was a few years older than Father and had five sons, three of whom he had exiled. One had been unwise enough to disagree with him, and two others had failed to marry into our family and give Gythorn a foothold in Valenia.

A month ago, Guthric, the ambassador from Noermark, had brought news that Gythorn had been thrown from his horse, breaking a bone in his leg. A child would be back on his feet, with the bone splinted and a crutch to lean on, in a week or so, and healed in six. A young man might need a few more weeks.

By the time we heard the news, Gythorn's accident was several weeks in the past, and he was still not on his feet. Secretly I wondered if he would ever heal enough to walk again, let alone ride.

"I hope he gets better soon," I said.

"Wishing our old enemy well?" Father raised an eyebrow.

"At least we know him," I said. "I'd rather deal with him than Beorn. If Beorn comes to the throne, there may be raids again." Secretly I worried about my father being injured the same way. If Gythorn didn't heal well, would he?

"What happened this morning?" Father asked. He set the boar spear carefully in the rack with the others.

"Not what I expected," I said, "though I don't know what I expected. Maybe your boar."

"What did you see?"

"Nothing. That's the problem. Willow was very nervous. She felt she was being watched, and I felt it myself. You know how the back of your neck goes tickly and your skin crawls?"

He nodded and folded his arms, watching me.

"I felt that way the whole time. Willow was edgy, too. She couldn't keep still. I don't think I've ever seen her that nervous. She helped haul in the cloth so we could get out of there sooner."

"And what happened?"

"Nothing until Aislin was getting the last piece of cloth. Then she fell in the pond. She didn't trip—she said after the ground under her feet just disappeared. She went in over her head. We pulled her out before she drowned, and by then the pond was bigger. Six or eight paces bigger anyway, where we were. Maybe the bog, too. It seemed closer."

"Did it?" I almost didn't hear him, and then he cleared his throat. "Did it, then?"

"I think so. Father, what's wrong?"

He waved my question off, and his tone when he spoke was light, almost mocking. "So you didn't see anything in particular, no boars, no bog-walkers?"

"No-o," I said, "but there were two scary things. Three, if you count the pond getting bigger."

"I think we have to count that," he said. "What were the others?"

"Well, all the birds stopped singing at once, right before Aislin fell in. And the bog breathed. I know it sounds odd, but that's how it seemed."

"Breathed."

"Yes, as if it had been holding its breath and let it out, the way you do when you shoot an arrow. I felt something was watching us. And then Aislin fell in, and the feeling went away."

Father said nothing.

"And while that was happening," I said, "it felt as though time had stopped. I could *see* Aislin overbalancing, but nothing was moving, not the water or the grass, or anything."

"Is that everything?" he asked.

"Not quite," I said. "Nobody else heard the breath. Nobody felt the air move, not even Tuan. He was keeping watch, the same as I was. I'd expect him to notice something that strange. I think it's something magical. I think it was meant for me."

"Did it feel angry, like it wanted to hurt you?" he asked. The question stopped me cold. I thought back to that endless moment, to the feeling of being watched, to the breath. I couldn't remember feeling that what watched me had wished me ill. On the other hand, lots of things can kill you without wishing you any ill at all—falling rocks, a charging boar, water.

"No," I said. "But then Aislin might have drowned. Why?"

"Something from your great-great-grandfather's time, I believe. Coren the second. That was an unlucky generation. He came to the throne because his older brother Terrel died in a hunting accident, unmarried and leaving no children. Coren was thirty or thereabouts when he was crowned, and also unmarried. Right after the coronation, he married a woman of the court."

"Who was she?" I asked.

"Her name was Ellian, and it's said she was the daughter of the captain of the guard. He'd probably known her all her life. They had a son and a daughter, and perhaps ten years after his coronation, he died of the lung fever. So did the queen, and their daughter. His son survived, Tirian, but he was only eight or nine years old."

"What happened?"

"Lucky for him, his grandmother was still alive. The men swore allegiance to him, but she was the one who held the reins, so to speak. Then a young man turned up who said he was Terrel's son, born to a woman of Dendale. He said Terrel had married her in secret but died before bringing her to Valenia."

"Did he really do that? Why didn't he tell someone? Why didn't the woman?"

"Nobody knows. Maybe after Terrel died, she hadn't the heart to fight for her son to be recognized. Or maybe it was all a lie. Either way, he was the right age, and Terrel had been in Dendale for the marriage of his aunt to the king there, about a year before the young man said he was born.

"This man, Connar, claimed he was the rightful king, because he was Terrel's oldest, true-born son. And with Tirian still a child, some felt it would be better for the kingdom to have a man on the throne.

"There was trouble, of course. Some sided with the young man, though most stood by the old queen."

"Did she believe him, the grandmother?"

"She might have, but it didn't stop her from driving the young man out. She banished anyone who took his side and held to it. There was one battle, not a big one, but bad because it was Valenians fighting Valenians, as well as Dendalesmen. Connar was killed, and his supporters fled."

"What about their families?"

"I don't know. I suppose if they swore to the young king, they could stay. A hard choice to make, it was. But for the few weeks Connar was around, things were unsettled, and it's said the bog flooded up the creek and washed over the whole of that pasture, all the low ground. My father told me the land wasn't under water anymore when he was a lad, but it was still wet. By the time he came to the throne, it was dry as before, and they could use it for grazing."

I felt more uneasy than ever. If the bog had grown once, it might do so again.

"Do *you* think the bog grew because Connar contested the throne?"

Father shrugged his shoulders. "I don't rightly know," he said. "But something caused it, and then for some reason, it pulled back."

I thought of the bog taking over the lower pasture for a whole generation, and then receding.

"It has to be more than a wet summer," I said. "Unless it was thirty years of them. And that doesn't explain this morning."

"No," Father said, "it doesn't. I don't know what would. But I can't say I'm happy about it."

"I'm not either," I said.

"It frightened you," Father said.

I nodded.

He held out his arms, and I went to him as though I were still a little girl, not a grown woman and a fighter. He was still tall enough to tuck me under his chin. Then he kissed the top of my head and pushed me gently away.

"At least you came back none the worse," he said, "and now you're warned and can be on your guard. Whatever it is won't take you by surprise. And it isn't a boar. There's that."

"It worries me that something magical singled me out."

"Yes," he said, thoughtfully rubbing his chin. "In the meantime, we should probably stay away from the bog. All right?"

I nodded. It wasn't a promise I needed to make. I couldn't think of anything that would make me want to go within sight of the bog and whatever power was lurking there.

CHAPTER

FIVE

When we came out of the armoury, Tuan and Willow were waiting for me. Both still wore clothes muddied and wet from the bog. They started over to us, and Father patted my shoulder and walked away before they arrived.

"How's Aislin?" I asked.

"She's all right," Willow said. "A change of clothes and a hot drink in the hall. She's sleeping now."

"Even without nearly drowning, I'd be tired from being up to my waist in cold water," I said. "Father says we're not to go back to the bog, at least for now."

"I want to see if the pond stays wide or recedes," Willow said. "If what you felt was magical, maybe it was something trying to drive us off. The pond might have gone back to normal after we left."

"And it might stop being normal if we go back to look."

"At least we'd know," she said.

"Know what? That something in the bog hates us?" I knew this wasn't strictly true. There hadn't been any feeling of hatred, or a sense that something wanted us gone. All we had felt—except for me—was the sense of being watched.

"We don't know it hates us," Willow said. "At least, it might only hate, well, humans. Not swanfolk."

"That's why it tried to knock you out of the air that time." I said.

"Whatever it was," Willow said, "all that really happened was Aislin falling in. If the bog was shifting, that could have happened anyway."

"There's something else," Tuan said, looking at me. "It's the king, isn't it?"

I nodded. "He says I don't need to be frightened of whatever was in the bog, but he won't say any more about it, except to stay away. But the look on his face—there's something he's not telling me."

"It can't get us here," said Willow. She began to look over her shoulder but stopped. It was no comfort to know she was nervous.

"The bog expanded quickly this morning," I said. "Where did all that water come from? And how did it move closer? If it can do that much in the time we were pulling Aislin out of the pond, maybe it *could* flood right up to the castle, or over it. Maybe in one night while we're asleep."

"It couldn't." Willow said, but her voice was uncertain.

"Maybe not," I said. "But if it flooded that part of the meadows, we'd lose the farther fields, and places to get mushrooms and wild greens, and some of the summer grazing."

"Is he thinking of the old way?" Tuan asked. "The king?"

Willow snorted.

"What old way?" I asked. Tuan looked at Willow, who shrugged and shook her head.

"Go ahead," she said. "Tell her, then. I don't know why you bother knowing these things."

"What things?" I asked.

"It's only old tales the elders tell," Willow said. "I bet hardly anyone remembers after they grow up."

"What old way?" I asked again. "Is this about the king-light again?" I knew a little about the mysteriously invisible light that shone from the true king or queen of a land. Somehow it told others—whether or not they could see it—the person who had it was bound to the land and cared for it.

"A little," Tuan said. "It's about the king and the land."

"And it's not a proper legend," Willow said. "It's something in the middle of one of the tales about Amala and a human land she visited."

"Valenia?" I asked.

"Maybe it was," Tuan said. "One of the human lands she visited would kill the king if he was ill or weak. The story says that if the king was weak, the land was weak. A new, strong king would make the land strong again."

"Father still goes out on patrol," I said. He was still strong, even if he'd gone only once since the spring and preferred to stay near Mother.

"It's not only about fighting," Tuan said. "If there was a drought, a bad harvest—"

"A flood," Willow interrupted.

"Yes, or a flood," Tuan said. "That could also mean the king was weakening."

"His people would kill him for a drought?" The idea was horrifying. "We've had droughts," I said, "and floods in the spring. We've had hard winters with almost not enough food to get by. Nobody ever thought killing Father would make it better! It couldn't have been Valenia. We don't do that!"

Tuan said nothing.

"We don't!" I repeated. "We didn't! And nobody is going to kill him now for this!"

"Of course not," Willow put her hand on my back and rubbed between my shoulders. "I told you it was stupid, Tuan. It's an old tale, Kiar. Don't think about it. Nobody is going to kill the king. Nobody would dare!"

"No, they won't," I said. "Because I won't let them!"

"It's an elders' tale," Willow repeated, still rubbing my back. She glared at Tuan.

"I'm sorry," he said.

"My father has told me all sorts of things about our past. *If* our ancestors used to kill kings, I'm sure he would have said." Now I was glaring at Tuan as well, angry for a reason I couldn't pin down.

"I didn't mean to frighten you," he said.

"I'm not afraid! I'm angry!" I was almost shouting now.

Tuan took a step back, and then bowed slightly and walked away. Furious, I opened my mouth to call him back, but closed it again. The truth was, I was frightened. I didn't want to believe Tuan, but I suspected that something in what he was saying was true.

Droughts or spring flooding, or a long, hard winter—those were natural things. The king could lead his people through those. I'd seen my father carrying water or ditching against flooding along with his men. None of us in the royal family ate more or better than any servant in the household when times were lean.

If the bog, or something in it, were trying to take over our land, that smacked of magic, and a will set against ours. If my father had no way to fight such magic, would someone try to kill him to make way for a new ruler? And if that ruler was me, as everyone knew it would be, how would I know what to do any better than he did?

CHAPTER

SIX

A groom had led Kestrel into her stall, but now I went to brush her down. In places, her hair was matted with sweat; she must have been frightened, too. The white feathers around her fetlocks were clumped and brownish. I brought a cloth and a bucket of water and washed her legs and feet clean of the bog water and specks of peat, then combed out her mane and tail. The warm, sweet smell of hay and horses soothed and comforted me.

Willow had followed me to the stables and was brushing Whiffle several stalls down. Lightfoot wasn't in his stall, and I wondered for a moment if Tuan had gone back out, riding off on some errand of his own. Willow might know. A year ago I would have asked her. Now I felt an unaccustomed hurt that he had gone without telling me where, and a stubborn reluctance to ask about him.

As I carried the bucket out of Kestrel's stall, Willow leaned over Whiffle's door.

"Sianna might know something about the bog," she said. "Did you want to go and ask her?"

Sianna, the wisewoman, lived half a day's ride away. For the last few months, she'd been healing from our confrontation with Orla, a fight that had left her with burns on her hands and an injured knee. She had also used a great deal of magic in that fight, and done some hard magical and physical work the next two days destroying Orla's things. She probably still needed time to heal and rest. I didn't want to disturb her unnecessarily.

"Ask her what?" I said. "I mean, what can I ask her about? This morning Father said the bog used to be bigger than it is now. Now it's bigger again. Maybe it always happens all at once. Maybe that's usual."

Willow twisted one side of her mouth up and raised her eyebrows. Her whole face said she didn't believe me.

"What would I tell her? Adana said it was probably nothing, that she might have been spooked by what Grandmother said."

"But you heard something breathing, and felt it, too."

"So what? Nobody else did."

"Yes, that's true," Willow said. "But nobody else saw what was happening with Orla and Gil, either. You were right, and everybody who didn't see it was wrong. If you say you saw or heard or felt something, and nobody else did, I believe you. And Tuan does, too."

I watched her, thinking about this.

"The elders' stories," she said. "I remember some of them. They stick in your head. It's hard to believe they could be true, though, when everything is so ordinary. Maybe they aren't anything but old tales. But if there's some truth to them—well, maybe it's better to know. Then you won't be caught by surprise."

"It sounded," I said, "as though Tuan thought my father would have to die."

"That's not true," Willow said. "He was asking if your father might be thinking that himself, because of the old tales. I don't know how it is with human people, but a swan whose mate is hurt or sick often fails, too. They grieve and worry and forget to eat. The king hasn't been the same since the queen—" She paused. "Stopped talking. After Orla."

"I know," I said.

"So if something is coming after him from the bog, we could be prepared. We could protect him. And if he's thinking of going off by himself to challenge it, we could stop him somehow or at least get ahead of him."

I turned to look at her. "Is that what you think? Really?"
She nodded.

My eyes burned. "I can't imagine my father not being there anymore."

"But Kiar, everyone dies. Nobody goes on forever. Sometime you'll be queen. You'll have to know what's happening with your people, even if it's bad." She paused. "Maybe especially if it's bad."

"I suppose you're right." I sighed and stroked Kestrel's neck. "When Tuan comes back, I'll ask him to tell me what he was going to say before."

"Good." She kissed Whiffle's nose and came out of the stall. "Now you're talking like a queen."

That afternoon I took my sword and went out to the practice pells, man-high pieces of oak trunk set into the ground behind the east guardhouse barracks. I worked with my sword until I drew a sweat, first with a stationery pell, then with one that spun when hit off-centre. The spinning ones had arms sticking straight out to the sides and spun quick enough to thwack a slow opponent.

When I finished, I went to the bathhouse. The hot water eased my muscles and quieted my mind. By the time I was dry, dressed again, and walking back to the castle, I felt calmer than I had since going to the bog.

Near the gate, a groom led a brown and white horse, light and long-legged, across to the stables. I stopped to look again, and as the horse moved, the markings changed, and I saw that it was a brown horse, marked with sweat and foam. Someone had ridden him hard. A girl stood speaking with the guard. She was probably no more than ten or eleven, and her hands were clasped together over her grey riding cloak.

I walked towards the gate, and the guard pointed to me.

She nodded and came running towards me. She'd barely stopped before she bowed her head and went onto one knee. "Princess Kiar," she said.

I felt my face heat up. "Get up," I said. "Kneeling's for the king."

"Yes, Lady," she said, and stood. She had dark rings under her eyes, startling against her pale face. She was clearly exhausted. "High Moor was attacked last evenin', Lady, jus' at nightfall."

"Attacked? Who attacked you?"

"I don' know, Lady," she said.

I put my hand on her shoulder and felt her trembling. She must have ridden all night at a walk, and then pushed her horse and herself hard today. If she didn't sit down soon, she would fall.

"What's your name?" I asked.

"Corvie, Lady."

"Well, Corvie of High Moor," I said, "come in. You can sit and eat while you give your news."

I sent someone to find my father and took Corvie straight to his council chamber. What had happened at High Moor to make them send a girl out into the night with the message? And alone?

"Wait until my father comes," I said. "Then you can tell it only once."

She nodded, and when the food came—three slices of hot pork with stewed apples, bread with butter, and a cup of milk—she watched it from the door to the table.

"Eat," I said.

Corvie promptly pulled out her small knife and started on the pork, eating almost as fast as she cut it. She was halfway through the second slice when Father came in. She dropped her knife onto the plate and jumped to her feet. She swallowed her mouthful and made to kneel.

"Sit down," Father said.

She stopped in mid-movement, and then almost fell back into her chair.

"This is Corvie of High Moor," I said. "They were attacked last evening at dusk."

"Who?" Father said.

"I don't know, Sire," Corvie said. "Da said they were comin' out of the trees, but he didn't say who. He jus' put me on Sparrow an' sent me to you for help."

"Did you hear anything else?" he asked.

She shook her head. "No, Sire. But—"

"But?" he said.

"I stopped, see, when we reached the field, 'cause I thought, well, I wanted to see who 'twas. So I could say. There was still some light, see? An'—" She stopped.

"Did you see who it was?" Father asked.

"'Twasn't a who," she said. "'Twas—" Her voice fell to a whisper. "Trees."

"Trees?" I said.

She nodded.

"You're sure?"

"No," she said, "But they weren't people. Least, they had legs an' heads an' that, but they ran different from people. They moved different. Jerky, like, an' quick, almost jumping. An' they were all brown."

"How many?" Father asked.

"I counted twelve," she said, "least, twelve I saw runnin'. There were ones at the wall already."

"Get the men together," Father said to me. "We'll want as many as we can take from the night watch as they'll be best rested. We can't move fast through the night, but we can get a good start before dark if we hurry."

"It's been almost a whole day," I said to Father. He knew what I meant; we might need wagons for the wounded, and to salvage anything that the raiders hadn't stolen or destroyed.

"We've a good wall," Corvie said. Her eyes flicked from Father to me. We all knew the wall wasn't the solid stone of the castle wall. Solid and strong as it might be, it was wooden, and wooden walls can be burned.

"And I'm sure your father and his people know how to defend it." Father turned to me. "Order the wagons to follow, but we'll go fast and light now. And send messengers to warn the other farmsteads."

"Yes, Father," I said.

In less than an hour, we had thirty fighters mounted in the courtyard.

"I hadn't planned for both of us to go," Father said when he saw me, with Willow and Tuan flanking me. I said nothing, but I didn't move to leave the group. He smiled briefly.

"If it's more than a farmstead raid," he said, "I want you back here as fast as you can go without killing the horses. We'll need a defence, and either you or I should be here. That is a command, Kiar. Do you understand me?"

"Yes," I said.

"Then you can come. But if I give the word, you leave."

"I understand."

"Good."

We rode out of the gate.

CHAPTER

SEVEN

The first part of the journey went quickly. The horses were fresh, and the light was still good. We made the best of it, cantering for short stretches where Corvie's horse had left a clear track towards High Moor in the northeast, trotting as much as possible. All too soon, the sun dipped behind the forest to the west, and the quick autumn twilight was upon us.

When it became darker we stopped long enough to light a single torch, and one of us went ahead to check the ground. We had to walk the horses then. Willow rode up on my right, and Tuan on my left.

"What do you think she meant by trees?" Willow asked.

"I don't know," I said. "Maybe they were carrying branches, so nobody would notice them against the forest."

"But they'd be easy to spot on open ground," she said.

"I know. It doesn't make sense. Anyway, she didn't say they had branches, only that they were brown, and ran differently from people. They made her think of trees."

"She was scared, and the light wasn't good," Tuan said.

"I know," I said. "Maybe it was armour, something made of leather. But armour shouldn't change the way you run." I thought for a minute. "And there's something else. Why attack at dusk?"

"So they won't see you?" Willow asked.

"But it didn't work. And it's hard to fight in the dark. Better to attack at dawn. For one thing, unless they're expecting an attack, more people are asleep. They might have one on watch at a farmstead, or maybe only the dogs. You'd still have a kind of twilight, and then you'd be able to see what you were doing afterwards."

"It's hard to miss a whole farmstead," Willow said. "Besides, they'd light torches."

"Or set it on fire," Tuan said.

We all looked ahead, but the only light came from the east, where the moon was rising.

"I guess not," Willow said. "We'd see it from here, wouldn't we? It wouldn't burn completely in one night?"

"Even if it had, we might smell smoke," I said. "It carries a long way." Nobody said what we all knew—that if High Moor hadn't been burned, it could still have been taken. One breach in the wall would let them in.

The dusk attack bothered me. Torches were more trouble than help. Looking into one blinded you for a few seconds and ruined your night vision for longer, and you had to be careful not to set yourself or your friends on fire. The only reason to take fire into a fight was to use it on your enemy.

"I wish I knew who they are," I said.

"Or what," Tuan said.

Willow leaned forward to look past me at Tuan.

"I wish you hadn't said that. I'm getting back in line." She reined in Whiffle behind Kestrel again. We rode on in the failing light.

I didn't notice the moment at which the horse ahead of me went from being a darker shadow in the dark to merely the sound of hooves and harness. We rode into the night, keeping our course northeasterly by the stars.

The day caught up with me—Adana's warning, the events at the dyeing pond, my work at the pells—and I dozed in the saddle for brief snatches, waking as my head fell forward onto my chest. Surely at least some of the men who were here would normally be asleep. I knew the threat of an enemy would jolt me awake when we got to High Moor—if an enemy was there, and if High Moor itself was still there—but I wished for my bed.

Near the middle of the night Father called a brief halt.

"We'll sleep for two hours," he said. He set guards to keep watch and rouse us when the time was up. We unsaddled and picketed the horses. I laid my head on my saddle for a pillow and was asleep before I knew it. It seemed no time at all before someone shook my shoulder to rouse me.

We saddled up again by torchlight and continued northward at a walk. I wiggled my fingers in my gloves and my toes in my boots to warm them up, all the while wishing for a hot drink.

At least we'd brought water and bread and dried meat. After our brief sleep, the hours of riding seemed to stretch on longer than the hours before it. Finally, when I'd stopped looking for it, the sky to the east turned a shade less dark. The man at the front put out the torch, and in minutes I could see Whiffle ahead of me and Willow's back fade into shape out of the brightening air.

Shortly after dawn, we came on a stream and stopped to water the horses and rest for a few more minutes.

"When we come to High Moor," Father said, "If it's under attack, half the force will come forward with me, and the other half will stay back with Princess Kiar and sweep around the other side of the farmstead. If it is more than a raiding party, Princess Kiar alone is to ride straight back to the castle and prepare a defence. The rest will stay with me and do what we can before falling back to the castle. Understood?"

"Yes, Sire," a few of the men said. Most of us nodded.

"If there is no attack happening, or if the farmstead has been taken and burned, we will stand off and Tarin, you'll scout for survivors and signs of ambush. Wave your right arm slowly three times if it's safe to come in."

"Yes, Sire," said Tarin. He was one of our best scouts, and his little brown horse was fast and light, nimble as a goat. If he had to scout, he'd be in and out quickly and miss little.

"Good. Let's go on then."

We mounted and rode on, our group fanned out now and watching for anything out of place. The land changed from deer-grazed wild pasture to fenced grazing, and then to stubbly harvested fields.

"The fences haven't been damaged," Willow said.

"Lucky, that," Tarin said. "they could have burned them and set fire to the grass and stubble."

When the walls of High Moor came into sight, we halted. There was no sign of movement. Tarin clucked to his horse and cantered ahead. He rode in a wide arc to the south, away from the forests that bordered the lands of High Moor on the north. I watched him ride out of sight behind the walls, then back out from behind them on the north. He pulled the horse to a walk, then a halt. After dismounting, he examined the ground, then the walls of High Moor.

"Can't see anything burned this side," someone said. "No spears or arrows, nothing sticking in the walls."

"Could have taken them when they left," someone else answered.

"Walk up to a wall to draw a spear? Get a rock dropped on you, or boiling water, easy as not."

"Hmmph."

Someone waved from inside the walls, and I heard a voice, though I couldn't make out the words. Tarin called back, then re-mounted and turned the horse to face us. Three or four people came out of High Moor and stood near Tarin, talking and waving their hands and pointing at the forest. After a few minutes, Tarin faced us and waved his right arm three times over his head.

The marks of battle were easier to see as we drew closer: trampled ground, scoring in the timbers of the wall, arrows and spears still sticking where they'd struck the earth.

"There's nothing in the walls, no arrows, no spears," I said. "Everything in the ground seems to have come from inside High Moor."

"Maybe everything from the intruders landed inside," Willow said.

"Nobody's that good. If they retreated, then they stopped to get their weapons. Who does that?"

"Or maybe they had none," Tuan said.

"Can you imagine attacking a walled farmstead with no weapons at all?"

"I can't imagine why anyone *would* attack one," Willow said. "It's not as though a farmstead would attack you first."

"For the stored food, horses, livestock," I said. "Or to show us they could. Remember Hafor's little raid."

"They killed a sheep," Willow said. "They didn't attack Stony Ridge."

"Same thing," Tuan said. "Just bigger." He and Willow exchanged a glance.

By the time we arrived at High Moor, it seemed almost everyone in the farmstead was outside the walls. Some of the younger children were running around in sheer relief at no longer being cooped up. Older ones, who had likely been part of the defence the night before, stood quietly with the adults. No toddlers or babies were present outside the walls.

A grey-haired woman, her eyes dark with fatigue, came before Father.

"You are very welcome here, Sire," she said, "and we thank you for coming so quickly. I am Rheann. My son would welcome you himself, but he was injured in the fight. How is my granddaughter?"

"When I left, she was finishing her supper. She was tired, but unhurt, and when it's safe for her to come home, I'll send an escort with her. She did bravely. What happened?"

"An attack, Sire, but not men. They came out of the forest at dusk, when the sun was down but the sky was still barely light. They left before dawn, then came again last night at dusk. They didn't come throughout the day yesterday, but we still had watchers on the wall anyway. If you would come in and eat and rest, Sire."

"Thank you, Rheann," Father said. "Some of us will watch while some sleep. Your people must be tired. Let's get within walls, and then hear about the attack."

Willow leaned close to me.

"Not men, he said. Maybe Tuan's right, and they didn't have weapons."

I rode up to the wall, Willow and Tuan following. The gate was made of timbers and planks worked to fit closely together, but the wall proper was tree-trunks set in the earth. The outer wall stood twice the height of a tall man. Behind it, I knew, was an inner wall, a little shorter, that strengthened the outer wall and supported it. As far as I could see, there was no charring anywhere, not so much as a smudge of black.

"No burning," I said. "Why wouldn't they use fire, if they wanted to take the wall down?"

Long, pale gouges marked the outer wall, mostly vertical, or nearly so, as though something had been trying to climb the timbers like a wildcat. Whatever it was, the shape of some of the gouges showed where its weight had dragged it down. Chips and curls of pale wood littered the base of the wall under the marks.

I stood in my stirrups and reached up the wall. I could put my hand above the topmost mark, but barely. The top of the wall was less than an arm's length above my fingers. Whatever had tried to climb the wall had come frighteningly close to succeeding.

EIGHT

Sheep were penned in the farmstead's garth, in folds made of hurdles tied together. A few milk cows stood tethered to stakes in the ground, and there were people everywhere. The noise, the crowding, and the livestock seemed like a fair day, but the working clothes and the sense of wariness in the air said otherwise. Our horses were turned into the paddock, and those that could not fit were picketed near it. Before the last knot was tied, men brought hay and water, and we went into the farmstead house.

The main room of High Moor was much smaller than the castle's great hall. Our party almost doubled the number of people on the farmstead. Most of us stood, after hours of being in the saddle, while the High Moor folk sat on benches. Rheann took Father to the best chair at the head of the room. I stood at Father's right, with Tuan next to me, but Willow slipped away from us and stood with the men. Rheann served us wine, bread, and cold meat, while some of the farmstead folk took food and drink around to the rest.

A man perhaps ten years younger than Father limped into the room, his left arm bound up in a bloodstained sling.

"Sire," he said. "Thank you for coming. I am Harrel of High Moor."

"Sit down," Father said. "An injured man shouldn't have to stand."

"Thank you, Sire." Harrel lowered himself onto a bench and one of his men helped him stretch the leg he limped on along the bench before him. He leaned his right arm on the table.

"What happened?" Father asked. "Who did this? Your daughter said trees."

"At first, that's what we thought, trees moving in the evening airs," Harrel said. "But then they came out, like trees running out of the forest. We had no warning. Lucky the harvest is in, or more of us would have been out there. There were few out, and they got safely in at the gate." He paused. "As for what they were, Sire, I thought men at first. But I never saw such men. Brown, they were, dark brown as earth, an' thin. They moved stiff-jointed, but fast all the same. They had no weapons, no armour, far as we could see."

"Cattle were in the north meadow," Harrel said, "set to come in to the paddock. Soon as those things came near, the beasts broke an' ran. The two cowherds ran, too, no blame to them. Neither man nor beast could have got back to the walls. Most of the herd got away safe."

He stopped and licked his lips, then swallowed. "Some of the things chased after the cattle. They caught one of the cows, an old girl. She's—she was a bit lame, but—any road, one of them caught her an' she started bellowing. An' there were three, four others on her before you could think. They tore her up, Sire." His hands twisted together, though his face was wooden. "They tore her up. An' they weren't fast about it, neither. She cried for help an' we couldn't help her. I saw the men shooting from the wall, but they—the things were all over her."

He stopped.

"Go on," Father said.

"I got Corvie on a horse an' out the back gate. I did it while we were still getting the front closed, while the cow—" His voice broke at last, and trembled as he continued. "What father could send his little girl out at such a time? But the things were on the other side. She's light an' a good rider, an' she wanted to help. I put her on our fastest horse. Better that than fighting or waiting inside with the little ones to be overrun."

"You did right," Father said.

I had to agree. As awful as Harrel clearly felt about sending his daughter out alone, she had been the right one to send for help. I would have preferred riding through the dark to waiting in a besieged farmstead myself.

His expression lightened a little. "Thank you, Sire."

"How many were there? Did you get a good look?"

"Too good, Sire. I'll see 'em in my sleep the rest of my life. They were like leather men, same as we've found in the peat bog west of us. Tanned, same as boot leather, their clothes, and their skin, too. An' their eyes gone, but it didn't seem to slow 'em down. An' strong to go with it. They had nothing but their hands an' they all but pulled the gate open before we got it barred. Then they came at the walls, climbing with their nails dug in. We hit them with rakes, shovels, rocks, anything we had. Some of 'em we had to pry loose, or break their hands to make them let go. That's how I got this." He touched his arm. "I was leaning over the wall, hitting 'im in the head with the sharp edge of a spade, an' he got his hand onto my sleeve an' started to haul me over. Dunno how I did it, Sire, but I pried 'im off me an' then fell off the inner wall. Broke the arm."

"You hit his head with the sharp edge of a spade?" I asked. "And he didn't fall?""

"That's right, Lady. Not fall, or so much as cry out. An' there wasn't any blood on the spade. I dunno what to make of that."

The men stirred, murmuring to one another, but none of the High Moor folk made a sound.

Father let the noise die away before he spoke again. "Something that doesn't cry out when struck," he said.

"Not at all," Harrel said. "I've not had to fight often, but from what I know, I'd say most men will yell when they do it, at least when they charge. These ones said nothing, not a word or a cry. They came at us all night. We knocked them off, an' they kept coming back. A long night, Sire, when the men—when what you fight won't lie down an' die."

"But they left in the end. What happened?"

Harrel shrugged with his good shoulder.

"Dawn, I'm thinking. Nothing else that I could see. We kept knockin' them down an' knockin' them down. We tried boiling water, but they paid it no mind. There's eerie, to see something coming at you through water hot enough to cook your flesh an' never a sound or a sign. We took the hands off a couple, but barring that they kept climbing." He stopped again, and I could see his hands shaking.

"Then they quit," he said, "sudden-like, as if they'd been called off. Dropped off the wall, turned around, an' walked away. One or two of 'em were draggin' spears, still stuck in, an' some had arrows in 'em. They took no notice, just walked back into the forest. Took us a while to figure out they were all gone, because we couldn't see 'em outside the torches. But by the time we could see beyond the walls, the last were disappearing in the trees."

"Do you know how many there were?"

Harrel shook his head. "No, Sire. As many as we have folk here, I think. Couldn't be many more, or we wouldn't have been able to turn them back."

"Did they leave any behind, wounded or dead?" Father asked.

"No, they didn't. No bodies at all. Maybe they took them when they left."

"And last night?" Father asked.

"The same, Sire, but we were ready for them. Some of 'em were the same as the first lot, which we knew because of the arrows an' one still draggin' a spear. We didn't waste arrows or spears on 'em the second night, an' we had more rocks. Even they noticed a rock dropped on 'em." He laughed, a brief chuckle, but his eyes didn't change.

"They got no farther, but it's wearying work fighting all night an' trying to repair and rest in the day. Hard on the body an' hard on the spirit. If they keep coming back, we'll keep fighting, but flesh an' bone an' heart can only take so much,. An' harvest's over now, nothing to mind but the cattle, but in spring, there'll be work to do an' none with strength to do it. We'd have to flit an' build again."

Abandoning an established farmstead would mean a dreadful amount of work. Only desperation would make Harrel mention it. I glanced at Willow. She mouthed "magic" at me, and I shook my head very slightly. Of course there had to be magic in this, but I didn't want it mentioned aloud, at least not here with everyone listening. I believed Gil when he said it wasn't Orla behind Grandmother's warning, but the events of the spring were still only a few months old. Orla had done the most destructive magic known in Valenia for years. It wouldn't be strange if others suspected her—who knew what a wisewoman could do, even after her death?

"They did leave something, though," Rheann said. She took a cloth-wrapped bundle from another woman. I thought at first of Dar bringing out Hafor's sword, but this bundle was shorter and thicker, knobbed on one end, possibly a club.

She set the bundle on the table, and the High Moor folk shrank back a bit. When she flipped the cloth open, I drew in my breath.

There on the table, dark brown and corded with lean, shrunken muscle, lay the forearm and hand of a right arm, snapped off right below the elbow.

CHAPTER

NINE

"How did this happen?" Father's voice broke the silence.

"When we closed the gate on the first night," Rheann said. "Some of their hands were nipped, but this one didn't get his arm out in time. We were making a lot of noise ourselves at the time, but I'd swear this one didn't scream when we shut the gate on his arm."

"He must have pulled free somehow." Father pushed aside his cup and plate and picked up the arm. Close up, the skin was leathery and smooth, with brittle-looking hairs. A whiff of peat smoke, or something like it, caught at the back of my nose. Father pulled the fingers, curled into a loose fist, straight. They came without resistance, but when he let go, they slowly returned to their flexed position. The skin between my shoulders shivered. It didn't seem like shrunken tendons had pulled the fingers in, but rather, as though a person had deliberately closed his hand.

"What do you make of that?" Father asked me.

"I've never seen a dead hand do that," I said.

"Nor I. Did this one come back the second night?" he asked Harrel.

"Not that I saw, Sire." He raised his voice. "Did any see a one-armed attacker?"

The farmstead folk murmured together for a few moments, then a woman's voice said, "No, not on the north."

"Nor the east," said a man.

"Not at the back wall," said another man. "Not to be sure of. But it was hard to tell, an' I'd not swear to it."

"That's something," Father touched the arm with one finger. "This one, at least, might be out of the fight. How much damage did they do?" he asked Harrel.

"None inside, at least, an' I'm the only one hurt this bad. If they'd had fire, they could have done worse."

Father looked around at the drawn, solemn faces. There was more damage here than would have been done by fire.

"Tarin?" Father asked.

"Two or three places where the outer wall has been clawed half through, Sire. They'll want some work, maybe an extra log or two set up. Gouges from the climbing. Nothing serious."

"They might not come back," Harrel said, but his voice didn't match his words. After two nights, chances were good they'd come again.

"We'll set a watch," Father said. "If they fought by day, I think they'd be on us by now. Everyone who can sleep, should sleep. Wake by mid-afternoon, and we'll have a council of war and set our plans."

"As you say, Sire," said Rheann. She helped her son to his feet. "If you'll come with me, Princess Kiar, you and your friend," she said, "I'll find you a room." Willow obediently came to stand with me, and Rheann took us to a small room with a bed. A toy dog made of sheepskin with some of the fur worn off lay on the pillows.

"My granddaughter's room," Rheann said. She pulled the curtains across the window. "Sleep well, Lady."

As soon as she was out of the room, Willow pulled off her boots and outer clothing.

"I don't know if I can sleep with the sun up," I said.

"I can," Willow said, and yawned hugely. "At least lie down and rest. We could be up all night."

"Yes." I undressed to my shirt, lay down, and closed my eyes.

The next thing I heard was tapping on the door and a voice saying, "Lady, the king asks for you." The finger of light slanting across the bed told me it was late afternoon.

The hush of the house when I left the bedroom made the hair on my neck prickle. No matter how quiet they're trying to be, thirty people in a farmstead make noise. Add our numbers, and the place should have hummed with activity, especially with a battle coming on. The quiet didn't sound right; the voices and sounds I heard from other parts of the house seemed both urgent and furtive.

When I found the main hall again, most of the tables had been put away against the wall and a few men slept at the far end. That might explain the quiet. I stood in the doorway for a moment, at a loss about where to go, then Rheann appeared beside me.

"This way, Lady," she said, and led me to a smaller room. Father sat at one end of a table and waved me over to sit beside him. Tarin, Maithey, Arlen, and Bron, all seasoned fighters, sat on either side of the table.

"Will you have food and drink now or later, Sire?" Rheann asked.

"Later," Father said. "We won't be long."

She bowed and closed the door behind her.

"Is the wagon gone?" Father asked.

"Yes, Sire," Arlen said. "All the children and two women who were nursing, and whatever food stores we could fit in for them. They're well away by now and should make the castle in two or three days."

"Good. Livestock?"

"Harrel sent a boy out with the sheep to find the cattle. No problem there. You can see the swath the cows trampled when they ran. You know how cattle are when they get 'run' into their heads. The cowherds'll have their work cut out getting them stopped. Harrel told the shepherd to stay out the night and make for the castle if he hears nothing from us tomorrow, and to tell the cowherds the same if he catches up. Barring the horses, no beasts underfoot, as far as we can manage. We couldn't find anyone to herd the poultry away."

We all smiled in spite of the seriousness of the situation.

"I doubt these raiders are here for a chicken supper," Father said. "Well done. Maithey, how are the defences?"

"We set some logs in the places torn up the worst. They didn't touch the outbuildings, Sire, not a one. They only went for the big wall, where there were people."

"Anything else for defence?" Father asked.

"I'd favour putting in a fire moat, if we're going to be here any length. It'll take a few days. I made a start marking it out."

"No saying that would stop them," Arlen said. "If they don't mind boiling water, they might not mind fire. Chances are they'd carry it in to set the walls alight."

"We don't want to set the plains on fire either," Father said. Fire in the dry grass would burn for miles; it could catch up with the wagon carrying the children.

"We cut some stakes and dug them in, pointing outwards," Maithey said. "They didn't have to be tall enough to stop a horse, only two, three feet, maybe. It'll slow them down a bit. And we dragged over a couple of wagonloads of limbs and branches. Tangle their feet for them."

"Good," Father said. "Now, pushing them off the walls over and over isn't going to defeat them, and neither is shooting them full of arrows and spears. What does stop them, it seems, is being cut to pieces."

"Or having a piece cut off," Bron said. "Hard to climb with one arm. Hard to walk missing a leg."

"What about the head?" Arlen said. "Most folk slow down a good bit without a head."

I remembered the way the hand had closed that morning, as though it were still living. I wasn't sure losing a head would stop these things.

"Arms will be easier," Father said. "Take off the arms and they can't grab you. Then the head, or legs, or whatever you can hit. Don't stab them. Slash and chop."

"We're going to ride out?" I said.

"Yes," Father said. "We'll let them get started on the walls, so they aren't all on the ground. We'll try to lure them around, away from the gate. Then we'll charge out, wheel around, and take them from behind. Half go out at a time, fifteen riders each. We need to be light and quick rather than hitting them as a wall. I want everyone to get in, slash and cut, and get out. Then go back in. If you can draw one away from the pack, take off a leg if you can and then leave it. Go back and pick out another."

He paused, looking at each of us until we nodded. "Each of us here takes four riders. Arlen, Tarin, you'll come with me on the first sortie. When we need a breather, or if it's going badly, Kiar, you bring your lot out with Maithey and Bron and take over. Everybody understand?"

"Yes," I said. Whether the others spoke or not, I couldn't have said. I was surprised by how normal my voice sounded, because from the moment Father told Maithey and Bron to take their orders from me, my mouth had been dry as ash.

"Good. Let's get some food and see to our weapons."

The men left the room. Father stayed behind.

"Kiar, a minute," he said, as I reached the door.

I walked back to the table.

"I'm glad you're here," he said. "I wasn't happy at first about it. I'd have preferred to have one of us at the castle, in case of attack."

"Dar knows as—" I began, but he waved me to silence.

"I know," he said. "But what Dar doesn't know—what nobody here knows—is how to fight magic. Nobody's saying it, but we all know there's magic in this. The men will feel better having you here. You're the only one with any experience in that."

"Once," I said.

"That's once more than anyone else, and you won. What that child said about the attackers could have been fear, dim light, disguise. We might have been facing only men. But after hearing what the farmstead folk said and seeing that arm, I'm not sure what we're fighting."

"I've never seen such a thing."

He shook his head and looked away, as though trying to recall something. "I don't know if anyone has, ever," he said at last. "I've never heard of the like of it, outside of bog-walkers, and who's ever seen one of those?"

"Maybe everyone here, now."

"Maybe so. Kiar, it'll hearten the men to have you here. Whatever you know, whatever you can do, however little, is something. If we have someone who can fight magic, it's better to have her here with us than a day's ride away."

"Thank you, Father," I said.

"The men respect you," he said, "especially after the way you dealt with Hafor. They know you can keep your head and won't ask them to do anything stupid."

"I'm not a wisewoman," I said. "I can't say words and make these things go away."

"No." He gave me a crooked smile. "Worse luck, eh? Well, we'll do what we can. Nobody can ask more."

"I'm scared," I said. "This isn't like fighting Hafor. He was a man. These things are— well, they're not. They're uncanny."

"Yes," Father said. "I'm afraid, too. I'd be worried if I wasn't. Someone who has no fear, who doesn't know what he can or can't do, gets careless and stupid. Then he dies, and if he's a leader, maybe the people around him die, too. Some fear is good. That's the warrior's little secret, daughter of mine. We all know it—we just don't talk about it."

He winked, and although my fear didn't disappear, I could shove it back into a corner. There were things to be done before dusk.

CHAPTER

TEN

"I never thought until now how similar to us the Noermarkers are," I said to Willow and Tuan.

We were saddling the horses. In a few minutes we'd be waiting in the courtyard between the gate and the farmstead house, with Father's force ready nearer the gate and mine right behind them.

"What do you mean?" Willow asked.

"Mostly, I know how Noermarkers are going to act. I know what they want. It's the same as what we want."

Willow's eyes rolled upward. "If you mean you both want Valenia, you're right."

"More than that," I said. "They want to be warm and fed in winter, to raise families and protect them."

"Well, so do swanfolk," Willow said, "and rabbits and foxes and wildcats, for that matter."

"Noermarkers think about it the same way we do, mostly. We knew what Hafor wanted, and what would make him go away. What do these things that attacked High Moor want?"

"What do you mean?"

"I mean, they want in, but what will they do then?" What they'd done to the cow, I thought.

"I'm sure they won't shove them out and take up farming," Willow said.

I laughed as much from nerves as from imagining the monsters settling to something as ordinary as farming. "I wish," I said, "I'd seen these things before we had to go out and fight them. Then maybe I could think of more ways to slow them down."

"Harrel said they don't notice arrows or spears," she said. "But what if there was something tied to the other end?"

"What kind of thing?"

"A rock to weigh them down, or a rope to tangle their legs?"

"You can't shoot an arrow with a rock on it!"

"All right, but what if—what if you dropped a net with rocks tied to it?"

"That might work. You'd need two people to do it. They'll have nets to keep birds off the fruit. They could use some of those. They won't hold anything forever, but their might slow them down. Run ahead when we go out, Willow, and tell Rheann. She'll know where everything is."

"I will," she said. "Did they try fire-arrows?"

"We don't want to use fire," I said. "They might bring it right back to the walls."

"Two spears," Tuan said. "A net and two spears."

"Yes! That would keep them farther away!" Willow said. "Maybe hold them until daylight!"

"Too late to do that tonight," I said. "You'd need practice throwing spears at the same time. I wonder what would happen to the attackers in daylight."

"Burst into flames, shrivel up, turn to dust, and blow away."

"The arm didn't do any of those things."

"We don't know if it was out in the sun," Willow said. "Rheann had it all wrapped up."

"That's true," I said. "Maybe we could see what sunlight does to it."

"Tomorrow," Tuan said.

"Yes," I said, "There'll be pieces of them all over the ground, if Father's plan works."

"It'll work." Willow handed Whiffle's reins to Tuan and slipped off to speak to Rheann.

"Are you afraid?" I asked Tuan.

"Why?" he asked. "Whether we are or not, we have to fight. I will stay with you and Willow."

I glanced sideways at him. His pale skin made his profile stand out against the falling dusk. He looked, for a moment, like a young warrior from an old story, and my heart jumped. Had I been angry at him only yesterday?

"I'm glad you're here with us – with me," I said.

He turned his head and when our eyes met, a shiver ran up my back.

"Where else would I be?" he asked. "My place is with you."

He mounted Lightfoot, and I mounted Kestrel, and together we rode out to the courtyard. Willow wove among the men and horses and took Whiffle back from Tuan.

"Rheann has gone to get the nets. She said she should have thought of it herself."

Then there was nothing to do but wait to see if an attack would come. Farmstead men and women stood on the inner wall, spaced to cover as much of it as possible. They had pitchforks, hoes, and spades in their hands. One man held a length of rope with a lump of iron on it, and a young woman gripped a cleaver that could split a man's skull.

Nobody spoke. My father, strange and fierce in his helm with black and white tails of horsehair falling down the back, waited near the gate. I couldn't remember ever seeing him wear his helm except on patrol. During those outings, he talked with the men, and his face looked the same as it did every day. Now it was closed-in and watchful. I could feel the same look on my own face, and a bird fluttered in my stomach. But this was no longer my first fight. I remembered Dar telling me how he'd thrown up on his horse's neck right before his first fight and wondered about Willow and Tuan.

"Do either of you feel—" I stopped, as though the word "sick" itself might make them throw up.

"What?" Willow said.

"Nothing. I'm going up on the wall to look."

Tuan took hold of Kestrel's rein as soon as I moved to dismount. I went as quickly as I could through the horses towards the west side of the wall, where the closest ladder was.

The man on the inner wall moved over to make space for me. The outer wall came up to my shoulders, and I could see the forest to my right. The sun was down, the sky red in the west and fading to blue-grey. The forest was only the dark, pointed palisade of firs and pines. Then, between one breath and the next, I saw them.

"There!" someone called from the wall over the gate. They came out of the trees, faster than I had imagined. In a flash I understood Corvie saying they weren't men. They had two legs, two arms, and a head, but there was nothing about the way they moved or looked that made me think of people. Harrel had said they were stiff-jointed, and I'd thought that meant their joints didn't move at all. I'd imagined them limping or shuffling. Instead, they almost sprang in long, jarring strides that covered the ground at a runner's speed, as each leg pushed off, then swung forward in time to make the next jump.

Then I remembered I had to be with my force. I pounded down the ladder, slid through the horses, and swung myself back into the saddle.

"What are they?" Willow asked.

Heads turned towards me all around.

"Nothing I've ever seen," I said. "and they jump like hares. Taking a leg might not be hard after all. Watch yourselves." Someone pressed forward to pass the word to my father. I saw him nod, but he kept his eyes forward.

The men on the wall over the gate yelled and waved torches. One threw a piece of hide knotted to a rope over the wall and jerked it to draw the things' attention, then sidestepped along the wall, away from the gate. A woman on the other side banged two pots together and screamed, "Over here! Over here!" All around the wall, the farmstead folk tried to get the attackers' attention away from the gate. We held our places and said nothing. A young man pressed his ear to the gate, looked at my father, and nodded.

Father held up his left hand, and the gate cracked open. Father brought Cloud up to the gate, and then thrust his arm forward. Then Father's first force went from standing to full gallop as they thundered through the gates. Almost on the heels of the last horse, two of the farmstead's men dragged the gates closed and dropped the bar.

"I want a lookout," I said. "Someone to tell me when we need to get out there."

"I'll do it, Lady," Rheann said. She had her arms full of bird-netting, and she was old enough to be my grandmother, but she fairly ran up the ladder on one side of the gate. She passed the nets to a man, who took one and passed the armful to the next man, then grabbed up his spade and thrust over the wall. I saw the first thrust stop as though he'd hit something, and he drew back his weapon. I found Rheann again and watched her. Between the din the defenders were making and the pounding of my own blood in my ears, I couldn't hope to hear anything she said. I'd have to rely on her giving me a sign I could understand.

The minutes dragged by. I moved Kestrel closer to the gate and the rest of my force fell in, my own four behind me, then Bron and Maithey's teams. Rheann turned and clasped her hands together over her head. Father's men must be winning. Then she nodded and I saw her mouth move.

"Now!" came faintly over the noise of battle. I drew my sword.

"Open the gate!" I shouted. The hinges rasped, and the gate cracked open again. In the fading evening light I saw movement flicker across that narrow space. Then the space widened, and I urged Kestrel toward it. In three paces, we were through and galloping out into the battlefield.

CHAPTER

ELEVEN

In front of me a creature leapt at a man on horseback. I set Kestrel at the pair. The creature had hold of the horse's neck and the animal whinnied long and high and shook its head, but its attacker paid no attention, scrambling up the neck. The rider struck at it three times while I galloped forward, and the creature took no notice at all.

Suddenly, its head snapped around. In the breath that followed, I saw the thing's face so clearly that it came back in dreams for years afterwards.

Its eyes were sunken in, and its skin clung to its skull as though there was no flesh between skin and bone. A long slash opened one cheek, but whether it was an old wound or a fresh one I couldn't tell; there was no blood.

Its mouth opened, and it screamed and flung itself away from me, pawing at its face and chest. Then it sprang up and ran, disappearing into the dark.

The sound seemed to be inside my head, ringing through my bones. I blinked against the shock of it and nearly dropped my sword. Kestrel never faltered but galloped straight on course. Her shoulder brushed the shoulder of the other horse. The creature was long out of sight. I wheeled back to the horse and rider.

"Are you hurt?" I asked.

"No, Lady!" I recognized Arlen's voice.

I looked around for Father. The light was at its worst now, neither clear nor dark. Colours faded into one another, and I couldn't pick out Cloud's light grey.

Finally, I saw the horsehair crest of Father's helm at the northeast corner of the wall. He urged Cloud forward, away from the wall and the light of the torches. Between us were three other riders fighting with High Moor's attackers.

"Go on, Lady!" Arlen said, and I headed towards the nearest tangle of man, horse and creature. The horse wheeled and bounced, striking out with its hooves. One creature clung to the back of the saddle and clawed at the rider; the horse kicked twice while I rode up, but it took no notice. A second leapt at the rider. One arm flapped from the elbow, but the other hand reached to seize the rider's helm. If the helm didn't come off, both rider and creature would be on the ground.

Tuan on Lightfoot swooped around me and set on the creature clinging to the saddle. When he struck, it let go of the saddle and turned in mid-air to wrap its arms around Lightfoot's head. Lightfoot whinnied, a high, panicky sound, and jerked his head as the creature dug one foot into the horse's breast and began to climb. For an instant I hesitated between Tuan and the other rider, then turned towards the man now leaning sideways out of his saddle under the weight of his attacker.

And again, before I was within striking distance, the thing snapped its blank, blind face towards me, opened its mouth and screamed before bounding away. Like the other, it beat and pawed at its skin, then fled. I turned Kestrel towards Tuan, and as I approached, the same thing happened. The creature climbing over Lightfoot's neck beat at its body as though a swarm of bees were on it, clinging to the horse with its legs. Then it dropped off and bounded away.

"They're afraid of you!" Willow shouted. "Just get near them and they'll run! Come on!" Together we rode towards the next tangle of fighters, and again, the creatures stopped whatever they were doing and ran away in long, slow bounds. Every one of them shrieked; my head rang with the noise until it was hard work to see, but none of them stayed to fight. I couldn't get close enough to lay a sword on a single one.

"I'll get around as fast as I can," I said to Willow. "Get anyone injured inside. They're running now, but they might come back."

She and Tuan galloped away. Without looking back, I rode at the next fight, and the next, and the next. My head pounded with the echoes of screaming. Hadn't Harrel said they made no sound? All the same, time after time, the creatures released their hold, stopped tearing and grabbing in mid-movement, dropped to the ground, and bounded away. Some of our men rode after them, chopping at them as they fled. Others struggled with panicking horses, or turned to follow me.

I was running a race, trying to reach all the men on the field before more were hurt or killed. Other riders struck at the attackers, spurring their horses past me to set on them, three or four at a time. Whatever the creatures were, their skin was tough and turned swords almost as though they wore leather armour. All the same, the men took the legs of one at the knee, and when I came close, I saw it could no longer run. It dragged itself along the ground, screaming while the men hacked at it.

There were always some of our men around me, joining and falling away as I rode. At each new fight, they galloped ahead to fall on the creatures before I arrived, and they fled. I don't know how long or how far I rode from fight to fight. I doubled and turned so often that I lost track of whether I'd circled the farmstead or only come back on my own track. I was never able to strike a blow, and my head pounded until I was dizzy and seeing double from the shrieking. I turned and rode yet again across the front of the farmstead, and saw Cloud and my father again.

Cloud wheeled and circled at the edge of the torchlight. His hindquarters were pale against the darkness that had fallen while I rode, and as he backed closer, the light caught my father's sword, rising and falling, and the thing he fought against.

At first I thought that it was dizziness or the pounding of my head from the screaming that made me see a tall, cloaked figure, half again as tall as a man. It followed Cloud, crowding the horse as he backed away. The man, if it was a man, swept the cloak around in a wide arc. The cloak didn't ripple, but struck Cloud's neck with a sound like a staff against flesh. Cloud grunted and stumbled, and my father jerked to stay upright in the saddle. He swung at the cloak, and part of it sheared off, falling into dark strips as it tumbled down past Cloud and disappeared into the darkness.

I charged forward, but the thing was already striking again, this time from the other side, and again Cloud grunted and stumbled. This time he missed his step and went down onto his knees, screaming, then rolled onto his right side. I heard Father's voice, loud and hoarse as he cried out, but I couldn't see whether he had got clear of the horse as he fell.

The next few breaths went on forever. I counted every beat of Kestrel's gallop—one, two, three, one, two, three—as her hooves hit the ground. I heard my own breath rushing past my teeth, and my voice as I called for my father, but it was all slow, slow as a tree growing, or a summer night falling. The cloaked man bent over my father. Father raised his sword, but his right leg was trapped under Cloud, his right side on the ground and his arm hampered. The man swept Father's sword aside with the other edge of its cloak, then bent and seized the king with both hands. Against Cloud's pale hide the arm I saw was thin and knobbed as bone, and I smelled again that sharp, peaty aroma. The creature struck Father's head with its chin and mouth, as though it were going to bite, with a force that jolted them both, then shook Father as though he were no more than a doll.

Time sped up again. The attacker dropped Father and straightened, and although I couldn't see his eyes, I knew he saw me. Even from horseback I had to look up to where that unseen face must be. The cloak disappeared as though it had folded behind him like wings, and he stood for an endless instant, then bowed his head slightly before vanishing into the darkness. Kestrel's speed carried us past Father and Cloud, into the dark.

I could see nothing, and when I pulled to a stop, the only noises I could hear were the voices of our own men and horses. To my left and right something swished briefly in the long grass, then thumped down, then swished again, then were gone as though they had never been.

I headed back to Father. When I reached him, he was still on the ground, with Cloud grunting, panting, and still lying on his leg. I knelt at his side. His leather body armour was punctured, and blood ran from the holes. His eyes were shadowed by his helm. I tore off my glove and licked my fingers. When I held them under his nose, I felt the stir of his breath. Cloud's sides heaved and his breath came hard and noisily, with small, whinnying grunts.

"Father!" I said, "Can you hear me? Please say something!"

"Kiar," he whispered.

"Hold on," I said. "They're gone. We'll get you inside."

"Are you hurt?" he asked.

"No, but Cloud—"

"His leg," Father said. "Needs the knife."

"Yes," I said. "We need to get you out from under him."

He closed his eyes, and my heart jumped. Then he opened his mouth a little and closed it again.

"Hold on," I said again, and then men and torchlight were all around, and Willow's hand was on my shoulder.

"What do we do?" she asked.

"Someone kill Cloud. He's broken a leg. Then we can get Father out from under him." Before I'd finished, I heard footsteps. Someone said, "Hold his head."

I tried not to hear the sounds of Cloud's death. My father hissed between his teeth as Cloud kicked in his final struggle.

"We need a stretcher," I said.

"Someone is fetching it."

"Are they gone?" I asked. "All of them?"

"All gone, Lady," said Bron. "Every one."

Then there were ropes, and lengths of log and poles to raise Cloud's body enough to pull Father's leg out.

Tuan bent and stripped off Father's leather glove. "Bite on this," he said.

Father bit down on the folded glove as we pulled him out and lifted him gently onto the stretcher. One of the men slid Father's helm off and another laid a blanket over him. Someone put a hand under my elbow and pulled.

"Stand up," Tuan said. "Let's go."

I walked beside Father all the way back to the gates and into the room where he'd slept the day before. Rheann came to me as the men began cutting the straps of Father's armour.

"Come out, Lady," she said. "You'll do him no good standing over him, and I'll need space to work. I'll call if you're wanted." She led me out of the room and once I was in the hall, she looked over my shoulder and lifted her chin to beckon someone.

"Get her a hot drink," she said.

"Yes, Rheann," said a woman before gently pulling on my elbow. "Lady, come and take your armour off."

I turned and went with her, tugging at the strap of my helm. My fingers didn't seem to remember how to undo the buckle. Finally, I undid it, and by that time we were in the main room of the farmstead. The men were there, some of them still half in armour, some having wounds tended.

I set down my helm and took off the single glove I still wore. Where had the other one gone? Oh, yes, I'd dropped it beside Father, when I checked to see he was still alive. I'd need to find it tomorrow. Then the farmwoman came back and put a wooden cup in my hand. I smelled mint, lavender, and honey.

I took a sip. The sweet, fragrant tea felt hot on my lips, and I realized how chilled I was. A fire burned in the hearth against the outer wall of the hall. The men with wounds were closest to it; others stood or sat farther away. Of the men who had been with me, only Bron was injured. His left arm rested in a sling. Other men were hurt, but none from my force. I walked over and sat beside Bron.

"Take off your armour," he said. "You'll be easier for it."

I saw most of my men were still in their armour, and several were clustered around Tuan.

"What about the others?" I said. "I should be ready, too—in case they come back."

"Ah, well," Bron said, "I think you could go out in your shirt and trousers and not be harmed, from the look of it."

I undid the buckles on my body armour and lifted it over my head, then unbuckled the leather over my arms and thighs and laid all of it on the floor beside me. My shirt clung to my back with sweat. Maybe it would dry before I had to put my armour back on. I picked up the cup and drank more of the tea.

"What happened?" I asked. "I couldn't get near them. And that screaming— I thought they couldn't make sound."

"I heard no screaming, Lady, but it looked as if they were running away from you. I saw the first ones. Even the ones you weren't near weren't as bold. They chased off easier, seemed to me. And after the king was down, they all ran."

"I don't understand it, Bron. I never struck a blow. I couldn't get close enough to hit them! Why would they run from me?"

"It's a mystery, right enough," he said. "But we can be glad of it, especially the king."

"Cloud's dead," I said.

"That he is," Bron said. "It was quick, if that's any comfort. I did it myself."

"Thank you," I said, and meant it. I drank the rest of my tea and went over to the group of men with Tuan. As I approached, they turned to me and saluted. I recognized Maithey, Kearn, and Talles.

"We should keep some armed in case they come back," Tuan said. "Harrel has a watch on the wall."

"I agree," I said. "And I need to go out with any sortie."

"Lady, you'll need to sleep sometime," said Kearn.

"Yes, but I can be wakened."

"We can't keep simply driving them off," said Maithey. "If they come back, we'll have to kill them to finish it. You can't stay at High Moor forever, Lady."

"I know that," I said. "We were outnumbered tonight, and that might not be all of them. And what of our dead and injured? How many have we lost?"

"None dead," Tuan said.

There was a brief pause. I saw again the blood running from punctures in Father's armour.

"Bron's shoulder is bad," Maithey said. "Two of them pulled his arm loose of its socket, but Rheann and one of her women put it back. He won't be lifting much for a while. And Mulloch was torn to the bone on one arm. They're stitching him up now. We'll see if he loses it or not. Apart from that, some cuts and bruises, two limping, another with a twisted knee who can't sit a horse. We got off light, Lady, and that's the truth."

"Can Mulloch ride?"

"I'll find out when the women are done with his arm," Bron said. "He won't like being sent home. He could stand watch, at least."

"That's six injured," I said. "If they come back again, we won't be as strong. I could stand watch outside if they're afraid of me, but I can't be everywhere, and they'd get up the wall again. And what of the other farmsteads? We don't know if anyone else is under attack. If they are, if two are attacked at once—"

I didn't have to say any more. After losing six fighters in one short battle, we would be weaker going into the next fight. Even if we sent a messenger for more forces, we would have to stand the invaders off for one more night before they arrived, and maybe two. Defending two farmsteads would cut deeply into the guard; defending all ten was impossible.

"If we beat them here, they may not attack anywhere else," Kearn said, but his tone said he didn't believe it.

"The problem is, we know nothing about them," Maithey said. "We know Noermark's strength, and their speed, and their borders. We can tell from the fighters they send how much they have in reserve. We can see their movements, and if we can't, the queen's folk can see them from the air."

"Why didn't they see these, then?" Talles said, "Begging your pardon, Lady, but Princess Adana never said anything of this, did she?"

"No," I said. "And if they've flown, they left in the last day or two. I don't know why she wouldn't have seen these creatures or known of them from other swanfolk."

"What will we do, Lady?" Maithey asked.

I thought for a minute before I answered. "Watchers on the wall," I said. "They can be ours or farmstead folk, but they must stay alert. Change every two hours. The injured and the rest will eat and sleep. Maithey, I'll need to plan for tomorrow and tomorrow night. Will you help with that?"

"Gladly, Lady."

"At first light, I need messengers. One to the castle, four to ride to the other farmsteads and take the word."

"What word?" Kearn asked.

"That they are to bring all people, livestock, ready food and stores to the castle."

"The grain pits, Lady?"

"No, leave them. They're hidden. From the look of these creatures, whatever they are, they won't dig up food. Tell each farmstead to bury or hide any stores they can't bring. They must leave early in the morning and travel as fast as they can."

"I'll choose the messengers, Lady," said Arlen. He began picking his way through the room, stopping to speak to his chosen men. Kearn bowed and left me with Maithey and Tuan.

"Tuan," I said, "tell Willow I need her to go for Sianna at first light, and be back here before dark. And then get some sleep."

"I'll stay with you," he said, "after I talk to Willow."

"No," I said. "I need you rested. I don't know if Grandfather's taken the flock south yet, and I need you to find out. If he hasn't, speak to Adana, see if she's heard anything or knows anything about what attacked us."

"And if the flock has left?"

"Then I'll need you in the sky," I said. "to see if you can learn anything about them from the air."

"I'll do that," Tuan said, and took my hand. My fingers were dirty and marked with Father's blood, but he kissed them before he left.

"I don't think Bron's shoulder will let him sleep," Maithey said. "So we might as well include him in the planning."

"Maithey, do you ever remember all the farmstead folk coming to the castle before?"

"No, Lady," he said. "Nor heard of it being done, either."

"I don't know what else to do," I said. I wished Father was with me. He would know whether I was doing the right thing or simply panicking. Father took advice—now, so had I. And, like him, I'd made a decision. My people would follow me, and it was my responsibility to lead.

CHAPTER

TWELVE

I don't know how long Maithey, Bron, and I had been talking when Rheann came into the little room Harrel had given us so we could speak without disturbing the men sleeping in the main room. She was pale with fatigue, and her apron smeared with blood and dirt, but she was calm.

"Pardon, Lady, but the king's wounds have been treated, and he is asking for you."

I was on my feet before she'd finished. Once out of the room she said, "He's resting well enough, with a bit of something to ease the pain. He may fall asleep on you, and that's all to the good."

"How is he?"

"The bleeding has stopped," she said, "and he's coughed none up. There is no foaming nor whistling where he was bleeding."

"What does that mean?"

"That the wounds didn't reach his lungs."

"So they aren't serious?" When she didn't answer right away, I asked again. "Are they serious?"

"Lady, they were deep, and curved, and reached the bone in two places. I've cleaned them as well as I can. I've never seen a wound made by any of those creatures before now. Whether there's more to them than a cut or a stab I can't say. Those things are uncanny."

"What about his leg? Was it broken under Cloud?"

"Everything feels to be in place, but it's hurting him deep inside. I believe it's cracked badly. I've put a splint on it to keep the bones lined up. It may not be needful, but better to be cautious. And I've given him something for pain."

"Can he travel?" I asked.

"He can't ride. He'd have to go in a wagon, or a litter. We have a wagon, but it would be a rough ride, hard on an injured man. A litter would be better. We don't have one, but maybe we could fix something up for the horses to carry. This way," she said, and opened the door to Father's room.

He lay on the near side of the wide bed, looking long and flat under the covers, except for a bend at his right knee. I went quietly to the side of the bed and took his hand. His fingers squeezed mine, and he opened his eyes.

"Here you are." Father's voice was hardly more than a whisper, and the lines between his nose and the corners of his mouth were deep. A dark bruise reached from the bone above his left temple to his eyebrow.

"How are you feeling?"

"Like a horse rolled on me." He tried to smile at his own joke, but pain twisted his mouth. "You scared it away – the thing."

"What was that? It was different—taller. And it didn't run like the others did."

"Ah," Father said. "No. I think—the lost, lost—" He coughed, and I put my arm behind his head and tried to raise him.

"Not so good," he said when he stopped coughing, but he patted my arm. "Ask Tuan."

"Don't talk," I said. He closed his eyes and his face slackened. My heart jumped, but the blankets rose and fell with his breath, and I sat down again, holding his hand.

"I don't know what happened," I whispered. "I couldn't get near any of them."

I thought he might be asleep, but he squeezed my fingers. I wanted to ask him if I was doing the right thing. I wanted to ask what he would do. But maybe Rheann was wrong, or maybe his lungs had been hurt when the thing shook him. I didn't want to make him speak.

"Are we leaving?" he asked. "Or staying?" His voice was hardly above a whisper.

"Leaving," I said. "But not right away. I'm sending for Sianna at first light. Maybe she can help somehow, make it easier for you to travel. Fix your leg, and your breath."

He shook his head.

"Sooner," he said, and opened his eyes. "Morning. Pack tonight."

"Don't talk, Father, please. If we stay another day Sianna will be here, and they'll have time to make a litter for you."

"You can't." He opened his eyes again. "You can't waste time for one man, Kiar. There is more—" He stopped and took two shallow breaths. "More at stake than my life."

"It's not one man!" Tears sprang to my eyes, and I dashed them away impatiently. "You're my father, and the king! I won't leave you!"

"Stubborn," he said, "I am—your king, you know."

"Would you leave me behind?" I demanded.

He didn't answer.

I took his hand in both of mine. "Well, then," I said. "That's settled."

He sighed and closed his eyes again.

"I'll tell them to pack up tonight," I said. "We can send off everyone who isn't needed to fight, and whatever stores they can take. And the men will have time to make you a litter, and the rest of us will leave early the next morning." But he was already asleep.

I sat for a little longer, holding his hand and watching the rise and fall of his chest. His face had relaxed in sleep. The lines in it were deeper, and his eyes more shadowed than when he was awake. He might give me advice, I thought, but right now I had to lead.

"I'm not ready to be queen," I whispered. It was on the tip of my tongue to ask him not to die, but it would surely be the worst sort of luck to say the words.

Finally I stood. I kissed his forehead; his skin felt too warm.

"Sianna will be here tomorrow," I said, as much to comfort myself as anything.

When I came out of the room, one of the farmwomen was hurrying by, her arms full of linens. She stopped when she saw me.

"Lady," she said. "I'll get Rheann." She hurried off before I could answer, and I stood where I was, feeling tired to the bone. I hadn't struck a single blow. Why had the thing that attacked Father jumped away when I rode up? Did it bow to me, or was that only a trick of the light and shadow? Nothing made sense, and my thoughts ran in circles that tired and annoyed me. It was a relief when Rheann arrived.

"Your men told us to get ready to leave," she said. "Is this true, Lady? We'll leave at first light?"

"I want Sianna to see Father before we move him," I said. "Some of us will be staying, but I want all the injured, and all your folk to leave, except a few to share watch with us."

"Lady, you don't mean to spend another night fighting those things!"

"We may not have to fight," I said, "Or at least, not much. They don't want me near them. If I can keep moving around the walls, I can probably stop the worst of it."

"Our men are making something to carry the king," she said. "It will be ready in a few hours. This stretcher will fix to the harness, and we can balance his weight with packs on the other side. It's smoother than a wagon, and we could all leave at dawn."

"He has a fever, I think," I said.

"Yes. That's to be expected. But, Lady, better for him to be in a safe place. He'll recover faster. I know I'm no wisewoman, but if it were my own father, I'd want him away. Sianna can meet us at the castle, or along the road."

I thought her words over. I hated to move Father before Sianna saw him, but Rheann's advice was sound. And Father wanted everyone out as quickly as possible. I could still send Willow for Sianna, but then ask her and Tuan to warn the farthest farmsteads. It would save time, and I didn't know how much we had, or whether other farmsteads were already under attack.

"Very well," I said at last. "How many wagons do you have?"

"Two," she said, "and a small cart, and the panniers."

"Wagons followed us from the castle," I said, "but they might turn back when the children reach them. I don't think they would continue right into an attack."

"We'll manage without," Rheann said.

"We may need to put one man with a wagon," I said. "The one with the torn arm."

"We may," she agreed. "We can put him up with the driver, or pack him in among the stores."

"Like a bag of grain," I said.

"Just so, Lady," she said. "Will you get some rest? My folk know where everything is, and we can pack what we can and hide the rest while yours keep watch."

"Thank you," I said.

She bowed briefly and went to tend to the business of leaving. I watched her bustle away and then went to find Bron.

When I told Bron about the change of plan, he blew out his breath in a long sigh.

"I'm glad you've thought better of staying, Lady," he said. "Truth to tell, I'd rather we were away, and I'd leave now if it were only me. Those things, whatever they are, aren't right. We might as well be fighting dead men, if you ask me. They don't seem to feel pain or fear, except of you."

"Too bad there's only one of me," I said. "If I could be at all the farmsteads at once, I could protect them all."

"You are," Bron said, "by calling them to the castle. It'll be crowded, but that's part of why it's built."

"Yes, but this can't be permanent," I said. "I don't want to think of having everyone there all winter. We'll run out of food, for one thing."

"Lady, we can only do what's before us," Bron said. "There may never be another attack, not here, not anywhere."

"I have to think about what happens if there is," I said. "This is a defeat, Bron, letting them drive us out of High Moor. I don't want to be driven out of the farmsteads, and we haven't enough lands around the castle to feed everyone, supposing those things never attack us there."

"You're right," Bron said, "and I like it no better than you. Nor does the king, I'll wager. But bloody battles to the last man are better in songs than in life."

"I know," I said. "Tell the men we're leaving in the morning. Call me if I'm needed." We both knew what I meant.

When I got to the room Willow and I had slept in the day before, she was still awake. A single candle burned on the window ledge.

"I have your glove," she said, and laid it on the bed between us.

"You're supposed to be asleep," I said.

"We're all supposed to be asleep," she said. "It's nighttime. Nobody should have to stay up all night. We're leaving in the morning, aren't we?"

"How did you know that? I spoke to Bron just this minute."

"And Rheann before that, and the farmstead folk are running around like ants, and the wagons are out and being loaded." She turned, and the candlelight flashed briefly in her eyes. "They're building something, too."

"A litter for Father," I said.

"How bad is he?" she asked. "And I'm sorry about Cloud."

"So am I," I said. I couldn't remember a time when Father hadn't ridden Cloud. "Rheann says his leg hurts him, as though it's cracked." My stomach flipped at the thought, and I swallowed before I went on. "But he won't be able to ride. He has a fever, too."

"Did the thing hurt him, too, or was it only from Cloud falling?"

"He has a bruise, here," I put my hand to my own head. "I saw the thing bash its head against his—its mouth and chin." Remembering that moment, I felt suddenly as though something about the movement was familiar. The feeling niggled at the back of my mind, but I couldn't think why I should recognize anything about the creature.

"Its claws went right through his body armour," I said. "Rheann said it got through to the bone in two places."

Willow's eyes widened. The boiled leather of our armour was tough, thicker than metal armour and hard to puncture.

"I want Sianna to meet us as soon as she can. Tell her we'll be riding southwesterly from here to the castle. Then I want you to go on from there to Near Fellstead and Far Fellstead to tell them to pack up and come to the castle."

"Stony Ridge is on the way to Near Fellstead," Willow said. "I'll stop there, too."

"That's a lot to do—getting Sianna and warning three farmsteads. A rider could go to Stony Ridge."

"I'm going right by. Send a rider somewhere else. I'll be faster, Kiar, you know it."

"All right. A rider would take two days from here to Eastenstead. Tuan can warn Eastenstead and then go southeast to Hill Farm. Then riders can go to Treegirt, Oak Vale, Riverbend, and West Steading. High Moor will already be gone.

"Give Eastenstead a day to pack, three, maybe four days' travel with the wagons. They're farthest from the castle. With any luck, everyone can be safely inside the walls within five or six days, maybe sooner."

"All right." Willow yawned. "I hope they don't come back," she said, and lay down. "Good night, Kiar."

"Good night." I pulled off my boots and trousers and slid under the blankets. In the moment before I fell asleep, I remembered as a child seeing two swans fight. One had struck the other with its wings and beak, and I suddenly knew why the darting movement of the creature that attacked Father had seemed familiar.

The next thing I knew, a tap sounded at the door.

Tuan's voice called, "Kiar, wake up. We're leaving soon. Are you awake?"

I opened my eyes. There was no light at the window, and for a moment I was confused, before I recalled my own orders.

"Yes," I said, and shook Willow. I got my feet onto the floor and pulled on my trousers. I opened the door a crack and saw Tuan, dressed and armed. Last evening at dusk, I'd seen him as a young warrior. Today, somehow, he seemed older, and it came to me that last night was the first time he'd ever fought outside of practice. I could see what he might look like at Father's age, and I thought, *I want to be there to see that.*

He smiled when I peered out. "Good morning."

"Good morning. You still have to fly today. I'm calling everyone to the castle, and I need you to tell Eastenstead and Hill Farm to get packed and moved."

He looked left and right and then kissed my nose. "As you command, Princess."

I took his hand. "There has to be someone I can't command," I said. "I'd like to think it was you."

"In private," he said, "I'll be as disobedient as you like. Will I kiss your nose again?"

"No," I said, and he promptly kissed my nose. Before I could say anything, he pulled me close and kissed me, or I kissed him, or both, until we ran out of breath.

"I don't want to leave you here," he said.

"I know."

"Be careful."

"You, too."

It was hard to let go of him.

"There's breakfast," he said. "Hurry or you'll miss it. They're bringing the king out soon." He turned away, and I hurried to finish dressing.

The tables in the hall held ends of loaves, and platters of cheese and cold sliced meats. I folded a slice of bread around some meat and cheese and ate standing. Pitchers of water stood on the table, along with ale. Clearly, we were finishing leftovers from the kitchen. There would be no baking or cooking today at High Moor, and I wondered if there ever would be again.

Outside the hall, four men shuffled by, carrying Father on a stretcher. Rheann followed them, carrying a bag and my father's boots. She wore his sword belt over her shoulder, and the sword clunked against her leg at every step.

I caught up and took the sword from her.

"Let me carry that. Is he better?"

"He's still fevered, Lady, but I think no worse." Her smooth face and light tone of voice worried me.

"But no better," I said.

"When the wisewoman sees him, she'll be able to tell you more," Rheann said. "It does no good to fret over him. He'll rest easier if you can be calm, Lady."

"All right," I said. "I'll try."

"Good." She nodded to me, and I hurried to catch up with the stretcher.

The litter wasn't a flat board, as I'd expected, but made with bends in it at hip and knee. It hung from the harness on one side of a heavy-boned, brown horse. The men stopped by the litter, and I caught up. Father was awake.

"Morning," he said. "I fell asleep on you."

"Did you sleep well? How are you feeling?"

"Very well." I wondered which question he was answering. "I see we're leaving."

"I decided to take your advice," I said.

He smiled and closed his eyes. Then Rheann came up to direct the men in getting Father onto the litter, and I moved out of the way.

Maithey walked over, leading his horse. "They never came back at all," he said. "We saw nor heard nothing on the second watch. You scared them truly, Lady."

"Did everybody get enough rest?"

"Those that didn't will sleep in the saddle." He grinned. "Least 'til they fall off. We'll go at a wagon's pace, so it'll be no worse than falling off a bench."

"And Mulloch? Can he ride?"

"He says he can, but there's a place for him on one of the wagon seats if he needs it." I thought if he couldn't ride, a bumpy wagon would be harder.

"Don't you worry, Lady. I'll stay near him."

"Thank you, Maithey."

The gates rumbled open. The forest was a dark wall, but beyond the tops of the trees the northern sky showed barely lighter and brightening as I watched. Willow came up beside me, and Tuan joined her. Both wore cloaks against the chill air, and both were barefooted.

"We're ready to go," she said. "Our clothes are in the back of the second wagon. Talles has our swords."

"Be careful," I said.

"It's flying," Willow said. "We've done this since we fledged. And whatever the creatures are, they don't have arrows. Pick something else to worry about."

"I suppose it's no use telling you to go to the castle when you've given your messages. That's where the scouts are going."

"None at all," Tuan said.

"Our weapons are here, and so are you," Willow added. "And we'll be faster, even with farther to go. We'll catch up with you tonight or early tomorrow morning."

"Travel safely," I said, and hugged her. Then I hugged Tuan. I wanted to hold onto him, snuggle into his arms and forget about everything else. But I had to be the leader. I had to look sure and strong, not anxious about every decision. I let him go after a few seconds.

"Tonight or tomorrow morning," he said. He looked like he might have said something more but for all the people around us. We were hardly private. He followed Willow out through the gate and into the field beyond. They separated, and the walls hid them, but the glow of the swan-magic as they changed shape brightened the air in the open gate. Two swans flew up. One went northwest over the forest, and the other flew away to the southwest. I turned my eyes away before they disappeared; to watch until they were out of sight would mean a longer parting. I went to saddle Kestrel, only to find Kerliss leading her out.

"Thank you, Kerliss," I said. "Has someone got Lightfoot and Whiffle?"

"They'll be following one of the wagons, Lady. It'll be a long journey. Most of the farmstead folk will be walking, and with the wagons—"

"I know," I said. "But we should be safe enough through the day, and I hope we'll be far enough away by dark that there'll be no trouble."

"As you say, Lady." He looked past me, and I turned to see four horsemen—Tarin among them—trot out the gate.

"The messengers are away, Lady," he said. "I wonder can we get this lot moving quickly?"

My men were dressed and ready, with blankets and packs already tied behind saddles and horses ready to start. The farmstead folk were half-ready, with bundles on the ground and their people running here and there. Some were still packing the wagons, and two women tucked cloths around the bulging tops of the panniers on one of the pack horses. Several other horses were piled with bulky but light cages of chickens, and two roosters challenged each other by crowing in turn unceasingly. Rheann was leading the horse that carried my father.

"Ask Arlen and Maithey to get the men mounted up," I said. "That will show them we're ready to go. Does anyone know how many people from the farmstead are still here?"

"Harrel has the count. There are no children at least."

At that moment, Harrel himself came through the main door of the farmstead. He pulled it shut and laid his hand on it. There was no bar or bolt on the door; after a moment, he walked towards us.

"Everyone is here, Lady," he said. "The stores are buried or locked into the storerooms or the cellar. Ploughshares an' such, too, that we can't take, an' getting them back out will be a job when we come back. With any luck they won't find the cellar. I'd hate to lose the beer."

"Well done," I said. A heavy, rhythmic banging came from the farmstead, Over Harrell's shoulder I saw two men pounding nails along the sides of the door.

"We barred every door an' window," Harrel said, "but whoever thinks they need to bar a door from the outside? Nail it shut, an' the devils will have to work to get in. Either that or tear the walls down, one."

"Hard work for you to get back in, too," I said.

"Truth to tell, Lady, I'll welcome that work. I never thought to leave here. My father, rest him, was born here, an' so was I, and it's hard to leave." He sighed. "But harder to die, I think."

Around us, my men mounted up and Harrel saluted me, fingers to forehead.

"Time to go," he said, and turned away. "All right, let's be off!"

All the confusion and disorder redoubled as the last bits and pieces were slung around. Someone brought a last wicker cage of chickens to load onto a horse. Several of the guard rode to the gate and the wagon drivers clucked and got their teams moving. Whiffle and Lightfoot trailed the second wagon on lead lines. Gradually people followed, leading horses and the two milk cows who had been inside the farmstead walls.

More of my men fell into place, flanking the ragged column of walkers. I mounted, and Bron rode up to me with the four men he'd led the night before. His left arm was still in a sling.

"We'll bring up the rear," I said. "If anything comes after us, I want to be there."

Bron nodded. "Yes, Lady."

We rode out of High Moor. Two of the farmstead men waited by the gate.

"We'll bar the gate behind you," one said, "and come down over the wall."

When I rode out, I saw a knotted rope hanging from one of the timbers, and a ladder set up by the wall. The bar of the gate dropped home behind us, and we waited and watched as the men climbed down the rope to set their feet on the ladder. The second man threw the rope back inside, and then the two of them picked up the ladder and trotted past us to catch up with the others.

"When those things come back tonight, they'll be surprised," said Kerliss. "Barred tight as a clam and nobody inside."

"You think they'll return?" I asked.

"They didn't seem all that smart."

I had to agree, but still I wondered if they would come to an empty farmstead or if, somehow, they would know it was empty and come after us instead. They'd left the outbuildings alone, after all, and only attacked where there were people. The sky was already much lighter, and I wanted to be far, far away before the autumn day drew to dark.

CHAPTER

THIRTEEN

Cloud's body, a grey mound on the grass, lay where he had fallen. His saddle and bridle were no longer on him. I hated to leave him there. He should be buried or burned after falling in battle, but there was no time.

After what Harrel had said about not finding any pieces after the first night, I was surprised to find bits of our attackers littering the ground. There were arms and legs, and one body tangled in a net and hacked to bits. The net was shredded by the sword-blows that had cut the creature up. I rode clear of the pieces, remembering the arm Rheann had shown us. I didn't want anything grabbing Kestrel's ankle, or leaping up from the grass at me. Nothing had burst into flames, or turned to ash, or shrivelled up like leaves in the sunlight. Maybe it was still too early.

The late autumn day left few hours to put distance between us and High Moor, but I couldn't recall a day that had seemed as long. The urgent need to hurry gnawed at me constantly. Whenever I looked over my shoulder, the farmstead seemed to have become no smaller, the forest around it no farther away than the last time.

If it had been only myself, or my own mounted men, we could have galloped away, far enough that I didn't feel the threat of last night breathing on my neck. We could have trotted or cantered for part of the time. But we were held to the pace of the slowest, and the farmstead folk had suffered two attacks in two nights, and had spent much of last night preparing to leave the protecting walls and make this journey. They were tired, worn by fear and labour.

Daylight gave us all a second wind after the night's exertions, and for the first few hours we made a brisk walking pace. As far as the eye could see, the trodden grass of our ride two nights before showed the most direct way back to the castle.

"At least we have a road," Kerliss said.

"There is that," Bron answered. "And the wagons will be along."

"They'll have turned back when the wagon with the children met them."

"No, Lady," Bron said. "They may not come the whole way. Wagons in an attack are as useless as trousers on a boar. But if the king sent the children out, there might be others coming, and I'd lay odds the men will stay where they are and wait to see."

When High Moor was a bump on the horizon, I rode up the column of walkers and riders to where Rheann led the plough-horse carrying Father.

An open cage of wickerwork held a cloth above his head to shield him from the sun. The litter was padded with a folded blanket, and more blankets supported Father's right knee. I hoped he was able to sleep, but I also wanted the reassurance of talking to him. I pulled Kestrel into step with the horse carrying the litter and he opened his eyes.

"How do you feel?" I asked.

"Very strange," he said, and my heart jumped, but he smiled. "I've never been in a bed that moved. Riding while lying down. Always something new." His voice was much stronger than last night's whisper.

"Are you in pain?"

"No," he said. "Rheann gave me something vile. Where are we?"

"Riding southwest towards the castle. We've left High Moor well behind, and I don't think anything will be coming after us today."

He closed his eyes again and nodded, pressing a hand to his ribs.

"Are you sure you don't need something for pain?" I asked.

He snatched his hand away and let it fall by his side again.

"I'm sure," he said. "Itches, that's all. Is there water?"

I unslung my waterskin and pulled out the peg.

"Open your mouth," I said, and held the waterskin close.

He turned his face towards me and let his jaw fall open, and I trickled water into the side of his mouth, pausing to let him swallow and then doing it again, a little at a time.

"Enough. Thank you." His colour was better, too, I thought. Maybe that was the effect of sunlight instead of candlelight, but it was heartening all the same. I slung the waterskin over my shoulder again. "Don't worry about me."

"Sianna's coming," I said. "She's going to meet us along the road, or else at the castle. She'll look after you, and everything will be all right."

"Well done, Kiar," he said. "Well done." He closed his eyes, and I rode beside him for a few minutes. Either he was asleep, or he wanted me to think so. I moved up beside Rheann. She held the lead rope of the litter horse. With her skirts kilted up above her knees, she walked through the grass as matter-of-factly as if she'd done this every day.

"Thank you for taking care of him," I said.

"What else would we do for someone who came to our help, let alone the king?"

I couldn't find anything to say to that. I nodded and rode up the column. A few of the farm folk were riding on cart horses or pack horses, but there were too few of those for everyone. One or two of the walkers had their heads down and lifted their feet barely enough to clear the ground. I didn't see anyone stumble, but several were clearly very tired. Behind the last wagon, I paused to pat Whiffle, tethered to the near side by a lead line. Lightfoot looked over at me, but he was out of reach.

"They'll be back tonight or tomorrow morning," I said to the horses. I continued up the column until I came to the front. "We need to slow down a little," I said. "People are flagging, those walking."

"If we slow down any more, we'll be walking backwards," Arlen said.

"I know, I know. I want to go faster, too, but they can't. I wish we had more horses."

"We could take some of them up pillion," Arlen said. "And they could trade places with some of the riders."

"Get some up on wagon seats," another man offered, "or in the wagons."

"It's harder on the horses, but it'll make the trip quicker," I said. "Can we get everyone mounted or on a wagon? It's just past midday. We could stop to eat and do it. We'll still be going at a wagon's speed, but we'll be a little faster."

Arlen looked at the sky.

"We should be quick, Lady," he said. "Eat standing and move on as soon as everyone is mounted or on a wagon. As it is, we'll be out in the open one night and the closer to home, the better."

"Look after it, then," I said. "Saddle Whiffle and Lightfoot."

"I'll take care of it," Arlen said.

"I'll go back to the back of the line," I said.

"Can't someone else do rear guard, Lady?"

"Only if you can find one to make those things run screaming."

Arlen grinned. "That's a rare talent, Lady. You should teach it to us."

I rode back down the far side of the line, pausing to pat Lightfoot on my way.

We stopped then, in a strung-out, ragged line. As soon as we did, many of the farmstead folk sat down. I did a quick count. Without the children and two women Father had sent out on the morning we arrived, there were twenty-three people from the farmstead. We had twenty-five horses, two without riders. Several of those, including Arlen's, had claw and bite wounds. Mulloch's face was grey with weariness and pain. If he agreed to ride in a wagon, we would have one more horse.

Kerliss rode down the line, with Whiffle and Lightfoot following at the ends of their reins. "Arlen says if we put one person up with the driver on each wagon, and then one on each of the draft horses pulling, that's six. The horse pulling the little cart is lighter; if we put another on her, we can't put a second on the cart. That's seven. The pack horses can each take someone light. It's not the most comfortable seat in the world, but it'll help. That's two more. Whiffle and Lightfoot can take one each. That leaves twelve to ride pillion among twenty-three of us."

"Get Mulloch into a wagon," I said. "His horse can take someone, too. That means there are half us who aren't carrying double. We can ride guard."

"Some of the horses are wounded and tired, too," Kerliss said.

"I know. We still have to make the best speed we can."

Most of the farmsteaders sat on the ground, some chewing on food or drinking from waterskins, and some clearly too tired even to do that. "We should get them moving," he said. "It's going to take time to sort this out. I'll start with Mulloch."

"Good." I dismounted and took Whiffle and Lightfoot. As Kerliss rode over to help Mulloch off his horse, I led the two over to a group sitting on the ground.

"We'll move a little faster if you're all on horseback or in wagons," I said. "Two of you take these horses, and I'll find riders to take the rest of you up behind them."

My own men got the farmsteaders, by ones and twos, into wagons or riding pillion behind someone else. It took longer than I wanted, and our shadows were leaning out behind us by the time we were moving again. I managed to get Rheann into the back of a wagon with Father's pack-horse walking behind. He kept his eyes closed, but his mouth was set, and I thought that in spite of Rheann's medicine, he was in some pain. I didn't speak to him; if he was resting at all, I wanted him to rest. I ached from the long ride to High Moor, the fight, and the journey back, but I hadn't been injured and was better rested than the farmsteaders. I couldn't imagine how much he and Mulloch were suffering, or how tired the farmstead folk were.

Even so, I could tell we were moving more quickly. I thought about the long night's ride to High Moor and remembered we'd slept for two hours in the middle of it. We hadn't rested at all today, except for the break shortly past midday. If we kept on at this pace, we might make enough distance to put us beyond reach of whatever had attacked High Moor.

As the sun fell, I watched the sky, hoping to see either Willow or Tuan flying towards us. Sianna would be riding from her home at an angle to meet us; with luck she might reach us before we reached the castle. I was anxious for her to look at

Father and Mulloch; however good a healer Rheann was, both were still badly hurt. If Mulloch were going to lose his arm, it would be better to do it soon, before the pain of the wound ate much of his strength.

As the light waned, Bron came looking for me. He, too, was drawn and tired, but not grey with pain or fatigue. Like all of us, he'd slept in his clothes, and not too well at that. His arm was still in its sling, and he moved it restlessly now and then. He smiled wryly when he saw me looking.

"It's hard to get used to being one-handed," he said. "There's a good camping place a few miles along—another hour, maybe less, a little rise with a hollow in it. We could defend the top, and they'd be attacking uphill."

"What about the horses? Is there room to picket them?"

He shook his head.

"Not in the hollow, Lady, and if we had a battle, we'd have panicky horses and panicky people. We could put a few torches around the top, set a watch at the base and a mounted guard at the top, but most of the horses would have to be picketed below the rise."

"You saw what they did to Arlen's horse," I said.

The skin of the horse's neck was clawed in four long, parallel slashes, and there were punctures on his poll and one ear, all from the thing trying to climb over him to get at Arlen. "And what Harrel said about the cow."

"I know, Lady. I'm not happy about it, but I can't think of anything better. If they're picketed, they can't run. If they're left loose, we'll be rounding them up half of tomorrow."

I sighed. "Let's get there first and have a look. At least we'll have the advantage of ground."

Bron nodded then swung around and looked towards the forest. I was about to ask what he saw when a dark-grey horse walked out of the trees. I peered at it; the light made it hard to see who was riding, or if the horse had a rider at all. But then, the horse trotted a few steps and broke into a loping canter towards us. The rider's garment billowed briefly, and in the shape of it, the flash of several colours, and a glimpse of light dapples over the horse's shoulder, I knew it was Sianna.

I whooped in excitement and relief, and several people near me started with surprise. Then I slipped Kestrel between Father's draft horse and Lightfoot, carrying Harrel, and galloped towards Sianna. When I reached her, I was laughing and crying, and brought Kestrel jostling up to Night Wind so I could throw my arms around her.

She returned my hug and then pushed me gently away.

"I got your message," she said. "What's happened? Willow said something wounded the king."

"Yes," I said, "something, but I don't know what."

As we rode I told her about the attack, Cloud's death, and the decision to abandon High Moor. She listened in silence, and when I finished, she said nothing.

"What do you think they were?" I asked. "And did you see any sign of them in the forest on your way here?"

"No sign," she said. "Everything was ordinary. As for what they were, all I can think of is bog-walkers. But I've never heard of them coming out of a bog. I've surely never heard of such an attack. Still, Harrel might have the right idea."

"People drowned in bogs, you mean? But how could they? They're dead, drowned. Dead people don't come back." I remembered Orla and added, "Not ordinary ones. Not as flesh."

"That's a mystery," Sianna said. "This will bear thinking. For now, let me do what I can for your father and Mulloch."

She rode immediately to Father. I dropped back to let her speak to him privately. She felt his forehead and hands, then lifted the blanket back and saw the chest wounds. She ran her hand over his right leg, replaced the blanket and spoke to him again. Then she turned and rode past me to look at Mulloch.

When she came back to me, her face was grave.

"I know you're worried about your father," she said, "but Mulloch's injury is much worse than it was. I want to tend to him first, and the king second."

"Yes, of course," I said, but my stomach sank. I glanced at Father in his litter, swaying ahead of us.

"Thank you," she said.

I wondered what she would have said, or done, if I'd refused her request. I knew what Father would have said.

At the hollow in the rise, she immediately made a small fire and set water to boil, then sent for Mulloch. Two men supported him to the fireside; it was clear he couldn't have walked on his own. After that, whether by some magic of Sianna's, or simply because we were too busy setting up camp, I didn't see her or Mulloch for some time. Then, when darkness had fallen, she brought him to one of the fires, walking slowly, but upright and on his own feet.

Then she came to me, where I sat on the ground by Father's litter, holding his hand. Rheann brewed a tea against pain on the fire beside us. Half a dozen of the men had dropped their saddles and blankets around her little blaze.

"We need to take him over to my fire," Sianna said.

Rheann stood up. "I'll get the stretcher poles," she said. "if you find men to carry him." By the time I came back with three men, Rheann had worked the poles through the loops on the stretcher cloth that still lay beneath Father. I took the foot end of one pole and together the four of us lifted Father and walked him over to Sianna's fire. We had to step carefully, because she had set up eight slender, knee-high sticks enclosing a space ten paces across. Inside that space, the light was that of a clear summer evening instead of an autumn night with dark closing in.

When we laid the stretcher on the ground, the three men walked away, but I stood where I was. "I want to stay," I said.

Sianna sifted a handful of something powdery into the steaming pot and stirred it without speaking. Then she took out the spoon and tapped it on the side of the pot, just as Nias might do, and turned to me.

"Can you sit and be silent, no matter what happens? Can you not cry out, or move, or reach for your knife? Can you leave your hands on your knees and keep your heart quiet in your breast, whatever you see or hear?" she asked. "If you can't, then you may disturb my work and endanger your father."

I wanted to say yes. I wanted badly to stay with Father, to see Sianna lay her hands on him and make everything right, to walk with him away from her fire and back to our own. Sianna waited. I watched my father's chest rise and fall, once, twice.

"I think I could," I said, "but thinking isn't good enough, is it?"

"No," she said. "Only knowing would be good enough. The sooner you leave, the sooner I can start."

I knelt beside Father and kissed his forehead. It felt as hot as it had the night before. "I'll see you soon," I said. Then I stood and walked out of Sianna's space. When I turned to look back, the fire was a dim glow, and Sianna and my father no more than shadows moving inside.

Bron was at the fireside when I returned.

"We've sorted out the horses," he said. "We picketed them in lines, one tether at the end, and a single rope passing through the bridles on five or six horses. That way if we need to release them, we can cut the rope and release six at a time instead of untying each one. And they're on the west side, farthest from the forest."

"Well done," I said. Bron laid his hand on my shoulder.

"He'll be all right," he said. "It's nothing she can't cure."

I nodded, but I knew there were some things Sianna could not cure.

CHAPTER

FOURTEEN

As full dark fell, I gave up hoping for Willow or Tuan to come back until the next morning. It was perfectly reasonable for them to be gone the whole day. I'd sent Willow to Sianna, and then she was to warn three farmsteads, and Tuan had to warn three as well. Each time they would have to tell the story of what had happened at High Moor and convince the farmsteaders to leave. And that was if no other place was under attack. I didn't want to think about having ten farmsteads all under attack at once and sending to the castle for help.

No matter what I told myself, I still wished my friends were there. I wanted badly to talk to Tuan about the day, about riding past Cloud's body and the long journey, and Sianna's arrival. I wanted to have him next to me, quiet and calm, deadly efficient in a fight, and tender with my feelings.

We set a watch at the base of the rise and changed it every couple of hours. I took the first one, wanting to be out of sight of that dim place where Sianna worked to help Father. If I sat at the fire, I couldn't keep myself from glancing over every few seconds, and turning my back meant only that I looked a little less often and twisted my neck to do it. The need to be alert on watch helped stop the worry for Father from running around in my head like a squirrel.

Standing guard at the castle was usually an easy duty. The castle had never been directly attacked. Anyone who tried had to come uphill, climbing the dun on horse or foot, and then face thick stone walls, well supplied with places for archers to pick off approaching attackers.

Standing guard at the foot of a hillock, without walls or defences apart from my own weapons and skill, was a different matter. The air chilled rapidly after the sun went down, and I wiggled my fingers in my gloves to keep them warm. Every familiar sound—rustling grass, the thump of a horse's hoof, or the night air sighing in the trees—made me prick my ears. Was that a hoof, or the first sound of the long, leaping approach of those nightmare attackers? When my relief came down the hillock, my shoulders hurt from the tightness of my muscles. I went gladly up to the fire.

Father's litter lay empty where we had left it when we moved him, and I could no longer be sure exactly where Sianna's fire was. There seemed to be no space big enough to hold a large circle, a fire and two people. I thought of going down to the pickets to check if Night Wind was still there, but that might look as though I didn't trust Sianna. It felt important to trust her, as though checking on her might hamper her in helping

Father. I turned away to spread out my blankets among the others sleeping around Rheann's little fire.

Rheann slept by the fire, her blankets wrapped neatly and snugly around her. A wooden cup stood near my blankets and Kestrel's saddle. When I sniffed it, it smelled of mint, and the lingering warmth was comforting on my fingers and mouth. I hoped she hadn't put anything in it to make me sleep; all I could taste was mint and a little honey. I drank it and lay down. A good guard slept when she could. If I was needed, someone would rouse me. All the same, it took me a long time to fall asleep.

I woke up cold in the dark before dawn. The fire had burned to dark coals. When I held my hand over them, I felt a little heat; I blew on the embers, and a small edge of orange glowed. I patted the ground around the firepit and felt cold, dew-wet grass. There was no wood, not so much as a twig. I stood up and folded my blankets by feel, then waited for my night vision to improve while I rubbed my arms and shook out my legs.

Whether it was the cold or the sounds I made, others began to stir around me. Rheann sat up and blew on the fire. When the coals glowed, a flame started, and Rheann held shreds of bark kept dry in her blanket to the embers. In a minute or two she had a small fire of twigs crackling. I squatted by the fire and held out my hands to it.

One by one, more fires sprang up around the hollow. I looked over my shoulder, and saw Sianna in the dim light coming up from the east, bending to pull up the slender sticks that marked her camp. Her lips moved, but I couldn't hear her voice. Father lay, still on his back, beside the fire with blankets tucked around him. When Sianna straightened up, she beckoned me over.

"Is he better?" I asked when I reached her.

Dark rings of fatigue marked her eyes. "A little. He won't die today. It will help when we can get him into a warm room and his own bed."

"Is that—" I swallowed. "Is that all?"

"I know it's not what you hoped for."

"I saw Mulloch before you treated him," I said. "He would have died but for you. And if you say we can get Father home, I'll believe you. Thank you. I'll find someone to get Father back onto the litter, and we can get going."

"Good," she said. "The sooner we're in out of the cold, the better for everyone."

People moved a little more quickly than they had the day before, and we were riding again under a low, grey sky before full daylight arrived. We put the farmstead folk at the front of the column and those of us who had nobody riding pillion spread out around the sides and back.

"We were lucky last night," I said to Bron. "We didn't need to do more than keep guard."

"That wasn't luck," he said. "That was you, Lady. They're afraid of you."

"I don't know why," I said. "And if it's something I do, I don't know what, or how."

"Doesn't matter," Bron said. "Word goes around—Princess Kiar scares the monsters. They feel safer with you here. 'Course, everyone knows you can fight magic, so nobody's surprised."

I looked at the skies to the northwest and southwest again. Surely either Willow or Tuan would be coming soon. I stared at the clouds as though staring hard enough would let me see through. A movement flickered at the edge of my right eye, and when I turned, the flicker became wings in the distance. A bird, a large bird with long wings, and then another, and in a few minutes two swans glided down and came to land directly behind us.

"Get their clothes," I called up the line, and heard the message passed.

The swans stood, watchful and still, muttering to each other, until a man came jogging back to us, a linen bag over his shoulder and two pair of boots under his arms. As he arrived, both swans rose up and spread their wings, and we had to close our eyes against the flare of magic. When it faded, I slid off of Kestrel, seized the linen bag from the messenger, and ran to Tuan and Willow.

"Thanks!" Willow said, grabbing the bag from me and tipping the clothes out onto the ground. "This is why you're supposed to go south for the winter, you know!" She hauled her shirt over her head and then reached for her trousers. "You really need to grow feathers. Brrr!" She took her boots and hopped around on one foot while she put her boot on the other, then switched feet.

"I was beginning to worry," I said. "What happened? Sianna arrived last night, just before dark."

"Were you attacked?" she asked.

"No. We stood guard, but nothing. You?" I looked from Willow to Tuan as he tucked his trousers into his boots. He shook his head.

"No," he said. "Not at any I visited."

"Far Fellstead had a raid last night," Willow said. "Not as many as we saw at High Moor, maybe nine or ten, they said. The attackers stayed all night, but they pushed them off the walls. They thought of the nets, too. If you can get them tangled, they stay on the ground, at least. It wasn't as bad as it could have been."

"But they're coming, aren't they?"

"I don't know. They caught three in nets, and when the sun came up they chopped them to pieces with axes. Far Fellstead think they can defend themselves.

"Far Fellstead is the farthest away from here," Tuan said.

"You mean, farthest away from Kiar," Willow said.

He nodded.

"How is the king?" Tuan asked.

"Better, both him and Mulloch. Sianna reached us last night. Right now, the important thing is to get everyone to the castle."

Someone yelled something from the front of the group, and in a moment Kerliss cantered down and stopped in front of me.

"Wagons, Lady," he said. "The wagons from the castle. And fresh horses."

"You did tell me, Bron," I said.

In less than an hour we met the wagons Father ordered. It seemed so long ago, now, that we had set out. The cart horses from High Moor were unharnessed and four fresh horses put in their place to pull the wagons. Some of the High Moor goods were loaded into the empty wagons, and the folk riding pillion made seats of bundles and bags. At midmorning, we were moving much faster. The fresh cart horses, pulling lighter loads, went at a brisk trot, and there was nobody on foot to hold them back.

Father's horse was the only one that couldn't move faster than a walk. I wanted everyone to stay together, but he refused.

"Get the rest safely inside," he said. His voice was stronger than the night before, and his forehead, when I touched it, was cool. He batted my hand away.

"We'll stay with you," I said. "You need a guard."

He didn't argue. Once Willow and Tuan were again on their own horses, we rode together and I led Father's horse, with Sianna and half a dozen of the guard. At a horse's walking pace we made better speed, even if we weren't keeping up with the rest. By midafternoon, we were climbing the dun towards the castle gate.

Inside the castle was as busy as an anthill. The wagons were off by the stables, horses probably already unharnessed and being groomed and fed. Some of the High Moor families were still in the courtyard, children clinging to parents. Dar came out to where Willow, Tuan, and I stood by Father's horse and immediately went to Father's side.

"Tir," he said. Father raised his right hand and Dar clasped it. Father said something too softly to carry, and Dar answered, "I'm not surprised. Let's get you settled." He snapped off orders, and in minutes, four men had lowered Father's litter and carried him into the castle. Dar watched them out of sight, then turned to me. "Your pardon, Lady."

"Please don't," I told him. "What do you know?"

"Most of it, I think," he said. "Rheann all but took me by the ear to tell me. A managing woman, that one."

"Her son is head of the farmstead now," I said.

"Is he so? Poor sod." Dar said.

"I sent word to the farmsteads," I said. "We could have them all here in a few days."

"Is it that bad?" Dar asked.

"I don't know," I said. "But Willow says there was one other attack. There might have been others since, or the farmsteads nearer High Moor might have been attacked."

"Not the southern ones, surely," Dar said. "These things came out of the forest."

"The ones at High Moor did," Willow said, "but there are no forests near Far Fellstead. It's all pasture and field, and scrubby trees wide apart. Rocks and water, marsh. Their farmstead wall is rock. They haven't enough trees to make a wall."

"Then where did they come from?" I asked.

Willow shrugged. "They weren't there, and then they were. Maybe nobody was watching."

"There haven't been any messengers, like Corvie?" I asked.

Dar shook his head. "None at all. What are your orders, Lady?"

In that moment, I felt the weight of the castle and all the farmsteads, and all the people, settle on my shoulders. Dar— my father's friend, the man who had taught me weapons, the captain of my guard, and the man I looked up to second only to my father, was asking me for orders.

Until Father recovered, I was responsible for Valenia.

CHAPTER

FIFTEEN

The first thing I wanted was a bath, but I settled for a pail of hot water in my room and a scrub with a rough cloth. When I was done, I wet my hair and scrubbed my scalp with my fingers, then dried and dressed. Combing out my hair, I gritted my teeth at the tangles and also at the time it took. After one attempt to braid it, while the wet hair clung to my fingers and refused to go where I wanted, I flicked the comb through it again and left it loose.

Tuan met me on the stairs as I came down. I stopped, one step above him. Our faces were almost level; I only had to raise my chin a little to look into his eyes.

"I washed my hair," I said. "It doesn't fix any problems, but I feel better." He tucked a dripping, curling strand behind my ear. "I see."

I put my arms around his waist and leaned my head on his shoulder. He held me close, wet hair and all, and I turned my face to rest against his neck and breathed in the smell of his skin. Stories never talked about that—how comforting someone's smell could be.

"I haven't washed at all," he said.

"I don't care. You smell good." I sighed and stood upright again.

"I'm not ready for this, Tuan. I didn't expect Father to get hurt so badly."

"None of us did," he said.

"Now I have to be—" I stopped.

"For now," Tuan said. "Sianna is with the king. She'll do everything that can be done."

I twined my fingers together.

"Remember, in the stable?" I said, "Before all this happened, you were trying to tell me something. I'm sorry. I should have listened to you."

"It's all right," he said.

"No, it's not. Will you tell me now? I'll ask Nias to send us some food to Father's chamber."

"If you want to hear it," he said.

"I do. I might not like it, but I think I need to know."

"Then I'll tell you."

I asked Willow to join us. Whatever Tuan had to say, I wanted her there, too.

Upstairs, I sat in Father's chair, and Tuan in Mother's, next to it. Willow took one of the chairs across the table from me. When we had finished the little meal Nias sent in, Tuan took my hand, and I twined my fingers in his.

"These things happened long ago," he began. "The elders I heard them from learned them from their elders, who heard them from elders before them."

He paused and I nodded. Swanfolk lived very long lives, longer than humans. What Tuan was about to tell me might have happened five hundred years ago, or longer.

"The king-light," he said, "shows everyone who the king, or queen, is. People who can't see can still feel it somehow. It shows the care the king has for his people, and his bond with them, and with the land they live in. When the king-light is strong, that bond is strong, and when it weakens, the bond does, too."

"You told me this part before," I said. "When we had to fight Orla."

"Yes, but there's another part. Once no king's light ever faded. The elders said that it was partly because there were more battles in old times, before the borders of Valenia, Noermark, and other countries were settled. Kings sometimes died in battle, before they grew old. But those who survived battle were sometimes killed by their own people. If crops failed, or the hunting was bad, they'd claim the king couldn't keep the land strong."

"Oh!" I said. "I think Father said something similar. Years ago, now. I can't remember why he told me, but—"

"So it happened here, too," Willow said.

"The kings couldn't have simply let themselves be killed! They must have fought."

"I don't know," Tuan said.

"They might allow it," Willow said, "if they believed it was good for the kingdom and the people. You went out to fight Hafor for that, and you could have been killed."

"That's different," I said. "That was doing something, not standing there and waiting for him to stab me or cut off my head."

For a minute, we were silent. A question chewed at me, annoying as a biting fly, and as hard to ignore. Finally I looked at Tuan and asked it. "The attack at High Moor," I said. "Father wasn't hurt before that. Do you think this happened because Father is worried about Mother? How could that be?"

"It's not only that," Willow said. She put her hand over mine. "I know you don't want to hear it, but the king looks and acts much older than he did last year. We watched the bog spread out a few days ago. You were there. Then the attack on High Moor—all of it almost at once."

"Do you believe that?" I asked Tuan. "That Father—that it's caused all of this? Just getting older?"

"I don't want to believe it either," he said. "Not of your father. But kings failing, bad things happening to the land—they're in the stories for a reason."

"And why were those things afraid of you, and not him?" Willow asked. "Unless there's something else happening that we don't know about."

We sat in silence for long minutes. Finally, I could no longer avoid the question nagging me. "If those—things—could attack before he was wounded, what will happen now? He can't fight, he can't even stand. But none of our people would turn on him! None!"

Willow turned to Tuan. "We shouldn't have said anything. It's not their way. And if it was, we couldn't stop it, the three of us on our own."

"You think we won't be able to—"

"I'm sorry," she said. "I only meant you should know where an enemy might be. I didn't mean we thought it was right, or that we would stand by and let anyone kill him."

My relief must have shown in my face.

Willow squeezed my hand. "If anyone tries, we're with you, aren't we, Tuan?"

He nodded. "Always. No matter who it is."

"Well, nobody's going to kill him," I said. "First, I won't let them, and Dar won't let them, either. There's his guard and my guard. Anyway, if someone was going to try," I said, "Don't you think they would have tried after the fight at High Moor? It wouldn't have been hard to do."

"That's an injury," Willow said. "Fighters get injured all the time, don't they?"

"But he has a fever," I said. "Everyone must know he's sick."

"Dar says a fever isn't unusual with a wound," Tuan said.

"What happens to the swanfolk's king?" I asked at last. "Does someone kill him when he becomes weak?"

"No," Tuan said. "There's no need. A swan who is ill or injured is usually killed by something, a wolf or a wildcat. Or they stay behind when the flock migrates."

"You don't take care of them?"

"We can't," Willow said. "At least, not the same way humans can. We can protect them from a predator, but if the flock has to go south, we have no way to bring them along if they're not strong enough to fly."

"You don't look after sick ones?"

"Not as well as humans can," Tuan said.

"If we get sick, we usually die," Willow said. "When I had the lung fever last winter, I wasn't nearly as sick as some people, but I thought I would die. Sometimes it's better to be human."

"I never thought of any of that," I said.

"We live longer," Tuan said, "but we die faster."

"If your father hadn't brought your mother back here," Willow said, "she would have died. She would have been outside the flock, where a predator could get her. Or—" she stopped.

"Or Grandfather would have killed her?" I asked.

"He has to protect the flock," Tuan said softly. "Even if he loves her, he can't allow her to endanger the flock. If she didn't leave, he'd try to drive her off."

"I never thought of how hard it is for you," I said. "All I ever thought about was flying."

"There's no reason you should have to think of it," she said. "The swanfolk aren't your concern; you have your own people to look after. That's hard enough."

"But they're my family," I said. "And you're my friends."

"That's another thing," Willow said. "I can be your friend, even though you're the heir. And you call Tuan your friend, but if you were in the flock, he would be your mate, or nothing."

I remembered when Prince Othar of Noermark, years ago, had given me the moss-stone necklace and said, "I hope to be friends with any woman I marry." But his people would never have been friends with my swanfolk people. It had hurt to break off with him, but my people had to come first.

"Here you can be both," I said. "Isn't it better to have a mate who is also your best friend?"

"Maybe it is," Willow said. "It's not how we think of it—at least, not in swan form."

"Swans don't fall in love?"

"Mm," she said, tilting her head. "Not the way you mean. I only know about it from watching Gil and Adana, and you and Tuan. Mostly, we feel the need to make a nest."

"Some of that with humans, too," Tuan said. He smiled at me, and I felt suddenly shy. Making a nest seemed so much simpler than all the fuss of betrothal and marriage among humans. Even now, anxious for Father and all of Valenia, part of me wanted to just fly off with Tuan, make a nest in some quiet corner of the lake.

"Yes, but they don't say it right out," Willow said. "Why is that?"

"It's hard to explain," I said. Now I could feel myself blushing.

"How hard could it be?" Willow asked. But she let it drop, and I was grateful.

I badly wanted to see Father, but I couldn't simply go and interrupt Sianna. I had to speak to Dar about defences. When I'd done that, I came back to the hall. I couldn't help looking up the stairs again, as though staring would tell me what was happening. Then I went to the kitchen to speak to Nias about food and what to do with the stores the High Moor folk had brought.

"It's not that we don't have room, Lady," Nias said. "We can bed people in the great hall and such. The food will crowd the people, you might say, and the more farmsteads empty to come here, the more people, and the more food."

"That's a problem that will solve itself, I'm afraid," I said. "I don't think any farmstead has enough wagons to bring all their stores. Of course, they'll bring cattle."

"Pity they can't bring the hay," Nias said.

"Yes. If the attacks continue all winter, we'll be killing cattle before they starve."

"Will everyone be here all winter, Lady?"

I sighed. "I wish I knew, Nias. I wish I knew how many are coming and how long they'll have to stay. What I do know is that we can't keep everyone here forever. We'll have to take back the farmsteads sometime."

"That's far in the future," Nias said. "Right now, whether we take the farmsteads back or not, we have to sort out where to put things and people We'll have to make do." She rubbed her hands together, and the look of satisfaction on her face was unmistakable.

"Nias, I swear you're pleased about this!"

"No, but it's a bit of a puzzle, you might say, where to fit things in. I don't mind a puzzle now and again."

"Rheann of High Moor could help you, if that's all right," I said.

"I'd be glad of some help, and that's the truth. But don't you fret about it, now. I'll send a message to Rheann. You look after what you have to do, and I'll figure out the rest."

"Thank you, Nias. I'm sure you'll take care of everything," I said. And I was. Only a few days ago, she had spoken to me about our own grain stores. Now she was taking charge of a whole extra farmstead of people to feed, and possibly more to come, as though it was a great game.

I came away from the kitchen and stood at the bottom of the stairs, wondering again what was happening in Father's room. I watched as Eleni came down, carrying a basin and stepping gently so as not to slosh water.

"Sianna says if you want to go up, Lady, you can," she said.

"How is he?" I asked.

"Resting," she said. "All the better for his own bed, too."

"Thank you." I ran up the stairs two at a time.

Father's door was ajar, and I pushed it gently open. Someone had hung a heavy, dark cloth over the window, and the room was dim. The candle beside Father's bed was the brightest light. Sianna sat by the bed. When I came in, she stood and put her finger to her lips.

I stole over to the bed. Father's face was no longer pinched with pain, and he breathed evenly with his mouth open a little. After a minute or two, I turned to Sianna, and she pointed to the door. We tiptoed out and stood in the hall.

"Is he going to be all right?" I whispered.

"He's not as badly hurt as all that," Sianna said. "Rheann did well at cleaning the punctures, and I have a cold cloth on his leg for the swelling. When that goes down, I can tell more about how much his leg is hurt."

"Rheann said it wasn't broken," I said.

"Nothing feels out of place," Sianna said. "I think the bone may be only cracked. For now, sleep is a good medicine. The body heals faster when the mind is quiet. I'll stay by him until he wakes."

"I'll have food and drink sent up for you. What about the claw wounds in his sides?"

"I've washed them out with woundwort and treated them with a salve to keep them clean. They'll be sore, but they're not dangerous. They're already starting to close and should heal well."

I felt as if a stone had been lifted off my heart. "Thank you," I said. "Thank you for coming, and for looking after him."

"You're welcome," Sianna said. Then she slipped back into Father's room and closed the door gently behind her.

CHAPTER

SIXTEEN

Late that afternoon, two ox-drawn wagons arrived from Treegirt, the northeastern farmstead. Five young children and two older girls rode in the first one, sitting on bags of clothing and bedding. A young woman drove that wagon, and the second, piled with bags of food, was driven by an elderly man. Corrin came to find me, still in the clothes he'd fought and ridden in. I knew how much he wanted a bath—my cold-water wash hadn't changed that for me.

"They got the children out as soon as your messenger came," he said, "and what they could throw on a cart right away. The rest are a day behind, he says. Treegirt hadn't been attacked when he left, and that was the night after we drove them off. We may have hurt them worse than we thought."

"I'd like to think that," I said.

"And the cattle and sheep from High Moor might be in today, too," Corrin said. "Eating their way to us, you might say."

"It's going to get crowded," I said. "If Treegirt escaped attack, I hope others will, too."

"You sent the message, Lady, and they'll give it in the king's name. They'll come. We can always be hawks and owls, and half sleep by day and half by night."

After he left, I wondered if Nias's enthusiasm would fade with that many people to feed and bed. I wasn't happy about the farmsteads either, and was most worried about Stony Ridge and Treegirt. Both were near the northern border, and if Noermark heard they were abandoned, they'd consider it an invitation. The bog-walkers might not dig up stores and burn buildings, but Noermarkers would.

The next two days brought the farmstead folk of Stony Ridge, Riverbend and Eastenstead, with more wagons, more people and stores, and more cattle. We doubled the guard on the wall to keep an eye out for any sign of attack and built extra paddocks on the southwest side of the castle, farthest from the bog. There was no lack of hands to build; as more and more farmstead folk came in with none of their usual work to do, they willingly built walls of tree-trunks and stone.

The old fire-moat around the castle was stripped of turf and the pieces turned earth-side up on the moat's bank. We filled it with sticks and brush and laid firebark every ten paces. A few well-placed fire-arrows would set it ablaze. It was a last resort; nobody wanted to set the grass on fire.

By the third day, messengers had arrived from Oak Vale and Near Fellstead; the farmstead folk would be here within a day and a half. Already it was almost impossible to find any place away from other people. Father's chamber offered a quieter place to talk, although the sounds of voices and children's play and dogs barking came through the heavy door and the single window.

Father's bedroom was also quiet. Sianna kept a rolled blanket against the foot of the door to cover the gap at the floor. When I pushed it back into place, the room fell almost silent, in spite of the crowd and bustle outside. The curtains were closed, too, and the first time I visited his room, I went to draw them back, let in some daylight.

"Don't move it," Sianna said. "You'll tear the spell."

I let go of the curtain and turned to her. "What spell?" I hadn't felt anything, and since wearing an iron necklace for a year, I often felt ill, or ill at ease, around magic.

"Something very mild, to keep it peaceful, help him rest and heal," she said. "You can't ask children to be quiet all the time. This keeps most of the noise out. The blanket at the door, too."

Sianna and Elena cared for Father, and I visited every day. His fever was lower, and the swelling on his leg had gone down with cold compresses, but the holes in his sides had refused to heal. He still slept a great deal, in part because of the medicines Sianna gave him for the pain.

"Why aren't his wounds getting better?" I asked Sianna.

"I don't know," she said. "They aren't infected or bleeding. It's as though they've simply stopped healing. They're no better but no worse. I've seen men with injuries like this back on their feet, or on horseback, and complaining only of soreness or itching."

"But not Father," I said.

"No, not your father. None of the lore says that bog-walkers have any command of magic, but we know almost nothing of them. Tonight I'll see if I can learn whether there's magic here, and what can be done about it."

"Is there anything I can do to help?" I asked.

"See that I am not interrupted," she said. "And sleep well yourself. Your people need you."

"I will," I said.

There was no lack of work to tire my body, but it was hard to keep my mind from jumping like a squirrel bouncing from branch to branch; Noermark, the farmsteads, the bog-walkers, and every other thought of my father and his wounds that wouldn't heal.

After supper I made sure there was a guard between Father's room and any approach, and one at the foot and the head of the stairs to keep people quiet there as well. As dark fell, I retreated to Father's chamber with Tuan and Willow for some peace. We'd barely settled when the guard at the door opened it with a message.

"Lady Kiar, the gatehouse says a man from Noermark has arrived and is asking for you."

"One man? Alone?"

"That's right."

"Guthric," Willow said. "But why is he asking for you instead of the king?"

"I don't know. You're sure he asked for me?"

"I didn't hear him myself, Lady, but that's the message I was given. Will you go, or will I send a message? What shall I tell them?"

"I'm coming."

"Yes, Lady," the guard said.

Willow looked at me with wide eyes.

"Either Gythorn is worse," I said, "or they've heard about Father. I can't think of any other reason for Guthric to come now."

"He didn't say it was Guthric," Tuan said.

"Well, who else would it be?" Willow asked. "Nobody's courting Kiar, and I doubt if they'd come politely to announce a raid."

"I hope not," I said, "But I can't imagine he's here for anything good."

CHAPTER

SEVENTEEN

I walked out to the gate with Willow and Tuan following. One of Noermark's small, swift, beautiful horses stood by the gatehouse. In the light of the torches, its dark coat could have been nearly any colour, but a white blaze stroked down the narrow nose to the wide nostrils.

I didn't recognize the man standing by the horse, holding the reins in one hand, until I had nearly reached the gatehouse. Then I knew him.

"It's Warulf," I said. "Hafor's man from his little sheep-thieving, remember?"

"The one who spoke to you after the fight," Willow said.

I hadn't thought of Warulf; I'd assumed he had gone into exile with Hafor in the spring. I couldn't imagine what would have brought him into Valenia alone. He straightened as we stopped in front of him.

"Warulf," I said. "What brings you here? And at this hour?"

"Princess Kiar." His voice was rough, and he was clearly weary. "I have come— There is a thing you only can help."

"Have you come alone, all this way?" I asked.

"Alone," he said. "no sheep-reivers." He grinned briefly, then his face fell back into lines of fatigue. "My king forbids. I am outlaw now. I cannot go back."

"It could be a trick, Lady," Corrin said.

"It is no trick!" Warulf put his hands on his belt and Corrin drew his sword. Warulf gave him a sneering look and unbuckled his belt. It fell to the ground, weighted by his sword and dagger. With two fingers he slid a sheathed knife from his sleeve and dropped it beside the belt, then raised his right hand and bent slowly until he slipped his left forefinger into his boot and hooked out another knife, which he also dropped. He stepped away from the little pile of weapons and put his hand on his horse's bridle; the animal had hardly moved.

"Unarmed," he said. "No tricks, no army. Princess Kiar, I come to ask help. I am outlaw now. No raider, my oath."

He stood still, watching my face. I'd met Warulf twice before. Once was when he'd come with Prince Hafor's raiding party, testing our defences when my father was away. That time he had spoken to me courteously after I'd defeated Hafor in a duel. The other time was when Hafor came to court Orla. I'd only spoken to him then to bid him farewell.

"He might have another knife," Willow said.

"You look, swan girl," Warulf said. "You look." He held his arms to each side and smiled at her.

"Corrin," I said, "see that his horse is stabled and fed. Maithey, take the weapons, please, and keep them safe. Now, where can we talk quietly?"

"The west guardhouse, Lady," Maithey said. "There's a fire there, and food. I'll let the others know you're not to be disturbed."

"Thank you," I said. "Warulf, come with us. Whatever you have to tell me, you may as well have a seat by a fire while you do it."

We walked without talking to the west guardhouse. I led, and Willow followed close behind. Behind her was Warulf, then Tuan. Inside the guardhouse, two benches flanked a narrow table. A small cask of beer sat on a three-legged stool at one end of the table, and a tray holding bread, cheese, apples, and half a dozen meat pasties in the centre.

I sat down on one side of the table and nodded to the other bench. Warulf sat. Willow stood at my left, and Tuan behind Warulf.

"Please, eat," I said. Tuan poured a cup of beer for Warulf, and he drank it thirstily, then picked up a meat pasty and bit half off. When he finished the pasty, he drank half of his second cup of beer and then set it on the table.

"What brings a man of Noermark here for my help?" I asked. "I thought Noermark didn't believe in the strength of women."

"Noermark, no. But I," Warulf said, putting his hand on his breast, "I see you, a warrior maid, from the songs."

"There are warriors in Noermark," Willow said.

"And kenningmen," Warulf said. "And kenningwives."

"Kenningmen, kenningmen," I repeated. Then I understood. "Wisemen, wisewomen!"

He nodded.

"There is a thing," he said. "From the fen. Our kenningmen seen not such a thing."

"What is the fen?" I asked.

"The mist place, the quaking ground. The fen."

"The bog," Willow and I said together.

"What's come out of the bog?" I asked. "What have you seen?"

"I have not seen," Warulf said. "Not the thing, no. What it did—" He drew his fingers down his face and throat and punched one hand against his breast, then ripped it away, fingers curved as though holding something. He flexed his fingers once, twice. "Hert."

"It ripped someone's heart out?"

He held up two fingers.

"Two men? It killed two men?"

"One wif takes weaving to the fen. Her man, too."

"Like Eatha and Aislin," I said. "Did the woman fall in, Warulf?" He shook his head and shrugged his shoulders.

"Did she fall?" This time I made a fist and let it drop below the table. "Did she fall in?"

"Na, na," he said. "The thing catch her. Then her man."

"Someone must have seen it," Willow said, "if you know how it happened."

He tightened his lips in a grim line and put his hand at table height. "Tochter." He pointed at Willow and again put his hand at the table height.

"Oh, hells," I whispered. "Their daughter saw it."

"Did she say what it was?" Tuan asked. It was the first time he'd spoken, and Warulf turned towards him. Tuan stood, arms folded, looking down at the Noermarker.

"What was it?" he asked again. Warulf put his left hand into the front of his shirt and pulled out something long that tapered towards the end, flat and yet curved, with a rippled edge. Stiff and brown, it confused me for a few long seconds. Then, as Warulf handed it to Tuan, I saw what it was.

"Oh, no, no, no," Willow said, almost a whisper. "No, it's not true."

I met Tuan's eyes. He looked shocked as I'd never seen him. In his fingers he turned the shaft of the peat-stained flight-feather.

"Fen-stalker," Warulf said. "Swan."

EIGHTEEN

"It's an elders' story," Willow said. She pointed at Warulf, and her voice was almost a snarl. "There's no such thing! It was a wildcat or something. Wolves, bears, but not that, not that! You made it up!"

"Willow," Tuan said. He spoke quietly, but she shut up. Slowly, she let her hand fall to her side.

"Let me be clear," I said to Warulf. "You're telling me that this feather, this swan's feather, came from the bog-walker? The—what did you call it? The fen-stalker?"

He nodded once, his eyes on mine.

"Why come to me with it?"

"We do not know swans, not the other ones. Their ways, their strength. How to fight."

"You do well enough with arrows," I said. "I've seen it once and heard of it on my own lands."

Warulf bowed his head as though to grant me the point.

"Arrows do not harm these," he said. "Or stop. No blood."

"You said 'these'. More than one."

"Ya." He held up his hands, fingers spread, then closed his fists and opened them twice. "So many. They fight one wick, one, ah—" He made a circling motion with his finger to take in the room.

"A farmstead, a steading?" I asked, and shaped a house with my hands and sketched a wall around it.

"Ya," he said, "Farrumstead."

"When?" I asked. "How long ago?"

He held up his hands, four fingers on each. I counted back.

"The day before High Moor," I said to Willow and Tuan. I turned back to Warulf. "Did they attack any more farmsteads, wicks?"

"Trey," he said, and held up three fingers.

"Does he mean three, or three more?" Willow asked.

"Does it matter?" I said. "Now Noermark is under attack, too." I turned back to Warulf. "What do you want from me, Warulf? Do you want me to fight Noermark's enemies for you?"

"Na! Na!" He thumped his fist on the table and half-rose.

Tuan dropped the bog-walker's feather at the first thump and the snick and slide of his knife coming out of the sheath stopped Warulf in the act of getting up.

He raised both hands, palms out, and slowly sat down again. "Pardon, Lady," he said. He laid his hands on the table, fingers splayed against the wood, worn smooth over many years of guards' mugs and plates and games of knucklebones. "Pardon, Lady," he said again.

"Granted." I said.

"I know not all right words. This fen-stalker, not ours. Not yours." He swept a circle on the table. "All fens, this fen-stalker. Everywhere. Every fen. There, here. Make all fens one."

"What does that mean, all fens one?" I asked. But I already knew. The bog was already a little bigger. Adana had seen it from the air, and we had witnessed it ourselves at the dyeing pond. Willow, Tuan, and I exchanged a look.

"He'll flood us out," Willow said. "Just what you said that day."

"Look, Warulf," I said, "How can he come from all the bogs? They're not all joined. Ours ends before the border with Noermark. Yours doesn't touch our borders."

He shrugged. "The king's kenningman said. Saw in the smoke, this fen-stalker, all fens everywhere. Old, old and angry. Hard to kill." He stopped.

Behind me Willow drew breath to speak, but I held up my hand and she said nothing.

"Kenningman—" Warulf said to me, "he say speak to swan-kin. Only swan-kin, swannen seoster – sis-ter, will know. I know you—swannen seoster. You kill her, you kill fen-stalker."

"He's talking about Orla," Willow said.

Warulf nodded. "Ya," He looked up at me. "You kill her."

"Not exactly," I said.

"So you told Gythorn that Kiar could kill your fen-stalker for you?" Willow asked.

Warulf snorted.

"Na. Not stupid. Kenningman say, ask help in Valenia."

"What did the king have to say to that?" I asked.

Warulf drew his finger across his throat. We all caught our breaths. Nobody killed a wiseman or wisewoman. They were too useful, and too few, for one thing. For another, who knew if one might not exact vengeance even after death? We had all seen what Orla could do.

"He killed a wiseman?" Willow said in a hushed voice. "Is he crazy?"

"Kenningmen die, swan girl, like other men," Warulf's eyes held mine. "Please, Lady. I know you, sword-maiden, warrior maiden, friend of kenningwif. My king forbids to ask for help. I come here, outlaw now. This fen-stalker kill here, here, here." He stabbed the table here and there with his finger. "Everywhere. All men, wif, wick."

Willow said, "We have only his word for it, even that the wiseman died."

"We have the feather," Tuan said. He picked it up.

"Let me see." I held out my hand, and he gave it to me. I brought it to my nose and sniffed.

There—faint, elusive, but undoubtedly present—was the smoky peat smell I remembered.

"Tuan, a cup of beer. Willow, find me some salt." Tuan drew a cup from the keg, and Willow rattled among the shelves behind me, returning with a brown clay bowl, small enough to fit in my palm. She put it on the table.

I tore a small piece of bread, no more than a large bite, from the half-loaf on the platter and pinched salt out of the bowl with my thumb and two fingers. I dipped the bread in my beer and sprinkled the salt over it. Then I held the piece out to Warulf.

"Bread, beer and salt," I said. We both knew what it meant. It was akin to the guest-bond. If he accepted this, ate half the piece while I ate the other, he was my ally. He would forswear his allegiance to King Gythorn, and his right to return to Noermark. He would owe me truth and loyalty, and I would protect him from Gythorn's vengeance, should he decide to take any.

"If you want my help against the fen-stalker, I want your allegiance," I said.

"Kiar, don't do this," Willow said.

"Can you think of another way to be sure it isn't a trap?" I asked. She said nothing.

Warulf took the other end of the bread. The beer-soaked piece tore easily, and he put his half in his mouth, chewed twice, and swallowed. I ate mine, the salt crunching briefly and stinging my tongue and the roof of my mouth.

"I oath you, too, swan girl," he said to Willow, and grinned.

Willow's lips thinned into a line, but Tuan broke another piece of bread, dipped and salted it, and offered it to Warulf. When that piece was gone, Warulf looked at Willow again.

"My oath," he said. This time he tore the bread, dipped and salted it, and held it out to her.

"I'm not royalty," Willow said. "He's her betrothed. I'm a friend."

"Friend is ally," Warulf said. His face was serious, and he held out the bread. Finally Willow took it. The piece all but fell apart in her fingers, but she ate it, and Warulf ate his.

"I don't know what the king is going to say to this," she said.

"I'll deal with that when I have to," I said. "Warulf, you look like you could sleep."

"Ya," he said. "Long riding from Noermark."

"Tuan, can you find Dar for me?"

Tuan went out and returned a few minutes later with Dar, once captain of my father's guard, and now of mine.

"You wanted me, Lady?" he said as he came in, then saw Warulf sitting across from me. "I know you. You were with that firebrand Hafor when he came looking for trouble."

"I know your sword," Warulf said, and grinned at him. Dar carried the sword that Hafor had used to fight me. Our swords were leaf-shaped, broader in the middle and tapering to a point, but Noermark's swords were a straight taper from hilt to point, and made of steel that rippled like water in the light. Noermark's swords were as fine as their horses, and as recognizable.

"Warulf is our sworn ally," I said. "I want you to find him a bed in the barracks. I don't want Mother to see him."

"I understand, Lady,"

"Give him back his weapons. They're at the gatehouse."

"So Tuan told me," he said. "Mind if I know why we have one of Noermark's finest on our side?"

"It's a long story," I said. "For now, let's say we have an enemy in common."

"That'd be our friends of High Moor," Dar said. "Never thought I'd see Gythorn admit trouble he couldn't handle."

"Warulf has come for help without Gythorn's permission."

Dar whistled. "Well, well. Outlaw today, ally tomorrow. I look forward to hearing about this. Come on, then, man of Noermark, and we'll find you a bed."

After they left, I picked up the feather again. Willow sat down beside me, and Tuan sat where Warulf had been. I turned the feather in my fingers. It was dull, without the sheen a flight-feather usually has, and brown as the peat-dyed wool we'd taken from the dyeing pond. It reminded me of something, but I couldn't think what.

"If we're to believe Warulf," I said, "this belongs to a bog-walker. But it smells the same as those things that attacked High Moor. Has either of you ever seen a bog-walker? To know what it is?"

"Not me," Willow said. Tuan shook his head.

"Me neither," I said. "I thought they never left the bog. Even Sianna said she'd never heard of it. Anything I've heard about them says they live in the mists. Those things that attacked High Moor, they arrived in the dark. They left before the light."

"Bog-walkers? Out here?" Willow said.

"Harrel said they reminded him of bodies you find in the peat, didn't he?"

"Yes, but those are dead! Dead things can't come to life and attack you. At least," she said, "only as spirits, like Orla. Even she didn't have a body."

"Yes," I said. "Except, these aren't alive the same way we are. They don't bleed. They can take a spear through the body, and it doesn't stop them. Boiling water doesn't hurt them. The only way to stop one is cut it to pieces. And none of us had ever seen a bog-walker before, so what do we really know about them?"

"What are you saying?"

"I don't know," I said. "Are they a different kind of alive?"

"How many kinds of alive can there be? I never thought they were real," Willow said. "Only a way to keep us away from the bog. I always thought, why not tell us the truth? It's bad enough without monsters. You can get lost in the bog, fall in, and drown. You can't see where you're flying in those mists. You could hit the ground and get hurt, or die."

"But this," I twirled the feather, "what was it that made you say it wasn't true'? And you," I said to Tuan, "you were upset by it as well. Why?"

They exchanged a glance.

"You'll tell it better," Willow said.

I looked at Tuan.

"It's the Lost King." He reached out and touched the feather with one finger.

"You told me that, I think," I said.

"No," Willow said, "I told you, and I didn't tell it right. Tell it properly, Tuan. Tell her everything."

"It starts with Queen Amala," he said. "She was the last Black Swan."

CHAPTER

NINETEEN

Queen Amala was the first Black Swan born in ten generations of swanfolk. She was the daughter of the king and queen, but her older brother was the heir. Before she gained her adult plumage, she was already more powerful in magic than any other Black Swan had ever been. She could make the cloak-of-feathers illusion, which, until then only kings and queens had done. She learned to take the forms of other birds and land-creatures, so skillfully that she could move among them and learn their ways.

When she became full adult, free to fly where she would, she studied the ways of the landfolk, watching them secretly, learning their ways, and then walking among them. She went among the truce-folk first. These were the landfolk who did not hunt swans. Long ago, a swan prince had loved a human woman, and although he could not marry her, he and she made a truce that none of her people would ever kill a swan. Amala learned their magic and healing from a wisewoman of the truce-folk.

Then she went among the herding-folk of the east, the ones who do not build but move around their grasslands from summer grounds to winter grounds, as swans do. She even went among the northmen, the swan-hunters. In every place, she learned their ways and how to seem as one who belonged there. It was not only the human folk she went among; she could take any form she chose, and live among the deer, the wolves, the ravens, and the trout in the water.

At first, she came back to her own people every year to travel to the winter grounds. Later she stayed among the landfolk for many years, learning their magics.

When the old king died, Amala's brother became king in his turn. He sent for Amala, asking her to use her wisdom to counsel him. She returned from her travels and lived among her people again, a wise, kind, and loving sister and counselor to her brother. She no longer travelled among the landfolk but went with her own folk from the summer grounds to the winter grounds.

Near the lake where her people spent the summers was a bog. The swanfolk shunned it, for it was not the same as the bogs in other places. In other bogs, the sun shone through the mists, and wild orchids bloomed in the spring. In summer the otter mothers brought their kits out to play in the pools between floating islands of spring bog-moss. In the autumn bright berries shone from hummocks of rough grass around the rim of the waters. In winter the deer and wolf and boar ran over the frozen ground without fear.

The bog the swanfolk shunned gathered its mists around it, white and thick, but dark with a darkness that made the heart low and the mind fearful. Deer never went into it, or near it. Frogs and fish stayed well upstream of the place where the creek entered the bog. As far out as the fields bordering it, the minds of those who came near became clouded or confused.

When nesting time arrived, Amala's brother flew out while the queen, his mate, sat on the clutch. He left alone and did not come back. After several days, Amala went among the land-creatures and the truce-folk to learn what she could.

From the deer she learned that the landfolk had come past the bog hunting and had shot something from the air. From the landfolk she learned that a hunting party had seen near the bog a beast in the air like a bird and bat at once, with razor claws and red eyes. One had shot an arrow, and both arrow and beast had disappeared.

Amala was greatly puzzled by this beast, for she had never seen anything to resemble it in her travels. So she spoke to the ravens, who are wise in themselves, and who furthermore see through illusion. From the ravens she learned that the beast had been her brother as he flew over the fields near the bog.

"The landfolk were afraid," the chief raven said. "They shot an arrow at it, and your brother swerved to avoid it and came too close to the bog. The dark mists struck him out of the sky as a wildcat takes a grouse and pulled him into the heart of the bog."

"Then he is dead," Amala said.

"Perhaps not," said the oldest raven. "We have heard something crying out in the bog. It moves from place to place. Your brother may still be alive."

Amala decided to go into the bog to rescue her brother. But when she took the news of what had happened back to the flock, the queen cried out in despair, broke her eggs, and flew away. The folk begged Amala not to leave them, and she reluctantly stayed as queen. She took a mate and raised an heir, biding her time in patience until he was old enough to rule.

When her son came into his full adulthood and had learned the things a king needs to know, Amala waited until the flock was back in their summer grounds. Then, she left secretly one night and flew away. Her mate stayed with the flock, hoping for her return, until he died. Her son, granddaughter, and great-grandson all came to rule and grew old, and no word ever came to say where Amala was.

Then, many years later, the raven chief sent a message to Amala's great-great-grandson. The message said that the young ravens, who made a game of daring each other to fly high over the bog, had seen, in its very heart and centre, wild orchids blooming.

CHAPTER

TWENTY

When Tuan finished, neither Willow nor I spoke for several breaths.

"Tuan," I said, "you could have been a bard. I had no idea you could talk like that."

"He can tell all the stories," Willow said.

"Not a bard," he said. "I can tell them to you, Kiar, to Willow. Maybe one or two other people. Not a whole hall."

"I'll have to ask you to tell me stories more often," I said. "But this feather—you think it came from the Lost King?"

Tuan nodded.

"I think so, too," Willow said. "I don't know any other story about a swan being snatched into the bog. Do you?" she asked Tuan.

"No. That's the only one I've ever heard," he said. "And that story is very old."

"I remember Mother telling Orla about Amala," I said. "She said Amala was our many-times-great grandmother."

Tuan tapped on his fingers. "Seven times great, I think. Nine generations. It might only be six times great, but I think it's seven."

Swanfolk often lived to be a hundred, nesting and raising children around thirty. The shortest time between Amala and me was still over two hundred years, probably more. For the first time, I considered that if I married Tuan, I could grow old and die long before he did. I shoved the thought away. There was enough to worry about right now.

"Maybe five hundred years," Tuan said. "It might have happened that long ago."

"He couldn't live that long, could he?" Willow asked. "It's horrible to think he could still be alive, trapped there. He must be dead."

"You aren't serious, are you?" I asked. "It couldn't be the Lost King. That was so long ago. It has to be something else, nothing to do with him."

"It could be," Willow said, "but Warulf said it was a swan. The child must have said something about how it looked. And someone else got close enough to shoot an arrow into it, and they'd have seen it, too."

"You smelled the feather," Tuan said.

"Yes," I said. "At the bog, when Aislin fell in, there was that same smell. It's how Willow's feathers smelled when the bog tried to grab her. And it was all over the battlefield, and the arm Rheann showed us. Whatever this was, it at least smells like what attacked High Moor, and what was watching us at the bog.

"And whatever it is, it was once winged," Tuan said.

"And going from bog to bog," Willow added. "Here and in Noermark. And attacking out of the forest, and out of the earth, maybe, at High Moor."

"That can't be possible," I said. "I know the bog is inside Valenia. I've ridden all the way around it on different patrols. It doesn't touch the border anywhere."

"If the story is right," Willow said, "it means Amala is probably still alive—or was, when the story was first told. And maybe the Lost King is still alive, too. That would take magic. Maybe magic would allow him to go from one bog to another, because they're all the same kind of place."

"You might as well say I could go from the stables here to the stables in Noermark because they're both stables."

"If they were magic, or you were, maybe you could."

"Nobody goes into the bog," Tuan said. "Nobody explores it. We don't know what's inside."

"There's a good reason for that," I said. "I don't know if anyone could go in and come out safely. Aislin almost drowned, and that wasn't really in the bog. It was only the dyeing pond."

"It might be part of the bog by now," Willow said, "if it expanded again. We should go and look."

"I don't understand why this is happening," I said. "The bog has been the same for years. You saw the stakes Eatha had for the pony and to hold the rope. They were practically grey from weather."

"Kiar." Tuan took my hand, and his voice was soft. "When Eatha put that cloth in the water, Orla was alive. Your mother was still herself. Your father was the king. You can't pretend nothing has changed since then."

"No," I said. "But he's not dying, he isn't! Sianna will make him well again. And Mother will get better."

Willow put her arm around me.

"A monster with swan feathers," Tuan said. "Either it's something else wearing swan feathers, or the feathers are its own. The only swans anyone knows have gone into the bog for five hundred years are the Lost King and Amala."

"Whatever wounded the king," Willow said. "Could it have been a woman?"

"I didn't see it well enough," I said. "The face was dark and shrunken, and the light was bad. All I saw was the colour of it. And a dark cloak."

"A cloak?" Willow said.

"Yes. It struck Father with it, and then he cut part and—" I twirled the feather in my fingers, and then held it out at arm's length and dropped it to the floor. I watched how it fell, then picked it up and dropped it again. I remembered the way the pieces of the cloak had fallen when Father struck it, and how the whole thing had disappeared when the creature saw me.

"What are you doing?" Willow asked.

"It wasn't a cloak," I said. "It wasn't a cloak! It was wings!"

"What do you mean, wings?"

"Father struck at the cloak and cut the corner off it. I saw the pieces fall. They fell like feathers—I didn't realize it until right now. Then it hit him again with the other side of its cloak, only the cloak seemed stiff and hard. And when it saw me, the whole thing disappeared behind it like—"

"Wings folding," Tuan finished.

"And after we got back into the farmstead, he said something about 'lost' and told me to ask you, Tuan."

"How could he know about the Lost King?" Willow asked.

"Mother might have told him. Maybe he realized who he was fighting." I shook my head. "Maybe that's what he was trying to tell me."

"Five hundred years. If it was really the Lost King," Willow said, "he's mad by now. But why attack High Moor? And why Noermark?"

"I don't know about High Moor," I said, "but Gythorn had a fall, weeks ago. He broke a bone in his leg, and when we first got the news, he still wasn't standing up. That was a month after the fall."

"Is he better now?" Willow asked.

"I don't know," I said. "But if he killed a wiseman, I wonder if he's in his right mind. Father always said Gythorn wasn't stupid. If the leg is rotting, he could be in great pain." I watched their faces. "When I was little, one of the men cut his arm with a scythe. Gern, that was his name. The cut turned black, and it stank. I remember hearing Mother vomiting after dressing the wound."

"What happened?" Willow asked.

"Sianna came. I don't remember how long she was here. I asked Mother if she was going to make Gern better. Mother said she hoped so. But he died anyway. If Gythorn's leg did that, he's probably out of his mind with pain."

We were all silent for a few minutes. That would explain why Gythorn had killed a wiseman, and it might explain why he had refused to ask for advice. If the king was the land, as Tuan said, did Gythorn have the king-light, too? If he did, it was fading as he slowly died of a stinking wound. That weakness might have opened the way for something to push back the borders between Noermark and some other country, and send the bog-walker out into our world.

I didn't want to think that my father's sadness about my mother, or the way he had ridden after her in the spring, leaving Valenia in my care, had led to the attack on High Moor. But if I believed that Gythorn's decline had anything to do with the bog-walker that had killed two people, it was hard not to think that Father's present injury and illness wouldn't bring the bog-walkers down on us, and maybe harder.

"There's one good thing about this," I said.

"I'm glad you can think of one," Willow said, "because I can't."

"If these things are attacking Noermark as well, I can stop worrying about a raid on Stony Ridge or High Moor," I said. "Gythorn's going to be far too busy at home to come visiting."

CHAPTER

TWENTY-ONE

When we went back to the castle, the tables had been taken up in the hall and beds were being laid out in rows. Several blankets down for padding would help, but the stone floors would still be hard to sleep on.

"If everyone comes here, we'll have to sleep in layers," Willow said, "and even Nias won't be able to feed everyone all at once."

"I hope she'll be able to feed them at all," I said. "The thought of having all these people here for the whole winter—I don't know what we'll do."

"I know what I'm doing right now," Willow said. "I'm going up to bed. There must be at least ten people in every room except our chamber, and the king's."

"Even Mother's solar," I said. "That's where most of the babies are, because it's warmest. She seems to like them."

"Are you coming up, too?" Willow asked.

"No. I'm going to wait for Sianna to finish whatever she's doing and tell me what's wrong with Father. I've asked Kearn to let me know." Kearn stood guard at the top of the stairs.

"I'll wait with you," Tuan said.

"In the morning, then," Willow said, with a little half-smile.

In Father's chamber, I sat in the chair across from his. It helped me to think that he would soon be back where he belonged, and that this chair, where I'd sat almost every time I came into this room, was where I should be. Tuan folded himself onto the floor by my leg and held my hand. After a few minutes, I slid down beside him. The leg of the chair pressed into my back and the floor was cold on my legs and seat, but Tuan's arm around my shoulders was warm and comforting. I leaned against him and sighed.

"I hate waiting," I said. "I want to do something, fight the bog-walkers, make Father better, something!"

Tuan said nothing but held me closer.

"I don't know how you stand it," I said. "Don't you ever get tired of waiting for things to happen?"

"Yes." He shifted around and put his hand under my chin, then kissed me. "Very tired."

"That's not what I meant," I said, "But, me too." We kissed for a while, but even then my worry for Father kept getting in the way. We snuggled back together, and in spite of the floor and the chair leg, I dozed off leaning against Tuan.

Then he was jiggling me. Someone was tapping at the door, and Tuan said, "Wake up."

It was Kearn to tell me that Sianna had come out of my father's room.

"I asked if you could see the king, Lady," he said, "and she said if you were awake, you could come up."

I kissed Tuan and almost ran up the stairs. At the top of the stairs, I stopped and walked more quietly to Father's room. When I tapped at the door, Sianna opened it a little.

"Can I talk to him? Is he awake?"

"Yes, he's awake. I don't know how much he'll want to talk."

"Did you learn anything?" I asked.

"Yes," she said. "You should know your mother is also here."

"She's here?"

"She can help him," Sianna said. "Think of her as a nervous horse. Be as calm and quiet as you can."

My palms were damp with sweat, and my heart thumped. Still, I nodded, and she pushed open the door. The air of the room smelled of burnt pine with a sweet undertone I didn't know. Whatever Sianna had done, she'd cleared away every trace of her work.

Mother sat on a stool by Father's bed, one hand on his chest, the other holding his hand.

"Hello, Mother," I said.

She glanced up as I came in, then went back to watching Father as though I were of no interest. I stood on the near side of the bed, across from her.

"How are you feeling?" I asked. The bruising on his head was fading now, with yellowish patches at the edges.

"As though a horse rolled on my leg," he said. "I'll live." He sounded tired.

"Can I talk to you about something important?" I asked.

"What is it?"

"Someone from Noermark."

"Not Guthric?"

"Warulf," I said. "One of Gythorn's men. You might remember him—grey hair, grey eyes. He came with Hafor the first time—" I glanced at Mother.

"Go on."

"The bog-walkers have attacked Noermark, too. Three or four places, at least one of them before they attacked High Moor."

"That will keep them off our borders," Father said. "Why did he come?"

"Gythorn's wiseman told him to ask for help from Valenia," I said.

Father sat up on one elbow, so suddenly that Mother and I both jumped. The motion jolted his leg, and his mouth twisted, but he glared at me through the pain.

"Let them fight the bog-walkers themselves," he said. "I have no help to spare them, and if I did, I wouldn't send it."

"Gythorn didn't ask for help," I said. "He killed the wiseman for his advice." Even in his anger, Father was nearly as shocked as I'd been. I hurried on. "Warulf came by himself to ask. He says he can't go back, that he's an outlaw now."

"Bad planning on his part, then," Father said.

"He told me something more," I said. "The wiseman said the bog-walker is old and angry and hard to kill. That sounds like

Grandmother's warning. And he said it will attack everywhere, push the bog out to flood as much land as possible. Father, if he's right there *will* be more attacks, lots of them. If we can work with Noermark, maybe send a message to—to Beorn—"

"No messages, no help!" I'd rarely heard my father shout, and my heart began to race. I don't know how I found the nerve to speak again.

"But we could be—"

"No! I thought better of you, Kiar, than to believe such a story! How—"

"I swore him as an ally. He can't lie to me."

The silence was worse than the shouting.

"You swore him an ally." Father's voice was flat. "That is not your right, Kiar. That is my right as king. And I am still king, even if I'm on my deathbed like Gythorn. You are not queen, with the queen's rights, while I live."

"I did it to make sure he wasn't lying," I said.

"It was not your right." He lay back down and turned his face away. "Get out," he said.

"Father—"

"Out, I said." Mother stood up so suddenly that the stool tipped and clattered to the floor, then she froze in place like a hare.

Sianna took my elbow and pulled me gently from the room.

"Wait here a little while," she said. "I have to show you something."

I stood in the passage, trying not to hear my father's rage and disappointment again and again in my head. If I'd told him differently—but what could I have said that was different? Nothing would change what Warulf had told me, that Gythorn was mad enough to kill a wiseman who had foretold disaster for every land the bogs touched. This wasn't only Noermark's problem, and it wasn't only ours. I'd counted on Father's experience to lay us a clear plan of action. Instead I was on my own, and whatever I did, I was sure I'd be going against his wishes.

I don't know how long I stood there. Finally Sianna came out again.

"Quietly, now," she said.

I went back in. Father was sleeping, and Mother sitting again beside his bed. When I came in she stood up and drifted to the corner of the room, where she stood watching.

Sianna turned the top of the cover back. Beneath the blanket Father's chest and shoulders were bare, except for a pad of linen, soaked in something pungent-smelling and green. Sianna lifted that, too, and I clearly saw for the first time the injuries that the bog-walker—if that was what it was—had left on him.

Three ragged round punctures marked his right side, the side I could see. The flesh around them was darkly bruised. They were packed with a white salve, flecked with dark green and bitterly aromatic. My stomach lurched.

"This is why they weren't healing," Sianna said. She held her hand over one of the wounds and watched. Her fingers trembled, and slowly a ripple formed in the air over the mark, dark and shining as black water. It squirmed and divided, into two, and four, and soon too many to count, across the wound and the skin on either side of it, following the shape of Father's body, pulsing with his breathing. My stomach heaved, and I put a hand over my mouth and swallowed hard.

"Stop," I said, when I could speak again. Sianna dropped her hand and the ripple faded.

"It's magic," she said. "Dark magic, and a lot of it. Mulloch's arm was torn up badly, much worse than this. But it was a straightforward wound, with barely a trace of magic on it. I think it might have been left by accident. Maybe it was what made the creature capable of moving. But this—" She gestured at the wounds. "This was left deliberately."

"You mean it tried to kill him with magic?"

"It tried to kill him any way it could. If it couldn't injure him badly enough, the magic would eat away at him."

"It seems that bog-walkers can use magic after all."

"So it seems," she said.

"It doesn't look infected. Rheann said she cleaned it out."

"It's not eating his flesh. It's eating him, his will, his self."

"Is that why he wouldn't listen to me?" My voice caught and I swallowed. Father's anger had hurt more than I'd thought.

"It may be. Or he may be angry because he's not used to being helpless. How often has he been injured as badly as this?"

"Never," I said.

"But Kiar, this magic—" She pulled the cover up over Father again, then stood unspeaking, fiddling with the end of her braid, as though picking her words. "This magic was meant for him. Not for him as a person, Tir of Valenia, but for the king. This was put here by someone who wanted to kill a king, and who had the power of a king to do it. And it's swan magic. I spent time with the swans after Orla, and I know the signature of it."

"That's why you have Mother here," I said.

Sianna nodded. "She's swanfolk, and she's royal. All swans have some magic. When she's with him, her presence seems to slow the effects. But she can't cure him, and neither can I."

"Who can?" I asked.

"The one who gave the wound is the only one who can heal it."

"I think I know who that is," I said.

"Can you find him and bring him here?"

I stared at her. "Bring a bog-walker into the castle? And how would I find the right one?"

"I don't know," she said. "But if you can't find the one who wounded him and bring him and your father together, I cannot cure him. I can keep him alive, maybe for a long time, but he will never be well. He will gradually lose everything that makes him himself, and in the end he will die."

I don't remember leaving Father's room, or going downstairs. I must have got through the great hall without stepping on people. I must have passed the guards, and Tuan, but I had no memory of it. I felt nothing, saw nothing, heard nothing; but somehow my body brought me to the stables. Tuan found me there, standing in Kestrel's stall, with my face resting against her withers, breathing in the comforting fragrance of horse and hay. He said nothing, just stood next to me and put his arm over Kestrel's back. He kissed my hair and remained with me, not speaking, until I sighed and turned to put my back to my horse, and my arms around Tuan.

"What is it?" he asked.

"Impossible," I said, then blurted out everything: Father's anger, his refusal to listen, what Sianna had told me about the magic working in his body. I told him what Sianna had said, what it would take to heal Father's wounds, and what would happen if I failed.

"They don't look that serious," I said. "But they aren't healing, not at all, and she says they'll kill him. They'll kill who he is, and then his body will die, too. And I'm supposed to find the one who did that to him and bring him back here and get him, somehow, to take the magic off."

For a long time, we stood in the stall. Tuan held me, and I listened to his breathing and felt it ruffle my hair. Finally, he spoke.

"Then, my heart, we'll have to try."

CHAPTER

TWENTY-TWO

I slept badly that night; my dreams were full of dark, winged figures who had something precious of mine and were always out of reach, no matter how hard I ran. I woke unrested, with gritty eyes and a sticky mouth. Willow was gone. Downstairs, she was sitting at the family table with Tuan. As soon as I sat down, Tuan said to me, "Tell her."

"Tell me what?" Willow asked.

"I spoke to Father last night, about what Warulf told us," I said. "He was so angry about me swearing Warulf as an ally that he wouldn't listen to what Gythorn's wiseman said about the bog-walkers. He said he couldn't give Noermark any help, and he wouldn't if he could."

Willow stopped in mid-chew.

"The king always listens," she said, "even when he's angry. He goes quiet and serious—it's scary, but he listens."

"He wasn't listening last night, not the way he usually does. And he thinks I'm pushing him aside."

"What do you mean?"

"He thinks I'm trying to take over the throne, because I swore Warulf as an ally. He says that was his right, not mine. After that, he ordered me to leave."

"Have you talked to him this morning?" Willow asked.

I glanced around the room to make sure we weren't heard. "I haven't dared. Sianna said that the thing that wounded him put magic on the wounds. She showed me." For a moment I saw that shimmering blackness, pulsing with my father's breath, and the skin between my shoulder blades shivered. I shoved the memory away. "She says the wounds aren't bad, but the magic will kill him. Not just his body, but himself—his spirit. Who he is."

"Maybe that's why he's angry," Willow said. "It's probably the magic, Kiar. It's not really him."

"That doesn't change anything," I said. "I'm going to have to disobey him and return to the bog."

"That's dangerous," she said. "What if you run into those things?"

"Sianna says only the one who wounded Father can heal him," I said. "The bog-walker with swan's wings, the same one that came out in Noermark."

"The Lost King," Tuan said.

"Yes. And I think—and Tuan agrees—we have to try to find him and bring him here to heal Father. The only place I know to start looking is the bog."

Willow stared at me. "Queen Amala in quicksand!" she said through a mouthful of bread and honey. Several people looked around, and she lowered her voice. "You're both completely mad." When neither of us spoke, she swallowed her food and went on. "*How* do you think you're going to get in and out of the bog, let alone catch a bog-walker?"

"I don't know," I said. "But I have to do it. I'll start by finding out if anyone has ever done it before."

"I'd say no," Willow said. "I'm guessing, mind you."

"Dar might know something," I said. "And there's Warulf. If anyone went into a bog in Noermark and came out, he might know about it."

"What if they don't, either of them?" Willow asked.

"Then I suppose I'll be the first."

She shook her head. "There's one other little problem, too. You've noticed they all run away from you. Are you going to chase the Lost King around the bog, if you can find him? Because he's not going to come to you willingly."

"That's me," said Tuan. He took another bite of bread, as if he hadn't just offered himself as bait for a monster. "He'll come to me."

"Come after you, you mean!"

He shrugged. "If necessary."

"I'm not having any part of it!" Willow kept her voice low, but her disgust and anger were as clear as if she'd shouted.

"We could use your help," I said.

She shook her head. "You're mad, both of you. You'll get yourselves killed, and I won't be a part of it!"

I couldn't disagree. Even if we succeeded in capturing the bog-walker and didn't get killed doing it, there were so many other things that could go wrong.

Willow stood up and stomped away, anger in every line of her.

"I wish—" I stopped myself. Tuan put his hand on mine, and I said, "I'll go see what I can find out."

I found Dar at the gatehouse. When I came in, he stood up and laid aside the bit of leather strap he'd been mending.

"Lady Kiar," he said. "I wondered when you'd be coming by."

"I could use some help with our new friend," I said.

He pulled a chair out from the wall, and I sat down. I told him briefly what Warulf had told us the night before, and why I'd sworn him an ally. Then I recounted what Sianna had told me, ending with my plan to bring back the bog-walker who had injured Father.

"That's a hard task," Dar said when I was done. "And I don't see how you can do it. If you could bring this bog-walker out of the bog, the right one, why would he take off a curse where he's laid it? Dangerous from beginning to end. Tir wouldn't want you to do that for him."

"It's not his decision" I said. "It's mine. I'm responsible now." I thought maybe Dar would have more to say.

"If so, it's not wise to be running off on some dangerous quest," he said. "You're the heir, and the only one left."

"I think Father wishes he had another," I said.

"Now why would he wish that, Lady? You've taken the responsibilities you have more seriously than many an older man would, or woman. When the time comes that you have to take the throne, it'll be in good hands, and he knows it."

"That's the bad part. He's angry because of Warulf. He says it wasn't my right to swear an ally. I know he's right, Dar, but I didn't see what else I could do! I had to make sure Warulf was telling the truth!"

"Ah," Dar said. "That'd hit a sore spot, you doing that."

"And he said he was still king here, even if he was on his deathbed. I don't want him to die! And I'm not trying to push him off the throne while he's still alive. How can he think that?"

Dar laced his fingers together and looked at them, and then back at me. When he spoke, his voice was so quiet I had to lean closer to hear him.

"The king's lost a lot in the last half-year," he said. "Two of you girls gone now, and the queen not herself. And worse than that is thinking that his youngest wasn't the sweet girl he'd thought her. It's taken a toll on him, Lady. He isn't what he was last year. No man wants to know he's getting old."

"He's not old!" I said.

Dar said nothing. His hair was more grey than brown now, and there were lines around his eyes and mouth. It occurred to me that Dar might be older than my father was. I couldn't remember a time when Dar hadn't been there. I couldn't imagine my world without him. Maybe he didn't want to know he was getting old, either.

"He can't think I'd –" I began.

"No, no, of course not. Not if he was himself. But men say strange things when they have a fever on them, or great pain.

They do strange things, too. If there's magic on the wounds, well, you may find he's not himself."

I thought of Gil, in the grip of Orla's spell, pining after her and ignoring Adana, whom he truly loved. The hurt Father's words had made in me eased a little. "Thank you," I said. "And I'm not exactly running into danger. At least, not headlong."

"I'm glad to hear it," Dar said. "And it may not be my place to say, but I've known the king since we were boys. He's a fair man, more than you know. He's never been the sort of king to forbid this or that because he can. There's been a time or two when someone's gone against his word. If it works out well, Tir's a man who can admit to a mistake. If it works out badly—"

"If this works out badly, I doubt I'll be around for him to be angry at," I said. We were both silent for a few minutes. I wondered if it had been Dar who'd gone against my father's word, and what that word had been. Finally, I spoke again.

"I came to ask you if you knew of anyone who had ever gone into the bog and come out, and what you knew about it. I'd like to prepare as much as I can."

"I'm not saying it's never been done," he said. "All I can say is I've never heard of it being done. Not this bog, and not by a Valenian. When men go into the little bogs, the sunny ones, they go by marked paths, and even those are shifty. And they never go alone."

"I'm not going alone," I said. "Tuan's going with me."

"And your other shadow?"

"No. Willow says she wants nothing to do with it. She thinks we're both crazy."

Dar laughed, more a snort than a real laugh, but there was a little humour in it. "I agree with her. It's not your best idea, young Kiar."

I smiled to hear him call me by the name he had used when he trained me. "I'm going to ask Warulf, too. He might know something."

"He's still in the guardhouse," Dar said. "He understands that the queen would not be happy to see him, and so he's willing to stay out of sight. But you can't hide him forever, Lady. And there's not much you can do to keep that one from standing out. For one, you'd have to get him to cut that braid of his. He'll not be willing for that. And that would give him away no matter what he wore. His talk, too, although I doubt the queen would ever hear that."

"I'll have to take him with me," I said.

"Well, he came with a purpose," Dar reminded me. "And he'll be useful, no doubt, or as useful as another."

"I'll go talk to him," I said. "I'm not happy about going into the bog for another reason. Father asked me right before all this—the attack on High Moor—to stay away. It was after Aislin fell in. You heard about that?"

Dar nodded.

"So nothing I do is going to please him," I said. "But I can't let him die and not try. And I can't think of anything else to do. The problem is, the bog-walkers at High Moor all ran away from me, and I don't know why, what I was doing or how to stop doing it. Should I blunder around the bog waving my sword and yelling for them to come out?"

Dar gave me a crooked smile. "You could do that."

"But you wouldn't advise it," I said.

"No."

"Gythorn's wiseman, the one he killed, said that the thing could go from one bog to another."

"Well, now," said Dar, "it could be there's something about the bog itself that lets it do that."

"Willow said something much the same. It doesn't make sense, Dar."

"Tell me what makes sense about any of this, even one part of it. I'll tell you straight, I never thought I'd see this day. I feel the same as if I've lost two daughters myself, with Princess Orla dead and Princess Adana gone to be queen of the swans. The queen as she is, and now the king—Noermark asking for help, even if it's just one old renegade. I don't know if Sianna herself would have seen this coming." He sighed and raked his hand through his hair. "If there's magic in this," he said, "then you and your shadows are probably the best to deal with it. Gods know your father has no magic, and the queen, whatever she may have, is no warrior and never has been. You and young Tuan are among the best I've ever trained, and even Willow can be trusted not to whack off her own head, or those of her comrades. As for Warulf, he did not grow so old without sword skills."

"Willow says she's not coming. And Tuan and I don't have a lot of magic," I said.

"No, not a lot," Dar said. "But maybe enough. There's some in all swanfolk, sure. Do you know all of what you can do?"

"I can tell when someone's using magic, if I'm close enough." I said. "It makes me sick."

"And Princess Orla couldn't pull you to her, when she could pull that Hafor and the young harper."

"She said that was a small magic. She said others would work on me."

"Well, being proof against small magics is something," Dar said. "Even a pin will stab if you don't have a sword. Unless you want to ask Sianna if she'll go with you."

"No, I can't," I said. "I need her here to keep Father alive."

"I'd say go soon, the three of you. A small force moves quickly."

"You're right," I said. My hands felt suddenly damp, and not only from the prospect of going into the bog. I'd promised my father I'd stay away from it. But Warulf had come to me for help, and I'd sworn an oath of alliance. Now I had to follow through on that. And oath or not, I couldn't keep my promise to my father if it meant letting him die.

"I don't want to leave without any word," I said. "I don't know if Mother would understand what I'm going to do, and Father is—" I stopped.

"I know," Dar said.

"Besides, Sianna gave him something for the pain, and to make him sleep. I can't wait for him to wake up, and I haven't got time to argue with him anymore. And I'd rather not be openly disobedient."

Dar laughed. "No, sneakily disobedient is much better, if you're going to disobey anyway."

"I suppose so," I said. "If I left a letter, would you see that he gets it when he wakes up? If I'm not already back by then?"

"Will you not change your mind about this?" Dar said. "We'll need you here if those things come to our walls. We'll need you if Tir dies."

"Dar, most of the fighters here have more experience than I do. And I trust you to use them well. Sianna is here, and you, and as long as Father is alive, then there is a king. I promise, I don't intend to die in the bog."

He sighed. "Give your letter to me, and I'll see it delivered."

"Thank you, Dar." I stood up. "I'd better go and see Warulf."

CHAPTER

TWENTY-THREE

I found Warulf out behind the guardhouse, hacking at the practice pells. Fresh-cut chips lay about on the ground, points of brightness in the dirt of the practice yard. When he saw me, he stopped and sheathed his sword, then stood waiting, hands at his sides. As I came up to him, he nodded and tapped his breast with his fist.

"Princess Kiar," he said.

"Good morning, Warulf. Come and sit down. I want to ask you some things about the bog. The fen," I said.

We sat on a bench by the wall. The sun cast some warmth there, although the air was chill enough that I was glad of my heavy tunic. Warulf pulled his cloak around his shoulders. A guardsman brought out two cups, a pitcher of water and one of ale. Warulf drank two cups of water quickly. Practising at the pell was thirsty work. Then he poured himself a cup of ale, and I did the same.

"What of the fen?" he asked.

"Do you know if anyone has ever gone into the fen and come back out?"

"Ah," he said. "No man here has done?"

"Not that I know of," I said. "What about in Noermark?"

He turned his cup between his hands in silence for a few breaths. Then he looked up, his face serious.

"I never tell this," he said. "Not in all the years. Not friend, or wife, or son, not my king, you understand. It is—" He stopped, and his eyes flicked from side to side as though he were looking for something. Then he put his finger to his lips.

"Secret?" I asked.

"Ya. Secret."

I thought, yes, he was a man who could keep secrets. All I knew of him was what I could see: worn clothes, grey eyes, grey hair in a thin braid falling forward over his shoulder. His skin was weathered and lined, and a scar crossed his nose on the left side and ran down onto his cheek. I'd never thought of him having a wife and family. He'd left more behind than I'd thought to seek me out.

"I understand," I said.

"Before I tell this," he said, "we go into the fen?"

"Yes," I said. "We're going to go into the fen."

He nodded slowly. "And if I say, stupid to go there?"

"I know," I said. "But I have to. The king—one of them hurt him. Sianna, the kenningwoman, says he'll die if I don't bring the fen-stalker out to heal his wound."

"You go in for your king?"

"Yes," I said, "but also for my father."

Warulf nodded. "A good son does so. A good tochter."

"And they attacked us, too, Warulf. Seven nights ago, eight now, they came out of the forest and attacked a farmstead. It was the same as you said—arrows and spears didn't kill them."

"Your people, no one hurt?"

"A few," I said. "My father, one other man whose arm was torn. And some others were hurt, not as badly. But they had to abandon the farmstead. And Father is very ill. He'll die if I don't do something."

"I ask my king," he said. "I ask to go into fen, with some—" He held up three fingers. "Small, quiet, fast, ya?"

"Yes. Dar said that, too. What did he say, King Gythorn?"

Again Warulf sat silent, turning his cup. When he looked up again, his eyes were bright, and his lashes wet.

"My king is mad." He slapped at his shin with his hand. "The pain." He waved his hand around his shin and pinched his nose.

"His wound is rotting," I whispered. So it was true.

Warulf spun his cup between his hands. "He dies. Not soon. Not soon." When I heard the break in his voice, I realized he loved Gythorn. Somehow that had never occurred to me, that the man who had tried for years to take over my country, either by force or diplomacy, could have men who loved him as Dar loved my father.

"Does he know you've left?"

Warulf shrugged.

"We hope no, Princess Kiar, or he sends men for me."

"To bring you back?" I asked, though I didn't think it likely. He smiled at me and shook his head, then drew a finger across his throat.

"Your man, now," he said.

"Then let's do what you came to do." I refilled his cup. "Tell me about the man who went into the fen and came back out."

"Two," he said. "One man, one boy. The man is dead. The boy—" He spread his hand on his own chest.

"You've been in the fen and come out!"

"Long ago."

"What happened?"

It took a long time for Warulf to tell. In his own tongue it would have taken less time, but I didn't know enough of his language to follow the story. We picked through our words, helping each other along. Sometimes he drew in the dust of the practice ground with his dagger, sometimes he shaped things in the air with his hands. Piece by piece, the story came out.

Warulf had a brother, ten years older than he was himself, curious, eager for adventure, and more than a little rash. As Warulf described him, he reminded me of Willow. His name was Valtir, and Warulf had idolized him.

When Warulf was eight or nine, Valtir came up with a plan to explore the fen beyond the dyeing pond. Their father had forbidden any of his children to go near the fen. The year before Warulf was born, Valtir's twin sister, Halle, had ventured into the fen, lured by the bright, frilly pink bog-orchids, and never come out. The peaty, uncertain bottom of the dyeing pond was dangerous enough; in the unknown terrain of the fen, it was easy for a child or an adult to drown.

Warulf found out his brother's plan and begged to go along, and Valtir agreed to take him. They planned to be back that day, and to get as far into the bog as they could, marking a safe path to follow for later explorations.

They cut a large bundle of willow switches, as long as a man's forearm, and one thick stake. Valtir took a rope and a torch, and both took their swords. Warulf's weapon was not much longer than Valtir's dagger.

At the edge of the fen, they pounded in the stake and tied the rope to it. Valtir slid the free end of the rope through his belt, and then Warulf's. If one of them fell in, they would at least still be attached to the rope. They started into the fen. The air was a curtain that kept them from seeing more than a few feet ahead. It wasn't dark, nor was it misty or foggy, but when Valtir thrust his hand out at arm's length, his fingers faded from sight.

Valtir went first. He tested the ground at each step and let out the rope as he walked. Warulf followed close behind, setting his foot where Valtir's had been and planting a willow switch every few steps. With the pale markers to show them a safe path and the rope in case one of them fell in, they were confident of getting in and out safely.

Some way into the fen, Valtir stopped and crouched on the path. When Warulf crouched by him, he saw what Valtir had seen—a small hand at the top of the water. The flesh had fallen away until the bones showed brownish-white, and when Valtir slipped the point of his knife under the water and lifted out the rest of the hand, they fell away into the water and sank. On the arm that came up from under the water, the skin was dark brown and still held together. Around the wrist was a strand of stone beads. Valtir turned them as much as he could, holding them in his fingertips and sliding the bracelet around the brown wrist. Across one of the smooth grey stones ran a vein of pink. When he saw that, Valtir let go of the bracelet, and laid the arm gently back down. The bones beneath it ticked as the stones touched them.

"Halle," he said. "This is her bracelet. It was our mother's when she was a girl." He sighed. "Well, it is better to know. Sad news to bring, that Halle has drowned in the fen, but it is better for them to know what happened to her."

Valtir stood up again, and they went on. When half their rope was gone, they came to a place where even the dim light of the fen failed. It was as though they had stepped out of the world, into a place where no light could come. They stopped, and Valtir lit the torch. The fire did nothing to dispel the eerie darkness, but the fluttering sound of the flame, and its flickering light, heartened them. Now they went slower than ever, and Warulf had to follow so closely that he knew he couldn't use his sword without hitting his brother.

Warulf didn't know how far along the path they had gone at this snail's pace when Valtir stopped. Warulf ran into him, scraping his face on the hard coils of rope over Valtir's shoulder. He heard Valtir whisper something, and then he saw the girl.

She was about his own age and stood in light, as though the light came from her. Her fair hair hung in two neat braids over her shoulders, and her dress and linen apron were clean and unspotted. In her hands she held a posy, pink bog-orchids and other flowers Warulf didn't recognize. She smiled and held one out to Valtir.

At first Warulf didn't believe what he felt—his brother's body trembling. How could Valtir be afraid of a little girl? Then Valtir said, "Halle!" She dropped her flowers and stepped back, then flung her arms out as though to catch her balance.

"Valtir!" she called. "I'm falling, I'm falling!" She began to sink into the mud, crying and pulling her feet up one after the other. As she lifted a foot, the other leg sank deeper. She flailed with her arms, and dark mud splotched her dress and apron, her face and hair. She wailed, and then shrieked as dark water bubbled up around her, begging her brother to pull her out.

Valtir stepped forward, and his leg sank to the ankle in the bog. Warulf grabbed his brother's arm and leaned to pull him back, and all around the murky air of the fen closed them in, except for the place where Halle struggled and shrieked and begged, now up to her armpits in water and muck.

"Don't look!" Valtir said, "Don't listen!" He pushed Warulf back the way they had come. Before Warulf could turn or look away, the girl tipped her head back, gasping and scrabbling at the surface of the bog, then gurgling and choking as dark water trickled into her mouth. Warulf panicked then, and instead of backing away, he turned and bolted.

The rope that linked him to his brother pulled tight, and Valtir stumbled back and dropped the torch. Warulf heard the hiss of Valtir's sword coming out of its scabbard, and his brother's voice yelling for him to run.

He didn't know how he stayed on the path in the lightless murk of the inner fen. His feet knocked against the switches that marked solid ground, and he clung to the rope and somehow came out into the dim light of the fen's edges. Behind him he heard a shriek, and Valtir flailed out of the murk, gasping.

His clothes were ripped over chest and belly, and blood flowed from long tears in his flesh. It soaked his clothing and dripped from the folds. A hand gripped Valtir's shoulder, its long fingers clenched around the joint and digging into the armpit. A head loomed over Valtir's—dark brown, with no eyes but sunken hollows—and the thing's other hand grabbed at his throat.

Valtir swung his sword down on the rope, and it parted under the blade. Warulf took a step back to help him, but the creature dragged Valtir away into the murk of the inner fen. The sword fell from his fingers.

"I know then," Warulf said, "he died. No man lets go his sword." He patted the sword that hung from his belt. "Valtir's sword," he said. "Mine now."

He stopped speaking. For a moment, I could neither move nor breathe, still held in the spell of the story. The practice yard, ordinary and calm in the daylight, seemed unreal. I felt that I had been far away in a strange country.

"How did you get out?" I asked. "Didn't the thing, the fen-stalker, come after you?"

"Na," he said. "Too small game, me."

"Or maybe Valtir hurt it."

He shrugged. "I follow the rope, fall in, get out."

"And when you went home? You didn't tell them what happened."

He shook his head. "Tell Valtir drown in fen. Fader beat me." He took my hand and put it on his forearm. I felt a knot on the bone.

"He broke your arm?"

Warulf nodded.

"Arm, head, three—" He walked his fingers down his ribs. "Very angry. Very sad. But I lie, so Fader not afraid."

"I don't understand."

"Valtir's sister, Halle, a fen-sprite. Maybe Valtir a bog-walker, na? Better Moder and Fader think them dead. Better they never know I don't tell truth."

"Nobody I know has ever seen a bog-walker, except for you," I said. "Willow said she thought they were stories, made up to keep children from going into the bog."

"Your man knows true," Warulf said.

"Tuan? He knows all the old stories, at least, the swanfolk ones. I suppose he always did believe the bog-walkers could be real." I told Warulf. "I have to believe it, too."

"Now it comes out," he said. "We go get it, yah?"

"I think we have to," I said. "Will you come with us?"

"Ya," he said. "Your man now, Princess Kiar. I come."

CHAPTER

TWENTY-FOUR

"You're really going to do it?" Willow scowled at me. "Kiar, it's madness! How will you find it? How will you bring it back? And why should it heal your father when it tried to kill him?"

We sat in the east guardhouse, the closest quiet place I could find to talk. Using Father's chamber was out of the question; I didn't want to bring Warulf into the castle. Warulf leaned back against the wall, legs outstretched before him, and watched Willow with the hint of a smile on his face. Tuan sat beside me with his hands folded on the table.

"I don't know how," I said. "It sounds impossible to me, but I can't let Father die if there's anything we can do to help. Why would Sianna ask me to do something completely impossible?"

"It's a waste of time. It might get all of you killed. Then things will be worse than ever."

"Wyrd," said Warulf. "All walk it, swan girl."

"What is that—werd?" Willow asked.

"Wyrd is—" he thought for a moment. "road. Your road, your end. All walk it."

"All right, but I don't want to do it any sooner than I have to!"

"Hide and wyrd finds you," Warulf said. I thought he might be teasing Willow again, but his face was perfectly serious. "You walk road, not walk, end the same."

"Wait a minute," I said to him. "You mean no matter what we do, we're going to die exactly the same as if we didn't do anything? Or do you mean Father will die no matter what I do?"

"Na, na," he said. "Lady, all men die. All wives. So fight hard, na? Fight, not fight, all die. Better to fight."

"I think we can find the bog-walker," Tuan said. "If it attacked Valtir, it would probably attack one of us." He turned to me. "If anyone should stay behind, it's you. Warulf and I will have more luck getting them close if you're not there."

"And you'll be killed if they all turn up at once! Do you really think I'll stay back and let that happen?"

"I agree with Kiar," Willow said. "Two of you against all of them is foolish. You need more."

"You can't make me stay behind," I said. "Besides, I'm the only one who got a good look at the bog-walker that attacked Father."

"There won't be that many with wings," Willow said. "It shouldn't be hard to tell."

"How do you know?" I asked. "There could be other swanfolk lost in the bog."

"None in the stories," Tuan said.

"That's not certain proof," I said. "What if there was an older one, or one that came from another flock? You need me to make sure you have the right one. I'm coming."

"I still say it's a bad idea," Willow said.

"Can you think of a better one?" I asked.

She shook her head.

"You fly away, swan girl?" Warulf said.

Willow fixed him with one eye, her brow drawn down in a scowl. She didn't speak for several breaths. "No," she said, "I'm coming."

"Thank you," I said, and I meant it. Having Willow along made me feel much better. Whatever doubts she had, once she'd committed, I knew I could count on her courage and loyalty.

"You think I'm afraid?" she asked Warulf.

"Ya," Warulf said. His voice was quiet. He spread his hand on his chest. "Afraid, too. Good to fear. Makes you careful, swan girl."

"Willow," she said, still scowling. "My name is Willow."

Warulf grinned at her.

"If we're going to do it, at least we could take more than the four of us," Willow said.

"No," I said. "More people means more people to keep track of, more noise, harder to move. If there's only a narrow path, then we'd have a long, thin line of people to be picked off one by one, or fall in. With four of us, we'd all know where everyone is. We can keep track of each other and stay close together, back-to-back if we have to."

"Better only us," Warulf said.

"How will we do this?" I said.

"Quickly and quietly," Tuan said.

"I'm leaving a letter for Father, in case he wakes up before we come back. Dar says he'll keep it for me."

"What do we need?" Willow asked.

"Rope, sticks, water." He held his thumb and finger close together. "Little food."

"We should go soon," Willow said. "Today, or tomorrow. If we're going to do it, let's do it and be done."

The sun was already halfway up the sky. Once we were in the bog, probably the time of day would make no difference at all.

"We may be gone a few days," I said.

"There won't be anything to burn in the bog, I'm sure," Willow said. "If we have to sleep, we three can sleep in feathers." She looked at Warulf. "What about you?"

"You worry on me, swan girl?" he said, and grinned. "I sleep in my cloak."

"What weapons?" Tuan said. "Bows? Swords?"

"We won't be able to see to shoot," I said. "Swords and knives. And the archers' helmets. I want to have some chance of seeing what's coming at me."

"Good," Tuan said.

The archers' helmets were light caps of boiled leather with a noseguard. They didn't give as much protection as a full metal helm, but they were light and had no cheekpieces to block vision.

"Spears? Something that could keep an attacker at a distance would be good," Willow said.

"Good idea, spears," Warulf said.

"Maybe not," I said. "I need to catch this thing, not kill it."

"Spears won't kill it," Willow said.

"All right, but they won't catch it, either. What about a net? That was a good idea."

"I know where the nets are from the High Moor wagons," Willow said. "I put them in the armoury, just in case. I'll get one."

"Good," I said. "Then it's settled. Spears, swords, a net. Food, water, rope, and the archers' helmets. Give me half an hour to write my letter to Father. We'll go on foot."

"Out the back?" Tuan asked. The little postern gate to the west was the way I'd left when I went to look for Orla's body in the spring. It was a small door with three layers of planking, bound with iron and barred with a heavy beam. I could ask Dar to bar it behind us.

"Yes, out the back," I said.

"Fine with me," Willow said. Tuan and Warulf nodded.

"Half an hour," I said.

In my room, I found a slip of parchment and dipped my pen. I wanted to tell Father what I was doing and why, in words that would show him I never meant to overstep. I sat for so long that the ink dried on the nib. I couldn't imagine anything I might write to change the fact that I was about to disobey him and go into the bog. Finally I gave up trying to find the words that would make things all right.

"Gone to bog with Willow, Tuan, Warulf. Sianna said to find" I hesitated, then finished, "something to help you. Back soon." I might not be back soon, or late, or at all, but I wanted to believe I would be. I signed my name. I wasn't happy with my message, but I couldn't think of one I could write that I would be happy with. This was the best I could do.

I took my letter to Dar.

"You're sure about this, Lady?" he asked me. "We've had two messengers back. The folk from Far Fellstead and West Steading are on the way. There'll be others."

"I know I should be here," I said, "but I have to find the bog-walker. You can handle the defences, and Nias will manage the food and beds. I'm sure Rheann and the other farmstead mistresses will help her. Nobody can do this but me, Dar. I know what he looks like."

"You're your father's daughter, right enough," he said. "I'll keep this safe. Just you see that you come back. You're all he's got now. And the rest of us will be counting on you, too."

"I'll be careful," I said.

Dar put a hand on my shoulder and squeezed it. "Keep your eyes open," he said, "and remember what you know. You'll be fine."

"I will. Especially the part about throwing up." I thought it would lighten the mood, but Dar didn't smile for me.

"I'd better go," I said.

We found the other three at the postern door. Each of them wore a coil of rope looped over their shoulders. It was the thickness of my little finger, but strong and smooth. Willow held a second coil and handed it to me. I looped it over my shoulders, and Tuan handed me a waterskin and a lumpy linen bag of food.

"I might as well be a whole patrol by myself," Willow said. She handed me a spear.

Warulf and Dar wrestled the bar out of its sockets. The door turned stiffly on its hinges, and was so low that Warulf had to duck his head to leave.

"Be careful, now, young Kiar," Dar said.

"I will," I said. "I promise." Whether I would be able to keep that promise, I had no idea.

We crept around the castle wall to the paddock and circled it, crouched low. Beyond the far side of the fence the ground dropped a little, and we could stand again.

We started down the dun at a jog, spread out across the drying grass.

At the bottom of the slope, we slowed and continued up the next rise and over at a walk. Once we reached the top of the rise, I felt the impulse to turn and look back at the castle. At the same moment I felt that if I did turn to look, someone would see us and follow, but if I kept my eyes forward, we could continue unnoticed. I paused, but didn't turn back, and in a few steps I was far enough down the hill that if I had turned, I could no longer have seen even the banners at the corners of the battlements.

We walked down the hill, past the stone pens where the rams usually butted and jostled each other. Other years they would have been left a few more weeks before being taken to breed the ewes, but with the threat of attack, they were already moved in closer to the castle. The dogs that slept with the sheep were gone, too.

We turned east and followed the creek towards the bog. The last little stand of bush alder and mouse-willow was now only a dozen paces from peaty brown water spreading over the grass. The stems still stood up, but between them the water glinted, and the ground gave under our feet and oozed water. We stopped there, and Tuan unfolded a sheet of waxed linen. We piled our bows and quivers into it and folded the edges close. Tied and hung among the alders, the weapons would stay dry and safe and be easy to find when we came back out.

"No warblers," Tuan said. It was true. Although it was late in the fall the little, yellow-breasted brown birds should still have been hanging on the reeds, giving out their clear, bubbling calls. Even along the sedges and reeds that lined the creek there was not a wing, not a flutter or a rustle to show where one might perch. When I listened, the quiet pressed on my ears. Was something watching us now? I didn't feel the tickle on my nape that I'd felt before, and when I inhaled, I didn't catch so much as a whiff of that sharp, dark smell I'd caught yesterday. All the same, if the little birds had fled, or hidden, it was not a good sign.

Any little breeze made the grasses move and whisper against each other. Behind us the creek burbled and sang as it rolled over a spot where smooth, water-rounded rocks pushed up to the surface. But not a bird called, not a wing stirred. We might have been the only living things in the world.

"I think the mist has moved," Willow said. "I don't remember it close to here." She kept her voice low.

"I believe you're right," I said. "And the water's farther out, too. I didn't think it would be this fast."

Warulf grunted and pulled his knife. He began cutting long switches from the bushes. I wanted to tell him to leave the mouse-willow alone; I loved the little grey buds they put out in the spring, soft as furry baby mice snuggled all up the branches, but I held my tongue. Who knew if I'd ever be here to see the mouse-willow bud again? Better to have all the switches we needed to mark our way. I pulled my knife, too, and in a minute we were all cutting switches. We kept on until each of us had a bundle as big as two hands could span, then stripped bark to tie them in smaller bunches to our belts.

"This really isn't wise," Willow said.

"You don't have to come," I told her. "I know you think this is a bad plan."

"I'm not backing out now. Wyrd, right?"

I knew what she was saying. If it was all going to come out the same anyway, we were free to do what we thought best. Either we were going to get back, or not, and only the spirits knew which.

There was no dry way into the bog now; the path that we had taken no more than a week ago to the dyeing pond was slick and shiny mud, and then submerged under a knuckle's depth of water. In three steps, my boots were soddened. In a dozen, even the beeswax and oil rubbed into the leather and the seams couldn't keep a cold trickle of water from seeping in where the sole and the upper joined. I followed the path by sight as long as I could see it under the water. When it disappeared into the brown, I used a spear-butt to find it. We went slowly, planting our feet carefully on the underwater slick of bare mud, making almost no sound as we moved.

The landscape had changed since we last saw it. I didn't realize how close we were to the dyeing pond until I saw what I thought was a slim snake in the water. I jumped, and in the ripples the snake rolled and turned, unresisting. I saw it was one of Eatha's cords, left behind unsecured. The mist was a pace or two ahead of us.

I heard splashing to my right, and my heart jumped. I turned to see Willow swishing her boot in the water. I gritted my teeth; gentle as the sound was, it rang like shouting in my ears. I glanced at the mist ahead of us, looking for some movement, certain that the sound of moving water would bring something leaping out to attack us.

"The pegs for the rope should be here somewhere," Willow said. "Once we get into that, we'll want a line to follow out."

"Quieter," I said, and glanced at the mist. She caught my look and nodded, then moved her foot again, more slowly this time. We all searched by touch for the pegs that Aislin's rope had been braced against.

"Here," Warulf said. He bent and felt under the water, and nodded to me. I waded over and bent to feel the peg. The hole was there.

"Tie off," I said. "I'll lead. Second listens for movement to the side. Third sets the markers, last person guards the rear."

"I'll do that," Tuan said. We tied our ropes together, mine to Willow's, Willow's to Warulf's, and Warulf's to Tuan's. Tuan tied the free end of his rope to the peg. When he'd done that, Warulf took Tuan's and looped it over his other shoulder.

"Free your sword, na?" he said.

I tied one end of my rope around my waist, threading it under my scabbard. I couldn't imagine what might make me lose it, but I was taking no chances.

"When Tuan's rope runs out, we let Warulf's out, then Willow's, then mine. We'll stop if we need to change positions, or if we need to rest. Otherwise keep on as we are."

"How are we going to find the bog-walker?" Willow said.

"I don't know. I hope if we're in its territory, it will come to us," I said. "If anyone has a better idea, say so." Nobody spoke.

With my spear in my left hand, I waded two steps up to the mist and paused. For a moment I felt as though I was looking someone, another person, in the face, but whether it was friend or foe I wasn't sure. I listened with my ears, with my whole body, and for a fleeting moment, I heard a breath. Then a thought came into my head, as clear as speech, but without words. Whatever watched—and I was sure by now that something or someone did—it was – curious.

I drew my sword and stepped into the bog.

CHAPTER

TWENTY-FIVE

The chill damp of a thick fog swept over me as I stepped forward. My clothes were no shelter from it. The clammy damp touched the skin of my legs, arms, body, even my scalp, making me shiver with cold. The chill went to my marrow— everywhere except my sword arm; my right hand, clenched on the hilt of my sword, felt hot. My stomach fluttered, and I swallowed hard. Then the nausea died.

From the murky look of the bog from outside, I'd expected darkness within. Instead the space around me swam with mist, layers of it moving in swirls and curtains. There was no sunlight, yet I could see, a little, perhaps an arm's length, straight ahead. I couldn't see the ground so much as a step in front of me. An edge of brightness ran up my sword and disappeared.

Almost immediately, someone stepped on my heel, and I jumped forward.

"Willow" came in a whisper, and a hand touched my shoulder.

"Good," I said. I moved forward and turned my head to listen for Warulf and Tuan. "Everyone here?"

"Yes," Tuan said. "All here." His voice came as though from far away. I glanced back. Willow stood almost at my shoulder, an outline of a woman in fog. I could see her face, swirls of mist clinging to her hair.

I stepped forward again. My boots squished; the water had soaked the leather and pressed up from the sole when I stepped. The path beneath my feet, though, was no longer underwater.

Behind me, Warulf muttered something and bent to plant a switch. I prodded the ground ahead with my spear butt, testing for firmness.

We made slow progress. Every step had to be tested. The fog muffled every sense – sight, hearing, touch. I worked my fingers on the haft of my spear and the hilt of my sword, afraid they might be falling asleep, but each time they moved easily, and I felt my weapons firmly in my hands. Now and again I felt Willow's hand laid briefly on my left shoulder, but it seemed as though she was touching me through a thick blanket.

I don't know for how long we moved through the outer mist of the bog, how many times I prodded the ground ahead of me and took a step, then another. The mist muffled every sense, and time seemed to drift apart in the swirls that marked every movement I made.

Then, exactly as Warulf had said, I came to a wall of darkness. I had no other way to describe it. I reached my spear-butt into it, and the shaft and my fingers vanished into the air. I pulled my hand back and it appeared again. This was the darkness that Valtir's torch hadn't dispelled, the place his sister, the marsh-fey, haunted. I felt as though I were about to dive into deep water. I sucked in my breath and held it, then stepped forward again.

As soon as I stepped into the dark, I felt as though I was the only person there, that my companions were an illusion and I was, and had always been, alone. All I heard was my heart beating and the blood rushing in my ears. My own heartbeat sounded slow. *Thump*, pause, *thump*. Time itself seemed to have slowed. My chest felt stiff, and the base of my throat squeezed. I realized I was still holding the breath I had taken before stepping in, and I let it out. With that, time started again, and the dreadful aloneness fell away a little. I groped for the loop of rope around my waist and the feel of it, really there, was like waking from a nightmare. I looked behind me, and a hand came out of the mist, groping towards me. Willow's, I realized, and clasped it, feeling the rope looped over her palm to be let out behind us. The loneliness receded a little farther, and I dropped her hand and prodded ahead again with my spear.

At first it seemed to me that we were moving as quickly through this darkness as we had in the lighter mists. The path turned and twisted, left and right; I lost any sense of direction. I couldn't tell if the path was straight or twisted, whether we had looped and doubled back on ourselves, or even how far we might have come. I don't know how many times I prodded and stepped before I felt, between one step and the next, that I had to hurry. The sense of urgency was as sharp as I'd ever felt it in a horse race, or the sheep game, but without the feeling of play. *There's no time!* beat through my thoughts. Images of Father dead, of bog-walkers swarming the walls of home, of flooded meadows and dead trees, crowded my mind's eye. My heart raced. and I spun on my left heel to bolt back the way I had come.

As soon as I put my right foot down for that first retreating step, the ground gave under me and my right foot sank into muck and water, jolting me to my knee. I let go of my spear and almost dropped my sword. I caught my breath and leaned away from my sinking foot.

When I felt the path firm under my knee, I found my sheath and slipped my sword into it. As I patted the ground, feeling for my spear, the rope around my waist tightened and pulled. I found the haft of my spear as my foot began to pull free, and set the butt of it on the ground, careful to aim the point away from Willow. I pulled on the spear haft and pushed hard with the one leg I could trust. Slowly, with a sucking sound, my foot came up out of the muck, and I got it back onto the path.

Then Willow herself emerged from the mist and stood close enough to see. The rope in her hand bounced as Warulf followed it forward and faded into view, then Tuan behind him. We huddled close enough together to see each other; the mist of the bog clung around us, and every movement sent tendrils swirling.

"Did the path run out?" Willow asked.

"No," I said. "I think the bog got into my head somehow. I thought I had to get back right away. It won't happen again, now that I know about it."

"Good thing the rope," Warulf said, "or you are fen princess." He grinned, and his good humour raised my own spirits. I was suddenly truly glad to have him along.

"How much rope left?" I asked.

Willow stuck a thumb under the coil on her shoulder and showed about half of it still there. "And you still have yours," She held up her hand and turned her head. We fell silent while she listened.

"Did you hear that?" she asked Tuan. He nodded. "We need to stop," she said. "I've heard something behind us, twice now, but it won't come near. We'll have to be away from Kiar if we're going to get anything to come close."

"Ya," Warulf said.

"If you're here," Tuan said, "they won't come near us."

Willow took the rope off her shoulder and draped it over mine.

"You go ahead," Willow said. "When you pay out the rope, leave it loose enough to lie on the ground. Then none of us will trip on it. Whatever's behind us will come closer, maybe rush us, and we can catch it in the net."

"Warulf and I hold the net," Tuan said. "Willow, you be the bait."

"That should work," she said.

Warulf nodded.

"We shouldn't split up," I said. "I won't see you, and I might not hear you. I won't be able to help."

"It'll have to come from there," Willow said, and jerked her thumb back over her shoulder. "because it won't go near you. If you're on the path ahead, we'll only have one direction to worry about."

"Two tugs on the rope," Tuan said. "If we need help."

"It'll be loose. I won't feel it."

"Go," Willow said. "We'll reel the rope in tight if we need to. We'll yell and scream. Go, or we're here for nothing at all."

She was right.

"Then be careful," I said. Nobody answered. If we were truly careful, we wouldn't be here.

I turned again, keeping my feet well away from the edge of the path. One boot was freshly sodden now; it sucked as I raised my foot and squished as I put it down. Water spurted up between my toes with every step.

How far away was far enough? I tried to picture how far I'd been from any of the bog-walkers when they first noticed me. Twenty paces, I thought, would be enough. I could feel the bog—or whatever it was—trying to get into my head again as I counted the steps. The numbers squirmed around each other like a knot of worms. Now the squish of my right boot was helpful. I counted them on the fingers of my empty right hand, touching a thumb to each finger as I stepped.

Finally, it seemed I'd gone far enough. Although I wanted to turn back to face my friends, it seemed more sensible to keep my eyes forward. I hoped I hadn't left enough space for a bog-walker to slip in between me and the others.

I stood and listened for any sound behind me to tell me what was happening. I thought I'd been listening as I picked our way through the bog, but now the muscles around my ears and temples strained with the effort. If I could have swivelled my ears like a fox, I would have.

That wait was the hardest I'd ever done. While I watched and listened for something ahead of me, I also listened for any sound that might tell me what Tuan, Willow and Warulf were doing. The same sense of fear and urgency came back in waves, flicking images across my inner eye. Now, among the pictures of High Moor and my father, it showed me Willow drowning in the muck that had swallowed my leg, and Tuan dead on the path with black, bleeding holes along his ribs, Warulf turning on Willow and stabbing her through the throat.

Now! Now! You'll be too late!

I knew it in my body, in my pounding heart and racing blood and the jolt of nervous energy that came with every wave. In my head, I knew it was all a lie. I clamped my will down on my body like a rider's knees on a shying horse, and tried to slow my breathing. I gritted my teeth and set my feet against the urge to run back, clinging to my spear with both hands.

"You tried this once," I muttered. "Give it up. It won't work." My knees trembled with the effort of simply standing still. How long had I been here? Willow had heard following steps at least twice; surely once I left whatever it was would come after them soon!

Now! They're dying now! You have to hurry!

Then, when I'd seen my friends and father dead or dying, my home overrun, for more times than I could count, when I felt as though one more wave would sweep my will like sand, I heard Willow whoop. Even through the muffling of the bog's airs, her triumph was clear.

"Got him! Kiar, we caught him! Yes!"

I had to work to set my feet carefully as I turned and picked up the rope to follow back. It was already tightening as Willow hauled it in. I took a dozen steps back, almost halfway there, and then heard Warulf give a wordless yell and Willow shout, "No! Hang onto him!"

I hauled faster on the rope, torn between speed and having to feel my way with my feet. A shriek cut through the muffling air as none of our voices could do, then echoed as though the bog were ringed by cliffs.

I moved as fast as I could and cursed my slowness. By the time I reached my friends, any struggle and any chance to hold the bog-walker was gone. Willow held her hands out in front of her, looking at something spread between them. When I came up behind her and peered over her shoulder, I saw tattered net.

Tuan moved close, still holding his sword, and then Warulf, his left hand clutched around his right wrist. My relief at having all three of them back in my sight, and safe, was greater than I'd expected. The bog had so nearly convinced me they were dead or dying.

"What happened?" I asked.

"We had it," Willow said. "It came straight after me and ran right into the net, right in!"

"I heard you. Is everyone all right?"

"I'm not hurt," she said. "Warulf? How's your arm?"

Warulf nodded, rubbing his right wrist with his left hand. Blood smeared the skin above the wrist, but when he took his hand away, there was only a thin, shallow cut. "All goot," he said.

"It worked," Willow said, "but this one tore the net."

"Two of them got tangled at High Moor and couldn't get out. It wasn't torn when you took it?"

Willow gave me a look. "I checked. But Kiar, this is good. It had wings!"

"Did you see if one side—" I thought for a moment. "The left side, had some broken feathers? If it's the same one that attacked Father, he cut some feathers at the tip of the left wing."

"I didn't see," Willow said. Tuan shook his head.

"Ya," said Warulf. He put his hand to his right cheek. "Ya. Fen-stalker beat with the wing." He held up his right hand and bent the two first fingers down, then pressed them against his cheek. "So," he said, and bumped the knuckles of his folded-down fingers against his cheekbone.

"It's the right one," I said. "Where did he—"

"Ssh," Willow said, and Tuan also held up his hand for silence. At first I heard nothing, but Willow coiled up the rope I'd unwound as fast as she could. Warulf gathered up the useless net and threw it aside, into the muck of the bog.

"Go!" Willow said.

Then I heard them; long, slow steps, tiny, rippled water sounds from my right, then from the left.

I stepped back in the direction I'd just come from. Warulf fell in behind me, and I saw Willow start to turn before I moved too far away to see her. Once again I poked and stepped, poked and stepped. Now the ripples were in front of me, but as I stepped forward again they moved around, leaving my path clear, closing in behind. I wondered how far away they would stay, especially here in the bog. I wasn't certain they would still run from me, here on their own ground, but I was absolutely sure they wouldn't run from Tuan or Willow or Warulf.

Poke and step, poke and step. All the time the sound of ripples and quiet steps moved slowly nearer.

"Can't we go faster?" Willow said. There was no point not talking. It was clear our pursuers knew exactly where we were.

"Only if we want to fall in."

Poke and step, poke and step. Then I saw a small, faint blot of colour ahead of me, so dim I couldn't tell what colour it was. Poke and step, and the colour grew clearer. Poke and step. It was pink, bright pink. Poke and step, and the firm path brought me straight towards the colour.

"It's a flower," I said.

"What?" said Willow.

"A flower! A bog-orchid! Look, there's another!" Poke and step. Around the flowers the murky air cleared, and the little blossoms shone as though in summer sunshine. Now I could see the path, bordered in bog-orchids set a pace apart along either side.

"Don't trust them!" Willow said. "Marsh-feys carry them, right, Warulf?"

"Ya," he said. "Fen-sprites, to call you."

"It's not marsh-feys. They're growing in the earth," I said. "The path runs between them; I can see it!"

"We're losing them," Tuan said. "The bog-walkers. They're fainter."

Now I could see the path clearly, and the light crept upwards with every step we took. In a dozen paces the path had changed from damp, mossy earth to dry ground, set with coloured pebbles. The orchids became little white moonflowers, goldcups, tall flameweed, and other summer flowers. As I stepped onto the first pebbles, the light sprang up around me. I turned, and the bog had disappeared. Willow, Tuan, Warulf and I stood blinking in the brilliant sunshine of a midsummer day.

"You are welcome here," said a woman's voice behind me, and I saw Tuan and Willow both remove their helmets and kneel before I turned around.

Before me stood a tall woman, pale-skinned and blue-eyed as my mother. Her straight, black hair fell to her knees, and she wore a gown of black feathers that pooled around her feet, and a crown of stars.

"Welcome, Granddaughter," said Queen Amala.

TWENTY-SIX

I pulled off my own helmet and started to kneel, but she put out a hand to stop me.

"Kiar," she said, and smiled. "I've hoped for many years that one of my family would find this place."

"How do you know me?" I asked.

"Blood calls to blood," she said. "I would know any descendant of mine, even one who looks so human. Perhaps only one with human blood would have dared think to enter the bog." She came to me and kissed my forehead. "Such a warrior, my granddaughter."

She looked past me and beckoned. "Hwaelew, come to me." Willow rose and hesitated.

"Come, now. Don't be afraid. I'm very glad to see you, Hwaelew."

"Me?" Willow's voice was thin, and she walked forward as though she might bolt if startled.

"Yes." Queen Amala stretched both arms out and brought Willow into an embrace, then kissed her cheek.

"Do not be jealous, Granddaughter. I am glad beyond reckoning to see you. But Hwaelew—" She held Willow's hands in hers. "You will do me a great service."

I had seldom seen Willow speechless, but she was speechless now. Queen Amala looked at Tuan and her smile widened.

"Tiwan, you have cut your hair. Stand up and let me look at you. You make as handsome a man as you do a swan." To my surprise, Tuan blushed.

"Thank you, Majesty," he said.

"Warulf of Noermark," she said, and Warulf, who had not knelt, came up to stand beside me and bowed his head.

"Lady of the Fen," he said. "I am the ally of Kiar Swan-kin and her folk. All her folk."

Queen Amala answered him in Noermarken. I had a few words of the language, but from the way Warulf's face brightened, she spoke it very well. He said something back to her and touched his fist to his breast, and she answered again, in a tone that said he was welcome here, too.

"You put the bog-orchids there, Majesty," I said.

"Yes, to bring you safely to me."

"Why us, Majesty?" said Tuan. "Others have drowned and worse than drowned. Why bring us here?"

"A good question, Tiwan. Come with me, and I will answer everything."

She turned, and a pavilion took shape in front of her, a white silk awning with blue pennants fluttering from the tall black poles at each corner, and from the centre peak. Underneath the pavilion a round table, surrounded by five tall chairs, was laid with cups of wine and plates of cheese, fruit, cold meats and delicate cakes.

"Please, sit," Queen Amala said. "Eat and drink." I saw Warulf hesitate before he sat, and Queen Amala spoke to him again in Noermarken, and he sat down.

"It is safe to eat and drink," she said. "I promise you—this is no spirit world where you will live a hundred years in a single hour and go home to find all you know have grown old and died."

I was thirstier than I had realized, and the wine was light and tart. The first mouthful quenched my thirst as quickly as water.

"Tell me why you've come," she said to me.

"Majesty, a bog-walker injured my father, King Tir," I said. "The wisewoman says that I have to find him and bring him back because only he can heal the king."

She nodded, and turned to Tuan.

"And you?" she asked.

"I am her mate," he said.

Queen Amala smiled, and now it was my turn to blush; I could feel my cheeks growing hot.

"If there were a man of Noermark I would expect to see here," she said, "it is you, Warulf. It has been a long time."

"You know me, Lady?" he said.

"I do. Have you come for your brother?"

"Min broder," Warulf said, almost under his breath.

"He is not dead," Queen Amala said. Then she turned to Willow. "What brings you here, Hwaelew, at last?"

"I'm Kiar's friend, Majesty," she said. "I wasn't going to come, but I couldn't let her go without me."

"I am glad you did not," said Queen Amala. "Without you, her quest would have failed. With you, it will succeed. Tell me, Granddaughter," she said to me, "what do you know of the king-light?"

"I know that the king-light surrounds the king or queen, and that it fades sometimes. I could make Orla—do you know about Orla, Majesty?"

"I know something of her, yes."

"I could make her leave Valenia when Father couldn't. Tuan told me I had the king-light and that Father's was fading."

"Most people don't see the king-light," Queen Amala said. "But they feel it. When people revere and obey a king or a queen and will follow them anywhere, that is the king-light they feel. It is a bond with the land they care for, and everything living on it—power, but also responsibility. The king-light is around you, Kiar. It's why you ventured here at all, and it is also why you would fail if not for Hwaelew."

"I don't understand," I said.

"I don't, either" Willow said.

"My brother," Queen Amala said, "also wears the king-light. When the bog seized him, he fought with all his strength to come back to his folk. There is magic here, an earth-power, simple and strong. I have studied it for many years, and still I don't understand it. But somehow, my brother did not die, although he is not truly alive, either. He did not lose the king-light, but he has been bound to the bog. You could say he is its king, and within its boundaries, he rules. The bog-walkers, the ones you saw, are his people, those who have wandered into the bog and never found their way out. I've often wondered if the bog itself somehow wished for a king, and that was why it took him.

"But not all lost people here become bog-walkers, and not at all in other bogs. Most are only marshy places, but open to the sun, with flowers and fruit in their seasons, wholesome for birds and beasts. There is still danger, but there one can only fall in and drown, and the only attack is from biting insects."

"It's the mists," I said. "That's what makes it different."

"Yes," Queen Amala said. "but whether it is the bog that made the mists, or the mists that made the bog as it is, I don't know. The bog is old; it was old when my people first made the lake their nesting grounds. And I believe, too, that there were not always bog-walkers."

"I've heard of them all my life," I said.

"But I had never heard of them," Amala said. "When I was a cygnet, we knew to stay away from this bog, and from the skies above it. We knew it was dangerous and could twist the senses so you couldn't trust what you saw or heard."

"We've used the dyeing pond at the edge of the bog for generations," I said. "We never had trouble until this year."

"No," Willow said. "It tried to take me, remember? I thought it was farther away, and then suddenly it was right there, and it reached for me. You saw that I was too close, but I didn't."

"You never heard of bog-walkers, not anywhere?" Tuan asked.

"No, Tiwan. No stories at all. Doesn't it seem strange now, that such a terror was never spoken of, even as something that must not be named? A fear that great, to leave no trace in the wisewomen's and wisemen's lore, in the fireside tales, in the nursery?"

"When *did* the stories start?" I asked.

"When there were enough bog-walkers that people sometimes met with them and lived," she said. "But I do not know exactly when that was. I was here by then. I could see my kin, sometimes quite clearly, but other things were harder to find, and not as clear. That is how I saw you, Warulf," she said. "It was my brother who took Valtir and made a bog-walker of him, as he made all but the first."

"Who made the first?" Tuan asked.

"The bog itself. I believe it was the bog that made my brother into a bog-walker, the first of his kind. I know that many people must have been lost in bogs before and drowned. Possibly he was the first creature with magic to be lost in the bog. I don't know, and we may never know. There is some powerful force here," she said, "but it's too simple for me to understand."

I must have looked puzzled. I know I certainly felt confused. How could something be too simple to understand?

"Think of a flower and a stone," she said. "A flower has petals, a stem, pollen, leaves. You can see those parts and understand how it fits together. A stone, a round stone from the river, is smooth and simple, and has no parts to divide it into. It's harder to see how a stone came to be. It has no parts—you can only break it. Whatever power is in the bog is like that."

"But there are two stones," Willow said. "There's one in Noermark, too."

"Yes," said Queen Amala. "I remember when that bog was bright and open, when my brother was alive. Then, when Warulf was a boy, it was growing misty and had a small darkness at its heart. After that, when the rule of Noermark was settled again, the mist and darkness disappeared, and for many years it was a bog, the same as other bogs. Now it belongs to my brother once again."

"That fen is—" Warulf held his hands apart and then moved them close together.

"Smaller," I said. "Smaller than this one?"

He nodded. "No fen-stalker comes out, never."

"I've never heard of one coming out of our bog, either" I said. "Tuan, is there anything in the swans' lore?"

"Nothing," he said.

"Then the bog has to be a certain kind of place," I said. "The High Moor folk have found people in the one south of them, but drowned and buried in the peat. No bog-walkers."

"But some of them are changing," Willow said. She turned to Queen Amala. "The one Warulf went into. You said it used to be ordinary."

"I believe my brother is pushing the borders of his kingdom out into your world," said Queen Amala. "First, there was an imbalance in the magic. Then one king-light diminished, and another one is dying. There is room for him to take hold of more of the world."

"Gythorn is dying," I said, "and my father's light is fading. Tuan told me that. But I have the king-light now; he told me that, too. Why can't I keep the bog—your brother out of Valenia?"

"Because," said Queen Amala gently, "you are not yet the queen. The power is divided. You have enough to protect a space around yourself, enough to show an enemy who sees such things that you are strong and will be hard to defeat. But there is a bond that comes with taking the throne yourself. Until you are the sole ruler of Valenia, the power is divided. The land is bound to both of you, for as long as your father is alive. Neither of you can protect all of it."

"Can't you stop them somehow?" Willow asked.

"No," Queen Amala said. "My brother was king of the swanfolk before I was queen. He does not answer to me; I cannot rule him. I have tried for many years to draw him out of the mists and bring him here to me. If I could do that, I might see how to heal him." She turned to me.

"He will not fight you. He can see the king-light on you, and if you are close enough, it drives him back. His people see it, too, and run from you. You can keep them away from your own, but only in the place where you are, and no ruler can be everywhere."

"I've given orders to bring everyone to the castle," I said. "I can protect them there. I need to take the king back to heal Father."

"You will not be able to approach him," Queen Amala said. "He will not come near you, or let you come near him. He will not fight you, because of the king-light you wear."

"He fought my father. He wounded him, and put magic in the wound to kill him!"

"That itself must tell you how badly your father is failing, when my brother can wound him yet cannot approach you."

"That doesn't make sense," I said. "Kings fight battles, and Gythorn would certainly kill Father in a fight if he could. I'm sure he'd do the same to me. He wouldn't avoid us because of the king-light."

"Perhaps if the king-light were as clear to ordinary people as it is in the places where magic rules," Queen Amala said, "Gythorn would avoid your father. But he hasn't challenged your father to battle, has he?"

"No, Majesty."

"So he must know your father's strength. He would look for weakness, for Tir to falter. Since human people don't see the king-light, you have different ways of finding weakness, or knowing strength."

"The fen-stalkers come," Warulf said, "when king is weak, ya? My king, Kiar Swan-kin's fader, ya?"

"Yes," Queen Amala said.

"But when my grandfather died, nothing like this happened," I said. "Father was away, and there was no king at all in Valenia until he got back. Why didn't your brother attack then?"

"Balance," said Queen Amala. "For many years, hundreds of years, there has been a balance between the places in the world where magic rules and the places where it does not. Not a perfect balance, but enough. Have you ever walked on a log, Kiar?"

"Yes," I said.

"Then you know that you can stay on if your balance isn't perfect. It's the same between this place and yours. But something tipped it, this past spring."

"Orla," said Tuan.

"Whatever happened," said Queen Amala. "it upset the balance. It affected the rule of Valenia and perhaps Noermark as well."

"You mean she made Gythorn fall off his horse?" Willow asked.

Queen Amala laughed. "No, Hwaelew, nothing so simple! But there are always small things pushing the balance, and this was one more push, a larger one. It's as though it was a stone in water, where the ripples spread wider and wider. The balance was tipped, and that made a ripple that let this world grow. Kiar's mother, her madness, and her father's care of her over his people, disturbed the balance a little more."

"Why didn't we notice anything?" I asked.

"But you did, Granddaughter," she said. "The animals knew. The deer, the boar, the wildcats and wolves, they felt the bog watching, stalking and preparing to spring. They abandoned their own places, did they not?"

"Yes," I said. "Was that him, too?"

"Him, and the bog using him. When your king," she said to Warulf, "broke his leg, that was an ordinary injury. But when it sickened, and he began to madden with the pain, there was enough imbalance to let this world come out into yours again, in Noermark and in Valenia, and in other places, too, far from here. It allowed my brother to lead his people against yours, Kiar," she said, "even though he could only do it in darkness."

"And then he attacked my father," I said.

She nodded. "I am sorry, Kiar."

"How can we do what we—what I came to do?" I asked. "How can I bring the—" I stopped at the word "bog-walker." It seemed disrespectful now—and besides, he was my many-times-great uncle. "If he won't come near me, how can I get him to come back with us and heal Father?"

Queen Amala turned to Willow.

"Hwaelew," she said, "You say the bog tried to take you. It is because when you came close, my brother recognized you. Perhaps it is better to say, you look like your seven-times-great aunt. You are very like her, you know. She was my brother's queen, and you are descended from her sister. Hwaelew, I believe my brother will come to you, and I believe that you can bring him back to himself and free him from the bog. And when he is himself, he will go with you to heal King Tir."

TWENTY-SEVEN

"How do I do it?" Willow said.

"There is a price," Queen Amala said. "Before you consent, you need to know everything you are offering."

"Then what is the price?" Willow asked.

"When my brother has become himself again, you will be his mate," Queen Amala said.

For a few breaths nobody spoke. Then Willow looked straight at Queen Amala.

"I'll do it," she said.

I jumped up from my seat.

"Willow," I said, "Don't!" I turned to Queen Amala. "Tuan told me you were the most powerful Black Swan ever born, that you knew all the magic of all the peoples! If you can't change your brother back or bring him out of the bog, how can

Willow? None of us have any more than a little magic, nothing to compare with yours."

"Kiar," Queen Amala said, "My brother was here for many years before I was free to come and seek him out. He lived, but the bog has made him mistrustful of those outside. He believes the truce-folk, the old Valenians, tried to kill him. When trying to escape their arrows, he was caught by the bog. By the time I was able to make this small realm of mine, he no longer trusted even me. But I believe he still remembers and loves his mate, Falera." She paused for a moment. "Kiar, I would not ask for your friend's help if I could free my brother myself. He will not come to you, or me, or anyone else in peace, but he will, I believe, come to Hwaelew."

I turned to Willow. "Who you marry should be your own choice!"

"Who have I got to choose from?" she asked.

"Anyone! You know there are men at the castle who are more than half in love with you. Or you could marry one of the swanfolk!"

"No," she said, "I couldn't. You and Tuan are my flock now. I couldn't take a swan mate and leave you for half the year. And I won't marry a human and lose half my life the way the queen did. After you and your sisters were born, she could never truly be her swan self again. I'm sorry, Kiar, but it's true."

"Willow," I said. "You shouldn't have to take a mate you don't know to break a spell." I turned to Tuan and Warulf. "She shouldn't have to do it, right?" I asked.

Tuan shook his head, and I thought he would support me until he said, "Nobody says she has to do it. She could say no. She said yes."

"Her wyrd," Warulf said to me. His voice was low and reasonable. "Her road."

"It's not *just* to break the spell," Willow said. "It's to save the king, too."

"But I'm supposed to bring the Lost King back, not you. I won't let you do it!"

"Why, Kiar, I do believe you're jealous," Willow said, and laughed out loud. "How can you stop me if I want to do it? Anyway, think of it! I'll be the heroine of a story, going off to fight magic without the slightest idea of what I'm doing. And getting a prince—a king, I suppose—as a reward!"

She got up and came around the table to stand beside me.

"Besides," she said, "This is my choice. This is my best chance of having a mate and still being able to stay with you. He can't go back to the flock, you know. He has no place there. Your grandfather is the Swan King, and Adana is his heir. Maybe we can make a little flock of our own—you and me and Tuan and—I don't know his name. Shouldn't I know his name?" she asked Amala.

Amala smiled at Willow with a look so affectionate that for a moment, I *was* jealous.

"His name is Keilan."

"And how do I change him back?"

"Willow!" I said, almost in tears. I remembered her saying the Lost King would be mad after five hundred years. What if he hurt Willow, even killed her?

"How do I change him back?" she repeated.

"Quite simply," Queen Amala said. "I will guide you back into the bog. All you have to do is wait. He will come to you, as he tried to come to you before. In one way, it is like the tales. A kiss breaks the spell. Kiss him, and he will become himself again. But once you kiss him, you must keep hold of him."

"That's all?" Willow asked. "Kiss him, and hold onto him."

"That's all," Queen Amala said, "but it will be quite enough. You may find it harder to do than you think. You may want to rest first; you have been a long time arriving, and you are all tired."

"How long?" I put down the slice of pear in my fingers. I was suddenly afraid that years might have passed in Valenia while I spent an afternoon here.

"One day and a night," she said. "Don't be afraid, Kiar. Your father is still alive. There is time."

"It didn't seem that long," Tuan said.

"Time is different in the darkest part of the bog," she said.

"Lady," Warulf said, "Valtir, min broder. How to free him?"

"If you go out into the bog with Hwaelew, my brother will come to her, but the others will attack you. When my brother is restored to his own shape, so will they be. Then you can find your brother among them and take him home."

"If they don't kill you first," I said. "But I suppose that is your wyrd."

"Ya," Warulf said. "But your man first. Free me?"

"No," I said. "I won't free you." Willow drew in her breath, and I went on before she could speak. "I won't leave you without protection against Gythorn. I won't let you take back your oath. But go and get your brother. I'll give him the same protection, if he wants it."

"I'll go with you," Tuan said to Warulf. "You can't kill them. One might be your brother. You'll need help."

"I should go," I said. "If Warulf isn't close to Willow, the king can come to her, and the rest of them will stay away from me – from us."

"Too far away," Tuan said. "If they become human again, they can get lost, maybe die. Is that right?"

Amala nodded. "That is right. Without my brother's magic, I don't believe the bog can re-make them as bog-walkers. They will be as they were when they first entered the bog."

"It's not right," I said. "I should be out there, too. I can't let you—all of you—go out there to face them while I stay here!" I looked at Tuan and felt tears close to the surface. "What if you die? What if you die because one of them gets through your guard? And there's no one to watch your back?"

"I would have fought Hafor," said Tuan. "I wanted to fight him for you, but it was you who had to do it. He cut you twice. If you stumbled, if he misjudged his stroke, there was no one to protect you."

"You were all there, watching," I said. "and I have to wait here until you come back, or don't, and I won't know."

"I can help with that, Granddaughter," Queen Amala said. "I have watched my brother often through the years, and I can lend you that same sight for the time they are away."

It was not what I wanted. I wanted to be by Tuan's side, to face whatever he had to face. If what Queen Amala said was true, Willow would be in no danger, and although I was unhappy about her choice, there was nothing I could do to stop her. In any fight, especially where there were more of the enemy, it was better to have more fighters on your own side. Warulf, Tuan and I would be better able to stand off an attack than Warulf and Tuan alone, except that with me, there would be no attack.

"Thank you," I said. There was nothing else to say.

CHAPTER

TWENTY-EIGHT

When we were done eating, Queen Amala said, "Now you must rest for a short while." We stood, and the table and chairs, dishes and food, faded away. Dark blue curtains unrolled down the sides of the pavilion, and the summer day faded to twilight. As the curtains lowered, four low cots seemed to grow up from the ground, with pillows and soft white blankets. By the time they had appeared, Queen Amala, too, was gone.

I kicked off my boots and lay down on one of the cots. Tuan moved another until it was touching mine, and we lay side by side, hands joined. There was nothing I could say to keep him from going into the bog with Warulf, and if there had been, I didn't think I would say it. He wasn't a child, to be told what he could and couldn't do.

If I asked, he might stay because I loved him, or because I held, as long as Father was ill, the power of a queen. I didn't want that, either. It was impossible to know what I wanted, except to have this over and done, and Tuan back safe by my side.

I closed my eyes but couldn't fall asleep. Tuan's eyes were closed, and his breathing slow and even. Whether Willow and Warulf were asleep or not, I couldn't tell; both had their backs to me. I could well believe Warulf, at least, would be able to sleep.

My worries chased themselves around in my head. Was Father still alive? He'd be angrier than ever that I disobeyed him to enter the bog, even if I did it to save his life. Warulf and Tuan might be hurt, maybe killed, out in the bog. If Queen Amala was wrong about Willow kissing the bog-walker and turning him back to what he had been, would he kill her?

I don't know how long I lay there before the pavilion became as bright as the summer day outside. Everyone woke and stretched. I envied them their ability to sleep and felt unrested and gritty-eyed. As we rose, the cots disappeared as the table had done. The pavilion somehow divided into two, and Willow and I were on one side with everything we needed to feel refreshed after our sleep. There was even a mirror and comb, and I found myself smiling.

"What's funny?" Willow asked.

"Oh, I remember Sianna telling me when I went to find Orla that just because I was on a quest didn't mean I had to have straw in my hair."

"That *is* funny." She pulled off the cord that tied her braid and undid her hair, then combed it out. Instead of braiding it up again, she left it loose. "I don't suppose Queen Falera ever braided her hair."

"Are you really doing this?" I asked.

"Yes," she said. She left off smoothing her hair and turned to me. Her face was calm, even a little cheerful. "Don't look so worried! I can't imagine it will be any worse than if you'd married Othar. You'd have done that partly for peace in Valenia. It's the same for me."

"At least I had a chance to meet Othar first," I said. "And nobody was going to force me."

"Nobody's forcing me," Willow said. "And he might be a bog-walker right now, but he seems to like me. That has to count for something, doesn't it?" She gave me a crooked smile. "He came very close to me when we tried to catch him. Perhaps that's as good as an introduction. Anyway, his family approves of me—you and Amala."

I shook my head. "You're impossible, Willow."

"Please promise you'll try to like him."

I sighed. "I'll be polite. Will that be enough?"

"To start with," she said. She brushed aside the pavilion wall and stepped out. There was nothing to do but follow her.

Queen Amala stood a few paces away from the pavilion. She had put off her feather robe and starry crown and stood in a simple black robe that fell to her feet in soft folds. She smiled to see Willow and me. Tuan and Warulf joined us, each carrying a heavy staff. The birds started up in my stomach again. They had their swords, but it would be slow and awkward to draw them while holding an enemy off with a staff.

"What do we do now?" I asked.

"You will stay with me to watch," Queen Amala said. She pointed at the grass to one side, and the same path. bordered with kingcup and flameweed, appeared, leading into a wall of bright mist.

"That is your path, Hwaelew," she said. "Tiwan and Warulf, you are set on going with her?"

"Ya," said Warulf, and Tuan nodded.

"Then have courage," she said, "and luck be with you." She kissed Willow on the forehead, and then Willow hugged me and turned away. As Warulf passed, he patted my back—a pat that was almost a blow.

"Wyrd, na?" he said, grinning as though he were a boy going to play a game or ride in a race.

"You're enjoying this!" I said.

"They make a song," he said as he followed Willow to the misty wall.

"Good luck!" I called after them. "I'll see they make a good song!" Then Tuan came and took my hand.

My heart pounded; the thought of him never returning made my throat close up. "Be careful," I whispered. "Promise me you'll come back."

"I don't intend to die," he said, then kissed me quickly and caught up with the others. As soon as he reached them, Willow said, "Ready?" Without waiting for an answer, she stepped into the wall of mist. The other two followed her. In seconds, they were gone.

Queen Amala turned away from the misty wall. "Come with me."

I followed, and when I glanced over my shoulder, the wall and the path were both gone, with nothing to show where Willow, Tuan, and Warulf had been. Queen Amala stood by a wide, black basin set on a low, grey stone column. She held out her hand to me, and I stood beside her.

"Look into the water," she said.

The liquid in the basin was clear and still, and only a glimmer of light at the edge showed me the basin wasn't empty. The basin seemed to curve not down but up, as though it had been turned upside down. Then it reversed again and again, until I could no longer be sure whether I was looking at the inside of a basin full of clear water, or the underside of one upturned.

My head spun with the speed of the changes, and then, all in a moment, it stopped. I no longer noticed the basin, the water, or Queen Amala beside me.

Instead I was walking a few paces behind Warulf. Ahead of him was Tuan, prodding with his spear-shaft along the path, reaching past Willow, who was close in front of him. I saw them all quite clearly, but from their slow, careful steps, it was evident none of them could see their way well.

"I don't know how far we have to go," Willow said. "I'd hate to fall in and have to be dragged out. Not very heroic." Her voice sounded muffled.

"Fen-stalkers find us," Warulf said. He glanced back over his shoulder, but his gaze went right past me.

"Soon, I hope," she said.

At that moment, I heard the splash and ripple we'd heard before, signalling the approach of the bog-walkers. My three friends kept walking as though they heard nothing.

"They're coming," I said. When nobody answered, I said, more loudly, "Can't you hear them?" I tried to tap Warulf's shoulder and saw my hand resting on the scuffed leather of his armour-plated vest. I felt nothing – not the yielding resilience of the leather, nor the smoothed edge of the small metal cap on his shoulder. It was equally obvious Warulf couldn't feel the pressure of my hand.

The noises grew louder and louder until I wondered if my friends were deaf. Then Tuan stopped Willow with a hand on her shoulder and cocked his head, as though listening hard.

"Do you hear them?" she whispered, and he nodded.

"Finally!" I said.

I watched as eight or ten bog-walkers closed around them. From the sound, more were coming. Tuan and Warulf set themselves back-to-back, turning their heads and listening. A bog-walker stepped onto the path. His foot fell right on mine. I couldn't feel any weight on my toes, but without thinking, I stepped back. My foot pulled away from his, but he was already moving forward again, and Warulf's staff swung around and knocked him sideways from the path.

The bog-walkers howled, and if Warulf and Tuan couldn't see them, they could certainly hear them. Then three rushed forward, and Tuan and Warulf had to work fast with their staves to keep them off. Killing them would have been simpler, and far less dangerous. I couldn't simply stand by and watch.

I drew my sword and picked a bog-walker with its back to me. I hit it as hard as I could on the head with my pommel, but I might as well have thrown a mushroom at it. I saw the pommel hit, but I couldn't feel the blow in my arm. I stabbed at the bog-walker, but it took no notice of me, not as much as if I'd been a fly.

"Hells!" I yelled. In frustration, I stabbed and slashed at them. It made not the slightest difference that I could see.

I had somehow stepped off the path and into—or onto—the bog, but even the ground took no notice of me. Still stabbing, trying in vain to distract the bog-walkers from Tuan and Warulf, I drifted around to the side. Now I could see everyone—Warulf, Tuan, and Willow standing a little ahead, turning her head from side to side, fists clenched.

Tuan snapped his staff sharply on a bog-walker's shoulder, then dug the end into its stomach and heaved the creature into the wet.

He and Warulf were both breathing hard now, and striking a little more slowly. Their clothing was torn where the bog-walkers' claws had hooked and ripped. Tuan had blood on his left forearm and cheek, and Warulf's right glove was in shreds, the back of his hand scored and bloody. As the bog-walkers rushed again, Warulf's foot slipped, and he almost went down. His staff swung, and a bog-walker slid under it. Tuan shoved the bog-walker he was fighting and as it staggered back, he jabbed at the one coming down on Warulf, hitting it square in the face.

"Look out!" I said, as the one he'd shoved away lunged again.

He caught it under the ribs with the end of his staff, dug in, and pivoted to throw his attacker into another to his left.

Even as he swung back, there was another reaching for him. He and Warulf both had their work cut out. It would have been much easier to use swords.

"Hurry up, Willow!" Tuan said between his teeth, and turned to knock away another attacker.

"He's not coming!" she said.

"Call him, then!"

I couldn't remember hearing Tuan shout before.

Willow drew a deep breath and shouted, "Keilan! Keilan!" at the top of her lungs. Whether it was her voice, or the swan king's name, the cry cut through the muffling airs of the bog and echoed over and over.

While those echoes lasted, the bog-walkers stopped where they were and turned their faces towards Willow. At first I was afraid they would attack her. Tuan shifted the staff in his hands and took a step closer to her.

Then the echoes faded, and the bog-walkers turned their empty faces again towards Tuan and Warulf. As the first one stepped forward, the Lost King surged out of the darkness and stopped before Willow. All the bog-walkers froze where they were. Tuan and Warulf stood braced, watching the bog-walkers, though Tuan turned his head a little, as though to hear what was happening with Willow.

The king was taller than I remembered, or maybe it was only that I could see him clearly through Amala's magic. He, too, stood braced as if for a fight, his hands open and held out from his sides. His skin, brown as peat, clung to his bones. Ribs, hips, the joints of his arms and hands, the shape of his skull—all showed as though there was no muscle at all between the skin and the bone. His eyes were sunken under closed lids, his mouth hardly more than a slash in his face. He spread his wings, and the bog-walkers stepped back and crouched low.

Willow stood very straight and held her chin high. All the same, her fists were clenched, as I'd seen them so long ago when she first came to live with us. I wanted to stand by her, but I was afraid the Lost King would be able to see me and vanish as he had come.

The king lowered his face towards Willow, his peat-dulled hair swinging forward in an uneven curtain. He sniffed twice, then reached with one ragged-nailed hand and took a strand of her hair between his finger and thumb. He raised it to his cheek and rubbed it up and down, like a small child with a bit of blanket.

Willow reached up, moving her arms slowly and gently, unclenching her fists to slip her hands around the Lost King's neck. She pulled that terrible, dried-leather face down to hers, and he came without resisting. From where I stood—if standing was what I was doing—I saw her lips touch his mouth.

For a moment nothing happened. We all seemed frozen in place while Willow kissed the Lost King. Then everything happened.

The magic flared up from the Lost King, brilliant white as sun shining on snow, brighter than anything I'd ever seen, a hundred swanfolk changing form all at once. Whether it was the magic itself, or that I didn't have my body with me, closing my eyes didn't shut out the light at all. After a few seconds of clenching my eyelids shut in vain, I also realized the light didn't hurt my eyes.

I tried to see Willow, or any sign of the Lost King, in whatever form. The white sun at the centre of the flare hid them, but I heard Willow cry out, a wordless shout, and then the sound of large wings beating. The flare died back, and Willow stood clutching a swan, a cob, around the neck, a swan who beat his wings and struggled to get free.

He struck at her arm with his head, and then snaked his neck to pull free of her hold. Just in time, she shifted one arm around his body, and even as he pulled his neck free, she slid the other arm around him.

Now she held him around the body, and his wings as well as his beak were free to strike at her. She buried her face in his breast and tucked her shoulders up around her ears as his wings came forward again and again.

"Watch his feet!" I called to her, though I knew she couldn't hear me.

Almost as I spoke, the cob raised one foot and pushed it up and out against Willow's body. She made a muffled sound and pulled him closer to her. Again he struck with his wings at her head and then raised his foot and kicked up under her arms. This time she cried out, and when his foot raked down her tunic, it left blood on the leather. He'd cut her with a nail. She stumbled back a step as he pushed, still holding hard to the swan in her arms, and fell to her knees.

Tuan stepped forward to help her, and the cob hissed and thrust at him.

"No!" Willow shouted, and then said something else, too muffled to pick out. She turned her head, and there was blood running down her chin.

"I have him!" she said, and turned her face back into the cob's breast. His beak struck her head, and she cried out again. The cob's beak came away bloody, holding strands of her long, black hair. She tightened her grip again, and I realized what she was doing. If she squeezed his body, he would run out of breath. He had to be able to expand his ribs to breathe, and she wouldn't let him. He would have to stop fighting for lack of air.

He battered her with his wings again, but already the blows were weaker, slower. Under the movement of his wings, I heard Willow's voice. I couldn't hear what she was saying, but the tone was soothing and low. Finally, he folded his wings back and turned his head this way and that, his beak open as he gasped for air.

Willow smoothed the feathers at the base of his neck and lifted her face a little away from the swan's breast. "There, now," she said.

He dropped his head and I thought for a moment that he would peck at her face, but instead he laid his cheek against her head and closed his eyes.

"It's all right," she said. She might have been speaking to Whiffle. "It's over now. You can come back." Over and over, she said the same few words in a low, calm voice. She unwound her arms from the swan's body and rocked back on her heels.

For a few moments, he only breathed and flipped the ends of his wings into place while he shifted from foot to foot. Then he stood tall, curved his neck back and raised his wings. He beat them once, twice, and the magic flared up again. Willow jumped to her feet and stepped back. When the magic faded, a swan man stood where the swan had been. He might have been any man of the swanfolk but for one thing; his hair was not black, but as white as swan feathers.

He and Willow looked into each other's faces, and neither spoke.

Warulf was the first to break the silence. "The fen-stalkers," he said.

He pointed back along the path my friends had taken into the bog. The bog-walkers were gone. Where they'd stood were men. Some stared at their own hands, or felt their faces. Some looked about with an air of bewilderment. As we watched, more people joined the ones we could see, wading through the bog as if it were nothing more than a shallow pond. One by one, they stepped out onto the path. Most were men, but there were a few women among them. The path itself must have become wider; every new person who came out of the bog seemed to find a place on it without trouble.

It was clear Warulf, Tuan and Willow could see the people around him as well as I could. Whether it was some work of Queen Amala's or a result of the Lost King changing back to himself, the air of the bog, though still misty, was brighter. I wondered now if Warulf's brother had been one of the bog-walkers killed in an attack, either here or at the farmstead in

Noermark. No, Queen Amala had told him Valtir was still alive—surely she wouldn't have said that unless she knew for certain. I watched Warulf for any sign of recognition. Valtir had been gone for many years, long enough for a little boy to become a grizzled fighter. Perhaps Warulf wouldn't recognize his brother if he saw him.

Then Warulf thrust his staff into the ground and pushed through the people to a young man at the edge of the path, a young man whose right arm ended below the elbow.

"Valtir! Min brodor!" The man looked up but didn't move his feet.

Warulf caught him by the shoulders, grinning.

"Eldfader?" Valtir asked.

"Na, na! Ich Warulf eom! Broder!" Warulf said, still grinning.

"Warulf."

"Ya, Valtir!"

"Warulf," Valtir said again, and placed his hand at the height of a small boy.

"Ya," Warulf said. To my immense surprise, he threw his arms around Valtir and hugged him. I had no idea he would do such a thing. Valtir put his left arm around Warulf, and then laid his head on his little brother's shoulder and cried.

"Can we take them back with us?" Tuan said to Willow.

She stood beside the Lost King, one hand on his arm. "I don't know why we can't." She turned to the king but before she could speak, he put his hand to her chin and wiped away some of the blood.

"I'm sorry," he said. He took her hands in his and held them to his heart. I thought he might smile at her, but his face was quiet and stern-looking, someone used to command. "Thank you," he said. "I thought you were my queen. I see now you are not."

"I'm related," Willow said.

"And yet I do not know you." He tipped his head and waited for her answer. She seemed lost for words, and it was Tuan who answered.

"Queen Amala will explain," he said. "We should go back. Can they come with us?"

The king frowned. "Who are you?" he said. "One of my folk, I see. Are you a prince, to speak so to me?"

"No," Tuan said. "Willow, we should go back. Kiar's father."

"Yes." She turned her hands to take the king's. "Sire, Queen Amala is waiting for you. Do you know if these people can come back with us? And will you come, Sire?"

"Amala is here?"

"Close by," Willow said.

"I am not certain what will happen when these folk return to the world," he said. "And, Lady, you brought me back to myself. How can I refuse you anything?" Then at last he smiled. Without his stern expression he was a handsome man, and I was glad for Willow. When she turned to lead him along the path, she was smiling, too.

Tuan motioned Warulf back along the path the way they had come. As he wove through the restored people with Valtir close behind, I felt a pull below my ribs, as though my stomach were trying to come out through my back. Then the people around me disappeared, and I was bent over by Queen Amala's black basin, my sword still in my hand, retching in the sunshine.

CHAPTER

TWENTY-NINE

When I had finished throwing up, Queen Amala handed me a cup of water, and I rinsed my mouth. I sheathed my sword and pushed my hair back from my face.

"I hate that about magic," I said. "It makes me sick."

"You tried to help your friends," she said. "Drawing your sword here, while your spirit was there. It was hard work, and the iron tried to pull you back to your body."

"I see," I said.

"It was partly my doing, as well. I could have let you come back, but I thought you would rather be with your friends. I held you there, against the iron, and you are paying the price now."

"I don't mind," I said. "I couldn't stand by while they were fighting against those odds."

"No." Queen Amala smiled. "I can see you're not good at standing by. Come, let's go and meet them."

We walked away from the basin. Already there was a mist forming in the air, and I thought it must be the same place where Tuan, Warulf, and Willow had gone into the bog. Plants sprouted in two lines, putting out shoots and leaves, then long stalks, and buds that burst into bloom, until they bordered a path that led away from the mist.

"Did you see everything?" I asked Queen Amala.

"Yes," she said. "I did. All of you did well, and Hwaelew best of all." Her smile lit up her whole face. As I watched, stars appeared in her hair, a circlet of tiny points of light that spilled over her shoulders, until her hair was as full of stars as a clear summer's night.

"They're beautiful," I said. "The stars."

She smiled and drew a circle around my brow. A ring of stars danced above my eyebrows for a moment before they closed in and settled in my hair. I could feel them there, light and trembling as butterflies resting on my head.

"What about the people who used to be bog-walkers?" I asked.

Her smile faded a little. "They will live out their lives as they would have if they had not been lost. The people they knew have aged, or died. They will return after a long sojourn to folk who have given them up for dead."

"Valtir called Warulf 'eldfader'."

"Yes. It will be hard for him, when everyone he knew is dead and even his little brother is as old as a grandfather."

"The ones we killed," I said, "they won't go back."

"No, Granddaughter. Raising the dead is perilous magic. To bring the spirit back to a ravaged body is no kindness. Look, here they are."

Warulf stepped out of the mist first, his staff held in his bloody right hand, and his left reaching back. When he saw me, he grinned.

"Kiar Swan-kin!" he called. Then his hand appeared, holding by the forearm a man perhaps a few years older than I was. "Min broder—Valtir!" He pulled Valtir aside onto the grass, out of the way of the people still coming through that misty curtain.

"Valtir," I said.

Valtir looked at me through narrowed eyes and said something to Warulf. The only word I caught was "Valener." Warulf shook his brother's arm and spoke back just as quickly, then nodded towards me and said, "Kiar Swan-kin," again. Valtir shook his arm free of Warulf's grip. He raised his right arm, hesitated at the sight of the puckered end and missing hand, and then tapped that end over his heart.

"Kiar Swan-kin," he said.

"I tell Valtir, my ally, his ally," Warulf said. "He sees never a sword-maiden." Then he laughed, and I laughed with him. After a moment, whether or not he knew why we were laughing, Valtir joined in.

Then Tuan stepped out of the curtain. He limped on his right leg, and there was blood at his knee as well as on his forearm and face. I ran to him and stopped short, not wanting to knock him over.

"Are you all right?" I said.

He grinned as widely as Warulf had, put his arm around me and kissed me hard. "I thought you were watching," he said.

"I was, but—"

"After your father's wounds, these are nothing." He flicked a finger at my hair. "I like the stars." Then he looked at the people around us. They stood gazing at the sky, the flowers, and green grass, blinking in the sunlight they had not seen for many years.

They wore leather tunics and trousers as I did, or the woven trousers tied below the knee of the Noermarkers. One woman, her dark brown hair braided into many plaits, was dressed in a soft leather vest padded and stitched in a diamond pattern over a long shirt split front and back, and leather trousers that came only halfway down her calves. Behind her stood a man, similarly dressed, with his moustaches braided and hanging below his chin. Both had skin the colour of a dun horse, and wide, black eyes under heavy eyebrows.

The last lost person walked out into the sun, and then came Willow and Keilan. From his shoulders hung the feather cloak only royalty could show. He almost glowed in the sunlight, pale from head to feet. Beside him, Willow looked small, her head reaching barely to his shoulder, her clothes plain and more than a little grubby from our adventure. Blood spotted her tunic and had crusted on her chin. Still, she stood straight, her head up, and her right hand in Keilan's left.

Before anyone could speak, Queen Amala had her arms around Keilan's neck. Her face lifted to his as she wept and laughed at the same time. He put his arms around her and his head on her shoulder, and they stood together, embracing so tightly they seemed a single being of black and white, with stars shimmering and sparkling all through Queen Amala's hair. When they finally parted, Amala wiped tears from her face.

"Keilan, Keilan," she said. "You've come back at last."

"How much time?" His voice was low and calm, but Amala put her hand on his cheek as if to comfort him.

"A long, long time," she said. "Grandchildren of my great-grandchildren rule our folk now."

He bowed his head and took Amala's hand in both of his. The curtain of his white hair hid his face, and his voice was low. "I knew," he said, "long ago that my queen must be dead. And then I thought you were dead, too, and if that were true, I was condemned never to return to myself. I hoped to die for many years, but nothing could kill me."

"I'm so sorry, Keilan," Queen Amala said. "When you disappeared, I had to look after our folk. I came as soon as I could leave them in my son's care. I've worked for many lives of swanfolk and truce-folk to find the way to free you. And when I found it, I had to wait still. Only someone of Falera's blood could bring you close." She turned to Willow. "Hwaelew is that one."

"Hwaelew," Keilan said. "If what my sister says is true, I have no place among my folk, no name, nowhere to make a nest. If I had these things, I would ask you to share them and be my mate, but I have nothing to offer."

Amala and Willow exchanged a look.

"I knew that when I said I'd bring you back," Willow said. "If there isn't a place among the swanfolk for us, I know there will be one with Kiar's folk." Keilan raised his eyebrows.

"The truce-folk drove me into the bog," he said, "and now they offer refuge?"

"Not refuge," I said. I came to stand in front of him. "A home, if you want it. Willow—Hwaelew—is my friend, and her mate is welcome. Those people who shot at you, all those years ago, they didn't see you. They saw a monster flying in the air, and they were afraid. They're all dead now, and nobody in Valenia has hunted swans for many years."

He looked me up and down. I couldn't imagine he'd be impressed by what he saw—a human woman in tunic and trousers the worse for travelling through the bog,

"I know you," he said. "You brought the king-light onto the field, so bright we feared you. I could not fight you, nor could any of my people. My poor people," he said, almost under his breath. He turned back to me.

"Are you queen of the truce-folk, with stars in your hair?" he asked.

"No," I said, "but I'm the king's heir of Valenia. My mother is your—" I tried to remember the number of greats and failed. "She's Tianis of the swanfolk, your many-times-great niece," I finished.

"Do the swanfolk take mates among the truce-folk now?"

"Yes," I said. "We are allies. Please, I need your help. You used magic against my father, and he'll die of it unless you take it off. I know we've been enemies, but we aren't any longer. Please help him."

"Please," Willow said. "The king has been good to us, Tuan and me, and he would never have fought you if your people hadn't attacked High Moor."

"What of my people?" Keilan said to Queen Amala.

"Let them rest here until you have done what Kiar asks," she said. "I will take care of them until you return."

"He'll need clothes," I said to Queen Amala. "He can't go all that way barefoot, and with nothing to protect him against the weather. It's cold now, almost winter."

"Leave that to me." As Queen Amala spoke, she wavered in the air, and I thought she was going to vanish. Then everything else rippled as though covered with water. The light faded and dimmed. For a moment, there was nothing around me, nothing to see, hear, or feel, no air on my skin or anything under my feet, and then I felt that I stood on something hard. The light returned, much dimmer than before.

I was on the stone floor inside the door of my father's room, and the light came from a candle, shaded so as not to disturb his sleep. Mother came to her feet from her seat at his bedside. She stared at Keilan, standing beside me in his feather cloak, then knelt.

Sianna came out of a dark corner of the room.

"Kiar," she said. Her eyes went to the swan man.

"I've done what you asked," I said. "This is Keilan. He wounded Father, and he's come to heal him."

Sianna coaxed Mother to her feet and away from the bed. She lifted the shade from the candle and turned back the coverlet over Father, then stood aside to give Keilan her place.

I came to stand across from him.

Father seemed faded, scraped thin as the parchment covers we put over windows in the winter. His eyes were closed, and his breathing shallow.

"I can almost see through him," I whispered.

"Yes," Sianna said, and lifted the linen pad that covered the wounds. They were no worse, but neither had they healed. "The magic is working quickly." She looked at Keilan.

He nodded and rubbed his hands together as though to warm them. Then he placed his fingers carefully over the holes his claws had made and bent his head. His hair fell forward over his arms and face. When he blinked, I saw a strand move, caught in his eyelashes, but he was too intent on Father to notice.

I don't know how long he stood there. Sianna seemed frozen; from the corner of my eye, I could see the linen she held shining in the dim room, and it never moved. I couldn't stop looking from Keilan's hands to Father's face. Finally, Keilan lifted his hands and straightened up. Sianna and I both leaned forward to look at Father's body in the candlelight.

Where six deep punctures had marked his flesh, there were now only small dents, white and round and smooth. Even as we watched, Father drew a deeper breath than I'd seen him take since his injury. His eyes opened. I took his hand and held it in both of mine.

"How do you feel?" I asked.

"Old," he said. His voice was soft, and he sounded tired. I watched him, anxious for some sign his anger was done.

"Kiar," he said. "Was this more of your doing?"

"Yes," I said. "I couldn't let you die without trying."

He shook his head a little. "I should be angry," he said. "You aren't very good at taking orders."

"I'm glad you're still here to be angry with me," I said.

"It's hard to be angry when you did it for me." He smiled, and I smiled back. Tears blurred my vision and I had to wipe my eyes. Then Father looked at Keilan.

"I think we have met," he said. "and I have heard of you. Tianis told me. The Lost King."

"Even so." Keilan said. "I am Keilan. I have healed the wounds I gave you and taken off my magic. It was done in fair battle. Even so, I ask your forgiveness."

"Granted, granted." Father closed his eyes for a few seconds, then opened them again. "The swans flew," he said. "Before High Moor. But you know where they go." He turned his head toward me. "The farmsteads?"

"I think everyone is safe," I said. "Most of them are here anyway. Maybe all by now," I said. "I had good advice, and lots of help. All you have to do is get well again. I think the attacks are over."

Keilan nodded. "Indeed they are," he said.

"Well done," Father said.

Sianna pulled the cover up again and brought a cup. Keilan moved away, and I helped her raise Father. He took a sip and grimaced.

"You need to sleep," Sianna said. "You've been fighting your wounds instead of resting. Now rest for tonight. You can get out of bed tomorrow."

"Promise," Father said.

"I promise," she said.

He drank the cup, and we laid him back down on the bed.

Keiland had quietly left Father's side, and stood in the far corner of the room, bright in the dimness. Mother was rising to her feet before him. I went over, a small hope rising in my heart.

"Can you do anything for her?" I asked.

"What is the matter?" he asked.

"She took my sister's death in the spring very hard. She's better than she was, but still not right."

"In the spring," he said, almost to himself. "This past spring? She died by magic?"

"She drowned," I said, "but her spirit came back to make trouble. She's been banished now."

Keilan took my mother's right hand in his and turned it palm-up, then laid his own palm over it and closed his eyes. Mother never took her eyes from his face, even when I was speaking. Now a little line formed between her brows, the barest hint of a frown, but she didn't withdraw her hand. Maybe she couldn't. Clearly she saw him as a king among the swans. Perhaps she would have to obey him as she had to obey her father and Adana.

Keilan opened his eyes and looked into Mother's. He took her left hand and placed the palm against his forehead, then he stroked his hand over her eyes, and she closed them. He laid his right palm on her forehead, and they stood in silence. I watched without speaking, hearing the small sounds Sianna made as she tended to my father.

Finally Keilan opened his eyes. He took both of Mother's hands in his and folded them together.

"Open your eyes, Tianis," he said. He led her to Father's bedside, then stepped back and glanced at the door. Without speaking, I opened the door, and Keilan and I went out into the passage. With guards still at each approach to Father's room, it was the closest thing to privacy nearby.

"What happened?" I asked. "What did you do?"

"This is not an ill I have seen before," he said. "If she came to live among us, we would drive her out."

"Grandfather already has," I said.

"It's a darkness within her, like the mists in the bog. She has been holding to it hard, for an image she sees in it." He cocked his head at me. "Can it be your sister? She thinks it is her daughter, but—"

"My sisters take after Mother, at least, Adana does, and Orla did, before she died. I look like Father's family."

He smiled a little.

"I was confused," he said. "I thought the daughter she sought in the mists would resemble you."

"No," I said. "I'm the odd one. But could you—did you help her?"

"I did what I could," he said. "I was able to show her that what she sought was not there, and only dark and illusion."

"Will that help?"

"I hope so," he said. "I am sorry, niece, but I can't force her will. She will be lost in that place all her life if she chooses to cling to it. If she can accept that her daughter is gone, she can heal and come back to you. She may never be as she was. There will always be a scar."

"And Father?"

"I have removed what I put on him. He should mend as men do. His scars will be in his skin and bones, not in the heart and mind."

Sianna joined us in the passage.

"Thank you," she said to Keilan. "Tir is a good man, and a good king. I'm glad we could save him."

"Sianna sent me to find you," I said.

"Did she so? That was a long chance, and a dangerous one," Keilan said. "You might have been killed."

"Warulf says it is wyrd," I said. "I'll die sometime anyway."

"So will your father," he said, "but you would not let it be today."

"No," I said. "And thank you. Even if you only did it for Willow."

"Was she right, that there is a place here for us?"

"Yes," I said. "There's always a place here for Willow, and for you. I wasn't happy that she would have to take you as her mate. I thought she should have a choice. She was willing to rescue you as soon as Queen Amala asked. She's brave and good and loyal and—" I stopped, not knowing exactly how to go on.

Keilan frowned and looked aside. "I think I have known her before, met her somehow."

"She was with us at High Moor," I said. "I don't know how close she came to you there."

"Before that. She came close to me—twice, I think. Once not long ago, once in the air. I tried both times to reach her, but she fled me."

I remembered Willow flying away, trailing darkness from the ends of her feathers.

"Was that you, when the bog tried to slap her out of the air?"

"Did I so? I didn't know I would hurt her. All I wanted was to reach her. I thought she was Falera."

"And after that, was she on the ground? Near the edge of the bog?"

"Yes, on the ground. I reached out to her there." He tilted his head. "You were there, I think. I didn't see you at first, but when I reached out, there you were."

"The bog flooded the ground where we stood," I said. "Did you do that? To reach Willow?"

"I believe so," he said. His face was solemn. "She brought me out of a living nightmare, one I could not escape by waking, or by dying. Were she a grandmother with ragged feathers and a bad temper, I would be glad still to honour and serve her the rest of her days. Have no fear for Hwaelew." He put a finger under my chin and smiled at me. "Before I became a monster I was accounted not a bad king, nor a bad mate. I suppose I will get used to being no longer a king."

"When I saw you at High Moor," I said, "you seemed taller than Father. Now you're Tuan's height."

"I told you there was illusion in mist and darkness," he said, still smiling. "Perhaps that is why monsters don't come in daylight." He looked up and down the passage and at the stone ceiling overhead. "I would like to go back to my sister's realm," he said, "but I don't know how to reach—ah!" His cloak faded a little around the edges, and then he was gone.

"How long was I away?" I asked Sianna.

"Two and a half days," she said.

"Did Father wake up?"

"No," she said. "I've done everything I could to take away the weight of the magic, little as that was. All his energy and will went to fighting it, and he had none left to wake. Yesterday morning, Dar came to see the king. He told me privately that you'd left at noon the day before. He said no bog-walker would touch you, but he worried that you'd fall in and drown."

"He's as bad as a mother hen," I said.

"I'm sure he'd be a happier mother hen if he knew you were home."

"I feel a little at a loss," I said. "I did what I went to do, and now—"

"And now you're home, with all the details of running a kingdom waiting for you. If it's a loss of something to do, that won't last long."

"So now everyone can go home again. If I'd known how it was going to turn out, I needn't have uprooted them all to come here."

"If anyone knew how things would turn out, they might do them differently. But then, having done them differently, they might find that events did not fall as they thought, nor turn out as they expected."

"I don't understand that at all," I said. "Anyway, Tuan and Willow are still back there, and Warulf, and his brother—I have to tell you all about that—and the bog-walkers are back to being people now." I remembered the arm at High Moor. "Warulf's brother is the one who lost his arm. I wonder if it changed back to human when he did."

Sianna laughed.

"I'm sure all the lost lambs will come home," she said. "In the meantime, there's a considerable flock here to be looked after."

"We can send them home," I said, and a great weight seemed to lift from me. "Keilan said there would be no more attacks. I believe his word is good. I'll send scouts tomorrow to all the farmsteads to make sure everything's right, and then everyone can go home again."

CHAPTER

THIRTY

Once I was past the guard at the passage to Father's room, there were more people in the castle than I remembered before I left. From the way everyone went about their business with the briefest salute or "Lady" to me, they probably hadn't noticed I was gone.

The autumn evening was turning to darkness when I went to the east gatehouse. The guard on duty sent a messenger to get Dar. He came at a run, and when he reached me, I threw my arms around him.

"Oh, Dar, we did it!" I said.

He gently pushed me away until he held me at arm's length. "All in one piece, I see."

"And not drowned, either."

"I thought wisewomen kept secrets, not spilled them," he said with mock indignation. "But well done, well done indeed. So Tir will heal. Come and tell me about it. Where are your shadows?"

"That's part of the story. They'll be along. But, Dar, we have to send scouts to the farmsteads. The attacks are over, I have the word of the king of the bog-walkers."

"Have you indeed? I want to hear that story. There's a feat of diplomacy Guthric could learn from. Come, I'll send the scouts, and you can tell me about it."

"Stony Ridge and High Moor first. I don't want Gythorn—or Beorn—getting any ideas about crossing our borders."

"And a farmsteader along with each. A familiar eye will see anything out of place. Is that your order, Princess Kiar?"

"Yes, Captain," I said.

He saluted and shouted for a messenger.

There was no lack of volunteers to ride out to the farmsteads. Only the falling dark prevented the scouts from riding out immediately, but the farmsteaders, left to themselves, would have been off at once. They'd have the scouts in their saddles at first light, and lucky to have breakfast first.

Dar and I sat in the west guardhouse where, a few days and a lifetime ago, I had sat with Warulf and sworn him an ally. Dar listened with no interruptions while I told him about our preparations and the walk into the bog. When I told him about Queen Amala's realm in the heart of the bog, his eyebrows rose.

"I know it sounds unbelievable," I said, "but it's true. She's still alive. She's been trying all these years to get her brother out of the bog and bring him back. He was the very first bog-walker, you know."

"You're right," Dar said. "It's hard to believe. Go on."

When I came to the end, to Keilan vanishing from the passage outside my father's room, he whistled long and low and shook his head.

"That is a quest fit for the old songs," he said. "And to think Willow has gone and captured herself a mate from the bog. I look forward to meeting him."

"You will," I said. "But I don't know when. I hope they come back soon. Tuan was injured, too, and I want Sianna to look at him."

"I'm sure a black swan can fix a few scrapes and bruises," Dar said. "and if he's clever, he'll stay put until all the work of getting these wagons loaded up and out of here is done. I'd say a week, and we'll be back to ourselves. You're sure there'll be no more attacks?"

"I am," I said. "All the bog-walkers are human again. Besides, Keilan said they were over, and I believe him."

"If only because Willow wouldn't be happy about it?" Dar asked with a grin.

"That's one reason," I said. "It's going to be strange having a room all to myself."

Dar said nothing, but grinned wider than before, and I went to see Kestrel before going up to bed. It took me a long time to get to sleep, wondering when Queen Amala would send Tuan and Warulf, and Willow and Kielan, back to the castle, and what would become of those who had once been bog-walkers.

In the morning, I went to Father's room before breakfast. He sat on the side of his bed, and Mother was helping him into his shirt. He had both arms in and was pushing his head through when I opened the door.

"How are you feeling today?" I asked.

Mother looked up and then back to fussing with Father's shirt.

"Better," he said. "Which wouldn't need to be much, after the way I've been. Where's the stick?"

Mother handed him a knobbed stick and helped him to his feet. As he came around the end of the bed, I saw his right calf was tightly wrapped, but not splinted. He saw where I was looking.

"Not broken after all, Sianna says," he told me.

"That's good."

"Hurts as badly as if it were. For once I feel for Gythorn. Oh, don't look that way," he said. "I'm not rotting away while I'm still alive. And I'm glad to be out of this bed at last."

"I'm sorry I overstepped," I said. "I never meant to push you out of the way. I only wanted to take the weight and look after everything for you."

"I know you did," he said. "I know." He stroked my hair with his left hand. "Someday you'll have it all to do."

"But not now," I said. "Not while you're still around."

"No, but a little practice was probably good for you," he said. "And you did well."

"Thank you," I said. "Where is Sianna?"

"I don't know," he said. "She's left me in good hands." He patted Mother's arm, and she gave him a small, almost shy smile, but a smile nonetheless.

We walked towards the stairs at Father's pace. Mother stayed close to his side, and I walked on his left. He lurched a little with every step as he leaned on the stick. At the stairs, we slowed more yet, and by the time we came down to the hall, there was sweat on Father's forehead.

"If I break a leg again," he said, "or even do this—whatever I've done—just finish me off, please." He paused and added, "Poor old Cloud.

"I know," I said. "We'll get him buried. There wasn't time when we were leaving."

"What's left of him," Father said. That was the last we ever spoke of Cloud.

Father insisted on threading his way through all the tables and people to the king's traditional place nearest the door. By the time we got there, Nias was laying out breakfast. The bread was still warm enough to send up curls of steam when it was cut.

"I'm glad to see you on your feet again, Sire," Nias said, then turned to Mother. "Good morning, Lady. I hope you slept well."

"Yes, Nias." Mother sounded quiet and calm. When Father was settled, she sat down beside him and put her hand on his arm. Whatever Keilan had shown her, it seemed she was finding her way back. Perhaps helping Sianna to nurse Father had also helped her. I couldn't remember the last time she had sat at breakfast when I was there.

"I wish I knew where Sianna was," I said. "I don't know when Tuan and everyone will be back."

"I'm not sure," Father said. "Where is Tuan? And who is 'everyone'?"

"She's resting," Mother said. It took me a moment to realize she'd actually answered my question.

"Thank you," I said. "Thank you, Mother." I turned back to Father.

"Last night I had Dar send scouts to the farmsteads," I said. "to make sure the attacks were over."

Father raised his eyebrows.

"Not that I doubt Keilan's word," I said. "It seemed sensible, like something you would do. I thought when they came back, we might be able to start sending the farmsteaders home."

"I'm sure they'll be happy to get back," Father said.

"I'd like—if you think it's a good idea—to get Stony Ridge and High Moor back first, because of the border."

"Good idea." Father spooned honey onto the warm bread. "Has there been any word about Gythorn?"

"No, nothing."

"I suppose we should consider that Beorn might step into his father's boots," he said, "before they're even properly empty."

"I was wondering about that myself. But he's had troubles of his own," I said.

"What kind of troubles?" Father asked.

"Attacks, the same as the one at High Moor. Warulf told me about them. Three, maybe four. I think he hasn't time to bother us."

"Then it's not all bad news," Father said. "Tell me what you've been doing, and where Willow and Tuan are. And about the man you brought last night—what was his name?"

"Keilan."

"Ah, yes. Keilan." He touched Mother's hair, with its wide, white streaks. "He must have lived a long time, for his hair to be completely white."

"A very long time," I said. "Did you ever hear the swanfolk's story of the Lost King?"

"Not the whole thing," he said, and patted Mother's hand on his arm. "Only something of it. Tell me."

Over a long, slow breakfast I told him the story. Mother listened, too, truly listened, and even looked directly at me now and then. She hadn't done that much since Orla's death. Then I told them about our journey into the bog, and Queen Amala's realm, and all I had seen when Willow brought Keilan back to himself.

"So we've seen the last of the bog-walkers," Father said when I was finished. "I've heard of them all my life, and never seen them until now. And now they're gone."

"It doesn't mean the bog is safe," I said. "Queen Amala said that there's a power that was there before the bog-walkers, and I suppose it will be there still."

"It may well. One thing sure, though," Father said, "When young Aren comes around again, there will be more for him to make songs of."

"Oh, no!" I said. "One was bad enough. Promise you won't tell."

"I won't have to," Father said. "He'll hear it from any farmstead he stops at, long before he reaches this court. If you don't want songs made, you'll have to stop doing things they make songs of."

"I don't set out to do them." I remembered Warulf, grinning as he went back into the bog to fight against long odds. "But I know someone who'll be pleased if there's a song, so that's all right."

"I'm going to take a walk," Father said. "I've been lying down for far too long. For now, I don't care if I never lie down again, although I imagine I'll think differently tonight."

"I'd like to ride down to the bog," I said. "I want to see where the water is, and if anyone is on the way back. I don't know when Tuan and Warulf might be coming, or Willow and Keilan. Is that all right, Father?"

"I managed for a few years before you were born," he said. "I think I can manage for a few hours now."

Shortly after, I rode out through the gate and down the dun. The wind was brisk, but the sun warmed my shoulders as I rode. I let Kestrel walk; there was no hurry. Time was different. Queen Amala said, in the darkest part of the bog, and possibly also in her own realm. We'd been gone two and a half days, and yet it had seemed no more than a single, long day to me.

I tried to imagine that Tuan and the others had not yet slept, that for them it was still yesterday evening. It was difficult to think of, and made my head spin. They might not be back for another two or three days. Maybe they wouldn't even walk back, but come as Amala had sent Keilan and me.

At least I could see if the bog had receded or not. I could pull in the rope we'd tied to the stake. It would be a long job, but the rope was thin, light and well-made, and I should be able to pull it back myself. It would be a shame to lose it.

The mouse-willow by the creek showed ovals of white wood where we'd cut our switches on an angle. The water was still exactly where it had been when Willow, Tuan, Warulf and I had waded in, but the mist that marked the borders of the bog had receded. I left Kestrel by the creek, and she nibbled on the drying grasses while I pulled off my boots and rolled up my trouser legs. The warblers and kingbirds sang their autumn melodies, and it comforted me to hear them.

I waded towards where I remembered Eatha's stakes. There were still a few familiar landmarks—trees and bushes, an ancient, man-high stub of a long-drowned tree. I swished my bare feet more carefully through the water than I'd done in boots only a few days before. Soon enough I spotted the pale, rolling coil of one of Eatha's cords, and almost immediately, I found the stake.

The knot had pulled snug. I found the end leading away to the bog and lifted it out of the water, and immediately felt a surge of doubt. If I pulled this rope back, there would be no way for anyone in the bog to find a safe path out. There were so many to send back. Could Amala send them all, or would they have to walk through the bog? If so, they'd need the rope. For a long time, I stood watching the misty wall of the bog, feeling for any tug, any movement on the rope. I was about to drop it back into the water when I felt the tiniest tremor in the strand between my fingers.

I stared at the long arc from my hand back into the brown water. As I watched, I felt again that tremor, almost a thrumming, that told my fingers someone, or something, was on the other end of the rope.

As I waited, barefoot in the water, far from my horse, I never doubted that it would be Tuan at the other end. When at last the arc down into the water lifted up, and it was clear that someone held the rope inside the concealing mists, my heart beat faster. Then Warulf walked out of the bog. His right hand had been bandaged and he held his spear in it and slid his left along the rope. Behind him came Valtir, and then, one after another, the people who had been bog-walkers.

"Kiar Swan-kin!" Warulf called as soon as he saw me.

"Warulf!" I called back. "Is everyone with you?"

"Ya, ya! Swan girl, too, and her man. And your man!" he bellowed.

He sloshed over to me, and I hugged him out of sheer relief. He muttered something in Noermarken, then stepped back, holding me by the arms and grinning. "They make a song, Kiar Swan-kin," he said. "They make a song of valour of us."

"They will indeed." I turned to Valtir. "Is it good to be back?" Warulf translated, and Valtir grinned even more widely than his brother.

"Ya," he said. "Goot."

I counted the people as they came out; beside Valtir, there were twenty-seven who had once been bog-walkers. Then, at the end of the line came Willow, with Kielan behind her. Willow wore a coil of rope on her shoulder, and looped each new length of rope into the coil as she walked. Behind Kielan, with sword and spear, walked Tuan. I waded as quickly as I could to him. He managed to get his sword sheathed before putting his arms around me.

I held him close and kissed his ear, which was what I could reach. "I'm glad you're safely back," I said.

"So am I," he answered, then pulled me away far enough to give me a proper kiss. "Let's go home."

CHAPTER

THIRTY-ONE

We must have been a sight as we came over the last hill before the dun. I heard the guards on the walls but couldn't hear what they said. As we crested the rise and walked down to the base of the dun, we were a ragtag lot. We had one horse and a few spears, and most of us were too busy looking at the grass and trees and sky, and the few remaining faded asters, to seem very warlike at all.

When I came to the gate, Kerliss saluted me.

"Lady," he said.

"Kerliss, please send a message to the king. Tell him that we have guests from Noermark and other places. We ask permission for them to come in, food, and a place to sleep."

"Yes, Lady," he said, and called for a messenger. When the message was sent he turned to me. "Begging your pardon, but the only place we've got to put them is the west guardhouse.

There aren't any empty stalls. Half the horses sleep in the paddock as it is."

"The west guardhouse will do," I said. "As long as we have enough blankets."

"Blankets will be no trouble," Kerliss said.

In a few minutes, the messenger was back.

"Lady, the king says your guests are welcome, and to bring them to the hall."

In the hall, a space had been cleared, large enough to hold all of us, but not much more. At the front, Father sat on his carved throne with Mother on his right. To his left, my throne had been set out. Father was wearing his crown, a circlet of gold set with garnets. This was going to be very formal.

I leaned towards Tuan. "Can you take charge?"

"Yes," he said.

I took my place beside Father.

Tuan stepped forward and knelt. Immediately everyone but Keilan knelt, and he, too, finally followed, folding gracefully beside Willow. He's getting used to not being a king, I thought.

"Welcome home, Tuan," Father said. "Welcome home, Willow. Stand and tell us of your companions."

Willow and Tuan exchanged a quick look, and he nodded his head slightly. She took Keilan by the hand and stepped forward.

"Sire, this is Keilan of the swanfolk, once the Lost King and now my mate," she said. "We would like to make our home here, if it please you."

"It does please me, foster-daughter. I look forward to hearing this story. Keilan, if you are my foster-daughter's husband, you are welcome here."

"Thank you, Sire," Willow said, and Keilan echoed her. They stepped aside and Tuan waved Warulf forward.

"This is Warulf of Noermark," Tuan said, "sworn ally of Princess Kiar."

"I have heard of this," Father said. "You came uninvited, but my daughter tells me you have done good service to us."

Tuan went on. "This is his brother, Valtir. These others have lately been—" He hesitated. "They have been in captivity and are newly released. I do not know all their names, Sire."

"What do they want of us?"

"Only food and a bed. Many of them want to return home as soon as they may."

"We will grant this," Father said. "Warulf of Noermark, come here."

My heart jumped. Even if Father had forgiven me, there was no saying what he felt about having his former enemy here. Warulf came forward, bowed slightly, and touched his fist to his breast. I didn't dare look past Father to see Mother's reaction, but I heard no sound of movement from her.

"My daughter's sworn ally," Father said.

"Ya, so," Warulf said. "Her ally, your ally."

"I've sworn no oath with you."

"Na, Sire," he said. "but your tochter, Kiar Swan-kin, your ally, na? Her ally, my ally."

"Kiar Swan-kin." Father looked at me.

I looked back, not blinking. I couldn't tell if he was amused or offended by the name. I wasn't sure which would be worse.

He turned back to Warulf. "So you will not be going back to Noermark?"

"Na, Sire. Valener, now, or outlaw."

"Well, then. Will you swear to me as a true Valenian?"

"Ya, Sire." He drew his sword and offered it hilt-first to Father, then knelt. Father held the sword across his hands and made to stand, then remembered his leg and leaned forward where he sat.

"Warulf of Noermark, do you swear to be loyal to me and mine, to fight for Valenia and her king and to forswear all other loyalties save family alone?"

"I oath to you, King Tir. I oath to Valenia. No more of Noermark."

"That will do, I think," Father said. "Then take your sword from me, Warulf of Valenia, and use it well."

Warulf received his sword back, stood, and sheathed it. He bowed to Father, and to me, and returned to stand by Valtir. Although this was the second time he had forsworn his oath to Gythorn, his face showed no trace of emotion.

"As for the rest," Father said, "You are welcome to rest here until you leave for your own lands, as long as you do not disturb our peace. Tuan, take them over there." He waved towards the south wall of the hall. "Nias will feed them."

"Thank you, Sire," Tuan said.

Father reached for the stick leaning against the arm of his throne and stood up. Mother stood, too, watching Father, but calm and quiet. The change in her, her willingness to be close to so many people and her attention to Father, heartened me.

As Tuan led the group to the tables Nias had prepared, Father turned to me.

"Thank you for accepting Warulf," I said. "We knew something of what to expect in the bog because of him. When Willow brought Keilan back, Tuan couldn't have held all the bog-walkers off by himself."

"Good," Father said.

"You've made your point, I think," I said.

"It's not for you," he said. "It's for them. Does them good to know there's someone in charge, with all the trappings. Doesn't do your status any harm, either. If those men are going back to Noermark, they'll see that you're a princess with a princess's honours done you." He looked me up and down. "Even dressed in leathers and smelling of horse. I'm lucky you're not barefoot."

"Thank you, Father," I said, and meant it.

"Hmph. Thank you for sending the message. You should have seen them run to get this cleared and the thrones out."

"I wanted to make a point, too," I said.

"Well, you've made it. And now I'll thank you to sort out your guests and what they want to do. Having made my point, as you say, I'll leave the work to you."

He turned away, and Mother went with him, close to his side. People cleared a way for them to pass through the hall and to the bottom of the stairs. Father leaned on his stick with every step, but his back was straight. Mother stayed by his side, though I could see he didn't need to lean on her. I hadn't seen her with him so much since Orla's death.

Father might not ride for a while, but he wasn't dying, either of magic or rotting while he lived, as Gythorn was doing. If his injury and the time she had spent at his bedside had brought Mother closer to Father again, his injury wasn't altogether a bad thing.

I went over to my guests, as Father had called them, and slid onto the bench beside Tuan at one end of the table. The Valenians, or at least the folk dressed like Valenians, gave me the salute due the heir. The folk dressed as Noermarkers nodded. Halfway down the table, the two strangers with braided hair touched their right hands to their foreheads and mouths and held their palms towards me. It seemed respectful, so I nodded back.

"What now?" Tuan asked.

I lifted my chin towards the far end of the table, where Valtir and Warulf were having a heated discussion in Noermarken. "What are they talking about?" I asked. "Nothing good, from the look of it."

He shrugged. "Valtir wasn't happy about Warulf swearing to the king."

"I don't suppose he would be," I said. "He probably wants to go home."

"And take Warulf with him," Tuan said.

"Where are Willow and Keilan?" I asked.

"Flying," Tuan said. "He hasn't flown for five hundred years or more. They'll be back at dark. It's too cold to sleep on the lake now."

"Where they'll sleep here I don't know," I said. "We'll have beds in the passages."

"Nias will find somewhere for them," Tuan said.

I sighed. "I should talk to all of these people after they've eaten. I suppose the Valenians can go back to their own farmsteads. We should send everyone else home as soon as possible. The scouts left early this morning. We can expect to hear back about High Moor and Stony Ridge tomorrow night or the next morning."

"A few days yet, then," Tuan said.

The hall bustled with people even in the middle of the day. Someone had cleared the thrones away, and three little boys ran across the hall and into the open space, squabbling and yelling at some game with wooden swords. A woman shouted, "Go outside to play!" and as they ran through the hall, she followed up with, "Close the door!"

"Maybe we can start Stony Ridge and High Moor packing up tomorrow," I said.

"You should see your face," Tuan said.

"I don't remember it being so loud when we were children."

"Not as many," Tuan said, "and not as crowded."

"Eleven Noermarkers," I said, "and none of them armed. They can go back with Stony Ridge and High Moor. I'll have some of my guard go along to take them to the border."

"And the other two?"

I looked down the table at the grasslanders.

"I suppose I'd better talk to them first. I have no idea how we'll understand each other." I thought for a minute. "I have to get something. When they're done eating, bring them to me in the council chamber."

Tuan nodded. Under the table his hand found mine and squeezed it.

When Tuan brought the man and woman to me, I was as prepared as I could be. I'd had wine and four cups brought in and placed on a small side table. The map, made long ago of a single piece of parchment from one bull, covered most of the square central table.

Immediately on entering, both touched their eyes and foreheads again and held their right hands palm-out towards me.

"Sit down, please," I said, indicating the chairs.

They sat with their legs crossed and hands laid on their thighs. The woman was perhaps a few years older than I was, the man older again, but still young. She had gathered her many dark-brown braids together and tied them in a knot at the back of her head. The man had left his braids to hang over his back and shoulders.

I put my hand on my own chest.

"I am Kiar," I said. "Kiar." I pointed to Tuan, who was pouring wine. "Tuan," I said. I held my hand out to the woman. "What is your name?"

She said something, a long string of sound that meant nothing to me.

"Kiar," I said again, and held my hand out to her once more.

"Lee-ah-tah," she said.

"Lee-ah-tah," I repeated, and she smiled and said it again. "Liatah. Kee-aw-ah."

"Kiar, yes. And Tuan." Tuan handed me a cup of wine, and then one to Liatah.

"Tuwan," the man said as he took his cup from Tuan. Then he placed his hand on his own chest. "Way-lowse," he said. "Waylos. Keeaw." He said my name with a little breathy sound at the end, not quite the "ah" that Liatah had said.

"Waylos. Good. Now," I leaned over the map and put my finger on Valenia, on the drawing of the castle. "We are in here, in Valenia." I pointed around the room and put my finger again on the castle. "Here. Where is your home?"

I pushed the map towards them.

Immediately they began to talk very fast and point at various places on the map. Waylos laid his hand on Valenia and looked at me, pointing around the room with his finger.

"Yes," I said, "Valenia."

"Valeen-ya," he said, and grinned.

"Where are you?" I asked and swept my hand over the map.

Now he and Liatah bent their heads together. Then Liatah put her hand on the far eastern side of the map, past Eastenstead, past the arm of forest that embraced it to the east. "Sawahey." She pointed to Waylos, and herself, and then to the place on the map.

"Sawahey," she said again.

"The eastern grasslands," I said to Tuan. "This might be the first time any of them has been in Valenia."

I laid a blank piece of parchment over the map and drew a horse, then passed it across the table. Liatah smiled at me and nodded her head vigorously, then began to talk, spreading her arms wide and then making running motions on the tabletop with her fingers.

"A lot of horses, is that right?" I put my finger on my drawing and then tapped it across the page.

"Ayah!" Then she held out her hand and I gave her the pen. It scratched and spattered, but the animal she drew was definitely a cow with wide horns and a shaggy coat. Then she made the same spreading gesture. Waylos did it as well, two or three times.

"A lot of horses, and a lot of cattle," I said. took back the parchment and drew two more horses and two riders with many braids. I pushed it back to Liatah, then put my finger on the castle and traced a straight path to the eastern grasslands.

"Sawahey sa?" Liatah said.

"Yes," I said. "Sawahey sa. You're going home." Both of them made the palms-out gesture again, and Liatah held her hands up, fingers spread.

"Liatah," she said, wiggling the fingers of one hand. "Keeaw-ah," as she wiggled the fingers of the other. Then she folded her hands together, fingers interlaced. "Hama." she said.

"Waylos, Tuwan," Waylos said, repeating Liatah's gesture. "Hama." I leaned over the table and put my hand on Liatah's folded ones. "Friends," I said. Then I put my hand on Waylos' hands and said "Friends." He bowed his head to me, then looked at Tuan.

Tuan came around the table and put his hand over Waylos', and over Liatah's and mine, still joined.

"Friends."

After Liatah and Waylos had left, I wrote *Sawahey* underneath "Eastern Grasslands" on the map. I put down on the parchment all the words they'd used that we had meanings for.

"What are you going to do?" Tuan asked me.

"First, talk to Father," I said, "and then give them horses. I want them to think of us as friends. These two are the first I've ever met."

"Ever?" Tuan said. "There are many. We see them when we fly to and from the winter grounds."

"They've never come to our borders," I said. "And we don't know where their farmsteads are."

"They don't have any. They move all the time, north to south, as the swanfolk do."

"No farmsteads at all?"

He shook his head. "They live in tents and move from place to place. The grasslands are many times larger than Valenia."

I wondered if, somewhere far back, we might have known the grasslanders and forgotten that bond. Perhaps I could visit the grasslands someday, try to make a new bond with Liatah's and Waylos's people.

If that ever happened, I thought "hama" might be a useful word to know.

THIRTY-TWO

The rest of the afternoon I spent on my throne in the middle of the hall, with Tuan sitting beside me. After several hours, I'd spoken to all the Valenians and Noermarkers who had once been bog-walkers. Once I had names for the Valenians, I sent for someone from each farmstead.

Rheann rushed to throw her arms around a man younger than her son and called him by name. "Terrec, it's Rheann!" she said. "It's me, your wife!" She laughed and cried at once and raised her face to kiss him, but he stood stunned, and only slowly put his arms around her.

"Rheann?" he said. "I—you were—how did you grow so old?"

Her face fell.

"Time," she said. "Time is all. You've been gone for years, Terrec. We thought you were dead."

"I didn't know," he said.

"No, of course not." Rheann wiped her eyes and took her young husband's hand. "Come and meet your son." As she led him away, he looked around at the people in the hall. I wondered how many of his friends had died, and how many would truly be glad to see him, still young when they were old.

Some of the Valenians had been gone so long they remembered my grandfather as a boy, and his grandfather still on the throne. As each was claimed by someone from his farmstead, I saw again and again that lost and bemused look on their faces.

"I don't envy them," I said to Tuan.

"Some would say they were lucky to come back at all," he said.

"They haven't come back, not really. Whatever place they had, others have taken. Their families have grown and changed. Maybe the luckiest are the ones who've lost everyone they knew. They can start fresh, with people who are strangers to them. Poor Rheann, and poor Terrec."

When the last of the Valenians had gone from the hall, I called Warulf to translate when I spoke to the Noermarkers. When they assembled, they began to talk all at once to him. It took him some time to calm them down. Finally he turned to me and saluted, fist on his heart in the Noermarker fashion. There was a mutter among the Noermarkers, and he snapped something back before repeating his salute.

"Kiar Swan-kin," he said. "These men ask to go home."

"Tell them they're free to do so," I said. "We will see them to the border and provide them with food and blankets for the rest of their journey."

When he translated my words, one of the Noermarkers said something I could tell was derisive. Before Warulf could answer, Valtir took the man by the shirt-front and shook him, speaking angry words. The man turned back to me, fist on heart, and muttered an apology.

"Hard for them, Kiar Swan-kin," Warulf said. "This one thinks you flyte to them. Valtir say he is stupid, maybe rather be fen-stalker."

"I don't understand 'flyte'," I said, and he mimed pointing and laughter.

"Ah," I said.

"This one, this one, this one," Warulf said, as he pointed to three young men. "These boys very old, long, long away. Trey hunder' year, I think. Wicks," He put his head on one side and then said, "Farrumwicks they know, some gone."

"Their home farms are gone?"

"Ya," he said. "Others, not so long. Valtir the last."

"And how long has he been gone?" I asked.

"Fift' year. He called me 'eldfader'."

"I know," I said. "I'm sorry, Warulf."

"Wyrd, na? These have no home, no kin," he said. "but dead, or old, like me. And no trust to you, Kiar Swan-kin. For them, Valenia and Noermark—" He made two fists and pressed them together. "No home here. Maybe no home in Noermark, but they ask to go."

"If they want to go to Noermark, they can. Tell them three days from now they will be on their way. Until then, they are my guests. Will that do?"

"Ya," he said. "Guest-bond is good." He hesitated, and then said, "Kiar Swan-kin, I ask a boon."

"What is it?" I said.

"I ask min broder to stay, oath to you. But first, ask you. Will you oath to Valtir?"

"Swear him an ally?"

"Ya, so."

"Warulf, why would your brother want to stay here when he could go back to Noermark? Here he would have to learn a new language, and our ways of doing things."

Warulf tucked his thumbs into his belt and shifted his feet before he answered. "Lady, my king is mad. Killed a kenningman. These men," he said, jerking his head at the Noermarkers, "are unkent."

"I don't understand. What is 'unkent'?"

"Unkent," he said. "not know. From fen, na? Unkent, not—not kin, not—" He struck himself twice on the chest with his open palm.

"Strangers?"

"Na, na. like fen-stalkers, fen-sprites. Unkent." He held up his hands, curved into claws and made a snarling face.

"Monsters," I said. "Warulf, they're only men!"

"Fen-stalkers, now men. Maybe still fen-stalkers, here." He tapped his chest.

"You know they're men."

"Ya, Lady." He sounded tired. "Ya, men. But my king, he think not. May be so."

"Gythorn has counsellors, advisors."

Warulf snorted.

"King says kill, who say na? Killed a kenningman, kill them. These men are unkent. Dead long ago, na?"

"I see," I said, and I did. Maybe Gythorn would let the men live, if they could find their way back to their home farms, and if they didn't come to his attention. If they did, they might be monsters yet, and at least they should have been dead years before.

"You ask me to take Valtir," I said. "What of the others?"

He shrugged.

"Not my kin, Lady. Wyrd, na?"

"Warulf, you understand I must ask the king before I do that. I will give you an answer tomorrow. But if he approves, then, yes, I will swear Valtir as my ally, and he will be welcome to stay."

"My thanks, Lady," Warulf said.

"I've arranged the west guardhouse as a place for them to sleep. They can take meals there as well if they prefer, but someone will have to come and get the food from the hall."

"Ya, so." Warulf saluted me again and then spoke a few brusque sentences to the Noermarkers. Each of them gave me at least a sketchy salute before leaving the hall.

"I could sleep for a week," I said. "And I've done almost nothing. One ride down to the bog and a walk back."

"And a great deal of being a princess," Tuan said.

"Yes. I hope the Noermarkers will be all right. Three hundred years away! They won't know anyone."

"Maybe that's best, as you said."

"Maybe. I keep thinking that, well, Gythorn might have them killed. They're strangers to him. The only one he might know is Valtir, and he's young. When he should be old. And Warulf says Gythorn is mad."

Tuan shook his head and smiled.

"What?" I asked.

"You know what Warulf would say to that," he said.

"'Wyrd, na?' and go anyway?"

"Yes. Besides, they must have enough sense to keep out of Gythorn's way." He took my hands and pulled me up off the throne. "Let's get something to eat and then take a walk before it's completely dark."

When we went outside the walls, the eastern sky was darkening quickly, and the wind was brisk enough that I was glad of my cloak and its sheepskin collar. We walked around to the northwest side of the wall, where the large paddock stood. A dark-grey plough horse stretched his head over the fence and whickered.

"You'll be going home soon," I said as I stroked the velvety skin between his nostrils.

"There they are," Tuan said, looking to the west. Two birds, far enough away that I couldn't have said what they were, flew directly towards the castle.

"I promised Mother we would fly once the flock had left," I said. "I still haven't kept that promise. We should do it tomorrow. I'll ask her tonight when I talk to Father about Valtir."

Tuan nodded.

"Everything is so different," I said. "A year ago, we were all together still. Mother was herself, and Gil and Adana were here, and—" I stopped.

"But Willow and I are still here," Tuan said, "and the queen seems better than she was before the king was injured."

"I thought that, too," I said. "I'm glad you noticed. She must really be better then."

"Water and sky," Tuan said. He put his arm around me and kissed my hair.

"What does that mean?"

"Only the water and the sky are forever."

"Is that something swans say?"

"When we think of it. But even the water and sky don't stay the same. If they did, we wouldn't have summer grounds and winter grounds."

"Warulf and his wyrd, Willow taking a mate she's never met almost on impulse, and now you and the water and sky never staying the same. Am I the only one who isn't happy about change?"

Tuan turned to me, smiling. "I remember when you couldn't wait for change."

"That was different, getting my wings. That was a good change. One I wanted. I want things to go back as they were, before all this. And they won't.

"Things never were as you remember them," he said. "You forget the bad parts. And if we went back to a year ago, everything would have to be done again. You know that, Kiar."

"I know," I said. "I know. I feel as though I've lost something, and I don't know what."

He put his arm around me. "But you've gained something, too. The king knows it, and so do your people. You'll be a good queen."

"I don't feel very queenly," I said.

"Ask the king if he ever feels kingly," Tuan said. "I might do it myself."

"You wouldn't dare!" I laughed at the thought of Tuan asking my father, quite seriously, if he ever felt kingly. "Tuan, you really couldn't!"

"It would be easier than some other things I might ask," he said.

"What things?" I asked, still laughing.

"If you and I might marry at the midwinter festival," he said.

I stopped laughing. I forgot to breathe. He turned me to face him, his hands on my shoulders. He looked solemn, almost worried. "Kiar," he said. "I thought you wanted that, too."

"I do," I said, "Oh, Tuan, I do. Everything has been so wild. All the changes—I sometimes think I'll never get my breath back."

"And the king expects us to say something."

"Yes," I said, "I suppose he knows, but we do need to tell him formally."

"Tonight?"

"Yes," I said, "yes, yes!" I threw my arms around Tuan and the plough horse shied away, snorting. Then we were kissing, and laughing and kissing again.

When we stopped, it was almost full dark. The guard on the walls were lighting the torches. I found the Chariot in the sky —four stars to make the body, and three for the shafts.

"Remember the harvest festival?" I said. "when we stood looking at the stars? I thought you were restful to be with."

"Restful," he said. "Thank you."

"I mean I could be myself with you."

"Who else would you be? Would I wake up one day and find you'd turned into Nias? Or Rheann?"

"No! I mean I didn't have to pretend to be brave, or wise, when I wasn't."

"You never have to pretend to be brave," Tuan said. "But I'll have to, if I'm asking the king to agree to our marriage."

"He's not a dragon." I slipped my arm around his waist, and he pulled me close.

"Then why does he scare me more than a bog-walker?"

"Maybe you need to take a sword with you," I said.

"Maybe I do."

"Did you want to go and ask him now?" I asked.

"No," he said. He took my hand and swung me around, and we continued on our walk. "I've waited this long. I can wait until we get around the wall and back in."

CHAPTER

THIRTY-THREE

Inside, the tables in the hall had been taken down and stacked against the walls, and people were laying out blankets and pillows for the night. Most of the children were already lying down. From up the stairs to Mother's solar we could hear one baby still fussing.

Willow and Keilan sat at the bottom of the stairs to the men's and women's rooms. When they saw us, they got up. Willow had found clothes for Keilan, trousers and a linen shirt he hadn't bothered to tuck in. He was barefoot on the stone floor in the last month of autumn.

"Aren't your feet cold?" I asked.

"A little," he said. "But I felt almost nothing for so long. Even cold stone is good."

"You'll change your mind on that in a few weeks."

"Yes, Hwaelew has been telling me about winter. Most strange."

"You'll like it," Willow said. "I love it. And I'll teach you to ride."

"Kiar," Keilan said, "I owe you thanks. It was Hwaelew who brought me out of the bog, but it was you who brought Hwaelew in to get me."

"I'm glad I did," I said. "I don't think you'd have come to help Father otherwise, do you?"

"Most unwillingly," he said. "Perhaps you could have dragged me out at the end of a rope?"

For a moment we all stood silent, then Keilan's lips twitched, and Willow sputtered into laughter.

"Oh, Kiar, the look on your face!" she said. "What did you think?"

"I am a mortal being now," said Keilan. "No longer a tale to frighten children."

"If you're mortal, you'll need somewhere to sleep," I said. "Willow, you can have our room. I'll sleep in the council chamber."

"Thank you," she said. Keilan opened his mouth and closed it again.

"There's a carpet," I said to him, "and I've slept on harder ground on patrol."

"But you are royalty and—" he said.

"And you can't argue with royalty," I said. "Isn't that right, Willow?"

"Yes," she said, and grinned. She tugged on Keilan's hand and led him up the stairs. Tuan and I followed. A few steps up Willow looked back at us.

"Is there something I don't know?" she asked. "Tuan, you're not allowed up here."

"I have to speak to the king," he said.

Willow raised her eyebrows. "Oh," she said. "Good luck."

Tuan frowned at her, and she laughed.

"Oh, Tuan," she said. "I've been wondering for months when you were going to speak to the king! Everybody in the whole castle has known for years that you love Kiar. It's no secret, so you can stop scowling. If you use that face on the king he'll kick you downstairs!"

"He's not the only one who's nervous," I said. My hands felt damp, and now that we were on the verge of making everything formal, I felt a flutter of anxiety.

"You don't need to be nervous," Willow said. She dropped Keilan's hand and came back down the stairs. She hugged me and kissed my cheek, and then did the same to Tuan.

"I'm happy that you're going to speak to him at last," she said. "Go on and get it done, then." She skipped back up the stairs to Keilan and the two of them continued up.

We let them get well ahead and then followed. We passed the guard at the passage to Father's room.

"Good evening, Lady, Lord Tuan," the guard said. "He's still awake. The queen and the wisewoman are with him."

"Thank you," I said. I tapped on the door to Father's room.

"Come in," Father called.

I glanced at Tuan, and he nodded and squeezed my hand. I pushed the door open, and we went in.

Sianna was washing her hands in the basin, and Mother pulling Father's trouser leg down over a fresh bandage.

"How are you feeling?" I asked before anyone else could speak.

"I'm well," he said.

"That leg looks swollen," Sianna told me. "He spent a lot of time lying down, and that is not good."

"Five days," Father said. "You talk as though I was in bed for a year."

"Nevertheless," Sianna said, "you need to be up and about as much as you can, in spite of the pain."

"I will see to it," Mother said, so softly I almost didn't catch her words. I looked at Sianna, and she opened her eyes wide and then winked at me. She slipped out of the room and closed the door gently behind her.

"Do you two have something to tell me?" Father asked. He glanced at our linked hands, but his face was perfectly serious.

"*I* have something to ask you," I said. I let go of Tuan's hand and went to stand in front of Father.

"Warulf has asked me if I'll swear his brother as an ally. I said I was willing, but it depended on what you said."

"A second Noermarker in the ranks," Father said. "Hmph. He'll have to learn Valenian. That will be your responsibility, to see he gets instruction. So he wants to join his brother rather than go home?"

"Warulf wanted to find out if we were willing before he spoke to Valtir about it. It's obviously his idea, not Valtir's. He's worried about what's waiting for the Noermarkers when they go back. He thinks Gythorn might kill them. He isn't the man he was."

"No," Father said. "A dying king is one thing, but a mad one? I wouldn't run back to that in a hurry."

"Warulf says that if the others go back, it's their choice. They're not his kin. But Valtir is, so he has asked if we'll take him."

Father sighed.

"If he's willing to forswear Noermark and swear to you, then you can take him," he said.

"And the man and woman with braided hair, they're from the eastern grasslands. They call it Sawahey. I'd like to give them horses to go back. I think if we did that, they'd look at us as friends."

"They should look at you as a friend already," Father said. "They'd still be attacking our farmsteads and getting cut to pieces if not for you."

"But they don't know that. I wasn't there in my body when they were changed back. They saw Tuan, Willow, and Warulf. But if we give them horses, that is a bond directly with us."

"They may not be welcome back any more than Warulf thinks the Noermarkers will be," Father said.

"Maybe not," I said, "but if they are, then we have friends there, allies. Isn't it worth risking two horses for that?"

"We're going to have to call you Kiar of the Many Allies," Father said.

"So I can give them horses? And food for the journey?"

He flapped his hand at me. "You have it all figured out," he said. "What do you need my word for?" His voice was growly, but he smiled. "Go on, then. Is that all?"

"Not quite," I said.

Tuan came to stand beside me and then, to my complete astonishment, he knelt in front of Father. "Sire," he said, "I am not royalty among my own people. What I ask would be impossible among the swanfolk, but here I hope it is possible. Will you agree to marry your daughter Kiar to me at midwinter?"

There was a silence that seemed to stretch on forever. Tuan's gaze was fixed on Father's neck, as though he didn't dare look at his face. I could see from the way Father's moustache curled that he was amused at Tuan's formality. He reached for Mother's hand.

"Well, now," Father said. "Shall we agree to this?"

"I do not," Mother said.

"What?" It came out louder than I'd intended. "Why not?"

"He is not fitting." Mother said. Her face held no expression.

"Tianis, you chose who to foster," Father said. "You chose Tuan."

"What did you think would happen?" I asked. "You put us together, all of us."

"I gave Adana a choice," she said. "That is all."

"I don't believe that," I said. "If that was all, why keep Tuan here? Why bring Willow at all?"

"Tianis, be reasonable," Father said. He pulled on her hand to make her look at him. "Tuan loves Kiar. We all know it. And she loves him. Why are you objecting after all these years?"

Mother said nothing.

Tuan slowly stood up.

"You two go on," Father said.

I turned on my heel and stalked out of the room. I could hardly see through my anger. Once we were in the hall, with the door between us and my parents, I said, "This is because of Orla. She still blames me for banishing her."

"You don't know that," Tuan said.

"What other reason could it be?"

"Perhaps no reason at all. She was—" he paused, "not well, until a few days ago."

"Mad, you mean. If she's still mad, then Father should take no notice."

He drew me by the hand to the stairs and we started down.

"She's just starting to get better," he said. "The king has missed her while she's been ill. She's only now coming back to him. You can't expect him to do something that would push her away. Maybe in a few days."

"Or a few weeks, or never!"

"Kiar. Be understanding."

"I don't want to be understanding! And I don't want you to be so reasonable!"

"You want me to be angry, too?"

"Yes!"

At the bottom of the stairs he took my hands in his. "I would be angry if I could," he said. "But the king and the queen—their word is law. Among us, the swanfolk, we can't argue or question. Not 'don't', Kiar—we can't. I can't be angry. It's not how we are."

"You were angry at me when you caught up with me in Noermark," I said.

"That was different. You were in danger and I—" He paused. "Was afraid for you. And I love you."

We stood silently for a few moments. I tried to remember if Tuan had ever before said that he loved me.

"It will be all right," he said. "Not as soon as we wanted, that's all."

I nodded. Somehow, even through the anger and the disappointment, I felt a little bit better.

"Willow and Keilan," I said. "We should have some kind of celebration for them."

"Why?" Tuan asked.

"Well, because it's all happened suddenly, and it's not at all romantic. I mean, Gil and Adana were in love for years, and Willow and Keilan just met, and now they're mates."

"Like a song." Tuan smiled. "The princess rescues the prince, and they marry and live happily ever after."

"Oh, yes," I said. "I'm sure Aren will find that very romantic when he comes back around. Of course, he wasn't there watching you and Warulf getting bruised and cut about." Tuan grinned at me and the skin around the fresh cut on his cheekbone wrinkled.

"Two valiant men fighting against terrible odds," he said.

I stuck out my tongue. "I sometimes think this whole family is here simply to provide songs for him to write."

"You could stop doing things he can sing about," Tuan said.

"It never seems to be song-worthy at the time. But we should have a feast or something for Willow and Keilan."

"Swanfolk don't make the same kind of ceremony over taking a mate," Tuan said.

"They're not going to be in swan form while they're living here. And it seems too simple."

"Right now I think I'd prefer simple," Tuan said. "I'd think you would, too. We both hate being the centre of attention. And yet you keep doing things that make it happen."

That night when I went to Father's council chamber, I found that someone had made up a comfortable bed for me on the floor, and had left me a basin and ewer of water, as I would have had in my own room. When I lay down, all my anger at Mother for refusing to let me marry Tuan rose up again, and I didn't think I could sleep. But my body had other ideas.

Tarin, who had gone out to scout High Moor and Stony Ridge, came back late that night. The guard on the wall sent someone to wake me, and I went out to the east guardhouse, the only one that didn't have people sleeping in it, to meet with him.

"What did you find?" I asked.

"Nothing, Lady," said Tarin. "High Moor was as we left it. They'll need to bury your father's horse, even with the cold, but there's nothing to say those things ever came back after we left."

"And Stony Ridge?"

"Shut up tight and nothing to show any visitors," he said. "There wasn't a sign that someone had come looking, and not a mark on the walls."

"Well done," I said.

"Is it true what they're saying, Lady?" Tarin asked. "That there's no more bog-walkers, and never will be again? And their king was a swan, and Lady Willow changed him back?"

"I don't know about never again, Tarin," I said. "But, yes, he was one of the swanfolk, and when Willow changed him back, all his folk changed back, too. Now it seems the bog-walkers are gone, and all we have left are some folk going home after many years away."

"It's a wonder," Tarin said, shaking his head.

"It is. Thank you, Tarin." He led his horse away, and I went back to bed. The folk of two farmsteads could be packed up tomorrow and on their way the next morning, along with the Noermarkers who wanted to go home. I'd choose horses for Liatah and Waylos and get them on their way as well. By the end of the week, if the weather held, everyone could be back where they belonged, or as close as possible.

I hoped Nias would enjoy finding everybody's stores as much a she had enjoyed getting them put away.

CHAPTER

THIRTY-FOUR

The next morning, I spoke to Father about getting the folk of High Moor and Stony Ridge back to their farmsteads. Mother was in the room, but I ignored her. After I'd talked to Father, I gave orders for the farmstead folk to be packed up and on their way as soon as they could be. The hall and courtyard were more chaotic still, with wagons out to be reloaded, and Nias and the farmstead women finding their own stores.

I sent for Liatah and Waylos and escaped to the horse paddocks. Folk from High Moor and Stony Ridge were picking their horses out of the herd and taking them to the smaller paddock for the next morning. They moved gently through the animals and talked softly, and after the bustle of the castle and court, the paddock, even crowded with moving horses, seemed calm. I chose two horses from my family's stock, a dappled mare with a black mane and tail, and a bay stallion, both light and fast.

By the time Waylos and I had brought them out of the paddock, Liatah had found some rope and knotted two bridles. They were tied oddly, with slipknots in places where ours were firmly fastened, and they had no bits. Liatah slipped one over the mare's head and adjusted a knot, and Waylos did the same with the stallion.

"They can't ride with those things," one of the farmstead men said. "There's no bit. How will they get them stopped?" He pulled back with his hands as though reining a horse in, and Waylos grinned and swung himself onto the bay. Then he clucked and nudged the horse with his heels, and the bay broke into a trot.

Waylos let him go until he was a little down the slope of the dun and well away from the paddocks, then turned him this way and that with the rein against his neck and set him at a canter up the slope. As he neared the paddock, he pulled back, and the stallion stopped neatly on the spot.

He leaned forward and slipped his fingers under the cheek strap of the bridle. I put my fingers where his were, and he pulled gently on the reins. The whole bridle tightened over the stallion's head and nose and my fingers.

"He stops when you pull," I said. "No bit?" I put my finger across my mouth and Waylos grinned and shook his head.

"Sa," he said, and patted the horse's neck. Down the slope of the dun, Liatah put the grey mare through a few turns and stops, and trotted her back up. I decided to try the same thing with Kestrel; being able to make a bridle at need would be useful. When Liatah dismounted I handed her another piece of rope, and she made a third of those oddly knotted bridles.

Very shortly after, supplied with blankets, a waterskin and food, they walked their horses to the eastern gate. The blankets they spread over the horses' backs; I'd offered saddles, but they had refused.

"Kiaweh, hama," Liatah said, and held up her right hand, fingers spread. She waited, and I put my right palm to hers. Then she twined her fingers in mine. "Hama, wa samlos sawahey ay." She pointed to the sky, and then the earth.

"Hama," I said. "I hope you get safely home, and your people remember you, and welcome you."

"Kiaweh, hama," Waylos said. He held out his hand and clasped mine as Liatah had done. "Tuwan hama, sa," he said.

"I'll tell Tuan you said goodbye," I answered. "Travel safely. Arrive safely."

Then they rode down the dun and away to the east. They never looked back. Whatever they found among the grasslanders at the end of their journey, I hoped it would be a welcome.

The Noermarkers were leaving with the folk of the northern farmstead, but I still had to speak to Warulf about Valtir. I sent for them as soon as Liatah and Waylos had ridden out of sight, and asked them to meet me in the eastern guardhouse.

"Kiar Swan-kin," Warulf said when they arrived. He saluted me in the Noermark fashion, fist on heart, which made me smile. Warulf of Valenia he might be, but there were some things I thought would never change about him.

Valtir also saluted me in that way. "Kiar Swan-kin," he said. Although he didn't know Valenian, he said my name precisely as Warulf had.

"Please, sit down," I said. "Valtir, the king has agreed that I may swear you an ally, as I have your brother, and that you are welcome to stay. He says that you must learn our language; I have no doubt you can."

Warulf spoke at length to Valtir. Halfway through Valtir interrupted him and the two of them argued in short bursts of Noermarken. Then Valtir turned to me and said, "Kiar Swan-kin," and followed with something in Noermarken that I didn't understand, except that at the end he said, quite clearly, "Wyrd, na?" Then he put his right arm on his breast and gave the half-bow that Noermarkers used.

"Lady," Warulf said, "I tell my brother you will oath him. He thanks you, but his oath is to King Gythorn. He is sad that I break my oath. I say to him the king is mad, but—" He shrugged.

"Wyrd, na?" I said.

Valtir smiled and bowed again. "Ya, Kiar Swan-kin. Wyrd."

"Then you are free to leave tomorrow with your countrymen," I said. Warulf translated this, and Valtir rose and bowed again, then left. Warulf watched him out the door, his face wooden.

"Warulf, I'm sorry," I said.

"Min wif will take," he said. "but my king—" He shrugged and smiled, but it was the saddest smile I'd ever seen.

"Did you want to bring your wife here?" I asked. "I will welcome her if she wants to come."

"Na," Warulf said. "She angers that I leave. She will not. But she will take Valtir."

"Will she be in danger for doing that?"

Again he shrugged.

"She will—" He paused and thought for a minute. "She is—" He made two fists and shook them.

"Strong-willed?" I asked.

"Ya. Sword wif, but no sword."

"You miss her," I said. "You gave up a lot to come here for help. Your king should be grateful, Warulf. If it wasn't for you, the fen-stalkers would still be killing Noermarkers."

"My king thanks," he says. "King Tir. Valener now, Kiar Swan-kin."

"You are welcome here, Warulf," I said. "I'm glad you came to me."

"Good you listen, Lady. Thanks to you."

He bowed to me, fist on heart, and then left. I felt sad at how much he'd lost, and how little I could do for him. When he had first come to me for help, I'd hardly thought I could trust him, but now he was a friend. What I'd seen of Hafor's smooth manners and the deceit beneath them had left me warier than ever of Noermarkers. Warulf's rough-spoken honor had changed that.

More scouts came in through the day. Treegirt, Riverbend, Eastenstead, and Near Fellstead were all untouched. Now the courtyard and castle hummed with activity. By the end of the day both Stony Ridge and High Moor had all their wagons loaded and lined up, ready to have the cart horses hitched to them and be on their way at dawn, and folk from the other farmsteads were impatient for their turn.

At breakfast the great hall seemed almost as chaotic as the battlefield at High Moor. People from the two farmsteads dashed here and there—parents after children, children shrieking with excitement, blankets and bundles from the night before lying under benches. As each family left with their blankets to load onto the wagons, the noise faded a little.

Father and Mother sat in their usual places at the king's table, and Tuan and I took seats there, too. Willow came down to join us.

"Where is Keilan?" I asked her.

"He stayed in our room. Too many people," she said. She looked around the hall. "I almost wish I'd stayed, too. But I wanted you to know I haven't abandoned you."

"I wouldn't blame you," I said. "I've never seen this many people at once."

"Like a big flock of crows," Willow said. "But brighter. And noisier. How is your leg today, Sire?"

"Better, Sianna tells me," Father said. "I'm looking forward to giving up this stick. I'm tired of hirpling around like an old man." He turned to Mother. She smiled at him in the way she had always done.

"Not so old," she said. Her voice was quieter than it used to be, and I could barely hear her over the chatter that filled the hall. I was still angry that she had refused to let Tuan and me marry, but it lifted my heart to think that she was coming back to her old self.

"Willow," she said. "You have taken a mate."

"Yes, Lady," Willow said.

"A king," my mother said. "as a woman of your line has done before."

"Yes, Lady," Willow said again. Her voice was low and controlled, and her face was blank, giving away nothing. She put down her bread and honey and folded her hands in her lap.

I glanced at Father, and he was looking from Mother to Willow. I looked at Tuan. He, too, had stopped eating and was watching Mother.

"Have you met him, then, Lady?" he asked.

"Yes, Tuan, I met him when he came to heal Tir," Mother said. She turned back to Willow. "Will you rejoin the flock in their winter grounds?"

"No," I said. "Willow and Keilan will stay here for the winter, Mother." She gave no sign she'd heard me, only kept her eyes fixed on Willow.

"A strong pair could reach the winter grounds now," she said. "You both know the way. The flock is not long gone."

"No," Willow said. "Your father is the Swan King now."

"Cobs fight for place," Mother said. "My father is old, and your mate is still strong. He was king first."

Willow said nothing and kept her eyes on Mother's face.

"Tianis," Father said. She didn't so much as glance at him. I remembered the ripples of magic when Orla cast a spell. I couldn't see anything in the air between Mother and Willow, but something was there, some test of will I didn't understand.

"He could be Swan King again," Mother said. "Why not?"

"He is done with fighting," Willow said.

"Is he?" Again Willow did not respond.

Mother's mouth curved in a smile that made the skin on my nape shiver. "You would be queen," she said.

"Is that what you think I want, Lady?" Willow asked. "Is that why you think I brought Keilan out of the bog? To overthrow the Swan King and take the crown from Adana?" She took a deep breath. "I did it for Kiar, because she's my friend, and her father was dying. Not to be Swan Queen, or any kind of queen at all. I've seen what Kiar has to look forward to, the care and work. Do you think I want that?"

For a moment nobody spoke. Then Willow said, "I'm not Orla, to take what's not mine."

Mother rocked back in her chair and Father half-rose.

"That's enough," he said.

"Keilan doesn't want to be king again. I don't want to be queen," Willow said.

After a moment Mother relaxed, and Father sat down again. The tension was gone. I heard Tuan let out his breath and realized I'd been holding my own.

"Well," I said, when nobody spoke. "We should go and see them off."

"Yes, yes." Father pushed himself up from his chair and walked out of the hall with Mother by his side.

"What was that?" I asked Willow as we got up.

"Something I half expected," she said. "Keilan *was* king, after all, and your mother recognized it when she met him. He told me."

"That was five hundred years ago," I said. "He couldn't expect to go back to it. Could he?"

"He didn't die, and he wasn't defeated by another challenger," Tuan said.

"No, he disappeared and spent five hundred years as a bog-walker. The first bog-walker."

"There's nothing about that in the lore," Tuan said. "A king is a king."

I shook my head.

"I heard Valtir is leaving," Willow said.

"Yes," I said. "He said his oath was to Gythorn, and he wouldn't break it. Warulf says his wife will give Valtir a place to stay."

"Warulf has a wife?" Willow said. "I never thought of him as married."

The Noermarkers had assembled to one side of the line of wagons and horses. Warulf stood talking with his brother, holding the reins of his lovely horse. At my request, Father had made him part of the guard escorting his countrymen home. The three of us went over to the group.

"Travel safely," I said, "and I hope you find a welcome when you arrive."

Warulf spoke in Noermarker, and one of the men said something to me, and then to Willow.

"Lady, thanks to you for guesting," Warulf said. He turned to Willow. "Thanks to you for making men of fen-stalkers, Swan-wif Willow." To my surprise, Willow blushed. I had never seen her blush.

"Valtir, if you find no place in Noermark," I said, "you will have one here." When Warulf had translated, Valtir saluted me. He said nothing, but there was nothing he needed to say.

"Warulf," I said. "Take care of yourself, and your brother. I will miss you."

"I miss you, too, Kiar Swan-kin." Then he said, "When I come back, they make a song for us, of fen-stalkers and Willow Swan-wif."

"Yes," I said. "I know just the harper to do it, too."

Warulf mounted and saluted me. The line of wagons moved out through the gates. Along with the farmsteaders and discreetly spaced along the line were the guards Father had sent to escort the Noermarkers to the border. If any word came to Gythorn, or Beorn, about the farmsteaders' problems, it would come with news of a patrol, as well. The herds of cattle and sheep, penned until this morning on the far side of the dun, would follow when all the wagons had passed.

There was one more parting that day. Sianna packed her medicines and her clothes, and at mid-morning looked at Father's leg for a last time.

"It still hurts," Father said. "And it's swollen."

"Less than it was," Sianna said. "As for the pain, there's bound to be some when a horse rolls on your leg. It will mend. If the pain increases, or the skin darkens, send for me again. I've left you something to help you sleep, but use it sparingly."

She rose slowly, with one hand on her own knee.

"I have to go home," she said. "I need to be in my own place, just as your farmstead folk do."

"Won't the wood-woses look after things for you?" Father asked, and she smiled, but didn't answer.

It was said that the forest spirits protected Sianna's home against all danger and attack. Whether it was true or not, she would never say. I helped her carry her things down to the stable and watched her ride Night Wind towards the forest that ran between the castle and her own home.

Mother continued to improve. Although she sometimes fell silent, with a sadness about her mouth, she allowed Elena to braid her hair and pin it up, and she joined us in the hall for every meal. There were new lines in her face that would never leave, and the wide streaks of white in her hair reminded me of those bad months, too. She and Father were friendly again, sitting close together, talking and holding hands as they used to do. She and I rarely spoke. Maybe she didn't know what to say to me. I didn't know what I could say to her. Her refusal to let me marry Tuan stood between us like a wall.

Over the next three days, the folk of four more farmsteads left on the slow journey back to their homes. Everyone was anxious to return, not only because the farmsteads had been left empty, but also because the herds still had to be culled for winter. Despite bog-walkers and battles and kings out of legend, the work of autumn still waited for us all.

CHAPTER

THIRTY-FIVE

Once the farmstead folk had gone back to their homes and the castle was quieter, Keilan joined us in the hall for meals. The first time Willow brought him to the family table, he hesitated before taking a seat.

"Sit down," Father said. "Willow has been another daughter in this household. Certainly as troublesome as one." He winked at her. "Her husband is welcome at this table."

"I thank you, Sire," Keilan said, but he did not sit. "I am not used to breaking bread with a man I have tried to kill."

"Nor I with a man who has tried to kill me. However, I think that was a different man than the one before me now. Sometime I want to hear about that man. And whatever damage you did has been undone," he said, patting his ribs.

"Your leg has not yet mended."

"Anyone could have a horse fall on them. Please sit and be welcome."

So Keilan joined our family, and he and Willow took the room that had been Adana's.

That night at supper, Father stood up at the table. When everyone was quiet, he spoke.

"Our foster-daughter Willow has taken a mate, Keilan of the swanfolk," he said. "We wish them a long and happy life together." He raised his winecup, and everyone in the hall cheered. Father waved Willow to her feet, and she pulled Kielan up beside her.

"He likes attention as much as you do," Tuan whispered to me.

Indeed, Keilan seemed very uncomfortable. Willow, not at all abashed, kissed him in front of the whole hall.

Then there was dancing. When it ended, we four went outside for a breath of cooler air. Keilan stood looking at the stars as though he would never get his fill.

"The world is beautiful," he said. "Anywhere you are, you can see the stars and the sun."

"Sometimes it rains," Willow said. "Sometimes it's cold, like tonight."

"Even so. And you can stand in all of it under the open sky."

"And when you have chilled your toes under the open sky, you can warm them up in front of the fire," she said. "I'm going in." They went inside together. As unhappy as I'd been about Willow taking Keilan as a mate, I envied her. At least while we were outside, Tuan and I could stay together. I leaned against him and wrapped my arm around his waist.

CHAPTER

THIRTY-SIX

"What an ordinary day we have ahead of us," Father said at breakfast. "No monsters to slay, no magic to work, no hundreds of people needing meals and beds. I will walk, as Sianna bade me, in spite of the pain in my leg."

"But rest, too," Mother said. "It's still swollen."

"Yes, yes," Father said, but he put his hand over Mother's and smiled at her, and she smiled back. He looked at Willow. "You're the one who makes trouble as I recall. Any plans?"

"No, Sire," Willow said. "At least, nothing for you. I thought I might teach Keilan to ride."

"He could have Lady," I said. "She's hardly been ridden since Adana left, and she's gentle and easy. I want to try Kestrel with the new bridle, the one without a bit."

"I've never heard of such a thing," Father said.

"It worked for the grasslanders," I said. "You should have seen how well it worked."

"Probably some secret horseman's word. I wonder if it's the same one Sylard has," Father said. "Did they whisper into the horse's ear at all?"

"No!"

"Are you quite sure?" he asked. "Because you might want to see if Sylard will tell it to you before you start."

"Never mind," Willow said. "If she doesn't stop, Whiffle can catch her."

In the stable I put Kestrel's bridle on her and tucked the one made from rope into my saddlebag. If I was going to look foolish, I preferred to do it with only Willow and Tuan to witness. As for Keilan, he'd be too busy learning to ride to laugh at me.

We rode west along the riverbank, past the new pens that had held the farmsteaders' cattle and sheep, now empty. Ahead of us, across the long, rolling grazing lands, the evergreens stood dark and sharp against the grey sky. It was good to be out, and good not to have anything to think about beyond the concerns of an ordinary day.

When we were well away from the castle, I changed Kestrel's bridle for the rope one. She shook her head at the unfamiliar feel, but it didn't slip off. When I mounted again, I put her into a walk and tried turning her with the reins against her neck. She caught on quickly and went first one way and then the other for me. When I pulled back on the reins, she stopped.

"It works!" I said.

"It works when she's walking," Willow said.

"Yes, you can jump off if she doesn't stop," Tuan said.

I clucked to Kestrel and flicked the reins on her neck; we cantered straight away from the others and then I turned her and pointed her nose straight towards Tuan on Lightfoot.

"Yah!" I yelled, and she broke into a gallop. I leaned over her neck and felt her mane flicking my face. As I came closer and closer, Willow seized Lady's bridle and took both Keilan and herself out of my way, and finally even Tuan moved Lightfoot a few steps to the side. I curved Kestrel towards him again, and then, as he turned Lightfoot out of my path, I straightened and pulled back. Kestrel stopped as neatly and quickly as before.

"Good girl," I said, and patted her neck. "Good girl." As Tuan rode up I said, "See? It works. I didn't have to jump off."

"You're pleased with yourself," he said.

"I am. Now I have to figure out how to make one."

We turned to ride home. The low rolling land let us see the castle even from far away. We were near the bottom of the dun when a rider came around from the main gate and started his horse towards us. It took a moment for me to recognize the little brown horse coming at us nearly head on, and at dangerous speed down the slope.

"That's Tarin," I said.

"He'll trip if he's not careful," Willow said, "and then there'll be someone else with a horse on top of him."

"What could be so urgent?" I asked. "Unless—maybe there's news about Gythorn. Or Beorn. He wouldn't dare! Father sent twenty men!"

I flicked Kestrel's reins and set her into a gallop. Tuan followed close behind me. I was already thinking about how many men to take, and what weapons, and wondered what we might be facing. The High Moor folk should be home by now, even if their cattle were still on the way, and the guard Father had sent would be seeing the Noermarkers to the border. If High Moor had lent them horses, they could already be there.

We would have to move quickly. Beorn might already have engaged the guard Father had sent. I wondered if the Noermarkers' gratitude for their rescue would keep them from turning on my men.

Tarin and I met at the base of the dun in a swirl of circling horses.

"What happened?" I shouted over the thump of hooves and the sound of horses' breath.

"It's the king!" Tarin shouted.

"Gythorn? What about him?"

"No, Lady! The king your father! Come quickly, Lady."

Not until Tuan grabbed my arm and pushed me upright did I realize how close I had come to falling out of my saddle. My hands, my legs, my whole body trembled like a harpstring. "Don't fall," Tuan said.

"I'm all right," I said and tightened my knees on Kestrel's sides. I started her up the dun. We were still on the back side of the castle. I would have to ride right around to the eastern gate. I didn't watch the ground or see anything around me. Beorn could have had men camped all around the walls and I wouldn't have noticed them. All I could think of was Father.

Kestrel put her head down and blew, pushing hard up the slope of the dun. Above me on the wall I heard the guards call out, announcing my arrival.

"The postern's open!" one shouted down, and I waved a hand at him and turned towards the little gate on the west side of the wall. Bron was waiting to take Kestrel's reins.

"Where is he?" I asked as I dismounted.

"They got him up to his room," Bron said. "The queen is with him, and we've sent for Sianna."

"What happened?"

"All I know is that he fell out by the paddock."

"From a horse? Or was he kicked?"

"I don't know, Lady, truly. The men who brought him in said he was looking at another grey and just fell. He didn't look good, and that's the truth. But he was breathing."

I ran through the postern and the corridors to the great hall and the foot of the stairs. I must have passed people, but I didn't notice anyone. I pounded up the stairs to Father's room and pushed the door open without knocking.

Dar stood up from a bench on the near side of the bed when I came in. Past him I saw Mother sitting on the far side, and Father, stretched out on the bed between them, lying flat, so flat, with blankets pulled up over his chest. His beard and moustache seemed very dark; his eyebrows stood out in two thick lines, and then I saw that it was because his face was drained of colour, pale as linen. A fleck of blood clung to one corner of his mouth.

Mother sat beside the bed, clutching one of Father's hands in hers. Her head was bent, and I couldn't see her face. My heart seemed to jump into my throat and my lungs wouldn't draw air. I stared at the blanket; the three, narrow green stripes over Father's collarbone trembled, and then I saw that he still breathed, and my own breath came again.

Mother's face was tear-streaked, her eyes red. I walked softly over to the bed. Dar still stood by the bench; he had tears on his cheeks and dark marks under his eyes.

"Sit," I said, and pushed him down, then sat down beside him. I fumbled under the blanket for Father's other hand. It was cold, even in my fingers chilled from riding.

He opened his eyes and I saw them slide towards me, but he didn't turn his head. I leaned forward so that he could see me easily.

"I'm here, Father," I said.

"Good," he said. It was hardly more than a breath. "Good." He seemed to want to say more. I waited, but he only breathed, slow breaths that barely moved the covers.

"Rest," I said. "Sianna will come." He nodded and closed his eyes. I sat back, still holding his hand. His fingers pressed mine, a gentle pressure, and I squeezed back gently.

"Bron said he was looking at the horses. Did one kick him, or..."

"No," Dar said, still watching Father. "He said he felt tired, and then he slid down the fence. Couldn't even—" He stopped and took two deep breaths. When he went on, his voice had steadied. "Couldn't catch himself." He wiped again at the tears in his eyes.

"He said his leg hurt," Mother said. "More than it did yesterday. But nothing else, nothing." Her voice trailed off, and she reached to pull the edge of the blanket smooth over Father.

"Please, swanling," she said, "We sent the fastest rider we had, but—" There was no need to tell me who she meant. Sianna was half a day's ride away and on the other side of an arm of the forest; no horse could gallop all that road. The fastest rider couldn't get to her in time to bring her before dark.

I didn't want to leave Father's side. I had thought I was afraid for him when he was wounded, but now all I could see was the slow, shallow rise and fall of his breath. If I left his bedside, he might stop breathing. Willow and Keilan were still far away, and I'd left even Tuan behind on my ride up the dun.

Dar and Mother were looking at me. I laid Father's hand back on the bed and stood up. "I'll go," I said.

I ran back down the stairs, out through the great hall and straight across the courtyard to the gate. As soon as I was outside the gate, I pulled off boots and tunic, trousers, and shirt, and called the change to me.

Then I was in the air, flying straight as an arrow over the trees to Sianna.

CHAPTER

THIRTY-SEVEN

I didn't see the rider. He might still have been travelling down the side of the forest, looking for the shortest way through, or he might have cut across early to shorten the distance. Whichever way he took, I would be faster.

I had never pushed myself so hard or flown so fast. The castle fell behind and in mere breaths it seemed, I was over the forest, feeling the cooler, heavier air under my breast and wings. I thought of nothing but getting to Sianna's house. Whatever happened after that, I would deal with as I had to.

My shadow followed me, a little to my left, catching up as the sun rose higher. It was still following me, only a little closer beneath me, when I saw Sianna's round house, circled by gardens, and her horses, the grey Night Wind and Star, the chestnut mare who had once belonged to Orla.

I landed in the gardens and changed. By the time I was back in human form, Sianna stood at her open door, holding a bowl and towel and wearing a plain grey dress.

"Kiar!" she said. "Come in! What brings you to visit?"

"No visit," I said as she stood aside to let me in. I hurried inside out of the cold.

"What then?" She handed me a blanket. "Sit down and tell me." She ladled something steaming from a small pot on the hob.

"It's Father," I said. "He fell this morning, and he's hardly breathing. I don't know what's happened to him, Sianna! I think he might be dying."

She stopped in the act of handing me the cup.

"When this morning? It's not yet noon, Kiar."

"I don't know—not long ago. I went out for a ride, right after breakfast. We weren't gone long, an hour or so, and when we came back, he'd fallen. I came here right away. I was only with him a little while. He's very pale, and hardly breathing!"

"Is his face twisted?" she asked.

I shook my head.

"Did he have pain, in his chest or his arm?" She touched her left arm.

"No," I said. "Dar was with him. He told me Father said he was tired, and then he fell. Mother said he complained this morning that his leg hurt more that it did yesterday."

"Is he bleeding anywhere?"

"There was blood on his lip. Maybe he hit it when he fell. But he's so pale, Sianna, as though there's no blood in him at all! Mother sent a rider, but then I came home, and she asked me. I came, as fast as I could."

"That was good," she said. She tapped her foot a couple of times. "What will I need? Hmmm...." Now she was talking softly, thinking aloud, still with the cup forgotten in her hand.

"If you give me something to wear, I'll catch Star and saddle her for you," I said. "She's faster than Night Wind."

"How quickly can you have a horse down where Orla's house used to be?" she asked.

"If I were home, a little more than a quarter of an hour. But what good is that?"

"Star is faster over the ground," she said, "But I think there might be a way faster than Star. It will take me a while to prepare it, and I'll need your help."

"What do you need?" If there was a way to get her to my Father faster than the ride through the woods to the castle, I would do anything in my power to make it work.

"Will you carry something for me, something light, and put it where Orla's house was?"

I didn't hesitate. "Yes!"

"Then get a horse down to the place?"

"Yes, I'll do that. But what will that do?"

"There may still be a residue of magic there, in the earth itself. If there is, I might be able to—" She hesitated. "Sometimes we can fold distance, bring two places close together and step across from one to the other It's easiest between two spots where a wiseman or wisewoman has made a place of power. If I'm right, there might be enough magic left in Orla's to let me fold the distance between here and there. If there is, it will take me less than an hour to do what I must to be there.”

“And if there isn’t?” I asked.

“Then I will ride Star as fast as she can go, and be at the castle no later than dark.”

“That may be too late,” I said.

“It may, but sooner is better. And the sooner you are away, the sooner I can begin.”

“What do you need me to take?” I asked.

She showed me a pouch on a cord. The pouch was the size of my fist, light and stuffed with something that smelled of new-mown hay. When I took it, my fingers tingled and buzzed.

“Can you carry this around your neck?” she asked.

“Yes, I can do that. What is it? It makes my fingers feel odd.”

“That is the token. When you reach the place where Orla’s house was, open the bag and take out the token in it. Put it where her house stood, anywhere within where the walls used to be. Then, when you get to the castle, tell your mother to give your father a tisane of this herb. Two large pinches in this much water.” She cupped her two hands. “Give him as much as they can make him drink. Sit him up to drink, but otherwise leave him lying down.”

I put the cord around my neck. “I’ll remember.”

“If this works,” she said. “I will not be long after you. If it doesn’t, I’ll be there before sunset.”

“I hope it works,” I said. I changed quickly and flew back the way I had come. The pouch dangled beneath my breast and tapped my body.

From the air, a smooth circle marked where Orla's house had been. The grass had grown back within it but somehow different from what grew around it. Maybe Sianna was right, and magic was left there yet. I hoped so. I landed and changed, then opened the pouch and put my fingers in.

On top of the crisp leaves in the bag I felt a curved shape. My fingers buzzed and tingled when I touched it, and my gorge rose. I swallowed hard and fished the thing out with two fingertips. It was a circle, carved from some dark, reddish wood I didn't recognize, pierced through in a swirling design and inlaid with three small stones. I squinted at the thing, but the curves of the design flowed and moved, and the stones seemed to flicker with different colours. Looking at it made me dizzy. I bent and laid it on the ground, in the centre of where Orla had built her house, then backed away until my stomach settled.

I wanted to wait for Sianna, see for myself that she was here, but she would need a horse, and my father needed the medicine she had sent. I changed and flew to the east gate. It was not yet quite noon of the short autumn day. The guard at the east gate had my clothes ready for me.

"Send someone to take a horse down to where Orla had her house," I said. "Tell them wait there until Sianna comes."

"Yes, Lady," said the guard. I slipped into the gatehouse and dressed, then ran into the castle and straight to the kitchens. Everything stopped when I came in, and Nias hurried forward.

"Oh, Lady Kiar, the queen's been asking if anyone has seen you."

"Is there any word on my father?" I asked.

"No, no change," she said.

I fumbled with the knot on the cord around my neck until she came over and cut it for me with a little kitchen knife. I put the pouch in her hands.

"There, now, Lady. You'll want to go up to the king, of course. What's this?"

"Make up a tisane, two big pinches of herb in so much water. Bring it up to the king as soon as it's ready. Sianna said he should drink as much of it as he could."

"Right away," Nias said. "I'll make it up until it's gone."

"Thank you." I was already on my way out as I said it. I ran up the stairs again. When had I ever run as much in my life as today? From the end of the passage I saw Willow, Keilan, and Tuan standing by my father's door.

"Where have you been?" Willow asked.

"Getting Sianna."

"Have you eaten anything?" Tuan asked. "Or drunk?"

I shook my head.

"I'll get something," Willow said to him. "You stay with her."

"Is there anything you can do?" I asked Keilan.

"No," he said. "I saw him as soon as I arrived. This is mortal. I mean it is his own body, nothing to do with my magic, or any other's."

"I see," I said. I turned to the door and Tuan opened it for me and followed me in.

Dar and Mother sat as though they hadn't moved since I left.

"Sianna will be here soon. Before sunset at the latest," I said. "She sent a tisane. I gave it to Nias to make up. She said give him as much as he'll drink."

"Sit down," Tuan said, and I sat on the bench next to Dar. Tuan stood behind me, his hands on my shoulders. I leaned back against his warmth and closed my eyes, trying not to cry. Now that I was sitting still again, I felt my whole body still vibrating, right to my bones.

"She'll be here before sunset," I said again. I looked out the window. I felt a pinch of doubt. Unless she could make Star sprout wings and fly, I didn't see how Sianna could possibly be here before the sun went down. At the same time, her promised arrival seemed impossibly far away.

I wanted to hold Father's hand, but now Dar had it in his, and it seemed cruel to take it away. They had been friends since before my birth. Instead I watched those long, slow breaths, willing them to keep on. I put my hands over Tuan's, and he folded his fingers around mine.

Willow came in with a steaming cup, and Nias followed her with a tray.

"You have to eat, Lady," she said to Mother. She looked at Dar, a look that was almost baleful. "You, too, good guard that you are. You know better than to starve on watch." She swept the same look over me but said nothing.

Mother put the cup to her lips to test the heat of it. I went around to her side of the bed and helped Dar sit Father up. His eyes flickered open and Mother put the cup to his lips. We all watched as he swallowed again and again, one tiny mouthful after another until the whole cup was gone.

"There's more in the kitchen, keeping hot," Nias said. "I'll fetch it up. You three eat." Obediently we took the pieces of buttered bread and cold meat and sliced pear, and the hot tea, sweetened with honey. Every bite tasted no better than so much grass to me and it was hard work to swallow.

Time crept on like a snail. There was a candle to mark the time scored with lines a finger's width apart, but the distance between the flame and the top line never seemed to shrink. Nias brought another cup of tisane, and Elena brought candles in to be lit at dark. Outside Father's window, which faced north, the sky kept a grey, unchanging light.

Then a guard called, "A rider!" Almost immediately, there were hoofbeats, light and quick, on the flagstone courtyard— two horses. Then the token had worked. I felt the muscles of my chest loosen a little.

Willow dashed out of the room. Sooner than I would have thought possible, Sianna came striding in. Willow followed, carrying one of Sianna's bags while Keilan carried the other.

"I will need you, and you," Sianna said, nodding to Mother and Dar. "If the rest of you will leave, I'll have room to work."

I left, looking back over my shoulder at Dar, Mother, and Sianna—all bending over Father.

"Now lift," I heard Sianna say, and then the door closed behind me, and I stood out in the passage.

"I know you won't leave," Willow said. "We brought a chair," She made me sit down and tucked a blanket over me, then put a pillow behind my head.

"She got here in time," I said. "Didn't she?"

"Yes, you got her here in time," Willow said. "Nobody could have done it faster."

I closed my eyes, but I could not rest. I wanted to push back into Father's room and watch his breathing to keep him alive. I wanted to beg him to get better, to beg Sianna to save him. He had survived the magic that tried to kill him; he was walking again. Better than that, he was happy again, with Mother coming back to herself.

I sat dozing and waking, swinging from hope to despair. Once I dreamed that Father walked out of the room and laughed to find me sleeping in my chair, but when I opened my eyes, the passage was dark, and Keilan sat beside me cross-legged on the floor. In a white shirt, with his pale skin and white hair, he might have been a ghost from a story, but when he spoke his voice was soft and reassuring.

"Hwaelew made Tuan go to get some sleep," he said. "It is full dark now. I said I would watch with you until he returned."

"Thank you," I said. I rubbed my eyes. "There's no word?"

"Nothing," he said. "The wisewoman is still in there."

"And Mother?"

He nodded. "And his friend, too."

"I dreamed he was well," I said.

Keilan nodded.

"I wish I could do something," I said. "I can't just let him die."

"I know," Keilan said. "Not today."

"No," I said. "Not today."

"If you wish," Keilan said, "I will get Tuan, or Hwaelew, to sit with you. You should have a friend near, and I am almost a stranger."

"No, stay," I said. "I wish I could speak to Father again."

"I hope you may," Keilan said. "and he to you."

A thread of pale light showed under the door of Father's room, wavering as though someone were going back and forth in front of a flame.

"If I knocked, do you think she would let me in?" I asked Keilan.

"A bold act, to interrupt a wisewoman," he said. Then he stood abruptly, and the door to Father's room opened. Sianna leaned out; I knew her by her outline, the dark shape of her edged with pale light.

"Come in," she said. In an instant, all my worry swung to relief.

I'd expected to see Sianna's bottles and bundles set out, perhaps a mortar and pestle, poultices or potions. Instead, everything was neatly away, except for a basin with the corner of a wet cloth hanging over it and a trickle of aromatic smoke from a small bronze bowl.

"Are you done?" I asked. "When will he be up?"

"Come and sit with me, swanling," Mother said from her place by the bed. She held Father's hand in one of hers, and rubbed her thumb over and over the back of it. The other arm she held out to me.

"No," I said. I stared at the blanket. "No. He's still breathing. There has to be something you can do!" I was almost shouting, and I turned on Sianna. "There has to be something you can do!"

"I am sorry," Sianna said. "Sometimes after a broken bone or a bad injury, something happens that hinders the breath, and then stops it."

"What something? What could there be—he was getting better! You have to help him!"

"I've done everything I know to do." She spoke to me as quietly as if she were talking about mending a tear in a sleeve. I remembered Gern, and his wound that stank and refused to heal, no matter what Sianna did. I knew there were things that even Sianna couldn't heal.

"No," I said. But my chest tightened, and I knew she spoke the truth.

"Come, now, young Kiar," Dar said. He took my arm and pulled me down beside him. He put Father's hand into mine. "Say goodbye, now. Let him know he's leaving us in good hands. Tears still ran down his face. "Like a good daughter," he said.

I nodded and took Father's hand between mine. Another breath lifted the covers, ever so slightly.

"I'll look after things, Father," I said. "Travel—" I had to stop and struggle with my breath and my voice. "Travel safely, arrive safely," I said. On the last word, my voice broke again, and I began to cry. I leaned on Dar's shoulder, and he put his arm around me.

I'd never heard the death-rattle in a person's throat before, never been present when someone died, but the sound was unmistakable. His breath came out in a sigh, and he did not draw another.

Dar stood up and went down on one knee before me. I sniffed back my tears as he held out his hands, folded together.

"Queen Kiar," he said. I understood and put my hands around his.

"My friend," I said.

"Your liege man, my queen," he answered.

Some little time later, women came in to wash and dress him. By then I had worn out my tears. When I stood up, Tuan was there to put his arms around me, but it was Willow, her own face tear-stained and her eyes red, who took me away and put me to bed, and gave me the tisane that sent me down into sleep.

CHAPTER

THIRTY-EIGHT

It took most of the next day to build the pyre at the bottom of the dun, where once I had seen one built for Orla. All day Father lay in the great hall. He wore his crown, and his sword and shield lay beside him. Everyone in the castle came to speak to him. Everyone had some word of thanks or praise. Mother and I stood by, she at his head, and I at his feet, while the people came to say farewell and left again. The guard took all the banners down that flew from the castle walls and roof. Without them, the grey stone of the castle was one piece with the grey sky.

In the evening we carried him out to the pyre and laid him on it. Mother kissed his lips and took the crown from his head. When she stood back again, Dar and I each took a torch and lit the pyre, I on the north and east, he on the south and west. The men who built the pyre had done their work well; it caught quickly. The kindling and firebark blazed up fast and hot, and we had to step back from its fiery breath.

I began the mourning song, which we would sing as long as the pyre burned.

Oh-ah, wind and rain,

earth and fire and wind and rain.

Oh-ah, wind and rain

take his spirit home again.

Other voices joined mine until everyone standing in the circle around the pyre was singing. Through the night people would stop and then rejoin the chant, but as long as even one voice went on, the thread of the song was unbroken.

At first it was only the chorus, rising and falling against the fluttering sound of the flames. Our voices drowned out that early, quiet voice of the fire, but as the larger branches caught, it roared and snapped. It wove in and out of the chant, sometimes drowning out our voices, and sometimes yielding to them like a harp to the bard's song. The sound came in waves from the people all around the pyre. On my right I heard Mother's clear, light voice, and on behind me Dar's low, gravelly one, struggling with the melody. On my left Tuan sang steadily and quietly, his voice clear to my ears, and comforting.

We were lost in the chant for a time. My mother's voice faltered into weeping, then took up the song again. Then people began to weave words of praise for Father into the song.

"Brave in battle, wind and rain," came Bron's voice clearly from the other side of the circle.

"Earth and fire and wind and rain," we sang.

"Wise in judgment, wind and rain," sang Bron.

"Take his spirit home again," we sang.

Then I heard Dar's voice. "Careful king, wind and rain."

"Earth and fire and wind and rain."

"Loyal friend, wind and rain."

"Take his spirit home again."

One by one other people spoke their thoughts into the song.

"Open-handed, open hearted."

"Loved his people, brought them safety."

"Kept the peace, kept the borders."

"Bright his honor, and his courage."

"Best of fathers," I sang, "wind and rain, earth and fire and wind and rain, loved his daughters, wind and rain, take his spirit home again."

Then I heard Tuan beside me, Tuan who had never spoken in front of this many people, lift his voice. I was so surprised I almost lost the thread of the song.

"Honoured also, wind and rain,

earth and fire and wind and rain,

among the swanfolk, wind and rain,

take his spirit home again."

It took all that long night for the pyre to burn down to ashes and embers. I waited by it, almost asleep on my feet at the end. I welcomed my exhaustion. it made me too tired for grief. By the time the men of Father's guard came to rake the ashes together, it was all I could do to climb the dun and then the stairs to bed. I slept for a few hours, and in the evening Mother and I, Dar and Tuan, Willow and Keilan went down to disperse Father's ashes to the air, water, and earth, as it was his family's and friend's right and duty to do.

I wanted to lie down and sleep for a month; my body ached, my chest hurt, and my mind felt as though my head was stuffed with hay. It didn't seem real that Father was dead. But there was no time for that; by long custom, the coronation of the new ruler took place as soon as possible after the death of the old one. Mine would be tomorrow. If Queen Amala was right, only then would I be able to hold Valenia truly safe.

When we came back, Sylard was waiting by the hearth of the great hall.

"I took the measure of your helmet," he said. Then he held out in both hands the gold circlet set with garnets that was the crown of Valenia.

"It's beautiful," I said.

"Thank you, Queen Kiar," he said.

Mother said, "I've asked Sianna to stay until you're crowned."

"You've thought of everything," I said. "I'll leave it in your hands. And will you keep the crown until tomorrow?"

"I will," she said. Sylard handed it to her, bowed to both of us and left the hall.

"It feels strange," I said.

"I know, swanling." The way she spoke sounded just as she had when I was a child. She stood with the crown in her hands, straight and calm, as steady and sure as I had known her before Orla's death. She smiled a little. "I suppose I should watch where I call you 'swanling' now. It would never do for Guthric to hear the queen of Valenia called by a pet name."

"You never called me 'swanling' in front of him anyway," I said. "I doubt you'll start now."

"No, but in front of other people I'll have to show you the respect and honour due the ruler."

"That will be hard to get used to," I said.

"You will get used to it. Your father was so proud of you, Kiar. When you came back from fighting Hafor, he told me that you would make a good queen, who was careful of her people. He was almost bursting with it."

"I want to be as good as he was," I said. "I don't know if I'm ready."

"You're nineteen," she said. "He wasn't much older when he came to the throne himself. Maybe nobody believes they're ready. But whether you believe it or not, he did. And Dar does, and so perhaps you could trust their judgment until you do, too."

"Thank you," I said.

"Well" she said, "Tomorrow will be a long day for us all."

I expected an early night after a quiet day. Late in the afternoon, however, the guard Father had sent with the High Moor folk and the Noermarkers came back. As soon as they crested the last rise before the castle, they must have known something was wrong, because no banners flew from the walls. The guardsman who came to announce their arrival found me in the council chamber—now no longer Father's, but mine. His chair still smelled as though he had been in it a moment before, and the familiar shape of the cushions comforted me. There was other news besides the return of the guard.

"Majesty," he said, "the guard the late king sent out has returned. They saw the Noermarkers safely to the border, and found the ambassador Guthric on his way here. He is outside. Will you receive him?"

"Yes," I said, "in the great hall."

I took a deep breath. This was my chance to impress Guthric that I was queen, and in command. I needed the thrones, and Tuan, and Mother, and I wanted Dar and two other guardsmen and Willow and Keilan, and for the moment my wits seemed to have deserted me. The guard waited, with no sign of haste or impatience, while I pulled my thoughts together.

"Send for Tuan," I said. "And send the captain of my guard to me with two picked men."

"Lord Tuan, Captain Dar, and two picked men," he said. "Right away, Majesty."

I heard him shouting for messengers on his way out. I pushed myself out of Father's chair and found one of the castle women in the corridor. She bowed when she saw me.

"Tell my mother I need her here," I said. "And send for Willow and Keilan. And who brings out the thrones?"

"I'll see to it," she said. "Did you want to change your clothes, La— Majesty?"

I looked down at my tunic and trousers and pulled at the collar of my shirt to make sure it was straight. If I changed, that would delay things. Maybe it was good politics to keep Guthric waiting, but I wanted this over.

"No," I said. "But send water for me to wash, and I'll want my sword."

She bowed again and hurried off. After I'd washed my face and hands, I went into the hall. In an astonishingly short time, the three thrones had been set out in a row. Tuan came in first with my sword over his shoulder.

"Wear it or hang it up?" he asked.

"Hang it up," I said. "I need practice to wear it. I don't want it catching on the arm of the throne."

He nodded and hung the sword on the back of my father's—my—throne. By then, Dar was there with two guardsmen, and Mother, Willow, and Keilan as well.

"Right," I said. "Willow and Keilan, you stand behind Mother." Tuan sat to my left in the consort's throne, and Mother settled into the one on the right and smoothed her skirts around her. Dar and the guardsmen took their places behind me and Tuan.

I rubbed my palms on my trousers and then laid my hands on the arms of the throne.

"Ready," I said.

"Tell the ambassador from Noermark the queen will receive him," Dar called to the guard at the door.

When Guthric came in. I almost didn't recognize him. His face and head were both bristly, as though they'd been shaved and were growing back out. The two Noermarkers with him had also shaved, both head and face. As he came closer, I saw the marks of grief on his face. He knelt and looked from my mother to me.

"Queen Tianis, Lady Kiar," he said, "I bring news for King Tir. My king, Guthric, third of that name, died ten days past."

"I am sorry to hear it," I said. "He was in great pain and not himself."

"Yes, great pain for many days," Guthric said. "It was a release to him to die."

"Tell King Beorn," I said. "that we grieve for his grief."

"Thank you, Lady Kiar," Guthric said.

"King Tir," I said, "has also died. Two days ago."

"I am sorry indeed to hear that," he said. "Forgive my discourtesy, Majesty. I had not heard."

"Do not distress yourself," I said. "For now, rest and eat after your long journey, and your great loss. Later you and I will speak privately."

When he had withdrawn to the room he usually used, Dar turned to me.

"There's a meeting he won't forget in a hurry," Dar said. "You took every point on that one, Majesty, no denying it."

"I couldn't tell a thing from his face," I said.

"He's good at hiding what he thinks," Mother said. "I agree with Dar. You knew more about his affairs than he knew about yours."

"You talk as if it's a game. Beorn could declare war on us. He might try it when he hears this news."

"Not likely," Dar said. "You have the look of a fighter, Majesty. You may not be a king, but you're not their idea of a queen, either. Oh, they'll have some work to figure you out." He sounded almost delighted. "And word'll get around about the—what do they call them—fen-stalkers? No, I don't imagine Beorn will want trouble with you in a hurry."

"Good," I said. "Now I need to get out. I'm going riding. Who's coming?"

"I will," said Tuan. I looked around at Willow and Keilan.

"No," Keilan said. "Thank you. I have had enough riding for now."

Willow shook her head and mouthed, "Sore."

We rode out the main gate, down the dun, and east across the plain. At the bottom of the dun, I rode by the patch of scorched earth and blackened grass where the pyre had burned, but didn't stop. We rode past Orla's old place of power. There was still something there, I thought, if Sianna could use it to fold distance. I would have to take thought for that later.

Somewhere along here, too, I had ridden with Father and Guthric, talking of marriage to a prince from Noermark. It felt to me now that I was with Father and Guthric again, although neither of them rode beside me. I reined Kestrel to a stop and searched for any landmark from that conversation, but there was nothing I could recall.

"You're far away," Tuan said.

I shook myself back to the present. "Remembering," I said. "I was here—somewhere near here—with Father and Guthric, talking about marrying one of Gythorn's sons. It seems a very long time ago."

"A lot has happened."

"I have so much to learn about ruling, and I thought Father would be with me. Sitting there today and waiting for Guthric was worse than fighting Hafor. I still have to talk to him in private. And get through the coronation."

Tuan put his other hand over mine. "You need time."

"Yes, but there isn't any. This has all happened so fast. But after the coronation Guthric will go home for the winter. One thing about being queen, I don't need Mother's word to marry. We can start thinking about our wedding."

"Your mother will not be happy."

"It's not for her to say, not anymore. Father approved, and I am the queen."

"Yes," he said. "You're the queen, and sooner than you thought. You need time to get used to that all by itself, without any other big changes."

My heart jumped into my throat. "What are you saying? That we shouldn't marry?"

Tuan squeezed my hand. "No, of course not. Just not right away. Kiar, you have things to learn about ruling, you said it yourself. I want you free to have your mind on that for a while. Only a year, one year to get used to being queen, and to get others used to it, too."

"I don't want to wait!"

"Nor do I. But I think it's best, even to give your mother time to get used to the idea. You don't need division within the family. You have enough enemies outside."

"That's why I need you with me," I said.

"I will be with you. I'll be right here, where I've always been. And we will marry at the next midwinter festival, I promise."

"No matter what my mother thinks?"

"No matter what your mother thinks. A lot can happen in a year, Kiar."

If I spoke, I thought I would cry.

Tuan squeezed my hands again. "I'd rather wait until you're free to have your mind on marrying instead of learning to rule."

I nodded, and then the tears spilled over. Kestrel tossed her head and jigged away from Lightfoot, tearing my hand from Tuan's. He caught her reins and held her while I buried my face in my hands and tried in vain to stop the tears. The world I'd known seemed to be slipping away from me; Father dead, Mother rejecting Tuan, Willow with a mate, and now Tuan saying we should wait to marry. The work of being queen and learning to rule was suddenly a long, uphill road I would have to walk alone.

Tuan made soothing noises, but whether they were intended for me or for my mare I couldn't have said. Finally, I drew a breath that didn't come out in sobs, and then another. I wiped my face and took back Kestrel's reins. Tuan turned Lightfoot so that our horses stood nose to tail, and we could face each other.

"I'm sorry," he said.

I shook my head. "No. You're right. I thought I'd have Father here for longer, and now I have to learn everything without him. It's going to take so long."

"You'll have help. And at High Moor you did everything right, remember?"

"Yes." I sighed.

"It's one year," he said. "You waited much longer than that to fly."

"I know. But I want to marry you even more than I wanted to fly."

"Come, now," Tuan said. He gathered Lightfoot's reins and gave me a sly smile. "I'll race you back."

"You'd better not let me win," I said.

"Is that a royal command?"

Before I could answer, he'd flicked Lightfoot's reins, and was pulling away. I turned Kestrel's head and started after him. Leaning low over my mare's neck, I urged her on, and she picked up her feet and flew after Lightfoot's black tail. Slowly, we pulled closer, and in the wash of Kestrel's mane over my face, the rhythm of her muscles bunching and stretching as she ran and the sound of her breathing, I forgot about everything else but the joy of the race. We pulled slowly closer, until I could reach out my hand and feel the flick of Lightfoot's tail over my fingers. Then the land sloped up and Lightfoot pulled away again for a few strides. Both Tuan and I slowed the horses to a trot, and then walked them side by side for the last part of the way to the castle gate.

"Better," he said. It wasn't a question, but I nodded. The race had blown all thoughts out of my head for a few minutes, and I felt lighter and somehow, unreasonably, happier.

I went to the bathhouse and the hot water eased my muscles and loosened the knots in my chest and stomach. Afterwards, I took a meal in my own room and went early to bed. Mother brought me a tisane for sleep, but I hadn't drunk a quarter of it before my eyelids drooped.

As I lay down, I wondered if my father's spirit would come to me on this night before I took the crown that had been his for so many years. Whether or not he did, the next morning all

I remembered of my dreams was that I had dreamed of flying,
as I often had before.

CHAPTER

THIRTY-NINE

I woke up to Willow pulling back the curtain on my window. The fire had been made up already, taking the morning chill off the room, but the stone floor was cold against the soles of my feet.

"Good morning, Your Majesty," Willow said. "Breakfast will be right up."

"Don't *you* start," I said. "I need someone to remember my name in private."

"I believe that's your consort's duty, Majesty," Willow said, her face very serious. I scowled at her, and she broke into giggles.

"Oh, it was worth it for that look on your face!" she said. "Come on, Kiar, sit up by the fire and I'll comb your hair. You're to wear it loose today."

I sat on the high stool by the hearth wrapped in a woollen robe, and Willow combed out my hair. She was gentle, even with the little tangles at the back of my neck, where my hair always snarled on my collar. Before she was done, Elena came in with a tray—fresh, hot honey cakes, cheese, sliced apples and pears and a mug of hot mint tea. I wrapped my hands around the mug, grateful for the warmth on my fingers.

A few minutes later, Mother came up with a swath of rosy fabric over her arm.

"I made this last year." She shook out a dress in soft wool, embroidered with swans on the breast and sleeves.

"Thank you, Mother." I stroked the dress. The wool felt soft and supple in my fingers, and when I put it on over a linen underdress, it fell in graceful folds to brush the tops of my shoes. In the mirror my face looked rosier, too, and my eyes more green than brown. I'd usually chosen green or russet for my dresses, and I was surprised how much this colour suited me.

At the same time, my clothes made me feel vulnerable. There was nowhere in my soft house shoes to keep a knife, and I couldn't wear a sword with this dress.

"This is worse than getting ready for a fight. I wish I could have a sword."

"You don't have to fight," Willow said. "Just look queenly and everything will happen around you. Isn't that right, Lady?"

"It is," Mother said. "And you'll have a guard."

"Besides, nobody would dare draw a weapon today," Willow said.

"Except for the oaths," I said. That would be the longest part of the day—accepting the oaths of everyone in the castle old enough to swear for themselves. It would be almost all castle folk. There might be someone from some of the closer farmsteads, but the farther ones would barely have got the news. The first time I visited each of the farmsteads, my people there would swear to me. I'd have to do all that in the spring and summer, but I put the thought aside. Today would be long enough without thinking of what I had to do in the future.

When I'd eaten and rinsed my mouth and hands, it was time to go downstairs. The hall outside my room was empty. As I walked to the head of the stairs, my mother fell back behind me, and Willow and Elena walked a little behind her.

So I came alone to the top of the staircase. The castle folk waited at the bottom, making an aisle for me to walk into the great hall. All that attention, all those eyes on me, made my stomach flutter and my hands tremble. I felt the damp on my right palm as I placed it on the balustrade.

At the right of the staircase, closest to the bottom step, stood a man wearing a dark-blue surcoat. Under it, the wide sleeves of his shirt were banded in white and black from shoulder to wrist. It took me several seconds to recognize Tuan.

I took a deep breath and stepped down, mindful of my footing. It would be the worst sort of omen to trip on my way to the throne. There was not a sound from the people waiting below. When I was a few steps from the bottom, I looked at Tuan, and his eyelid flickered in a wink so small and quick that I barely caught it. My hands were still damp, and my stomach still fluttery, but his small signal made me feel a little better about the ordeal ahead. I passed and heard him move to follow me with Mother and Willow.

Everyone I passed bowed as I went by. At the entrance to the great hall, Guthric and his guards, their shorn heads standing out in sharp contrast to everyone around them, also bowed.

All three thrones had been set up in the hall, near the door where the king's table usually stood. Sianna stood to one side of the throne, and Sylard on the other. Behind the thrones and spreading out on either side, all the men of my own and my father's guard stood, in their armour and carrying sword, spear and bow. I recognized Dar to the right of the centre throne. He carried the sword I had given him, unsheathed and upright in his right hand, and on his left arm he wore his shield.

Beyond the thrones, the doors to the hall were open and the great, bronze fire-bowl stood in the courtyard beyond, surrounded by torches. The flames were almost invisible in the sunlight, but the hall was so quiet that I could hear them fluttering with the sound of banners blown in the wind.

Someone had picked asters and the last, late-blooming kingcups to spread along the final few yards of my way. I walked on a purple-and-gold carpet of blossoms as I came to the throne. As I reached it, I turned and stood facing the people crowded into the hall. Sylard was on my right, and Sianna on my left. Tuan and Mother moved to stand before their own thrones, Tuan on my left and Mother on my right, and I saw Elena sweep around behind Mother's throne and Willow take her place behind Tuan's.

I wanted to smooth my hair—I was certain it was flying every which way. I wanted to wipe the damp off my palms. Instead I stood quietly and thought about breathing evenly, while everyone who had been at the bottom of the stairs found places to stand in the hall.

When everyone was quiet, Mother spoke.

"We are met today to crown Kiar, trueborn daughter of Tir, as Queen of Valenia, to give into her hands the well-being of the land, and all the folk in it, animals, plants and speaking peoples. If there is anyone here who knows any bar to her right and duty to take the throne, let them come forward, state their cause, and defend it by arms against her champion."

Dar took one step forward. When the sound of his movement had died away, there was silence in the hall except for the flutter of torches. Even Guthric and his men stood silent in the place of honour given them, at the front of the crowd and on my left.

"Will any challenge the right of Kiar to take the throne of Valenia?" Sylard said.

No one spoke.

"Will any challenge her right to the throne?" Sianna asked.

Still there was silence.

Mother turned to face me.

"Kiar, daughter of Tir, will you swear to hold safe the land and peoples of Valenia? Will you lead, counsel and protect them in times of peace and war, plenty and need? Will you guard the weak and hold in check the strong, so long as you live?"

"I so swear," I said.

Mother stepped back, and Sianna came forward.

"Kiar, daughter of Tir, will you remember to seek counsel? For no one man or woman can know everything. Will you seek advisors among your own folk, and among the wisemen and wisewomen? Will you judge and follow their counsel in the light of the good of your land and people, and not for your own will or glory?"

"I so swear," I said.

Sianna stepped away and Sylard faced me.

"Kiar, daughter of Tir, will you honour the mysteries of steel, and those who know them? Will you keep your sword apart from works of treachery and self-will and maintain it in defence of Valenia and her peoples?"

"I so swear," I said.

Sylard and Sianna stepped back, and the people opened a way for me to the door of the great hall. I walked out to stand beside the fire-bowl. A breeze sprang up and blew a strand of hair across my eyes. I brushed it aside, and then Sianna, Mother, and Sylard were around me. People flowed into the courtyard, all around the great fire-bowl.

Sylard handed me a small, slender knife. I took it in my right hand and held my open left hand above my head.

"I bind myself to my land and my people. Let the spirits witness that my blood is the blood of Valenia, my heart is the heart of Valenia, and my strength is in Valenia's service." I lowered my hand and put the point of the little knife below my forefinger. A drop of blood sprang up before I felt the prick of the blade, and I pulled it quickly across my palm, opening a shallow cut that welled blood. Only then did I feel the sting of the slash I'd made. I felt my hand tremble, but to my eyes it held steady.

I held my hand up and flicked it towards the fire so that drops of blood fell into the flames. One trickled down my wrist to the edge of my linen underdress and seeped along the weave.

Then Mother held my hand while Sianna bound it. We returned to the hall, and I stood again before the throne.

Mother brought the crown forward, and she and Sylard held it between them. Sianna reached out to the crown but did not touch it. Instead she held both hands out, palms up, and I saw light gathering in the hollow of each palm, spreading out until it seemed she held a bowl of pale fire in each hand.

"Let the ruler's right pass from Tir to Kiar," she said. "Let her hold it by right of birth and blood and iron, by the strength of her arm and the wisdom of her heart." She turned her palms forward, and the fire in them billowed forward and lit up the crown, making the gold flash like sunlight reflected off water and the garnets blaze. I had to squint against the brightness. It lasted barely a heartbeat, but even after it faded, my eyes were still dazzled by it.

I saw a shadow in front of me and felt a heat around my brow, like the ripple from a hearth, and then a great weight, a wheel of stone that would press me into the ground. I held myself straight, and my knees trembled a little; then the weight disappeared, and the heat, too. I blinked and the dazzle cleared from my eyes. In front of me Mother, Sylard, and Sianna were stepping back, the hands they had used to set the crown on my head still raised.

"Long live Queen Kiar!" I don't know who said it first, but the crowd took it up and shouted it three times, then broke into wild cheering. Mother made a small motion with her hand towards the throne. I took a step back and sat down, my hands on the carved wolf heads of the arms. It was done. I was the true queen.

Tuan brought my sword, unsheathed, and laid it across my lap. Then my mother knelt before me.

"Queen Kiar, I pledge you my loyalty and service so long as you rule Valenia."

"I accept your pledge, and swear in return to protect and defend you from all harm so far as I can as a true queen."

She had barely risen when Dar came forward and knelt.

I remembered what my father had said to Warulf.

"Dar, do you swear to be loyal to me and mine, to fight for Valenia and her queen, and to forswear all other loyalties save family alone?"

"I so swear," he said.

"I accept your pledge, and swear in return to protect and defend you from all harm so far as I can as a true queen."

That was a long day, as every adult in the castle came to pledge me their loyalty and service. By the end, my throat was sore and my back aching. One after another they came, men and women of the guard, and of the household. Sometimes it hardly seemed real. I had known these people all my life. Some of them had been responsible for me when I was a child, and now I would be responsible for them.

Once I almost smiled, when Warulf knelt before me and said, "I so swear," as everyone else had done. I remembered him saying to Father, "I oath to you." I was touched that he had learned the words he so carefully said. Once I felt tears prickle in my eyes when Willow knelt to swear to me. Tuan had meant for years to stay with me; I had never been as sure of Willow.

Keilan, too, swore to me. The thought flitted across my mind that perhaps no other ruler of Valenia had accepted the oath of allegiance from another king.

In the end it was done. I was thirsty and hungry, and the smells of cooking and baking from the kitchen teased my nose and made my mouth water. When the last person had sworn to me, I called Guthric forward.

"Take our greetings to King Beorn," I said. "Tell him we share the grief he feels at the loss of a father. Tell him also that we hope our two lands may live in peace hereafter. There are enemies enough in the world."

"I will, Majesty," he said. He withdrew, and I was free to sheathe my sword and get up from my throne. All I wanted was to be alone.

"There's something to eat and drink in your council chamber," Mother said.

"Thank you."

In the council chamber, I took off the crown and laid it gently on the table beside the tray left for me. Looking at that slender circlet, I wondered at the weight I had felt when it was first put on my head. Then I turned my attention to the food and ate standing. There was a honeyed tisane, soothing to the throat, a few slices of cold chicken, bread and herbed butter and an apple.

As I bit into the apple, someone knocked at the door.

"Yes," I said. The door swung open and Kearn looked in. "Your pardon, Majesty. Lord Tuan is here."

"Come in, Tuan," I said. "I almost didn't recognize you today in those clothes. They suit you."

He came to me as the door closed behind him, and we kissed. I put my arms around him and rested my head against his shoulder, and he rubbed his hands up and down my back.

"Oh, that feels good," I said. "I never thought sitting in a chair would be such hard work."

"Nor did I," he said. "I hope we won't have to do much of that."

"Father never did," I said. "I won't, either, if I can help it." We stood for a few minutes, and then Tuan pulled away. He took my left hand in his, careful not to press on the bandaged palm.

"Did that hurt?" he asked. "I didn't know you had to shed blood to be queen."

"The knife was very sharp," I said. "I didn't feel it until the cut was done."

"I hope you won't have to shed blood often," he said.

"So do I." I sighed. "Now the feast and dancing, I suppose."

"I've never heard you speak of dancing as though you'd rather not do it."

"All I want to do right now is sleep. And tomorrow I should see Guthric and talk to him about how things are in Noermark and whether the men who were bog-walkers will be welcomed."

"Think about that later." He took a small bag from inside his sleeve and held it out to me. "I asked Sylard to make this for you."

I took the bag into my hand, and it shifted in my fingers with the weight of what it contained. I pulled the mouth open and spilled a chain of interlocked spirals into my palm. They were as delicate and skilfully made as the loops of my iron necklace had been, but they were silver. At the front of the chain the spirals grew larger, until the two front ones were a pair of swans, their necks intertwined and their eyes tiny garnets.

"Tuan, it's beautiful," I said. "Thank you. Will you fasten it for me?" I put the necklace to my throat and turned my back to him.

He lifted my hair out of the way. I felt his breath on the back of my neck and shivered. Then he took the ends of the necklace and hooked them together. The links lay cool over my skin, and the entwined swans rested in the hollow of my throat. Tuan put his arms around me, and I leaned into him and reached back to touch his face. We stood that way for a few minutes, then I turned and put my arms around his neck, and we kissed.

"It's beautiful," I said again. "Stay with me until we have to go back out."

"Of course, my queen," he said, and kissed my hair.

"Willow said it's up to you to remember my name when everyone else calls me 'Your Majesty'."

"Ah," he said. "I suppose that's a royal command itself."

I pulled back and he looked down at me, laughing.

"Even a queen needs a sense of humour," he said. "Maybe especially a queen. Can't I tease you a little?"

"If you can't, who can?" I said, and snuggled back into his arms.

CHAPTER

FORTY

The next day was almost as tiring as my coronation day. I had to meet with Guthric. I asked Tuan to be there, too. He said nothing, but I looked forward to discussing that meeting with him later and hearing his thoughts. It was a short meeting, but I was anxious, thinking of what I needed to say and to ask. I'd been included in Father's meetings with Guthric before, but I had never met with him alone. When we were done, I thought I'd given a good account of myself. Time would tell. I was tired from the strain of it.

Mother came to me in the afternoon.

"I've had everything moved out of the big bedchamber," she said. "I'll be in the next room to it, but the big bedchamber is yours by right."

"But that was always your room, yours and Father's."

"When Tir was crowned, his mother moved out of that room, too. It's always been the king's room. Now it's yours. I'll have your things moved into it today, and you can sleep there tonight."

As she turned to go, I said, "Mother."

She faced me.

"There's something I have to say. Tuan and I are going to marry. I know you don't like it, and I don't know why. We'd like you to agree to it, but we will do it whether you agree or not."

"Of course," she said. "You are the queen now."

"Will you tell me why you objected before?"

"It will make no difference," she said. "I do not object now."

"Do not, or cannot?" I asked. She smiled slightly and said nothing.

"Is nothing going to be the same anymore?" I asked.

"Maybe not, swanling," she said. "Him not being here, that alone is enough change." She swallowed, but when she spoke again her voice was calm. "We'll all get used to it in time, I suppose."

"Will we?" I asked. It didn't seem possible. I thought Mother would leave. Instead she stood in thought for a few minutes, and I waited.

"It has been a hard year," she said. "Hard for us all, perhaps hardest for you. Yes," she said as I opened my mouth to deny it. "You've shouldered so much this year. Hafor, the attack on High Moor, so much else. And more to come."

"All I did was what needed to be done," I said.

"And you did it well. Others—I—did not. I will be a help to you from here, Kiar, instead of a hindrance."

"Thank you," I said, when it was clear she was done speaking. "I know it was hard. I hope it won't be hard forever."

"So do I." She bowed briefly and turned away.

"Mother."

She turned back. "Yes, swanling?"

"If you're calling me 'swanling' in private, you don't need to bow. We can keep that for court."

"Of course." She was smiling as she turned to leave.

I went out into the courtyard. As I passed the kitchens I heard Nias's voice giving someone directions for supper, and the rattle of pans and knives. Outside, there were guards on the wall as usual, folk going in and out of the stables, kennels and other outbuildings. From the forge came a light, metallic ring as Sylard tapped on some piece of metalwork, making or mending.

I walked out to the paddock. Everyone I passed gave me the king's—the queen's— salute and went back to their work. At the paddock two of the men were checking a horse's feet.

"He'll need this one trimmed," one said to the other. They led the horse away.

Everything seemed to be going on as usual. We would have to start culling the herds tomorrow. It was already later than we usually started, but Father's funeral and the coronation had interrupted everything. I felt my world had been turned upside-down, and yet meals were still cooked, horses still cared for, cloth made, and crops planted and harvested, and every other daily activity carried out as it always had been.

My father must once have felt this way, I thought, and sometime some son or daughter of mine might stand here and feel the same. For a fleeting moment I saw that everything would be fine, and that a day would come when the thought of meeting with Guthric wouldn't knot my stomach. There would be a day when I would seem to everyone to know exactly what had to be done, as Father had always seemed to know.

I wanted his counsel badly. This would be a hard winter, with the crops ravaged by animals. We would all, no doubt, be hungry by the spring. He knew so much more than I did about how to keep the heart in people in bad times. Everyone had trusted him. His men would follow him anywhere, and his people loved him.

It would take me time to become that kind of queen, time and the good counsel of the people around me. I had several pieces of good fortune, at least; Valenia, and not Noermark, had defeated the bog-walkers. Beorn, too, was new to the throne. And winter was coming, when nobody made war. There would be a space of peace for me to learn at least something of what I needed to do.

A few flakes of snow drifted down. I leaned my arms on the paddock and watched the horses. I imagined my father on Cloud, riding out to hunt deer. Where the spirits flew to when the body was gone, nobody knew, but I wanted to think that Father and Cloud, who had spent so many years together, were together again. The thought of him with the horse he had ridden all my life eased the knot of grief in my heart a little.

I heard footsteps approaching and turned to see Sianna, in her coat of every animal, with the otter hood pulled up over her head. Flakes of snow settled on the dark fur.

"How will you go home?" I asked her. "The same way you came?"

She shook her head, smiling. "No, Majesty. That road is a hard one, and I'd rather not walk it again unless I must. I hoped you would lend me a horse."

"Gladly," I said, and turned back to the paddock. "It's the least I can offer."

"Thank you, Majesty."

I sighed. "That will be hard to get used to. Can't you call me Kiar, at least when there's nobody else around?"

"If you like," she said, and her voice told me she was smiling.

"Thank you." I said. "I'm sorry for how I spoke to you. I know you did everything you could. Everything anyone could do. I never thought he would die."

"Even an expected death is hard," she said. "I was taken by surprise, too. What happened to your father happens very seldom. But when it does happen, it is almost always death. I have seen it three times now, and never seen one live."

"But you tried to save him."

"Yes. He was a good king."

"He was."

We stood looking at the horses as the light faded. My toes began to feel the cold, even through my boots and the wool padding them.

"I will be leaving tomorrow," Sianna said.

"Do you need anything? Stores for the winter?"

She shook her head. "I have all I need, and you'll need all you have to get your people through."

"That's truer than you know. I hope I can get them through as well as he would have."

She didn't say, "You will," or anything at all.

I looked at the horses. "That little roan mare," I said. "She's quick and light. Will she do you?"

"Perfectly. Thank you, Kiar."

"Good." I straightened up. "Let's go in to supper."

Overnight, the weather changed. In the morning, the sky dropped snow in big, slow flakes like feathers. It melted on the ground, but winter had given notice. For all that, the air was fresh on the skin, and not biting at all. There was not much wind, but what there was came from the north; soon it would be much colder.

Guthric asked to speak to me, and I met with him in the council chamber after breakfast.

"I should take my leave, Majesty," he said. "This late in the year, it was only urgent news that made me come."

"Wait a day or two," I said. "You'll be riding into the wind and the snow all the way. It's a long journey."

"And I am an old man," he said. And older, I thought, for the death of his king. The stubble growing in was as much grey as red, and without his beard the lines of age and grief on his face were deep furrows.

"Not so old," I said. "But I've known you most of my life. I don't want any harm to come to you. You and my father were friends, in a way."

He smiled at that.

"I hope to be a friend to you, as well, Queen Kiar."

"If you're determined, then, leave now. If you make good time, you could reach Stony Ridge tonight. Stop there, Guthric. Don't camp out in this weather." I wrote a couple of lines on a piece of parchment and handed it to him. "Rafe and Marin of Stony Ridge will give you a welcome."

"Or a bed, at least, on your word. Thank you, Majesty. With your leave, I will start immediately."

He bowed and left. When I came out of the council chamber, Sianna was waiting in the hall with her packs.

"This is winter setting in," she said. "I need to be home."

"We've given you a hard year. Thank you for all you've done, ever since the spring."

"It's been a hard year for you, too," she said. "It will get better."

"You told me once that it's not good to tell people the future."

"No," she said, smiling. "It's not. But there is nothing wrong with encouragement."

"I can send someone with you to bring the mare back," I said. "I don't want you to have to feed a third horse all winter."

"The wood-woses will always find me a little extra hay." She put her hand on my shoulder. "Send if you need me. I will come if I can."

"Thank you," I said. "Travel safely."

She picked up her packs, and as she turned away I asked, "So the wood-woses do look after your house?" She smiled back over her shoulder at me and said nothing. I turned away before she reached the door. To watch her out of sight would mean a long parting. Although I didn't wish the hardship of winter travel on her, I looked forward to her return and hoped it would be soon.

Guthric and his men left shortly after. I had no qualms about watching them out of sight. Tuan had joined me to see them off. Guthric bowed to him, too, and called him "Lord Tuan."

When Guthric was gone, I turned to Tuan. "Tomorrow we'll have to start the cull," I said. "Right now I want to fly, but I'll settle for riding."

"Then let's ride," Tuan said.

We went down the south side of the dun, sheltered from the wind. The snow still melted when it touched the ground, but where it caught on the grass, it stayed.

"What are you thinking?" Tuan asked me.

"Of what it must be like never to have winter. The swanfolk never see winter. You fly away before it comes, and return after it's left. What is it like, where you go?"

"Like here, mostly. Water, sky."

"What about people?"

He shrugged.

"I've never taken human form at the winter grounds. There are no human folk there that I've ever seen."

"It sounds peaceful," I said.

He reached across the space between our horses, and I took his hand.

"You would be bored," he said. "Trust me. It's far more interesting here."

"I look forward to hearing you say that when food gets scarce," I said. "I don't think hunger will be interesting. At least, not a good kind of interesting."

"I would rather be here with you with the food scarce, than in the winter grounds with plenty but without you."

"I'm glad you're here," I said. "It'll be hard to wait until we can marry."

He gave my hand a little shake. "There'll be things to do while we wait. We'll be clearing a space for the sheep game before you know it."

"I suppose I can still do that," I said.

"Why should the queen not play the sheep game?" he asked. "Don't kings and queens do whatever they want?"

"Only in stories and songs," I said.

Tuan laughed.

"Kiar, you are already in stories and songs. You're part of the Lost King's story now, and Queen Amala's, and when Aren returns, no doubt there will be at least one more song about you."

"I'd rather it were about Warulf—he'll enjoy it more! So, you see, I can't always have things my own way." I wondered if Father had ever felt like that, and wished I could ask him. Had he ever been unsure, even when he'd just been crowned? Had anyone challenged his right, or tested if the new king could hold his throne? Had he ever fought magic before the bog-walkers? I was all too aware of how little I knew of magic, especially if I ever had to face it again.

Tuan's voice broke into my thoughts. "I've never flown in the snow." He tipped his head back, and snowflakes settled on his hood.

"Neither have I."

"It's not very cold. And I know a clearing in the woods to the west, with room enough. The queen may not have everything she wants, but if she wishes to fly once more before spring—" He kissed the back of my gloved hand.

"Yes," I said. "Yes! The queen does wish to fly!"

We turned the horses west and rode together through the snow.

ACKNOWLEDGEMENTS

As always, there are more people than the author involved in a book.

My friend Ravi Nair read an early draft of The Swan Harp and told me "You need to write two more stories, because young adult books always come in threes." I didn't think there was any more to write about Kiar and her world, but Ravi was right.

My friends and fellow writers of To the Point writers' group listened to and commented on large sections of this story. Their input has made it stronger. Thanks to all of them, and particularly to Gordon Graham for the title.

The things I learned from my friends and mentors in the Society for Creative Anachronism continue to feed my writing. Thanks also to Dr Roberta Frank for my first lessons in early English, which provided the basis for Noermarken, and to Dr Larry Raney for feedback on pulmonary embolism. Any errors or omissions are my own.

Thanks to Mary Vensel White, for encouragement and for her ex-cellent editing. It's a pleasure work-ing with her.

Thanks to the Ontario Arts Council for financial support during the writing of this manuscript.

And, as always, thanks to David Syme, my sounding board, my personal barista and my amuse.

ABOUT THE AUTHOR

Elizabeth Creith has been a storyteller and visual artist for as long as she can remember. For a large part of her working life she made her living as a printmaker and potter. She first became a published writer with a humor piece, "A Loom with a Zoo" in September 1990. Her dream gig as a writer was to have a humor column; she has had four—two online, one on radio, and one in print.

She reads fantasy, folklore, history, paleontology, archaeology, science, poetry, and almost anything she can get her hands on about art. She writes humor, fantasy, poetry, and non-fiction, mostly pieces under 2000 words, and wrote her first novel-length draft in 2006 during the Three-Day Novel competition. She also practices bookmaking (with pages, not ponies), paper engineering, painting, and printmaking.

Elizabeth lives in a hundred-year-old farmhouse surrounded by roses and forest with her husband, cat, koi, and a lot of wildlife.